PRAISE FOR
KYLIE CHAN
AND THE
EMMA DONAHOE NOVELS

"Chinese legend with the thrill of a
fast-paced martial-arts movie."
Publishers Weekly

"*White Tiger* is a fast-paced novel with liberal quantities
of romance, action and fantasy. The present-day setting
blends seamlessly with the solid grounding the book
has in myth and folklore. It is a rich tapestry of culture,
action and love and makes for good entertainment."
OzHorrorScope

"Packed with Chinese mythology, kick-ass action and
sexual tension…a smart, entertaining read."
Australian SpecFic

"[The Dark Heavens trilogy] is impossible to put down…
you're missing out if you don't rush out and get them."
Lunch.com

"The third book of the Dark Heavens trilogy delivers the
same dialogue-driven action as the first two books… The
showdown at the end of the book is not to be missed."
Library Thing

Books by Kylie Chan

Dark Heavens

WHITE TIGER
RED PHOENIX
BLUE DRAGON

Journey to Wudang

EARTH TO HELL
HELL TO HEAVEN
HEAVEN TO WUDANG

Celestial Battles

DARK SERPENT

And Coming Soon

DEMON CHILD
BLACK JADE

KYLIE CHAN

DARK SERPENT

CELESTIAL BATTLES
BOOK ONE

HARPER Voyager
An Imprint of HarperCollins*Publishers*

First published in Australia in 2013 by HarperCollins*Publishers* Australia Pty Limited.

HARPER Voyager
An Imprint of HarperCollins*Publishers*
10 East 53rd Street
New York, New York 10022-5299

Copyright © 2013 by Kylie Chan
Cover Design by Darren Holt, HarperCollins Design Studio
Cover images by shutterstock.com
Chinese characters supplied by author
ISBN 978-0-06-232906-6
www.harpervoyagerbooks.com

First Harper Voyager mass market printing: May 2014

Harper Voyager and) is a trademark of HCP LLC.

Printed in the U.S.A.

10 9 8 7 6 5 4 3 2 1

Gentle Reader, this is the seventh book in this story. Although you can choose to start here, you may find it more rewarding to read the story from the beginning with the first novel, *White Tiger*.

In response to readers' requests I've added a list of characters at the end.

Note for parents/teachers

My books are sometimes shelved as 'Young Adult'. This novel contains adult themes that a less mature reader may find disturbing. Parental discretion is advised.

For Stephanie Smith,
Mentor, Adviser, Advocate, Champion

The Serpent lies in the scalding cage;
it wakes, rigid with pain.
The King stands outside the bars,
her face twisted into a malicious smile.

The Turtle surges through the ocean,
but cannot enjoy its element.
The shredded wound cleaves them
and it shares the Serpent's agony.

1

Zhenwu

John pushed more of the blasted papers to the side of the desk, then realised that he didn't have anywhere to put the keyboard, so he added the papers to the pile of student files on a cabinet to his left. The stack was in danger of toppling so he bound it together with a thread of energy. He'd sort them out later.

There was a window above the cabinet, looking out over the western wall of the Wudang Mountain complex. The green hills of the Celestial countryside spread before him, dotted with the occasional small residence of those Shen who chose to live a more rural lifestyle. He took a moment to enjoy the outlook. It had been a long time — he had married Michelle and moved permanently to the Earthly Plane in 1995 — and the sense of being home, back where he belonged, filled him with satisfaction.

Emma was safe within his Mountain walls, Simone was strong and well able to take care of herself even without her yin, and his family was harmonious. His Mountain, although weakened by recent attacks, stood strong in the face of the demon menace. A few hundred more Disciples would bring it up to full strength, and his son's husband-to-be was doing a fine job searching the world for them.

He resisted the urge to go outside and do a sword set and turned back to the paperwork, then changed his mind and decided to do a sword set anyway. His personal assistant, Zara, would let him know if anything major happened.

Lord Venus is here to see you, Zara said.

Typical. Just as he was enjoying some respite the Jade Emperor had to send his most senior emissary.

Escort him in, then take stone form and record from your stand, John said.

He quickly grabbed all the papers off his desk, spun in his chair and dropped them onto the floor behind him as Zara opened the door. He rose and stood behind the desk as Venus floated into the room, slightly above the floor. Venus was in full Celestial regalia, with a Tang-style robe of many layers of transparent violet silk over his human form of a slim mid-thirties gentleman. He had his hair long and tied on top in traditional fashion and carried — John nearly sighed with exasperation when he saw it — a red lacquered box containing an Edict from the Jade Emperor.

Zara was in its androgynous human form with golden skin and gleaming white hair. It changed to its stone form, a fist-sized diamond, and took its place in its decorative platinum stand on John's desk, ready to record the proceedings.

John saluted Venus. 'Honoured Lord Venus, Emissary of the Celestial, Carrier of the Way. Welcome to Wudang Mountain.'

Venus bowed in return, still holding the box in front of him with both hands. 'Honoured Emperor Xuan Wu, Celestial Master of the Nine Mysteries. I thank you for your warm hospitality.'

John put his hand out, palm up, towards one of the chairs on the other side of the desk. 'Please sit.'

2

Venus bowed slightly again, placed the box carefully on John's desk, and flicked his robe before sitting, pulling his long sleeves out of the way.

John sat as well and eyed Venus across the desk. 'What brings your honoured self to my humble facility?'

'I am here in my capacity as emissary to present you with an Edict from the Celestial One Himself, may he live ten thousand years,' Venus said.

'Ten thousand years,' John echoed. He leaned back in his executive chair and waited.

'And it's been *far* too long, you ugly bastard,' Venus said. 'Fucking leave me and Number Two alone to handle his Celestial Temper-Tantrumness — we'll never forgive you.'

'Er Lang still hasn't spoken to me,' John said, leaning on his hand to cover his smile.

'Er Lang's madly in love with your woman, which is an achievement in itself,' Venus said. 'His dog's ready to tear her to pieces.'

John raised his hands in exasperation. 'What do they see in her? She's plain, over forty, slightly overweight from spending too much time on energy work, and hardly ever wears make-up or fancy outfits. She's the opposite of what an attractive woman's supposed to be and they all adore her.'

'I'll tell her you said that,' Venus said with amusement.

'So will I,' Zara said.

'Record. Do not comment,' John said, glaring at the stone in its stand.

'My Lord,' Zara said, its voice full of laughter, 'they don't all adore her. Many members of the Celestial regard her as an ugly, arrogant pain in the ass.'

'The little stone is right, if altogether too honest,' Venus said. 'Everything you said about her is true, and it has made some Celestials unhappy about her presence here.

She is strong-willed, outspoken and cares nothing for her appearance; these are not regarded as qualities that a good woman should possess.'

'Am I still pissing off half the Celestial?' John said.

'More than half.'

'Good.' He waved one hand over the desk. 'So what's in the box?'

'Take a look for yourself.'

John glowered at Venus, spun the intricately carved box to face him, and thumbed the clasp. The box sprang open, revealing the Edict within. John slipped the vermillion ribbon from around the scroll, opened and studied it.

The Celestial Emperor of the Northern Heavens, His Imperial Highness Emperor Zhenwu, is hereby instructed by the Celestial to undertake an information-gathering mission to the Western Corner of the World. It is this realm's opinion that demons are gathering in the far west of the nation known as England ...

John smiled slightly. The Jade Emperor had that part wrong, and it was a convenient loophole if John ever needed it. As far as they knew, the demons were up to something in Wales, not England.

... and the Celestial Emperor is hereby ordered to travel to that Corner immediately following Mid-Autumn Festival and to stay in the country known as Great Britain ...

John shook his head. Wales was part of Great Britain, which meant the loophole was gone, but did the JE really mean just Great Britain? He needed to spend some time updating the JE on the status of western Europe. The rest of the world, for that matter. He would bet money that the JE had never even seen the internet.

... until the demons are identified and located and the Shen of the West are contacted, or one month has passed, whichever comes first.

John frowned. A whole month away from the Mountain? Why a month? He glanced at Venus, who wore the serene expression he used when he expected someone to explode in his face. Did the Jade Emperor know more than he was sharing? John shook the scroll to open it further. Of course he did.

The Emperor Zhenwu is to return in one month and present himself to the Celestial Palace with the results of his explorations.
    Ten Thousand Years, etc.

John let the scroll roll back up and tossed it on the desk. 'Has he said anything at all about why a month?'

Venus carefully maintained his explosion-proof expression. 'No.'

'Did you tell him to say England instead of the UK? It's the sort of sneaky thing you'd do.'

'Nope, he did that one himself. I thought you'd like that. Then he changes it to Great Britain, which means he knows exactly which country he's specifying and you aren't allowed in Ireland.'

'Or the European continent,' John said. He leaned on the desk and rubbed his chin. 'That's much too specific to be a mistake.'

'Damn straight.'

As usual when he was distracted, John's hair came out of its tie, but he ignored it. 'Why do I get the feeling that I'm being set up for something extremely nasty?'

'The Celestial is the pure and divine ruler of the Heavenly realm and cares for us all with equal compassion and heartfelt warmth.'

'That doesn't answer my question.' John leaned back and ran his hands over the top of his head and through his hair, which had already become tangled. 'I suppose we have no choice but to trust him to do what's best for all of Heaven.'

'Ten thousand years,' Venus said.

'Even if it means sacrifice.'

'Ten thousand times ten thousand years,' Venus said.

'Fuck you.'

Zara made a high-pitched noise then quickly cut it off.

'Erase that,' John said, waving one hand at the stone.

'I didn't hear anything,' it said.

'Damn, I've missed you,' Venus said. 'No more women for a while after this one, eh? All of the Celestial suffers when the Turtle is being a Turtle. We've gone far too long without your reassuring presence.'

'I've vowed to Raise Emma and marry her and that is all I want from life. Apart, of course, from the safety of my family and protection of the realm.'

'It's good to have you back, my friend.'

'It's good to be back.' John opened the bottom drawer of his desk and pulled out a flask of fiery Sichuan rice wine. 'Zara, find a couple of wine cups. This has been sitting here for more than fifty years and it's about time I opened it.'

Zara disappeared from his desk.

Venus took the flask and examined it. 'Tiger's own cellar, eh?' He glanced sharply at John. 'Is this stolen?'

'Of course it is.'

John used energy to remove the wax stopper and waited for Zara to return.

My Lord, Zara said, sounding concerned, *Er Lang is here.*

'Come on in, Number Two,' John shouted at the door. He dropped his voice. 'Thanks, Venus.'

'I told him about the wine,' Venus said with amusement.

Er Lang let himself in and nodded to Venus. He saluted John. 'Lord Xuan Wu, Celestial Master —'

'Shut the fuck up and sit down,' Venus said. 'Ah Wu's opening one of the Tiger's special vintages.' He leaned on the chair to look behind him. 'Where's that damn stone with the wine cups?'

Zara floated in with a tray suspended above it holding the ceramic wine cups. 'Apologies.'

'Get another one for yourself,' John said as the tray drifted to land on the desk. He picked up the cups in turn and filled them from the flask, then raised his own. 'Venus, Er Lang, two of the greatest comrades in battle an old Turtle could ever wish for. Thanks for putting up with the Imperial bullshit while I was gone, and let's make sure those demon bastards never lay their hands on any of our charges while we still breathe.'

Venus and Er Lang raised their cups and sipped the rice wine, then both made a face.

'I have a good Californian vintage red back at my house; next time we should open that,' Venus said.

'I was about to say something similar,' Er Lang said. He raised the flask and studied it. 'Is this really from the Tiger's cellar?'

John poured himself another cup. 'I see that now I have returned I will have to give you two lessons on the fine art,' he drained the cup, 'of being ...' he filled their cups, '*men.*'

'That's very good coming from someone who only recently spent several weeks as a woman.'

John shrugged. 'I'm yin. I had no control over it.'

'And neither of us had a chance to see it,' Venus said. 'I've heard that you're a ...' He glanced at Er Lang. 'What's the expression?'

'Hottie,' Er Lang said with satisfaction. 'The talk of you in female form will keep the Celestial gossip mill grinding for many years.'

'Good, it'll move attention away from Emma's little bungle,' John said with feeling.

'I can't understand why you keep her around after she imprisoned half of you,' Venus said.

'She didn't do it. The Demon King did.'

'Still,' Er Lang said, 'I hear she's an interesting creature. Care to share what you discovered when you examined her?'

'Zara, bring up the file on my monitor,' John said, turning to face the screen.

'My Lord,' Zara said.

'Level one eyes only,' John said. He leaned his chin on his hand as he scrolled through the notes. 'Because of her Western nature it's difficult to quantify exactly what she is; she doesn't fit into any of our existing categories. There is some demonic character there, but it's unlike anything we've ever seen ...'

'As she demonstrated when I forced her into Mother form,' Er Lang said. 'Her demon form didn't have control over her, and she protected the students as fiercely as she did when she was human.'

'Even though she was full of demon essence and in Mother form, she protected humans?' Venus said in disbelief.

'She was ready to give her life for them,' Er Lang said.

'She was tamed, then?' Venus said.

'Nope,' Er Lang said. 'We know that for sure, because two minutes later the Dark Lord tamed her.'

'So she's a demon? You should have informed the Celestial.'

'She's not a demon,' John said. 'She's a human with characteristics of both Shen and demon without being either.'

'Impossible,' Er Lang said.

'I agree,' Venus said. 'Either you're Shen or demon. You can't be both. You can fall to be demonic or you can be Raised to be Shen, but you can't be both at the same time.'

John didn't look away from the screen. 'She's just enough demon to be able to accept an infusion of demon essence without it killing her. She's just enough Shen to change to snake form and manipulate shen energy. I speculate that she's the only one to exhibit these attributes because she met me and ...' He hesitated.

'Lived on the Celestial Plane?' Venus said.

'No,' John said. 'My Serpent took advantage of her inherent snake nature and was using her as a vessel to defend my daughter when I could not. That seems to have caused all of this.'

'What do you mean, a vessel?' Er Lang said. 'She said you were possessing her, but of course that is impossible.'

John sighed with misery. 'Keep this to this room. I *was* possessing her.'

'What?' Er Lang shot to his feet. 'Ah Wu, how could you do such a thing? That is unacceptable and I must report it —'

'Shut up and sit down,' Venus said. 'I think there's more.'

'There'd better not be,' Er Lang said, sitting.

'In her human form, she's faster and stronger than a normal human. We have another human here from Wales who's a similar type; his son is a half-demon who can take Snake Mother form. The Tiger's researchers say that his trait is attached to the female gene so only females show the full potential.'

'A male half-demon that can take Mother form? That's completely impossible,' Er Lang said.

9

'This young man is seriously disquieting,' John said. 'Someone over in the West has been interbreeding Shen, demons and humans, and Emma's the result.'

'And being possessed by you activated the other stuff,' Venus said, understanding. 'You're the only Shen on the Plane who is capable of something as demonic as that.'

John mumbled at the desk. 'I am fully aligned to the Celestial. I made my choice.'

'We know that, Ah Wu,' Er Lang said. 'We've seen you fight.'

'It sounds like too much of a coincidence that Emma would land in your lap like this, ready to be changed by proximity to you,' Venus said.

'It wasn't. The Demon King in his guise of Kitty Kwok set us up.' John sighed and rubbed his eyes. 'We will go to the West and see what is happening. Our Demon King seems to be involved; he was there overseeing the experiments on the Western men we are sheltering. They will come with us and guide us. Something serious is happening over there, and we need to know what it is.'

Venus waved one hand at the box. 'So that's what all this is about. Now I see.'

John explained for Er Lang's benefit. 'It's an Edict. I have to go over there directly after Mid-Autumn Festival and stay until I either find out what's going on or a month has passed.'

'Who are you taking?' Er Lang said.

'Emma and Simone — I must protect them. Leo, to guard them when I'm not. The two Western men — their names are Tom and Ben O'Breen.'

'That's an unusual surname; isn't it supposed to be O'Brien?' Er Lang said.

'Definitely O'Breen, it's spelt slightly differently because it's an older version. Same as Emma's last name, Donahoe.'

'Fascinating,' Venus said.

'My Number One, Ming Gui, and my Number Two, Yue Gui, will mind the Northern Heavens,' John said. 'The Lius and the Celestial Masters will manage the Mountain. Er Lang, you're on call to see to the defence of the Celestial Palace.'

'Wonderful, now Ah Wu's back I don't have to manage the defence of the entire Celestial Plane all by myself,' Er Lang said with cutting sarcasm.

John shrugged. 'An Edict's an Edict.'

'What do you think you'll find there, Ah Wu?' Venus said.

'A breeding program. Humans, demons, Shen, somehow kept captive and forced to have children. Emma's ancestors were exiled for marrying; someone was telling them when they could have a family, and who with.'

'Controlling who could marry? That's sickening,' Venus said.

'That's the way it was here until about a hundred years ago,' John said.

'We forget the cruelties of the past so quickly,' Er Lang said.

John deliberately focused his intent dark gaze on Er Lang. 'I hear you challenged Emma so that you could court Simone when Simone was only sixteen.'

Er Lang paled. 'I had no intention of courting her, my Lord, it was merely a ruse because I was convinced that Emma was a demon.' His voice rose in pitch when he saw John's face. 'Well, she *was* a demon! And I wanted to show the Celestial — I thought the Jade Emperor was too busy to know ...' His eyes widened as John continued to glower at him. 'I was defending the Celestial! I have no intention of pursuing your daughter!' He saluted John, who had summoned yin in dark cold strands through his long hair. 'Believe me, my Lord, I am here to protect the Celestial, and although it was once acceptable I know that it's no longer the way —'

'Calm down, he's toying with you,' Venus said.

'What?' Er Lang relaxed when he saw John smile slightly. 'Don't do that to me!'

John pulled the yin back and filled Er Lang's cup. 'You wouldn't be able to handle my daughter anyway. I daresay any man on the Plane will find her a challenge when she's of age and ready to choose a partner.'

'Hell yeah, she has a lot of her mother in her,' Er Lang said. He drained his wine cup and made another face. 'The Tiger saw you coming, my friend.'

'He usually does.'

2

Emma

I hefted the sheaf of papers under my arm and tapped on John's office door.

'Enter,' he said.

I opened the door, took three steps in, then fell to one knee with my head bowed. 'My Lord, I am here in my role as research assistant to help you in your pursuit of information on the Shen of the West, as directed by the Celestial himself. I offer no advice or guidance on the management of the Mountain or the Heavens.'

'I accept your assistance under those constraints,' John said. He leaned back and put his hands on the desk. 'Saying that once should be enough. Why do we have to say it every single damn time?'

I sat across the desk from him and placed the papers on it. 'Whatever, it doesn't mean anything —'

'Say it doesn't mean anything and you'll be blocked from doing this too,' he said urgently.

'I was going to say that it doesn't mean anything to me if I have to say the words a million times as long as I can work on this.'

'I understand,' he said. He rubbed his hands over his face. 'I just received an Edict.'

'Oh crap. How bad is it?'

'Nothing we hadn't already planned ... sort of. We have to go to the UK directly after Mid-Autumn Fest—'

'That was the plan anyway,' I said, interrupting.

He stopped and glared at me, his dark eyes sharp, then his expression softened and he smiled slightly and shook his head. 'We have to stay either a month or until we find out what's going on, whatever's sooner.'

'We won't be there a whole month,' I said. 'It shouldn't take us long to find out what's happening over there — we have some excellent leads and Ben's assistance. We'll be fine.'

'I hope you're right.' He saw the documents I'd placed on his desk. 'Is that my thesis?'

I raised the thick manuscript. 'What a freaking slog to read.'

'I hardly understand most of it myself without the Serpent,' he said. 'When I had the snake I could see patterns so quickly. Things just slotted together and the bigger picture became obvious. If I'd managed to talk to some Western Shen, I think I would have discovered something important. As it is, I found so many parallels that I began to wonder if we Shen are created by your storytelling and only exist as an extension of your combined consciousness.'

'I'm beginning to wonder that myself,' I said. 'Look at Campbell's work — Shen all over the world have close to identical stories, even when the societies had no contact whatsoever.'

'Or we could be the creations of aliens who visited this planet and left us behind as guardians,' he said, examining the documents. 'That fits as well. I was well on the way to finding the truth when I lost the snake.'

'That may be why you lost it — you were close to a discovery so they took it away.'

'We must ask it,' he said. 'Anyway, I only covered Arthurian legends and the parallels with Chinese myths of the Xuan Wu in my thesis. The Arthurian stories were heavily influenced by romantic ideals, so they've diverged dramatically from the original tales. What have you come up with so far?'

I spread the papers in front of me and put my tablet computer to the side. 'Three major European polytheistic strands: Greco-Roman, Norse and Celtic. Celtic you've touched on with Arthurian; I've been looking into Greco-Roman and Norse.'

'Do any of them sound like us?'

'They're sex fiends who spend their time fighting, screwing and getting into trouble on the Earthly with human men and women.'

'Sounds exactly like us.'

'Yep.'

'Both Norse and Greco-Roman? Aren't they completely different from each other?'

'There are variations, but when it comes to the basic elemental forces like yourself, you'll find definite similarities.'

'Celtic?'

'Much the same. When the Romans invaded Britain, they were surprised at how closely the Celtic gods mirrored their own. And on top of that, Buddhist missionaries went through way before the Romans did and the Celts made one of the Buddhas a member of their own pantheon. I suspect Kwan Yin may have been wandering much further than we know.'

'Fascinating. I must give her a call and see if she has anything for us. Any leads on what names we'll be looking for when we get there?'

'No idea at all. Each set of stories is equally strong.'

'I'll just have to make my way to Western Heaven and say hello then.' He leaned back. 'Good afternoon, sir, are you Odin, Jupiter, Zeus or the Dagda?'

I made my voice deeper. 'All of 'em, motherfucker, wanna take me on?'

He grew wistful for a moment. 'Now *that's* an interesting proposition.'

'Me or Odin?'

He smiled slightly. 'Another god of war. Someone who would be a challenge.'

'I see.'

He looked down at the papers. 'Holy Island?'

I shuffled through them, looking for the photo, then gave up and brought it up on the tablet. 'This is a pair of standing stones called Penrhos Feilw, three metres high and three metres apart, that have been there for three thousand years.'

'That's a gateway,' he said. He glanced up from the picture. 'Has the implant worked?'

'Stone?' I said.

'It's satisfactory,' the stone that used to be in my engagement ring said. It had been relocated to between my shoulderblades. 'We're still working on options for a backup plan in case I'm discovered or disabled.'

'We were thinking something similar to *The Bourne Identity*,' I said. 'A code or number tattooed onto me in an extremely private place.'

'What have you decided?' Zara said from her stand on the desk.

'Probably a phone number tattooed very high on my inner thigh.'

'How about an IP address in ultraviolet ink?' Zara said.

'Ultraviolet wouldn't work; if I've lost my memory I won't know it's there. But the IP address is a good idea. We can use a website to provide an info dump and contact point.'

'It would need some work to make it traceable from our end but not from hers, in case her captors find it,' my stone said.

'What's the Bourne Identity?' John said.

'Matt Damon,' Zara said with a huge sigh of bliss. 'I have copies of all his movies stored in my lattice.'

'DVD time,' I said.

'I see. Do you need me to order the IP business?'

'Stone,' I said, and stopped. I couldn't tell the stone to do this; it was too close to management of the Mountain. 'Yes, I do.'

'Do it,' John said.

'My Lord,' the stone said.

I collected the papers together. 'There's a Roman fort and a village that is several thousand years old on that island. It was the last place to hold to the old ways when the Romans swept through Britain. The islanders supposedly used magic to stop the Romans from invading.'

'Is the village the one from your dreams?'

'No, it's from the Iron Age and just ruins. The village I dream about is definitely the modern village called Mountain. I used Google Earth to pay it a virtual visit — the topography is the same.' I hesitated. 'The Welsh name for it is "Red Enclosure". I looked it up and there's some suggestion that it's called that because people were herded there and their blood spilled.'

'Is the hill — Holy Mountain — the one with blood on top in your dream?' John said.

I nodded.

'Don't be too concerned about the blood business.'

'In the dream, I thirsted for blood because it would bring me power.'

'That's what it does.'

'It was a freaking *sacrifice*.' I tried to control my voice. 'It was a human sacrifice, and I couldn't wait for the

17

sacrifice to die. I would have been happy to help the other snakes kill it if I could have a share of its blood. His or her blood.'

'I will find you and Raise you and marry you. Hold on to that thought. Now ...' He rose from his desk and pushed his keyboard to the side. 'I have a class with the junior Masters. Is there anything else?'

'No, sir.'

'Good. Dismissed.'

I jerked to attention and saluted him Western-style. 'Sir!'

'You are very cute when you do that,' he said as he walked past without looking at me.

I stamped one foot military-style. 'Sir, yes sir!'

He raised one hand behind him without looking back. 'That is extremely distracting.'

I gathered the papers together and shoved them under my arm to follow him. 'Excellent.'

* * *

Three first-year students, two girls and a boy, were waiting for us outside the office. John stopped when he saw them. 'Are you here for me?'

They stared at him, stunned, then one of the girls found her voice. 'Uh, no, my Lord, we're here for ...' She gestured helplessly towards me.

John glanced back at me. 'Oh, I see.' He raised his voice. 'Three more students to play the Game with you, Emma. Have fun.'

He strode away towards the training section.

I put my free hand on my hip. 'Okay, go for your lives — you have two minutes. What's the bet this time?'

'Fifty US dollars if one of us can do a simple salute,' the boy said.

I shrugged. 'As I said, go for your life.'

They all went stiff and their faces became taut with effort. The Chinese girl started to pant with the strain, then gave up and sagged. 'Okay. L …' She gagged on the sound. 'L …'

'You can't call me Lady anything, it won't work. Try ma'am.'

'M …'

The other two joined in, and the three of them hummed the M together, unable to take the word any further.

'Very musical,' I said. 'You should join the new Glee Club, they need more members.'

The stone broke in. 'Emma, quickly, the Serpent's made contact!'

I shoved the documents at one of the students. 'Do me a huge favour, please, and take these to —'

She stared at the documents without moving. 'I'm sorry, I want to, but I can't.'

'Dammit!' I said, and hefted the papers again. 'Where is he?'

'Infirmary. Run!'

I was at the infirmary before them. The junior Masters carried John into the ward and Edwin worked quickly. He tore open John's black jacket and inspected the wounds on his abdomen, then went to the other side of the room to grab an IV stand.

The students hovered over John, concerned. I stood at the back of the group, unable to ask them to move.

Edwin returned with the IV and began to set up the bag. 'Everybody except Emma out,' he said. 'Go find Master Meredith, and ask her and Master Liu to come.'

The students nodded and went out, shooting a few concerned looks behind them. I sat beside the bed and took John's hand. He had withdrawn into himself and didn't seem to register anybody's presence.

More wounds appeared on his abdomen, combined with a strong acrid smell. The wounds were oval and angrily red, some larger than others. As I watched, another appeared and grew to five centimetres across, again combined with the acrid smell.

Edwin touched one of the wounds with a gauze pad, raised it to his nose and jerked back. 'Hydrochloric acid. That *bastard*.' He quickly went out.

John made a soft sound in his throat and another burn appeared on his upper arm. I held his hand tighter and he squeezed it in return.

Edwin returned with bandages and a white paste. He smeared the paste over the wounds, then covered them with the bandages.

'What's that you're putting on it?' I said.

'Ordinary baking soda,' Edwin said. 'It will neutralise the acid, but the burns won't go away.'

A dark patch appeared on the fabric covering John's thigh, and Edwin quickly cut his uniform trousers away to treat the new burn.

'He can't do much more — the Serpent will die of blood loss,' Edwin said, almost to himself. He glanced at John's face. 'Come on, John, don't lose it now.'

John's eyes snapped open and he turned his face to see me. His eyes were completely black: the Serpent had connected to him through the suffering.

'Can you talk yet?' I said.

He shook his head.

'I'll wait.'

Edwin checked the flow on the IV, and pulled a light blanket over John. 'No more coming up; he appears to be done.'

'He's done, he's gone,' John said. He turned his head to see Edwin. 'Did you just call me by my first name?'

'No, I called you John,' Edwin said. 'Heat of the moment; I apologise, my Lord.'

'Since there are mitigating circumstances I won't

reprimand you,' John said. He turned his head back to me. 'There you are, Emma. Quickly — how much progress have you made in finding me?'

'We still have no idea.'

'How about I set up a major storm or something like that directly above me?'

'Frankly, John, that wouldn't be much of a marker. Without you out here moderating the weather, there's a constant stream of freak floods and storms.'

'I need to be back out on the Earthly protecting humanity,' he said. 'Okay, affecting the weather won't work. Are you sending in agents?'

'The King finds them and destroys them the minute they cross into the demonic side of Hell.'

'I'm out of ideas on helping you to find me, and my contact with the Turtle will be lost soon. When are you going to Wales?'

'After Mid-Autumn Festival.'

'Take care, love, you'll be lost.'

'I'm already taking precautions.'

'Good. My contact is slipping …' He closed his eyes. 'It feels so good to be almost one again. Still in two pieces, but closer than I've been in years …'

'Did someone deliberately separate you because you were moving close to a truth about your nature?' I said.

'I don't know, it just seemed to happen by itself,' the Serpent said through John. 'I don't remember much about it, except being angry and confused and in pain. I don't recall anyone else being there.' He opened his eyes again. 'Run quickly through the precautions you're taking against being completely lost.'

'The stone in my ring is a dummy,' I said. 'The real stone's been implanted between my shoulderblades so it can help when I'm lost. We're thinking of having something tattooed on me as well, in case the stone is found and removed.'

'That's what I was going to suggest,' the Serpent said. 'The Turtle's doing well.' He winced slightly. 'I thought for a moment George was coming back. He's planning something; he's spending much less time playing with me. I'm keeping my Serpent ears to the ground but not catching anything. How's Simone?'

'She's finishing high school and thinking about which university she'd like to study at.'

'What, on the *Earthly*?' the Serpent said, shocked. 'Wait.' His face went expressionless. 'The Turtle just shared an info dump. Don't let him do that too much, it drains him and he needs to heal. One of me needs to be up there defending the Celestial.'

'Okay.'

'Tell her that marine biology is an excellent choice, and I hope to take her swimming with both of me one day soon. Oh, and one other thing.'

'Yes?'

'I love you. I'm losing the link. Be very care ...' He took a soft, deep breath and let it out, and his eyes snapped back to normal. 'The Serpent says be very careful.'

'Both of you know I will be.'

'It's still yelling at me every chance it has for making that stupid oath.'

I squeezed his hand. 'Good. Now rest.'

Meredith and Liu hurried in, both wearing their dress uniforms — Meredith in a black silk pant suit with white cuffs, and Liu in his saffron Shaolin robes.

'Is the Serpent still here?' Meredith said, sitting next to John and leaning over him. She took his wrist and put her finger on his pulse. 'More burns?'

'It's gone, you missed it,' I said. 'Looks like the King sprayed it with hydrochloric acid.'

'His creativity is endless,' John said. He struggled to pull himself upright. 'How much longer before the ceremony?'

I slapped my forehead. 'Gold's child — I completely forgot in the excitement. I have to change, I can't go like this.'

'I must be there,' John said. 'This is too important for me to miss.'

'Everybody will understand if you can't make it,' the stone said.

'I'm aware of that, but it's my duty as its Lord to support it through this transition,' John said. 'Find me a uniform, Emma? Liu, ask Edwin to come in and tidy these burns up so I can attend.'

We all opened our mouths to protest and John raised one hand. 'I have to be there. I promise I will rest afterwards. If you like, someone can stand behind me to catch me just in case. Leo's the obvious choice, he's done it before.'

We shared a look, and Meredith and Liu both shrugged with defeat.

'I'll be right back,' I said, and went to the Imperial Residence to find him a uniform.

3

'Why didn't you remind me?' I said as I changed out of my jeans and T-shirt into a white cotton top with a mandarin collar and three-quarter sleeves, matched with a pair of plain black cotton pants — the uniform of a servant.

The stone's voice was rueful. 'I thought you knew, and you were just leaving things to the last minute the way you always do.'

'Oh, thank you very much.'

I found a spare Mountain uniform that would fit John and took it with me, pulling on a pair of cotton boat shoes as I went out the front door.

Everybody was gathering in front of Dragon Tiger Hall when we arrived. Amy and Gold were at the entrance, Gold's child floating at eye level with them. I stood at the back of the group, as was my place as a servant in this official engagement, and John stood near Amy and Gold, Leo alert behind him to catch him just in case.

'Just remember,' Gold was saying to the child, 'if you feel yourself taking something highly reactive like sodium or magnesium, let us know quickly so we can move the mortals away.'

'Don't *worry*, Daddy,' the stone child said. 'As if I'd take sodium and spend the rest of my life as a block of salt. I'll be something very precious, just you see.'

'You have no choice in the matter, little one,' the stone in my back said. 'Just think pure thoughts, and whatever you take will be wonderful.'

'I can't wait,' the child said. 'I'll have a name, and I'll be able to take a human form and hug my little brother and sister.' It jiggled in the air. 'This is so exciting!'

'All right, let's begin,' Gold said. 'Everybody move back and give the child room, please.'

'As I cannot take human form at the moment, I delegate my duties as senior stone here to my child Gold,' the stone in my back said.

'Why can't you take human form, Grandpa?' the stone child said, but was interrupted by Simone running across the square towards us.

'Wait!' she shouted. 'Don't start without me!' She stopped in front of the stone child. 'Sorry I'm late, my driving lesson went over time. Come here.' The stone child moved closer to her and she kissed it. 'That's for good luck, not that you need it.'

'Thanks, Auntie Simone,' the child said, obviously embarrassed.

There was a brilliant flare of white light and Kwan Yin appeared in her middle-aged human form. Everybody immediately fell to one knee, except for John, who took her hand and kissed her on the cheek.

She nodded to him in reply, then smiled around at us. 'There is no need, everybody, up you get.' She went to the stone child and touched it. 'You have my blessing, little one.'

The stone child didn't reply, it just hovered.

'I think it's a little awestruck, my Lady,' Gold said. He dropped his voice, 'Thank you.' He raised his voice again. 'Now if everybody will stand back slightly, let's see what this magnificent little stone has in store for us.'

We moved back to stand in a semicircle around the stone, and Gold turned to face the group.

'This stone child was born in battle from my own stone self. It has respect for its elders and venerates the Grandmother. Now it is time for it to take a mineral, a human form, and a name. May its form and deeds bring credit to its lineage. It is a grandchild of the Jade Building Block of the World, and a child of the Golden Boy.' He took a step back and gazed at the child. 'The Grandmother and the Goddess have blessed you, child. You are privileged. Now take a mineral and a form.'

The child lifted slightly, turned in the air and emitted a golden light. The light grew until it was blinding, then flashed black and disappeared. The stone was now black, with veins of silver flowing through it, and had grown to the size of an adult fist.

There was a stunned silence.

The stone glowed again, this time with a silvery light, and changed to a slim human girl of fourteen years, wearing jeans and a plain black T-shirt. She appeared as a perfectly normal Chinese girl except that her eyes were black instead of brown.

She looked around at everybody's stunned expressions. 'Did I do something wrong?'

Gold snapped out of it first. He pulled her into a hug — she was nearly as tall as he was — and kissed her on the cheek. 'Absolutely nothing at all. You are very beautiful.' He pulled back to smile at her and touched the side of her face. 'I'm very proud that you're something so precious.'

Kwan Yin went to her and took her hands. 'Do not be concerned, you have done nothing wrong. I will return to speak to you later.' She disappeared.

The stone child went to Amy and put her arms out. 'I finally get to hug you, Amy.'

Amy pulled her into a huge hug. 'This is something I've wanted to do for a very long time,' she said, her voice thick with tears.

'So, your name — what's it to be?' Simone said. 'What sort of mineral are you? Onyx? Agate?'

'Oh no, nothing as mundane as that. Remember who my parent and grandparent are,' the child said. 'I'm Black Jade.' She saw Simone's shocked expression and looked around at everybody again. 'Okay, now I'm sure I've done something wrong. What is it?'

'You don't know about *Dream of the Red Chamber*?' Simone said.

'No, let me look.' Black Jade went silent for a moment, then shrugged. 'Oh, I see, the character Black Jade was abandoned by her boyfriend and died of sadness or something. I don't see a problem — I'm not getting married any time soon. It's just a coincidence.'

Nobody replied.

'If it worries you, you could all call me BJ, but that —'

She didn't finish because Gold burst out laughing.

'What?' Amy said, then, 'Oh.' She pushed Black Jade affectionately.

'I'll think of something else you can call me if Black Jade is too scary,' the stone child said. 'Let me check the network ... processing ... I choose Darcy. That means dark, which is close enough. I like that — very Jane Austen.'

'I have two daughters now,' Gold said with wonder.

Darcy changed to a fourteen-year-old boy with the same colouring.

'And two sons,' Gold said, unfazed.

Darcy turned to the group, still in male form. 'I thank you all for attending my mineral-taking. I will go now to the temple and give thanks to the Buddhas.'

He bowed low to everybody, hands clasped in front of him, and Gold and Amy put their arms around his shoulders to lead him away.

'What's wrong with calling him ... her ... BJ?' Simone said. 'That sounds very cute.'

Nobody replied.

'Oh, come on, someone tell me,' she said, frustrated. She jumped. 'Oh my God!' She giggled, covering her mouth. 'I see!'

* * *

I returned to my office in the spare room of the Emperor's Residence and checked my email, scanning for a specific subject and sender — then felt a jolt of joy when I saw it.

> Subject: *Make Your Man-Meat Earthquake*
> Sender: *John Boscoe <JennySmith@wowadmin.ru>*
> Message: *all assistant, speeds, smart(ass) isn't 4G, family king camera royal upgraded Even and 5, spectacular ready voice it's of and and a useful iOS to we has good: part without Call*
> *Woman cannot respect man with small ...*

I deleted the spam part about penis enhancement, copied the random words inserted into the message to fool spam filters, then pasted them into the decryption program that Gold had provided. The real message came up:

> *Hi Emma, all's well here and we miss you! Good news — the boys felt strong enough and both went back to school. Mark had a couple of bad episodes on the first few days — we nearly took him back out again, but he wouldn't let us. It's settled down and they're not having as many nightmares any more, and Andrew even brought a friend — would you believe it a girl — over! They're very cute and loudly claim just to be good friends. It's so good to see something as normal as that happening for them.*

28

Jen's new husband, Greg, has been a complete treasure, and he's such a reassuring presence. Even though he never does anything 'special' it's good to know that he's there just in case. He says it's relaxing to be away from all the politics of being the Tiger's Number One and asked me to pass on his good wishes to Michael — because he says he'll need it!

Perth is lovely, the weather is beautiful, and to be honest it's a great feeling just to be 'normal' again and to live an anonymous life. We've had to find a good doctor now that we don't have the extra boost — I didn't realise that we would go backwards so quickly when we left there, and your father has felt it particularly badly, but if we mind our wellbeing we should be fine.

That was a blow — I had hoped that my parents would retain the health benefits from being on the Celestial Plane. I wished I could see them, but they wouldn't return to the Celestial Plane to see me, and I couldn't go down there — it would blow their cover and make them a target.

That's all I have for now. We're all fine and I hope that one day soon you will be able to visit us. Pass on our best to John and Leo —

'Busy?'

I jumped and looked up. I'd been completely immersed in the email and hadn't even heard Leo appear in the doorway.

'Absolutely not.' I waved at the screen. 'My parents send their best; all's well with them.'

'That's good to hear.' He wheeled himself in and parked on the other side of the desk. 'I'm just here to gossip. Don't give me any advice, I want to have a moan.'

'Moan away, Lord Leo.'

He smiled slightly. 'I still get a kick from being called that. Then someone kills me and I have to go put up with goddamn Pao Qing Tian. The guy's a pain in the ass.'

I leaned my chin on my hand. 'So what's up? What could you possibly have to moan about? You have the dream marriage —'

'Not a real marriage,' he said, glum.

'With the prince of your dreams, the job of your dreams, and you live in Heaven. What could possibly be wrong?' I dropped my hand and sat more upright. 'You and Martin haven't fallen out, have you?'

'No, no,' he said, waving one hand. 'That side of it is … well, as you said, like a dream. Damn, he makes me happy. I wish I could make him as happy as he makes me.' He sighed and leaned on the desk, rubbing his eyes. 'It's my job.'

'Not your dream job any more?'

'Completely. But like I just told the Dark Lord, there's nobody to recruit. In the past year I've brought in every single kid that showed remotely enough talent, and we don't nearly have what we need to fill the gap left by the latest attack.' He ran a hand over his bald head. 'The decision's been made: we're halting recruitment for two years to give younger practitioners time to train up. Until then it's just not worth going down there.'

'How short are we?'

His face went rigid, then he shook his head. My limitation on helping run the Mountain had kicked in and he couldn't reply. I shouldn't have said 'we'. I tried a different tack — letting him have a moan.

'So this must make you feel pretty useless?'

'Tell me about it. I just got my dream job and I can't do anything. The Mountain is still short a good two hundred Disciples, and there's nowhere to recruit from; the well is dry. I've done my best, but we may need to expel at least twenty of the latest batch I brought in because they're not up to scratch.'

'Damn.'

Chang appeared in the doorway, filling it. He wore his brown working robes of a Buddhist monk. 'Sorry, I didn't realise there was someone with you,' he said. He bowed to both of us. 'I will return later.'

Leo turned back to me, confused. 'How come he can bow to you?'

'Don't go, come on in, Chang,' I said. 'Because of his humble nature he can bow to anybody. He bows to butterflies.'

'Well, everyone should bow to butterflies, they are the essence of enlightenment,' Leo said.

'You are quite correct, my Lord.' Chang came in to stand next to him. 'I have a request to ask of you, Miss Donahoe. When should I return?'

'What, me?' I said. 'You can't ask me anything.'

'I would just like to bounce an idea off you. You know the Dark Lord better than anybody; you can guide me on what his expected reaction would be.'

I waved for him to sit. 'Go right ahead.'

'Do you want me to leave you to it?' Leo said.

'I would like to hear your opinion as well, if you would, my Lord,' Chang said as he sat. He hesitated for a moment, then said, 'I hear that you are having difficulty recruiting on the Earthly Plane. There are not enough talented youngsters to bring the Mountain back to full strength.'

'That's just what I was complaining to Emma about,' Leo said. 'If you're thinking of recruiting Shen instead, that won't work. There's no talented Shen of majority age left either.'

Chang clasped his hands in his lap. 'I have a longer-term idea. You know where I came from: I was an orphan left at a monastery to learn the Arts. Maybe the Mountain could start its own orphanage on the Earthly? Care for youngsters, give them a start in the Arts and an education, and if they wish to pursue the Arts they can come up here.'

I stared at him, stunned.

When Leo finally spoke, his voice was thick with emotion. 'You humble me more and more every day, Chang.'

'Do you think the Dark Lord would accede to this request?' Chang said.

'He would welcome it,' I said. 'We already have orphanages, but this could be a full-on educational foundation. What a brilliant idea. I can help you with funding through the Earthly assets.'

Chang leaned forward, intense. 'Do you think he'd let me run it?'

'I can't think of anyone more qualified than you,' I said. 'Over-qualified to run just one home, to be honest. I'd like to see you running a whole foundation with a string of orphanages across Asia.'

'So I should put this idea to the Dark Lord?'

Leo spun his chair around. 'Come with me, Chang, he's in the meditation pavilion right now. If you don't make his shen energy flare with delight at the idea, I'll buy you a new set of prayer beads. I'll buy you a new set anyway; this is the best idea anyone on the Mountain's had in a while.'

Chang rose. 'I don't require new beads, the ones I have are perfectly functional.'

Leo patted him on the arm. 'How do you reward the man who needs nothing to make him content?'

'Having the Dark Lord agree to this would be a lifetime's worth of reward in itself.'

I rose and found I was able to join them. 'It seems I can come with you since this is related to the management of the estate.'

Leo grinned. 'Excellent.'

John was sitting cross-legged in Celestial Form in the meditation hall. He'd opened the screened walls of the pavilion and the late summer breeze and the scent of the Mountain's pines wafted through the room. His massive dark form was dimly visible in the centre of a two-metre-wide cylinder of energy and water that surrounded him and rose to the ceiling. Ribbons of glowing shen energy and his own dark essence swirled around him with an audible wash and a deep bass thrum that could be felt through the floor.

'He's a living yin-yang,' Chang said with wonder.

Leo's deep voice was full of awe. 'The highest form of goodness is like water. Water knows how to benefit all things without striving with them.'

The top of the cylinder lowered until John's face was visible above its edge. 'The water greets the ones it benefits,' he said without opening his eyes or stopping the flow of the energy. 'I'm not really alive, I just exist.'

He took a deep breath and held it, and the energy-filled water shrank into a smaller spiral and disappeared into his heart chakra. He opened his eyes, changed to his human form and, without rising, gestured for us to enter. 'Three who seek the Tao. Come and tell me what the disaster is this time.'

Chang tried to kneel behind Leo and me, but we manoeuvred him to kneel between us. He was silent, awestruck, until Leo poked his arm and he jumped.

'Uh, Celestial Highness,' he said, obviously intimidated. He bowed low from his knees over his hands on the mat, then sat upright. 'I have a humble request ...' He stopped, appearing to be lost for words.

John reached out and put his index finger on Chang's forehead. 'What is your request?' He was silent for a moment, then nodded and dropped his hands into his lap. 'I see your plan. There are already orphanages in each of the Twelve Villages. This is unnecessary duplication of work we are already doing. Why did you let him come, Emma? You know all about the orphanages.'

'I thought we could integrate what he's proposing into what we already have,' I said. 'The Twelve Villages are always complaining about having to run them. Sorry to have wasted your time, Chang.'

Chang bowed low over his hands again and rose to leave.

'I did not grant you leave to depart,' John said without looking at him.

Chang fell to kneel on the floor again and bent low.

'Sit up,' John said. 'Look at me.'

Chang sat up, head bowed.

'Look into my face!' John snapped.

Chang looked up.

John put his index finger on Chang's forehead again. 'You wish to be given custody of a large number of children, boys and girls. What would you do with them?'

'Teach them,' Chang said. 'Only through education can we change the world. Give them a life, a home, knowledge and the tools they need to go out and make the world a better place.'

John dropped his hand. 'You are to go to my office and report to my secretary. It will either be in human form outside my office or in the shape of a stone on my desk. It is called Zara. Tell it that you have been given the task of reviewing the orphanages run by the Twelve Villages and expanding them as you see fit. Liaise with Miss Donahoe on the funding of this expansion directly from the House of the North. With your intelligence and ability overseeing the administration, I think we can easily double the population of the orphanages and remove management from the Twelve Villages, who have always found this task a drain on their resources. I approve your five-year goal to have twelve large residential schools connected to, but not run by, the villages. Dismissed.'

Chang sniffled loudly, wiped his eyes, and bowed again. He rose to go out, and Leo and I moved to join him.

'Emma, remain. Leo, go with him to ensure Zara carries out this task; sometimes she can be …' he smiled slightly, 'stubborn about obeying anyone but me.'

Leo saluted John and he and Chang went out.

John waved one hand at me. 'Sit, Emma.'

I sat cross-legged opposite him.

He glared at me from under his brows. 'There is no need for you to still be wearing servant's black and white.'

I shrugged. 'Couldn't be bothered changing. It's comfortable enough.'

'Not fitting.' He put his hands on his knees. 'His motives are completely pure, which is surprising considering his history with women when he was an assassin. He will do well.'

'It never occurred to me that his motives could be anything but genuine.'

'You're only human. It's to be expected.'

I gazed into his eyes. 'Am I?'

He looked deeply into my eyes. 'Yes. You are mortal, and forgetful, and prone to emotional outbursts and the occasional fit of ridiculous stupidity.'

I raised my hands. 'Guilty as charged.'

He gracefully rose and put out one hand. I took it and he pulled me into him.

'But it's the serpent side of you that really drives me nuts,' he said softly into my ear.

'You said taking snake form wasn't a good idea,' I said, matching his low tone.

'It isn't,' he said. 'Please, for all our sakes, don't change to snake.' He wrapped his arms around me and held me. 'It's a very bad idea. But sometimes bad ideas are the most enticing.' He ran his mouth down the side of my throat, making me gasp, then moved back to whisper in my ear,

'One day, both my reptiles will show your serpent pleasure like you've never known.'

I shivered. 'Why does that sound terrifying and exhilarating at the same time?'

He moved so that his mouth was close to mine and put one hand on the side of my face. 'Reptiles together,' he said, and closed the gap.

The cylinder of water rose around us.

4

The doctor in the medical centre at the Tiger's Western Palace opened the door to his office. 'Emma?' he said without looking up from the card he was holding, then he saw me in the waiting room. 'Oh! I'm sorry, I didn't realise it was you.' He held the door open for me. 'Please, come on in.'

I raised one hand before I entered. 'Do you know about the restrictions on me?'

He nodded. 'I do.'

I went in and sat in the patient's chair next to his desk. 'Thank you. Just call me Emma; that's all you'll be able to use.'

He tried to say 'ma'am' and choked on the word. 'I see.' He turned and flipped open a new medical file for me. 'What can I do for you, Miss Donahoe?' He relaxed when he realised he could call me that. 'What brings you to the West when your own medical facilities in the North are some of the finest on the Plane?'

'Fertility,' I said. 'Your fertility clinic is the best. I only have one ovary and I want to make sure that I'm capable of having children with the Dark Lord.'

He looked down and shook his head. 'Damn. That's a big assignment: assisting the Dark Emperor.'

'We don't need to test him; he's already fathered Simone on a human woman so we know it can be done. We've been trying for a year now and I'm not getting any younger. We need to isolate any problems now.'

'Date of birth, Miss?'

'October twenty-third, nineteen seventy-three.'

'So you're already past forty.'

'Exactly. My biological clock is ticking.'

He wrote my birth date on the folder. 'Not really. On the Celestial Plane your child-bearing ability will extend for at least another ten years even without attaining Immortality. If you attain Immortality, you'll never have to worry about it.'

'Even if I attain Immortality after menopause?'

'Even so. An Immortal chooses their form and physiology. If you take a younger form for a year or so, you can still bear children. Even though it is slightly draining, many Immortals have done it without risk.'

I leaned back and sighed with relief. 'Thank you. I didn't know that.'

'Most Immortals are past the point of caring about having families.'

'Except your father.'

He chuckled. 'Even my father. Having us is just a side effect for him.'

'I see.'

He turned back to me and raised his pen. 'Last menstrual period?'

I looked up, trying to work it out. 'About six weeks ago?'

He checked his calendar and wrote the date. 'Are they normally six weeks apart?'

'They're as irregular as anything. Can be anything from three to ten weeks apart.'

'That may be from having only one ovary and insufficient hormones,' he said, writing notes. 'Nothing to be terribly concerned about. I'll start with some basic tests, just to make sure that everything is working. Blood tests, maybe move on to some X-rays, then if we don't establish anything we can try a laparoscopy.'

'You don't have anyone who can look directly inside me?' I said. 'I know you have routine ultrasounds, but I thought you'd have someone on staff who could do it without any invasive devices.'

'Only as a last resort. It's considered degrading to use someone with enhanced vision as a scanner. We don't generally ask unless it's absolutely necessary.'

'I see.'

'We have excellent fertility therapy here, and if the worst comes to the worst we can always use IVF. You have multiple options.'

'Thank you.'

He pulled an empty vial out of a drawer and placed it on the desk. 'I still need a semen sample from the Dark Lord. He's in very different shape now to when he fathered the Princess. We have to eliminate the possibility that he's the cause of the problem. It would be silly to do multiple invasive tests on you only to find that the issue is with him.'

'I'll arrange it.' I smiled slightly. 'You're in for a surprise there.'

He glanced at me and raised one eyebrow.

'Black,' I said.

'No way. Really?'

'And cold. Just like him.'

He leaned forward. 'How cold?' He leaned back and waved one hand. 'Sorry, my curiosity got the better of me.'

'Not cold enough to hurt, if that's what you're asking. Just … cold.'

'Fascinating. We'll start these tests straight away. Oh, and one other thing.' He closed the folder. 'It's about young Clarissa Huang.'

'How is she progressing? The psychiatrist won't let me see her.'

'Not well. Her kidneys have failed; she is on regular dialysis. Her organs can't recover from what she went through when she was held by the demons because her kidneys aren't cleansing her system correctly. If we don't find her a donor kidney soon, we may lose her to complete organ failure.' He shook his head. 'She is deteriorating rapidly.'

I held my arm out. 'You just need a blood sample to see if I'm compatible, don't you?'

He rifled through his equipment trolley for a syringe. 'Are you offering to donate a kidney if you're compatible?'

'Absolutely.'

He nodded as he fitted the needle to the syringe. 'Let me see if you're compatible first, then you can decide. This is not a decision to be made lightly. Immortals or Shen can't donate organs; their organs will kill an ordinary human patient. The donor organ must be from an ordinary human and they're in a limited supply on the Celestial Plane.'

He tightened the tourniquet around my upper arm and took a blood sample.

'Is there anything else I can do for Clarissa?' I said.

'She is withdrawn. The psychiatrist counsels her, but she's not very responsive. She won't talk to her family.'

'What about Michael?'

'She refuses to see him. It is a tragic situation.'

'Can I talk to her?'

'The psychiatrist won't let anyone except family or Michael in; she said that outside visitors would probably do Clarissa more harm than good. Right now the poor girl needs to be completely sheltered from the world, and to be reintroduced to it very slowly when she's strong enough.'

'If we don't find her a new kidney she may never be strong enough.'

'True. I hope we can find a compatible donor in time.' He transferred my blood into the vial. 'You didn't ask me whether you being European and her being Chinese made a difference to the possible organ compatibility.'

'That's because I know, medical wise, there isn't a difference.'

He nodded. 'As far as we doctors are concerned, there's no medical way to identify race. Racial differentiation doesn't exist; we're just all human beings.'

'I wish that was true for people who aren't doctors.'

He smiled at me. 'Snakes, however, are something completely different.'

'Will I still be compatible even though I can change to snake?'

'Let me test your blood and we'll see. Since your human form is so mundane, I think it may be possible.' He labelled the vial. 'Wait until we establish whether you're compatible or not and we'll take it from there. You can't donate a kidney if we're working to get you pregnant anyway.'

'Clarissa's life comes first.'

'Nevertheless, we can still start work on making a little snake baby for the Dark Lord. Goodness, that *is* a scary thought.'

* * *

I wound my way through the red stone archways of the Western Palace. Even though summer was nearly finished, the morning heat was radiating off the bricks and most of the residents were indoors in the shade. I passed through a small garden with a fountain in the middle spraying water that shone with a rainbow. I took the stairs down the steep hillside from the palace to the riding flats spread below. Blue-green mountains rose from the other side of the plain, and stretched so far and high that they became invisible, their snowy tops merging into the sky. The riding area was green in some places with irrigated grass; in other places, its natural sandy soil was used as a base for the training arenas.

Simone was having a lesson on Freddo in one of the sandy areas. They performed a near-perfect half-pass diagonally across the arena, Freddo lifting his feet and placing them carefully to cross as he trotted. The arch of his neck and the collection over his back was impressive to see, although the strain was obvious: he regularly twitched his tail with the effort of holding the shape.

'All right,' the instructor said. 'Now go around and try it again, and this time don't start until Simone actually gives the *aid*.'

I recognised the instructor: it was Lisel, one of the Tiger's more senior wives, an Olympic dressage medal winner.

Simone and Freddo straightened up, powered down the long side of the arena and turned to do the move again.

'Stop, stop, stop!' the instructor yelled. She pointed at the ground. 'Come here.'

Both Freddo and Simone looked sheepish as they walked towards her.

I leaned on the fence and watched them. Freddo looked particularly magnificent; he hadn't started his shaggy winter coat yet and his smooth golden summer coat was glossy with bronze highlights in the morning sunshine.

'I said wait for the aid,' Lisel said, obviously exasperated.

'But I don't need it,' Simone said. 'I just tell him.'

'And she didn't even need to tell me, because I know what to do,' Freddo said.

'What if you're in battle and there's fifty demons screaming all around you. What then?' Lisel said.

Simone shrugged. 'I talk to him telepathically.'

Freddo shook his ears, agreeing with her. 'I give up my will and let my Simone control me directly.'

'No, no, no!' Lisel stomped in a circle. 'So that's what you two have been thinking. No wonder you're not progressing.' She put her hands out towards them. 'How stupid are the two of you? Freddo, would you give your life for Simone?'

'In a second,' Freddo said, turning his head to look at Simone. 'She's my whole life.'

'Do you want to be the best you can for her?'

'I want to obey her. I want to give her my will and let her control me completely.'

Lisel sagged with defeat. 'You need to work intelligently as a team member, not be a puppet.'

'She's right, Freddo,' Simone said. 'I need you to make your own decisions. Sometimes we may be overwhelmed and we'll have to work as a team. You'll need to watch my back. And if you surrender your free will and let me control you, that's an extra complication that I really don't need.'

'Simone understands!' Lisel yelled, raising her arms in triumph.

'This is too hard. I just want to do what Simmony tells me,' Freddo said.

Simone dropped her face into his mane and wrapped her arms around his neck. 'Oh, Freddo.'

'You are worse than useless if you just sit around waiting for orders,' Lisel yelled, really losing her temper with Freddo. 'You will get Simone killed with your laziness.' She turned her back on them and stormed off. 'Go clean up, and come back when you are ready to protect your owner, horse. Until then I want nothing to do with you. You are useless.'

Freddo dropped his head with shame but Simone didn't let go of her clasp around his neck. Eventually he turned, head still bowed, and shuffled towards the stables.

'Tell Simone I'll be up in the coffee house waiting for her?' I said.

The stone didn't reply.

With its new position in my back, I couldn't tap it to wake it up, so I pulled out my mobile and texted Simone to let her know where I'd be.

I turned and walked back up the stairs to the Turkish-style coffee house. It was full of bright blue and purple woven mats and dark wood benches piled with glittering cushions against the red stone walls. A few of the Tiger's wives lazed around on the cushions, chatting, reading books and working with laptops. I sat on the veranda overlooking the riding plain and waved at the barista behind the bar.

He brought me a frappé in a condensation-covered glass. 'I've been watching the Princess and her demon horse,' he said. 'They're magnificent; you should be proud.'

'I am.'

'You were coming out of the clinic before, Emma. Is everything all right?'

'Perfectly fine.'

'You don't have any issues at the moment?'

I grinned into my frappé. 'No, Adrian, I'm in outstanding health.'

'I see.'

I didn't give him any more and he wandered away, obviously still curious.

* * *

We scheduled an estate management meeting that afternoon in the Peak apartment. I could participate in family decision-making provided neither the Mountain nor the Northern Heavens were involved.

It was sad to enter the empty Peak apartment. We used it as a base in Hong Kong whenever we needed to overnight there, and some of the furniture was still there, but everything else had been moved up to the Mountain.

The memories of our happy times in the apartment were strong, but every time I returned to the Mountain the sheer joy of being in such a wondrous location on the Celestial Plane made those memories fade into contented history.

The dining table was still the main meeting area, and Simone, John, Gold and I sat around it to discuss our plans.

'You've had more than enough time to look into my options for the Earthly,' John said. 'Fill me in.'

Gold opened the folder in front of him. 'This is an unusual situation, my Lord. Your severed head was recovered and you were definitely declared dead. This means that you can't return to being John Chen Wu; you'll have to take a new identity. You won't be Simone's father or Emma's fiancé on the Earthly, and you can't assume ownership of the properties.'

'You mean I'm stuck with them?' Simone said with dismay.

'Emma can manage them for you,' John said.

'Oh, thank you very much,' I said, then saw Simone's pleading face. 'Don't worry, Simone, I'll manage everything for you.'

'Thanks, Emma, but I don't want them,' Simone said. 'They make me really rich, and I want to go to university down here. I want to be an ordinary student, not a target for gold-diggers.'

'I can arrange alternative identities for both of you,' Gold said. 'Lord Xuan, I can give you a set of identity documents from the Mainland.'

'Is my previous human identity, John Chen's father, still active?' John said. 'It's about eighty-something years old, isn't it?'

'I'll check. If that's still valid we can re-use it,' Gold said. 'Princess, I can make you anyone you like.'

'What about getting into uni with the false identity?' Simone said.

'That might be slightly harder. It depends where you want to go.'

'HKU, Cambridge or Tokyo,' Simone said. 'HKU because I already have a home here; and Cambridge is where Daddy did his doctorate.'

'I used that old identity to do that doctorate,' John said. 'All my colleagues are probably gone.'

'Then Todai in Tokyo maybe,' Simone said.

'Why Tokyo?' I said.

'Whales.'

'What about Wales?' I said.

'No, the animals, silly,' she said. 'I want to do something to stop the meaningless slaughter of them. Education is the best way.'

'I'm impressed. You have my full support,' John said.

'Thanks, Daddy. This is something that impacts on you as well — whales are a major source of protein for you guys —'

'I'm a biological specimen,' John said with humour.

'The ones the whaling fleets take are just used for novelty food or frozen and stockpiled. It's a waste when sea life like you needs that protein.'

'It's been years,' John said.

'Cambridge would be extremely difficult,' Gold said. 'We'd have to fabricate an identity and a set of academic records from here that would match what you've done at CH, and even then you may not gain entrance. Todai you could walk into tomorrow.'

'What about identity documents if I wanted to study in Tokyo?' Simone said.

'The House of the East runs Todai University,' John said. 'It's as Gold said: you could walk into any undergrad program immediately. A good proportion of the tech students are the Dragon's children.'

'I'm not so sure about going there now,' Simone said.

'So the decisions are made,' John said. 'Gold to either reactivate my old identity or find me a new one from the Mainland. Emma to continue handling the properties in Simone's name, and Simone to talk to the Dragon about entering Todai.'

'What?' Simone said, horrified.

'As I said, the Dragon runs it.'

'That's your job as my father.'

'I'm too busy,' he said.

Simone rounded on me. 'Emma, you have to help me here.'

The doorbell rang and John's expression darkened. 'Gold, escort Simone and Emma to the Northern Heavens —'

'I need to be involved in this, don't lock me out,' Simone said. 'Gold, stay and guard Emma.' She rose. 'I'll answer it. It's the Number One Son of the King of the Demons, Emma.'

'Not your place,' John said. 'We will remain here with Emma. Gold will answer the door.'

Simone and I stood at John's shoulders as Gold escorted the visitors in. The Number One son of the Demon King was in his mid-twenties gangster form, slim and good-looking, with blond slicked-back hair and a pale grey silk suit.

'What the hell,' I said when I saw that Number One was accompanied by our half-demon fung shui master, Ronnie Wong.

Ronnie was in his normal human form, but he followed Number One like an automaton.

'Are you okay, Ronnie?' I said. 'What's going on?'

'He took my wife.' Ronnie seemed to struggle for a moment, then spoke with effort. 'I must obey Number One.'

'No,' Simone said softly.

Number One raised his hands. 'Not a good way to start the negotiations, I know, but I needed to get in here and this one has access.'

'Where's his wife?' John said.

Number One pulled a gold chain with a Buddhist medallion over his head and showed it to us. 'I used her as bait, but she's not harmed. I won't harm either of them; I'm just here to talk.'

'Please help us, it's taken Ronnie's free will,' the medallion said in a woman's voice.

John rose and leaned his fists on the table. 'Ronnie Wong was a good friend and a treasured consultant for the House of the North, and you have as good as killed him. I should destroy you where you stand.'

'I have important news for you,' Number One said. 'After I've told you, you can do what you like to me.'

John stood straight and waved one hand at Ronnie. 'You've taken his will.'

'I'm bigger than him and he obeyed me. It just happened.'

John thumped the table with one fist. 'He's half-human!'

'It was necessary.'

John became icy calm and spoke to the medallion. 'What is your name, stone?'

'Silica, my Lord.'

'Go out of this room, turn right, and straight ahead there will be another room. Wait there for me,' John said.

'I won't leave Ronnie,' she said.

'Order him to go with her,' John said to Number One.

Number One handed the medallion to Ronnie. 'Do as he says.'

Ronnie took the necklace and went out.

John waved for Number One to sit, and sat himself. 'That was unnecessary. I would have given you audience if you had petitioned me.'

'I had to make it look good,' Number One said. 'Next

time I'll request that your people capture me or something; Dad mustn't know what's going on. This time it has to look like I'm blackmailing someone close to you.'

'Gold, take True Form and position yourself on the roof to hide us from anyone who could be listening.'

Gold changed to his stone form and disappeared.

I wanted to contribute, but this was too big and I was restricted.

'Here's the deal,' Number One said. 'Dad is working very closely with the demons of the West. He's made a pact with them, one that many of us don't want to see come to fruition.'

'Why?' John said. 'If they are successful, you will rule the world.'

'Pah. Gweilohs will rule us again,' he said, and the meaning of 'gweiloh' really was 'foreign devil'. 'The Westerners will take control and our own King will be a puppet for them, just as happened in the past. This is a stupid idea.'

'Your father obviously doesn't think so.'

'He's power-mad. He's been successful in trapping you, and he thinks he can do anything.' He shook his head. 'He wears military uniforms. Crazy.' He glanced up at John. 'Let me give you the details of his plans, anything that will help you stop him. I don't care if my head ends up on a platter in one of the Mothers' caverns. I can't let him give us to the West. Again.'

'You want me to stop him and give you kingship?' John said. 'Give you access to everything he built — all of Six's stone science, the Death Mother's copies, the elementals? You'd have them all as weapons against us.'

Number One sliced one hand through the air. 'He nurtured them while they built his toys, and when they were done he killed them. None of them are left, and he keeps their technology so secure that if he was destroyed nobody else would have it.' He smiled slightly. 'Believe me, I would

49

like to get my hands on it, particularly the copies the Death Mother was making. But Dad's locked everything up extra tight and told everybody that if he's destroyed, it's all gone, and with it goes our chance to walk the Earth again. It's with him or not at all.'

John leaned back and rubbed his chin. 'So what's he planning?'

'He has a pact with the demons of the West. There are no Shen there —'

'What, none at all?' John said.

Number One shook his head. 'Something happened a long time ago. Maybe the demons won, I don't know. Anyway, there's nothing to stop the demons there helping Dad to bring you all down. They're building a very special hybrid army there — he won't go into details. Something about snakes, about Miss Donahoe —'

'What about me?' I said, able to ask something directly related to myself.

'I don't know. Something about snakes, about Miss Donahoe, about stones in Wales. He's been dropping hints that he's building an army of invulnerable demons, together with a host of fake elementals and artificial stones. It sounds enough to take you all down.'

'Invulnerable demons? How invulnerable?' John said.

'To quote my father, "Shoot them, hit them, pierce them — everything will bounce right off. My babies will be indestructible." After he said that, I decided to come here and warn you. What he's doing is wrong.'

'Where is his base?' John said.

'Wales.'

'We know that. Where specifically?'

'A big house somewhere in the northwest.'

'That's not much to go on,' John said.

I raised one hand. I couldn't advise or contribute, but the stone helped.

'Emma has spent some time making virtual visits to the region, my Lord, and I have been assisting her. It's quite a remote and sparsely populated part of Britain, and I believe the number of really big houses there could be counted on the fingers of one hand.'

I nodded my thanks to the stone.

'She can't follow it up now and find the exact house,' Number One said. 'We all know about the Jade Emperor's little tantrum.'

'With good reason,' I said.

He focused on me. 'You are one of them.' He pointed at me and spoke to John. 'You would make a foreigner Empress of the Northern Heavens, ruling when you are not present. Once again, they are taking over, and you are letting them. Helping them.'

'My daughter will also assist in future and she is half-European,' John said without emotion. He raised his hands to indicate Simone and myself. 'Behold, demon, two women at my side, neither of them full-blood Chinese.'

Number One glared at him. 'After the Boxers, one would think you'd know better.'

'I do. Race or gender makes no difference; it is intelligence and loyalty that count before anything. And in your case, I think you are correct. The demons of the West will be loyal to their own, and the King is foolish in making a pact with them.' He rose and put one hand on the table. 'Do you need assistance in returning to Hell?'

'I petition that you break both of my legs and leave me unconscious in an alley in Dongguan. They will find me there.'

'No. Either I destroy you or I free you. I do not torture demons for pleasure.'

'Then release me and I'll pretend that I've escaped.'

John glowered at him. 'That would be seen through immediately. There is no escape from me.'

'Very well, destroy me. I will not turn,' the demon said. 'It is enough that you will stop the foreigners from taking over our Hell.'

John strode to Number One, who jumped to his feet. John took him by the throat and forced him onto his knees. 'Confirm you were telling the truth just then.'

'I was,' Number One said without a trace of fear. 'Just do it.'

'Very well.' John released him and stepped back. 'How much do you want to live?'

'I knew I was dead the minute I walked in your door,' the demon said, still on his knees. 'I'm dead already.'

'If I had a way of returning you to Hell unharmed and with a cast-iron alibi, would you do it?'

The demon stared up at John, expressionless. 'If they found out, my death would be very, very slow. Even more so because of what I am — I don't have a shell to break, I have blood and bones. They could play with me for a long time.'

'I'm aware of that. Do you have the courage to take that risk anyway, to stay alive and help us stop the Westerners from taking over Hell?'

The demon thought for a moment. 'It depends how cast-iron we're talking about here.'

John placed his index finger on the middle of Number One's forehead. 'Go to this place and stay for as long as you see fit. The staff there will be waiting for you.'

Number One stared at him, then grinned with disbelief. 'I know that place. I'm a regular. That's yours?'

'Even better if you are known to them,' John said.

'Can we meet there in future?' Number One said.

'There are better seals on this apartment, nobody can see what we are doing. I will give you leave to move directly between there and here. You will not need to hijack any

52

more of my associates in future. Just go there and the staff will show you the way directly here.'

'You're on,' Number One said, and disappeared.

* * *

John dropped his hands to his sides. 'Now for the fun part.'

Silica and Ronnie were standing clutching each other in the training room, rocking gently back and forth. Ronnie was silent, but Silica was quietly moaning 'No' over and over.

Ronnie heard us come in and pulled back to speak to Silica. 'I need to know that you'll be safe. As long as they can command me, you're not safe — and I can't live with the idea that I'll ever hurt you.'

'I'd rather be dead than have you do this,' she said. She moved closer to him, but he pushed her away. 'Don't do it!'

'I love you,' he said, his voice thick. 'You're the best thing that ever happened to me.' He brushed one hand down the side of her face. 'Goodbye.'

He spun towards us; his eyes were as red as hers. He fell to his knees. 'Lord Xuan, protect me, I am yours,' he said.

Silica fell to her knees next to him and buried her face in his shoulder.

'Make him take it back,' Simone said.

'It's done, sweetheart,' John said. 'Once the words are said, they can't be unsaid. He's tamed.' He went to Ronnie. 'Stand up and hold out your hand.'

Ronnie didn't hesitate. He stood, holding out his hand. Silica rose with him, sobbing quietly into his shoulder. John took his hand and fed the Fire Essence Pill into him, ensuring total obedience.

Simone choked a huge gasping breath and disappeared.

'First me, then Freddo, now Ronnie,' I said. 'This has to stop.'

John put his hand on Silica's shoulder. 'He was pursuing the Way, Silica. He is not completely demon, and he may eventually regain free will.'

'I will stay with him for as long as it takes,' she said. She touched his face. 'My Ronnie is still in there somewhere, I know it.'

Ronnie ignored her, concentrating completely on John as he waited for his next order. She turned away and wiped her eyes.

'Present yourself to L K Pak, the demon master of Wudang Mountain,' John said. 'Tell him what has happened, and to start immediately on finding a way to speed the recovery of your freedom.'

'I do not wish to recover, I wish to serve you,' Ronnie said, and disappeared, Silica with him.

We went back to the Mountain, and John landed us among the small cypress trees outside the Imperial Residence.

'Where did you send Number One?' I said.

'Number Eighty-Eight Spring Garden Lane. I had Gold take Number One's form, head straight to a bank and deposit a large amount of gold. Anyone watching will think that someone borrowed Number One's form to blackmail us while Number One was in the brothel.' His expression changed to horror and he stepped back. 'Oh, shit.'

'What?'

'Nothing, nothing. So what do you have planned for the rest of this afternoon?'

'Ha!' I said. 'You thought I didn't know about Number Eighty-Eight. I've been running things for ten years, John, of course I know about it.'

'You're not mad?'

'Of course not. The staff there are lovely. What —'

'What do you mean, the staff are lovely?' he said sharply. 'You've been down there?'

'Of course I have. I go down regularly to make sure everybody's happy. Cerise passed her Diploma of Administration two years ago and she's running the back of house. Niktor's been studying make-up and wants to break into movies.'

'You should not be seen to be associating with them, that is not fitting,' he said. 'Wait, who's Niktor?'

'New guy. Couldn't find a job doing anything else because he's so screamingly obvious, but the movie business may be an opportunity for him. I rescued him off a street corner. Leo's been trying, unsuccessfully, to get him to be more true to himself, but Niktor seems too scared to do anything but act out the stereotype.'

We started walking towards the administration area. 'I haven't had time yet to find out how the old staff are and meet the new ones,' John said. 'So much to catch up on.'

'What I would like to know', I said, 'is how you came to own the flagship of demonkind's underworld operations in Hong Kong a hundred years before Simon Wong emerged as a local power.'

'That's a very long story,' he said with humour.

'Stone,' I said, tapping my engagement ring before I remembered it wasn't there. 'John, give the stone in my back a tap, will you?'

'Jade Building Block,' John said.

The stone didn't reply and I felt a shot of concern. 'Stone?'

John put his hand on my back between my shoulderblades. 'It's definitely there. Just a sec ...' A flash of cold pierced my back and I yelped.

'Sorry,' he said. 'Stone?'

The stone still didn't reply.

'Don't do that again,' I said. 'It hurt! Let's find Gold and ask him to talk to it.'

'When was the last time it spoke to you?' John said, still with his hand on my back.

'A few days ago, at BJ's mineral-taking.' My stomach fell. 'It's been slowly fading, hasn't it?'

'Or it had too much to drink last night at the mineral-taking party and wants to be left alone,' the stone said, its voice sharp with sarcasm.

'Better check the wine cellar, John, you know about the stone's taste,' I said.

'I have better taste than most and I'm not afraid to admit it,' the stone said. 'And if you're nice to me, I may even be persuaded to advise you on the contents of the Mountain's cellar.'

'Stone, John's going to tell me the story of how he came to own Eighty-Eight. Can you record it for me, please?' I said.

'I even get a please,' the stone said, its voice softening. 'Don't worry, I'm not gone yet.'

'I'm glad,' I said.

'Let's go to my office and I'll tell you the tale of the Stone Turtle and the Brothel at Number Eighty-Eight Spring Garden Lane,' John said.

'Excellent,' the stone said. 'I've never heard that one before.'

5

Three days later, while I was studying the half-a-dozen books on Western mythology I had open on my desk in the spare bedroom of the Residence, the tower bells began to ring. I didn't bother asking anyone what was going on; I just summoned my sword and ran towards the offices.

Outside the armoury, Disciples were being issued with weapons and forming squads. The weapons master, Miss Chen, was supervising and yelling directions.

'Third- and fourth-year energy specialists to the west wall with Master Meredith; physical specialists to the west gate with Master Liu. Second years to the other three walls in case they mount a flanking operation. First years, divide into your teams and be ready to run supplies, wounded and messages. Master Au is your supervisor.'

The bells changed in pitch and Miss Chen looked up. 'They're close now, everybody to battle stations. Run!'

She glanced at her assistant. 'Are all the arrows out?' Her assistant said something and she nodded. 'Then let's head to the west wall and help defend.'

She stopped and pointed at me. 'Emma Donahoe, get your little white ass into the Imperial Residence right now or else.'

'No need to be offensive,' I said. 'I won't participate. I'll stand at the top of the wall near Lord Xuan and record for the Chronicles.'

She glared at me. 'I don't believe a word you're saying.'

'Isn't there somewhere you're supposed to be?' I said, heading towards the admin area and the western wall.

She muttered something unintelligible and disappeared.

John was standing on the southwest corner of the wall that joined his office, watching the demons approach.

'You are not supposed to be here,' he said without turning away from the view.

'I'm here to record for the Chronicles.'

He took Celestial Form, complete with his battle armour: plain black with the seven stars of the Big Dipper on his breastplate. His hair came loose and flowed around him as he grew to three metres tall. His skin was darker, and his square ugly face wore a thin black beard.

'Stay well back and keep yourself out of trouble, please,' he said with his usual voice. 'I would hate to lose you to these, because the King himself is among them.'

He changed to silent speech in broadcast mode. *This is a big group: two hundred level fifty plus, but non-Mothers. They're probably shooting for promotion. Behind them are at least twenty level seventy plus, and the King himself is at the rear flanked by two bull-head dukes.* His voice changed slightly. *They are all mounted on demon horse-hybrid steeds the like of which I have never before seen. It would be advantageous to take one alive and see what's inside. Take care, all, they may be poisonous.*

'Venomous horse-hybrids?' I said.

'Wait until you see them.'

He summoned Seven Stars and the dark sword appeared in his hand. He raised it and loaded the seven circular holes in the sword with his own chakra energy, lighting up the blade so that it sang with restrained power.

'These will be something of a challenge with our current depleted numbers, but we should overcome them easily,' John said. *Lord Leo, to the west wall.*

Leo appeared next to him and quickly fell to one knee. 'My Lord.' He saw me and glared. 'What the hell are you doing here? You should be inside the compound where it's safe.'

'Up, Leo, and stay alert,' John said. 'The King himself is with this group, and it's not a threat to the Mountain by any stretch. He may be planning to do something to the Serpent to disable me while he's attacking the compound. If he does, pull me inside the compound and notify the senior masters.'

'My Lord,' Leo said, moving to stand next to John. He took Celestial Form: a larger version of himself, the same size as John's form, wearing a Mountain uniform with armour over the top.

'Check with Ming Gui that there is no army gathering on the borders of the Northern Heavens,' John said.

'Prince Ming reports that there is nothing there that appears untoward,' Leo said. 'He has mobilised the defences just in case.'

'Good.'

The demons came into view, riding creatures that galloped on clouds. I rubbed my eyes as I tried to focus on them through the mist. At first glance, the creatures appeared to be horses, but had too many legs and their heads were strangely out of proportion. As they drew nearer it became clear that although they had the bodies of palomino horses, they were massively elongated and had four pairs of legs. Their heads were wider than a horse's, and they had a circle of eight eyes on top like a spider's, with fanged mouthparts hanging down instead of a horse's mouth.

'Dear god, they're ugly,' Leo said.

'The one the King's riding appears to be an ordinary demon horse,' John said. 'I'm glad Simone isn't here — it looks like Freddo.' He shifted slightly and Seven Stars sang through the air, leaving a trail of light as it moved. 'On my mark.'

'No parley?' I said.

'The Demon King used language one does not repeat in front of a lady when I offered parley,' John said.

'Good thing there's no ladies here then,' I said.

'Emma,' he dropped his voice, 'hold on to that sword. It's the only thing that will destroy him. And if it comes to that, don't hesitate to use it.'

'Seven Stars will take him down too, won't it?'

John glanced down at his glowing sword. 'Yes, it would destroy him. But his dark energy would obliterate the chakra energy in Seven Stars, taking my intelligence with it. Possibly for good.'

'What, permanently?'

'Could be. I could even lose my Celestial alignment. The Murasame is the only weapon that is safely capable of destroying this King.'

'So use yin if you have to.'

'I will.' He hefted the sword. 'Stay back where it's safe. As long as you're up here I'll be able to defend you.'

The west gate, covered from bottom to top with the image of a gold and white tiger, opened and a cohort of third and fourth years, guided by junior and senior masters, emerged to stand in ranks on the narrow roadway between the cliffs that led to the gate. Even though the demons could fly, they would be limited in their movement by the narrowness of the canyon. To our left, at the top of the wall, another group of third and fourth years armed with bows took position, ready to pick off any demons that attempted to fly over the wall. Five of the Academy's dragons in True Form landed next to them, ready to assist.

'It's about two to one to our advantage,' I said. 'For it to be an even match human to demon, it really should be about three to one.'

'I'm well aware of that,' John said mildly. 'But remember that I am here as well, and I am worth more than fifty by myself.'

The demons landed on the roadway and spurred their horses into a gallop, charging at the students. John spread his arms and leapt off the wall, somersaulting to land on his feet at the front of the group. Leo leapt to follow him, summoning his own sword, the Black Lion, as he fell. The demons surged around John and attacked the students.

The students fought in tight-knit groups, three or four of them to a single hybrid-mounted demon. The students on the wall used energy arrows to pick off the flying demons, complaining loudly that they couldn't get clear shots in the mêlée.

The Demon King stood at the back of his demon army, seemingly content to watch.

John stopped for a moment, brought his hands together around his sword and pulled it apart into two identical blades, the indentations on each joined to the other by a shining ribbon of coloured light. He swung the swords, one in each hand, and the rainbow band destroyed every demon he caught in it. He swung the swords over his head, the ribbon of light stretching wider as it swept around him, and demons exploded into black essence.

I concentrated on the Demon King. More than anything, I wanted to run up to him and take him down, but I'd suffered enough for my rash actions already. He was still watching, but also appeared to be speaking to someone.

There was a shout from below. John had collapsed, returning to his small human form and dropping the swords. They singed the vegetation around them, then lost their light and returned to the single blade, which disappeared. Leo knelt next to John, quickly checked him, then tossed him over his shoulder and ran to the wall. He ran up it to the top and gently dropped John onto his back on the stones next to me.

The demons redoubled their efforts, but the students held them off. The dragons lifted the demon horse-hybrids and threw them into the Mountain's walls, splattering them into demon essence.

'He's barely conscious and his pupils are constricted,' Leo said. 'No sign of head injury. If I didn't know better, I'd say he'd OD'd on an opiate.'

'Just let me sleep,' John mumbled, then turned over and vomited. I quickly stepped back to avoid it, but Leo wasn't as fast.

'Definitely looks like an OD,' Leo said, picking John up again and carrying him towards the infirmary, not seeming to notice the mess all over him. 'How did the King ...' He realised before I needed to explain. 'They did this to the Serpent.'

* * *

Edwin already had a bed ready for John, and quickly pulled back his eyelids and shone a light into his eyes. He went to the stores cupboard, found a testing kit and swabbed the inside of John's mouth. Leo held the reagent strip as Edwin ran the swab over it, then both of them watched it change, seemingly oblivious to the injured students being brought in and cared for by Edwin's assistants.

'Negative for everything,' Edwin said, confused, then his expression cleared as he understood. 'The drugs aren't in his system, they're in the Serpent's.' He looked around the infirmary. 'Anything major?'

'Cuts and bruises mostly; a broken wrist as well,' one of his assistants said. 'We're on top of it.'

Edwin looked back at John. 'Simone used techniques she'd learnt in school to fight the drugs they gave her at Angkor. Surely he'd have the same skills?'

'I think he's too out of it to be aware,' I said.

'I don't want to give him the antidote. Without the drugs in his system, it could do more harm than good,' Edwin said. 'We can't let him die, it's too dangerous. We need to wake him up and talk to him.' He shook John's shoulder. 'Lord Xuan, it is vitally important that you try to stay awake for us.'

'No,' John said. 'Let me sleep.'

'John Chen Wu, you listen to me right now,' I said sternly. 'Your Mountain is under attack, your students are in danger, and you need to wake up and defend them.'

That roused him. 'My students are in danger?' He groggily tried to rise.

'John,' I said urgently, 'the Serpent can talk through the Turtle. Can the Turtle act through the Serpent?'

'Don't want to, could rejoin,' he said, trying to focus on me. 'Why is it so dark?'

'The Serpent's full of opium,' I said. 'It's affecting you. Can you fix it?'

'Opium,' John said with distaste, dropping his head again. 'Never tried the stuff; it killed too many of my people. Wait.' He raised his head. 'In the Serpent?'

'The King's filled the Serpent with opium. It's making you like this.'

'We'll see about that,' he said grimly, and flopped back on the bed, closing his eyes. His face filled with concentration, then he took a deep breath in and out again. 'You're right. Someone put it in my food. Must have injected a litre of the stuff into the chicken they gave me. I wondered why it tasted so bitter. Just give me a moment.' His eyes snapped open, and this time his pupils were enormous. 'I've never taken opium, but I can see how it works and I think I can reverse the effect it's having on me ...' He took another deep breath and held it.

I held my own breath as I waited for him to let it out, but he didn't. After a couple of minutes I couldn't stay silent. 'Edwin ...'

'I know,' Edwin said. 'If he goes blue I'll do something.'

John spasmed as if he'd been shocked and released the breath. He panted for a few moments, then turned to look at me. His eyes were back to normal. 'Fixed.'

Demons are retreating, Liu said.

'This whole thing,' I indicated the injured students around us, 'it was just to try this out?'

'Unfortunately, yes,' John said. 'And they gained some valuable information as well.'

'What information?' Leo said.

'One, that I can act on the Serpent to clear any drug they try to use on it. And two, when I was talking to you, the Serpent was saying what I was saying. They know that I can speak through the Serpent — and therefore that the Serpent can speak through me.'

'Oh, damn,' I said.

'I have patients to attend to,' Edwin said, rising. 'You'll be fine. You may need to rest after the exertion.'

John tried to sit up, struggled with it, and gave up. 'Leo,' he said.

'My Lord?'

'Go take a shower, you stink.'

'With great pleasure, my Lord. May I suggest that you do the same because, with all due respect, so do you.'

'Give me a hand to the Residence?'

Leo grinned. 'Sure thing, Dad.'

John and I both stared at him in shock and said in unison, '*Dad*?'

'I'm engaged to his son, aren't I?' Leo said, the grin not shifting. He put one arm around John's shoulder and assisted him to stand. 'I think that gives me every right to expect a trip to the ball game with you.'

'Don't push your luck,' John said.

'Leo, be quick, you're needed back here,' Edwin said.

'Can you wait for me to help him back to the Residence?' Leo said.

'Go right ahead, there's nothing critical. But come straight back when you're done. An extra nurse is always good.'

'I'll take him, you stay and help,' I said.

'We're both covered in turtle vomit, we need to clean up,' Leo said, helping John towards the door. 'You can mind him when I get him home.'

'Do as the Immortal Lord says,' John said, wincing as Leo guided him through the door. 'He has precedence.'

'Damn,' I said, and followed them.

* * *

Later that day, as dusk was falling over the compound, John lay on the bed and I gently worked over the acid burns, performing mild energy healing. I couldn't fix them completely, but I was speeding up the healing process and in a couple of days he would be fine.

'The biggest you can take without the Serpent's help is about level sixty-five,' John said. 'The King would have torn you to pieces.'

'He raped my nephews,' I said.

'Is that good enough reason to kill yourself seeking revenge? We fixed that death wish.'

'My nephews will never completely recover and it's his fault.'

'Your family would never forgive you.'

'If he was gone, my family could come out of hiding and I could see them again!' I said, my voice strained.

He was silent at that.

'Can I come in?' Simone called from outside the door.

'Yeah, it's fine,' I said.

Simone stopped when she saw John's torso covered in burns. 'We need to do something about this, Daddy.'

He pulled himself up to lean on the bedhead. 'You concentrate on your schoolwork. Let me deal with this.'

She gestured towards his injuries. 'Cuts *and* burns.' She sat on the bed next to him. 'Give me back my yin and I'll sort this out myself.'

He held his hand out, his expression grim. She took it, and they sat motionless for a moment, hands clasped, neither of them breathing.

'Is everything okay?' a girl said from outside the room.

John and Simone snapped back with a visible jump.

'Sorry, Hickory,' Simone called out. 'I got distracted talking to my dad. My bedroom's the first one on the side there, around the balcony. I'll be right there.'

'Your father's in there?' Hickory said, her voice small. 'The Dark Lord?'

'Put a shirt on,' Simone hissed, and John conjured a black Mountain uniform. 'Come on in and say hello if you like, Hickory.'

'Uh ... I think I'll just go wait for you in your room, if that's okay,' Hickory said.

'That's fine,' John said with a small smile. 'Simone will be along shortly.'

Hickory squeaked and we heard her footsteps run towards Simone's room.

Simone glared at John. 'You like scaring my friends.'

'I don't do anything at all to them,' he said. 'They do it to themselves.'

'I suppose everybody's afraid of the dark, Simone,' I said.

Simone rose. 'How long before you can give me my yin back?'

'Do you really want it that badly?'

Simone gestured towards his chest. 'I want to stop them doing that to you.'

'I may consider returning it to you when you no longer want it for revenge.'

66

She sighed loudly. 'Yeah, I know the drill.' She bent and kissed him on the cheek and he rubbed her back affectionately.

'I have study to do,' she said. 'We only have a few more weeks until the final exams.'

'You'll be just fine,' he said.

As she went out, he sighed. 'I have enough to worry about without dealing with the pair of you wanting to go off and throw yourselves at a demon that has been working for years to make itself more powerful.'

'I won't let her,' I said.

'I'm very glad. I'm also glad that she won't let you.'

After John was asleep, I went back to my reference books. Hickory was loudly complaining to Simone in the room next-door to me, and Simone was trying to placate her.

'I opened it, and it was a *black* one!' Hickory said. 'I cannot believe this — he got me a black one. I told him I wanted a white one *six weeks* ago, and he goes and buys me a black one. My life is completely over.'

'But there's no difference,' Simone said. 'Look at this one — everything's the same.'

'Oh my god, see?' Hickory said. 'You have a white one. Honestly, how could any father get something so completely wrong?'

'This is actually a black one. Michael changed it to white a while ago to annoy me,' Simone said.

'Michael?' Hickory's voice grew sly. 'Michael who? There's no Michael in our grade.'

'Michael MacLaren.'

Hickory gasped. 'The Tiger's Number One?'

'Didn't you know he used to live in the House of the North?'

'No?' Hickory was breathless. 'He lived here?'

'Beside the point now, he's the Tiger's Number One,' Simone said. 'He made this phone white to piss me off. His father had to have a white one, so Michael stole mine and practised on it before he did his father's.'

'That is so cool,' Hickory said. 'You are so lucky. Look at me, my dad is so useless he goes out and buys me a black one. He did this deliberately to hurt me, I'm sure of it. If he loved me, he'd get me a white one when I asked for it.' She thumped the desk. 'I get next to no allowance and they make me *help* running the household. I have to *work*. I might as well be a slave. I just wish they'd *die*.'

'Hickory,' Simone said, her voice taut with restraint, 'your father is a dragon and he's mortal. He won't be around forever. How can you talk like that about him? God, my dad's freaking Immortal and I treasure every minute with him. I missed him so much when I was growing up —'

Hickory cut her off. 'It's all right for *you*, you have a white phone.'

'I'd swap a million stupid white phones for the ten years I lost with him,' Simone said. 'Now can we go back to the major phyla? If we don't get these memorised, we'll fail our finals and never be able to buy ourselves anything, black or white.'

'I wonder if I can take it back to the shop and get them to change it,' Hickory said.

'I can ask Michael to change the colour for you, if you like.'

'Let me get my hair done before I talk to him!'

'He's engaged to be married, Hickory.'

'So?'

'And his fiancée was tortured by demons. They deserve all the happiness they can find together.'

'God, Simone, sometimes you sound like my mother.'

'Sometimes I feel old enough to be your mother.'

6

The next morning, a large group of students gathered at the main forecourt where John was giving Michael a one-on-one lesson with the Tiger looking on. John and Michael were both in ordinary human form, but the Tiger was in full Celestial Form. His face was a cross between a man's and a tiger's and he was three metres tall, covered in short white fur and wearing a robe of white and gold. His mane of white hair fell all the way down his back and was loosely tied with a gold ribbon at his waist. He had his arms crossed as he watched, one furry clawed hand resting on his other forearm.

John carried Dark Heavens, his preferred weapon in human form. Michael was using the White Tiger. They had passed the kata stage and John was attacking Michael with swift random strikes. Michael was deflecting them easily.

'A click faster,' John said, and attacked again.

Michael didn't say anything; his face was full of concentration.

'Click,' John said, and ramped up the speed again. Michael's expression hardened, but he continued to parry.

'Click,' John said, and his attacks became almost too fast to see. Michael's parries were similarly fast, but on the eighth strike they both stopped at the same time. John's sword was millimetres from Michael's throat.

John swung the blade away from the side of Michael's neck and stepped back. 'That's really the best you can do?'

Michael nodded.

John grew and stretched and darkened, taking Celestial Form. He was half a metre taller than the Tiger, with a square, dark, ugly face. Some of the students gasped with shock and took a few steps back, nearly treading on me behind them.

John towered over Michael. 'Let's try it full-on.'

Michael changed to Celestial Form as well, with white and gold armour and his snow-white hair in a short ponytail. He was the same height as his father and his golden skin glowed from within. He took up a guard position, and John dismissed the sword and attacked him barehanded. Michael used his sword to parry and John deflected every stroke to the bracers on his forearms. Michael didn't touch him.

John moved faster, and Michael began to shift on the spot, moving more vigorously as he deflected the attacks with his sword, and unbalancing with the effort. Sparks flew from John's bracers as Michael struck as hard as he could to deflect the blows.

They stopped mid-move. The blade of John's hand was a centimetre from Michael's larynx.

The Tiger dropped his arms and turned away. 'Shit.'

John shrank to human size and stepped back. He crossed his arms and glowered at Michael. 'Who has been training you?'

Michael drooped with misery. 'The best in the West.' He nodded to the Tiger. 'The Emperor himself, when he has time. But nobody in the West is as good as you, my Lord.'

The Tiger turned back to face them and raised one arm towards John. 'Nobody anywhere is as good as him. Don't blame it on the West.'

'Can you spare him twice a week?' John said.

'No, but do whatever it takes. It's either send him over here twice a week or put up with him being continuously at the mercy of Pao Qing Tian in Court Ten.'

'How often are they calling him out?' John said.

'Dad ...' Michael gestured towards the group of students watching them.

'What?'

Michael sighed. 'Having the Horsemen going after me is enough. I'd prefer not to have senior Wudang Disciples calling me out as well. I'd be spending so much time dead I'd never get anything done.'

'Good point. Let's either lose the tourists or go somewhere a bit more private,' the Tiger said. 'Got a training room big enough to work in Celestial Form?'

'No, that's why we're out here,' John said. He nodded to the students. 'Dismissed.'

The students turned to go and I moved to join them.

'Please stay, Emma, I have something to ask you,' Michael said, and I waved one hand and waited.

John turned back to Michael. 'I'll order my Disciples not to call you out. They're more obedient than the Horsemen; you won't receive any trouble.'

'Well, fuck you too, Turtle,' the Tiger said.

John turned to the Tiger, summoned Dark Heavens and attacked him at neck height in one fluid movement.

The Tiger performed a handspring backwards, more cat than human, and summoned a short curved sword in each hand. 'Shit, Turtle, I apologise! I apologise!'

John swung Dark Heavens at the Tiger's head faster than was visible. The Tiger was hard put to block the blade with both of his paws crossed in front of his face. He swept the blades down, feinted with his right towards John's eyes and tried to get around his guard with the left into his side, but John moved faster, blocking both one after the other and locking the Tiger's hands together. He pushed the Tiger away and stepped back, readying himself to attack again.

'Seriously, Turtle, please, man,' the Tiger said, panting. 'I only just got the wife schedule under control from last time you executed me. I swear, it was a slip of the tongue —'

He didn't finish because John lopped his head off. It bounced a couple of times and landed near Michael.

'Well, thanks a lot,' it said. 'I haven't seen my favourites in weeks, they miss out again, and now I have to redo the schedule. Thanks a bunch.'

John dismissed his sword and prodded the Tiger's head with his foot. 'Keep a more respectful tongue in your head and you may keep both of them more often.'

'You know what to do, Number One,' the Tiger's head said.

'Sure thing, Dad, have fun with Judge Pao,' Michael said.

'Erk,' the head said, and it and the body disappeared.

'Speak to Zara about arranging biweekly training sessions,' John said to Michael. 'Two hours each session. Let's start again from the beginning.'

'By your leave, my Lord,' Michael said, and turned to call to me. 'Miss Donahoe, may I have an interview after this training? I have something I need to ask you.'

'Of course, Michael, I'll be in the Residence, in the room you vacated.'

'Thank you.' He turned back to John. 'Show me how to use the energy to speed it up again.'

* * *

Michael came into the spare room I'd set up as an office and smiled wryly. 'I can't even salute or anything. This feels really wrong.'

I pulled a chair over for him. 'You've always been family, Michael, no need anyway.'

He spun the chair so that it was backwards and sat on it. 'You offered to donate a kidney for Clarissa. I want to thank you personally for that.'

'I'm compatible?'

'No, you aren't. But we've found a generous wife who is, and Clarissa will be getting a new kidney this week.'

'That's great news.'

'When she's recovered, I wonder if you could do me a favour?'

'Sure, anything. Do you want me to speak to her for you?'

'Yes, I do.' He crossed his arms over the back of the chair. 'She won't see anybody. Her parents think she's in a hospital in China, and they're prepared to visit, but she won't see them. She might see you, however; she has a lot of respect for you.'

'I'm honoured.'

'So are we. Will you?'

'If she's willing to see me, of course I am.'

He rose and spun the chair back into its place. 'Thanks, Emma.'

Simone appeared in the doorway. 'Emma, there's a message for you from the Archivist —' She saw Michael. 'Oh, hi, Mike.'

He nodded to her. 'Princess.'

She leaned on the doorway. 'Cut it out.'

'I'll be going then,' Michael said to me. 'When Clarissa's ready to see you, I'll email and we can arrange something.'

'How is Clarissa?' Simone said.

'She's getting a new kidney, she'll be fine,' Michael said.

Simone went to him and patted him on the arm. 'I'm really glad, Michael. That's wonderful.'

He smiled down at her. 'We'll get there.'

She released his arm. 'I know you will. She's like a sister to me.'

'I have to go. I'll see you later.' He ruffled her hair and she winced.

'I hope you have gel all over your fingers,' she said. 'I just fixed it up.'

He leaned down to speak conspiratorially to her. 'I already have gel on my fingers; how else do you think I spike the front of mine up?' He turned and waved one hand at me. 'Later, Emma.'

Simone looked longingly after him for a moment, then snapped out of it. 'The Archivist wants to talk to you about your research on the West. He says give him a call so you can make an appointment.'

'I'm free just about all the time. The only arrangement I need to make is for someone to carry me.'

'I'm going to the library tomorrow morning to meet my study group,' she said. 'Are you free then?'

'Sure.'

'Let me see.' Her eyes unfocused. 'God, he's rude. He says 9 am.'

* * *

The Archivist had changed the appearance of the Archives again. It was no longer floating islands; instead it appeared as a concrete bunker surrounded by barbed wire on steep snow-covered slopes.

'This is unimpressive,' I said.

'Covert Ops,' Simone said. 'Boring. He spends way too much time playing it.'

She pointed to the edge of the compound where a group of snow-camouflaged soldiers were attempting an incursion, shooting at the guards in front of the bunker. The entrance to the bunker opened and the bullets whizzed around and sometimes through us. As we approached the Archivist's office, we could hear him shouting.

'Don't give me that shit, try-hard, we lost because of you. I am so kicking you off the clan.' He was silent for a moment, then his voice went up in pitch. 'Twelve years old? Twelve years old? I'll tell you who sounds twelve years old, mother—' He was interrupted, but shouted them down. 'I may sound fucking twelve years old but I got a few good solid centuries on you, asshole, and don't you forget it.'

We entered his office to find him in the form of a twelve-year-old boy, sitting on a couch in front of a first-person shooter on a large-screen television.

'So next time we're out and it's for ladder,' he shouted into his headset, 'you keep your fucking position when told.' He saw us. 'Never mind, I have to go. Work and shit. See you later, eh?'

He flipped off the headset and threw the controller to one side. 'Ladies.' He rose and gestured for us to sit across his desk, and took his seat behind it. 'So glad you could come.' He took out a wet wipe and wiped his hands, then tossed it into the bin. 'Miss Donahoe, if you don't mind, I'd like to speak to you alone.' He bowed slightly to Simone and gestured towards the door. 'Princess?'

Simone bowed stiffly back to him, unable to hide her distaste, and went out.

He leaned back in his executive chair, saw that the television was still on, and flicked it off with a wave of his hand. 'So when are you going to Europe?'

I stared at him. 'Not even a hello?'

He waved it away. 'You're a Westerner. You're all a bunch of rude bastards, so I can skip that bit.' He leaned forward over the desk. 'So when are you going?'

'After Mid-Autumn Festival. Lord Xuan wants to book the whole of first class on a single aircraft for his entourage; we're looking for a flight where that's available. At the moment there aren't any, so his staff are checking about chartering a plane.'

'Can't he just carry you himself? He's back to full Turtle strength.'

I leaned my chin on my hand. 'The Demon King can incapacitate him at any time. He's fallen out of the sky before; he's knocked down a couple of outbuildings at the Northern Palace.'

The Archivist glowered. 'I didn't know that. Keep me informed.'

'I'm adding to the Chronicles. I'll email you copies.'

He nodded, satisfied. 'Appreciated.' His expression went stern again. 'You shouldn't go to the West. None of you should. This is a damn fool mission and you could stir up something we really don't want to face.'

'You've been doing some research?'

He spread his hands. 'That's what I do. This hasn't really been a cause for concern since it's all so far away, but if you're heading over to the West you need to be prepared. Something's not right there.'

'I'm well aware of that. No Shen have been seen there in centuries.'

'That's just the beginning of it. You've been looking for the lost Shen, I know that, so I did some research into what's there right now. This Western god of theirs — it's seriously scary. Have you actually read any of your own holy book?'

'Not my holy book, and some of it, yes.'

'This god.' He put his hand on a book on the desk and shook his head. 'This god with no name — it likes the smell of burning flesh, and it kills its followers for breaking stupid petty rules that it makes up. It seems to enjoy tormenting the very people who follow it. It's heavily into genocide; it's helped its people to destroy whole cities and murder their entire populations. It told them to kill all the residents of the cities; men, women — hell, it told its soldiers to bash the children against rocks — '

'The Middle Kingdom was doing exactly the same thing in the same time period,' I said. 'That book was written by men of that period, and they were boasting of their exploits.'

'There are no Shen in the West. People blindly follow this god that has promised to destroy the world, and for some stupid reason they think this is a good thing. They're not allowed to question it, they have to give up all semblance of free thought and just do as they're told with this "faith" business. We've already lost half of Lord Xuan. I hate to think he might run into this ... thing and lose his other half as well.'

'My mother would have a heart attack if she heard you saying any of this. Her god is a god of love.'

'A god of oppression, you mean. Especially women. This god wants women to be silent, servile child-making factories.'

'Bah, you can speak. Only two of the Thirty-Five Generals are women.'

'Not any more, they resigned.' He spread his hands. 'Okay, let's not have this argument, because there won't be any winner.'

'In other words, you're losing,' I said.

He ignored me. 'I am concerned for your safety, so please reconsider this plan to go to the West. Send agents instead. We don't want to lose either of you.'

'We don't have a choice. He was ordered by the Jade Emperor.'

He sagged in his seat. 'Well, shit.'

'But any information you have on the mythology and what could possibly have happened to the Shen over there is most welcome.'

He grabbed a small pile of USB memory sticks to the side of his desk. 'Western mythology — all the resources I've recently gathered. Some of this stuff is from overseas libraries. I tried to talk to their version of the Archives but couldn't find one. I couldn't find any Shen at all. Until about two thousand years ago, their Shen were active on the Earthly, causing the usual trouble that nature spirits will, then they disappeared. From the looks of it, they had a battle in their Heaven, and one god took over both Heaven and Hell and threw everybody else out.'

'According to their own mythology, God and his most trusted advisor had a battle. God stayed in Heaven, and the advisor or Shen or whatever took over Hell.'

'I know that's the general understanding of the situation,' he said, 'but if you do more research into the nature of this Satan thing, it becomes even more disturbing. It appears that it's a serpent Shen that taught their people about free will and enlightenment — hell, its name is Lucifer, which means Light. The other god didn't want humanity to have any sort of knowledge or free will so demonised it as punishment. You're a serpent yourself, you know you're not inherently evil.' He touched the pile of USBs. 'But this god labels all women, all snakes, all things with a reasonable amount of intelligence and scientific curiosity as evil. It's all in here. Check my summary.'

'Could the rest of the Shen be in exile on the Earthly?'

'That's a distinct possibility. I don't know what the result would be if Shen were locked out of Heaven for such a long time. You saw what happened to Lord Xuan; they could have reverted to mindless nature spirits.'

'What about the Buddhas of the West — wouldn't they have stopped something as bad as this?'

'Buddhas cannot intervene on the lower Planes; they can only guide, advise and comfort. If something of that magnitude happened, they'd retreat to the Heaven of Perfection and Enlightenment and mourn.'

'I really don't think it's as bad as you say.'

'I hope you're right.'

I gestured towards the USBs. 'Anything on Atlantis there?'

He stared at me. '*Atlantis*? You have to be joking. That never existed, it's a myth.'

'According to modern archaeological theory, yes, but so is the Chinese god of the sea, the Xuan Wu. The Western god of the sea gave Atlantis to his sons to rule on Earth with their human wives. Anything on Nephilim, the evil children of angel/human pairings in the West?'

'That really is grasping at straws. There's nothing anywhere on Nephilim. I looked them up when one was the main boss for that Tomb Raider game fifteen years ago.' His expression cleared. 'I see where you're going with this. Powerful Shen having half-Shen children, and their children going bad.'

'It's happened before.'

'Where? I know nothing of this.'

'Just take my word for it, it has.'

His eyes burned into me. 'What happened?'

'I won't betray the trust given to me.'

'I see. Then it's obvious which powerful god is involved. I can understand him not wanting to share if one of his children went bad; they're nearly as powerful as he is.' He spread his hands. 'If I find anything on Nephilim I'll let you know, but so far I have nothing.'

I picked up the memory sticks and rose. 'Thanks for your help, Archivist.'

He nodded to me. 'Just stay safe, dear. I hate to think what would happen if the Dark Lord were to lose you. We need him more than anything.'

The stone broke in. 'I say exactly the same thing all the time, Archivist.'

'Keep her safe, old friend.'

'Don't worry, I will.'

7

I leaned on the doorway as Edwin changed John's dressings the next morning.

'You don't need me' I said. 'I can't contribute to the court cases, I just sit there.'

'I need your brains. I'm only half what I could be, and there are some cases that aren't related to the Jade Emperor's limitations on you.'

'If they're not related to the management of the Mountain or the Northern Heavens, then you shouldn't be hearing them.'

Edwin patted John on the arm to indicate that he was done, and John hopped off the bed and conjured his black robe.

'One of them is Freddo's father. He's requested a hearing.'

I pushed myself off the doorway, and John went past me and out into the courtyard outside the new infirmary. A young Japanese maple tree had been planted in the middle of the freshly sown lawn and it was already showing the first signs of the autumn colour change.

'Why are you wasting your time listening to a tame demon?' I said, following John towards the main square. 'I doubt he has anything important to say.'

We arrived at the square, where his mounted escort

waited, flanked by two black dragons and holding a saddled horse for him.

'Because his owner says we should listen to him.'

I hurried to catch up with his long-legged stride. 'Mr Ling loves him; this stallion's the best horse he's ever owned.'

'So we will ensure that the demon receives a full and fair hearing. Then we will destroy it.'

'Very funny,' I said, standing back as he mounted his horse.

He gathered the reins and raised his voice. 'Proceed.'

'See you there,' I said.

I walked to the back of the entourage and took my place on foot with the most junior servants bringing up the rear. I admired John as he rode, tall and proud, towards the centre of the court, then disappeared. We followed behind him, until the world changed around my group and we were in the great court of the Palace of the Northern Heavens.

John's son Martin and Martin's older sister, Yue Gui, waited at the front of the Hall of Dark Justice with a small entourage. They both wore Tang-style floating silk robes in the black of the House of the North, and Yue's long hair was bound with black pearls and silver ornaments that glittered as she moved. They prostrated themselves in front of John as he dismounted, chanted the greeting, then rose again.

Martin began the formal welcoming speech. 'The Palace of the Northern Heavens greets its master —'

John waved him down. 'Skip the bullshit, I have better things to do. Let's get this over with.'

He strode past them and ran up the steps two at a time. Martin and Yue shared a glance full of exasperated humour, and ran after him. John's entourage hurried to follow, but Firebrand, one of the administrators, stopped us.

'The Dark Lord is heading straight to the audience chamber to review the affidavits. Those of you who are on his personal staff are welcome to attend the residences.' He bowed to us all. 'This way.'

I hesitated, unsure of my role in this.

Stop dithering and get in here, woman, John said into my head. *I need you!*

I stomped up the stairs, grumbling under my breath. 'I am not letting him goad me into another full-on training session; I'm still stiff from the last one.'

'What did he say?' Firebrand said, still guiding the staff towards the residences.

'Oh, he thinks that if he throws enough obnoxious sexist rubbish at me I'll call him out, and then I'm to blame for all the injuries.'

'He should never cause you injury, Emma, he is way too good for that,' Firebrand said with concern.

I turned halfway up the stairs to speak to him. 'He's the one who's lost a couple of fingers and needed stitches protecting me from my own ineptness.'

When you have finished catching up on all the palace gossip, I would love to hear your opinion on this, John said into my head. *But make sure you share all the juiciest bits later.*

'He needs me, and you have stuff to do,' I said, and we shared a wave and headed in our separate directions.

I went into the Hall of Dark Justice and walked unnoticed past the guards at the double doors to the hearing room. As a servant, I was beneath their attention.

John was sitting at his desk on the dais in Celestial Form, glaring down at the demon stallion, who was standing next to his owner, Mr Ling. Freddo's father was much bigger than Freddo was; he must have been more than seventeen hands — as big as a carthorse but with the shape of a thoroughbred. His coat was unkempt and his ribs showed; he hadn't been eating well.

Lily, one of the administrators, gestured for me to join her at the desk at the base of the dais, and I sat next to her.

'This may not work, demon,' John said, his expression severe. 'What will we do with you then?'

'Let me try,' the horse said.

I jumped. He sounded almost exactly like Freddo, just with a slightly deeper voice.

'Run and I will destroy you,' John said.

The horse inhaled deeply, then whinnied so loudly that the clerestory windows high on the pagoda-like roof rattled.

Nothing happened.

John waved at the horse's owner. 'Take —'

The stallion called again, even louder, and another horse, Freddo's mother, popped into existence next to him. She was wearing a halter for leading, with an anti-rearing ring bit on it and the lead rope dangling. Everybody started talking at once, and Lily jumped up and ran to grab the mare's lead rope. The stallion's face was full of smug triumph; the mare looked around, obviously confused.

'Quiet!' John roared, and there was silence.

He rose from his chair behind the desk, flicked his robe as he turned, and stalked down the stairs towards the horses. The mare visibly quailed as he approached her. He put his hand on her head and she broke out into a trembling sweat, dancing on the spot with distress.

John spun and put his other hand on the stallion's head. The demon horse stood placidly waiting.

John dropped his hands, turned and strode back up the steps with his hands behind his back. He lowered himself to sit, and gazed at the papers on his desk for a long time.

Eventually he spoke. 'Wait here.' He disappeared.

The courtroom broke out into loud discussion again. I rose and went to Lily, who was standing between the horses.

'What's this all about? I missed the first part.' I nodded towards the mare. 'How was she able to do that?'

'I kept trying to tell everybody, but nobody would believe me, everybody saw her as a natural horse,' the stallion said. '*She* came to *me*. I never broke into her stable, she broke into mine. She's a demon, and I thought she'd come if I called her. I was right.'

'John should have picked her straight away then,' I said, turning back to look at his desk.

'He had to,' Lily said. 'That's the one thing we can rely on: his ability to pick them.'

'He'd never seen that mare before. It hid its nature so well I don't think anybody else saw it,' the stallion said.

'I am more impressed with you all the time, Lobster,' Mr Ling said. 'I should have listened to you when you said you didn't break out, but I believed Toi when she said you were there.'

The stallion dropped his head. 'I thank you, my Lord.'

'Lobster?' I said.

'He's gold and precious, like the finest lobster,' Mr Ling said.

'Lobster isn't gold,' I said, confused.

'Red, gold, same thing.' He nodded towards the dais. 'The Emperor has returned.'

John was standing behind the desk. He picked up a wooden block and slammed it on the table, silencing everybody. He came down the stairs again and stood in front of Freddo's father.

'I went to Miss Toi's residence and she has left the Celestial Plane,' John said. 'Her residence is deserted, her demons destroyed, and all her horses are gone. It looks like nobody's been there for a while. Can you speak, demon?' he said to the mare.

The mare just stared at its surroundings, uncomprehending.

'Low level, almost a natural animal,' John said. 'Probably half-demon. It was the only thing Toi took with her when she left. She obviously didn't have a good enough hold on it and it escaped here. Would you keep this one until I decide what to do with it, Ling?'

'I would be honoured.'

'The answer to your question is yes, you may put your stallion to her and get her in foal again while you hold her. And yes, the foal would be yours.'

Ling bowed to John, grinning. 'I thank you, my Lord, for answering the question before I even asked it.'

John dropped his voice to speak to Lily and me. 'This explains why Freddo had so many issues. He is three-quarters demon and inherited their oversexed nature.'

'Why did Miss Toi do something like this?' Lily said. 'She gave up everything she had on the Celestial Plane — what did she get in return?'

'She won every competition when she rode that horse,' John said. 'She did it for the prestige of being the most successful equestrian on the Earthly and Heavenly Planes combined.' He gestured dismissively towards the mare. 'It's probably more than half-demon and stronger than a natural horse, but because of its nature it's undetectable to anyone but me. She cheated every time she competed on it.'

He strode back up the dais, sat at his desk and scribbled some notes. 'I hope Toi finds the prestige worth the price, because she is to be marked as Fallen from the Celestial and her entrance to the Heavenly Plane is hereby revoked. The horse is confiscated and is to be held by Mr Ling at the convenience of the court.' He glared around at those present. 'Clear this courtroom; the demon mare and Miss Donahoe are to stay. Emma, hold the horse. Lily, summon Number One and Number Two, set up a conference table and bring tea.'

After everyone had gone, John changed to human form, came down from the dais and sat at the table. Lily poured the tea. He glanced at her, she bowed and went out. John sat and waited, his expression grim as he stared at the table, occasionally sipping his tea. I held the mare, who lifted and dropped one foot occasionally but otherwise was well-behaved.

Martin and Yue Gui entered, saluted John by quickly shaking their hands in front of their faces, and sat. Martin poured tea for them.

John ran one hand over his face. 'Of the other three Winds, only the Phoenix is able to come. The Tiger and Dragon have sent their Number Ones. I can see why Toi was willing to risk having this thing in her residence.' He glanced at Martin. 'Is that a horse or a demon?'

Martin looked at the mare, then back at his father and said with confidence, 'Natural horse.'

I made a soft sound of distress despite myself and Martin and Yue both glanced at me.

John eyed his teacup. 'Go up and touch it, and tell me that again.'

Martin rose and went to the horse, which watched him placidly. He stroked its nose and it rubbed its head on his hand.

'Is it a demon hybrid?' Martin said. He peered into its eyes. 'Now that I can see inside, it looks different somehow, but I've never seen anything like it before. I definitely don't see it as demon, though.'

I ran my free hand through my hair. It was still short and thin, but at least it wasn't falling out any more.

'I see it as completely natural,' Yue Gui said. She rose and put her hand on the horse's neck, then shook her head. 'Still completely natural.'

There was a tap on the door and the Phoenix, in her red robes, entered. Michael came in as well, in the white uniform of a Horseman, accompanied by another strongly built white-haired Horseman — the Tiger's Number Two. They saluted John and stopped at the end of the table. John rose to greet them. He and the Phoenix formally nodded to each other, and he accepted the salutes of the Horsemen. Everybody ignored me.

John gestured towards the horse. 'Ah Que, do you see that as demon in any way?'

Zhu Que studied the horse, then went to it and put her hand on its neck. Martin and Yue Gui moved back to give her room.

'I've never seen anything like this before,' she said with interest. 'I don't see it as demon, though, I see it as a natural horse, just with something slightly different about it.' She turned to John. 'Sometimes I am very glad we have your abilities, Ah Wu. I'm sure you are able to see its demon nature from very far away.'

John waved the Horsemen forward. 'Come and see what you think.'

Zhu Que patted me on the shoulder as she went past to the table. She picked up a teacup and filled it from the pot, then watched Michael with interest over the rim of her cup as he and the other Horseman inspected the mare.

'This is a demon hybrid?' Michael said. 'I can't pick it. Rohan?'

The other Horseman shook his head. 'Can't see it.' He ran his hand down the horse's neck. 'I know this one — this is Toi's mare. She boasted that she won so many ribbons on this horse that she had to build a special room to hold them. Cheating dragon bitch.'

'It's a part of our nature,' the Dragon's Number One son said with good humour as he approached us. He fell to one knee and saluted John and the Phoenix. He wore wide grey pants with a pale blue kimono over the top: the dress of a traditional samurai. His electric blue hair was held in a topknot and fell down to his waist, strands of gold shimmering through it. He stopped to clasp Michael's hand and thumped him on the back; then did the same with Rohan, the other Horseman. He nodded to Martin and Yue Gui, then studied the mare, gazing into its eyes. 'And you say this is half-demon?'

'At least half, could be more,' John said.

The dragon came to the table and poured himself some tea, then turned to study the horse again as he sipped from the cup. 'Dad'll lay eggs.'

'How far away can you detect it, Ah Wu?' the Phoenix said.

John glowered at his teacup. 'I don't see it as demon unless I touch it. Even then, as you say, it is something completely different. It doesn't seem to be demon at all.'

He turned to study me, his dark eyes boring into me, and I shivered.

Everybody was silent for a long moment, staring from John to the horse. Michael studied me appraisingly. From their expressions, Martin and Yue Gui were conversing silently.

'How old is this animal?' the Dragon's Number One said.

Rohan thought about it for a moment. 'Just checked the competition records back at the West. She started competing on it four years ago; at that time she said it was five years old.'

'This thing has been around for nearly ten years?' the Phoenix said, placing her teacup carefully back on the table. 'I will therefore ask the question that everybody else is thinking. How many more of these things are there?'

'Is it intelligent?' the dragon said, still holding his teacup.

'No, it's more like a natural animal than a demon,' John said. 'Same as the human copies — they were unaware of what they were until they were activated. I think this one has no sentience at all.'

'But the King could control Freddo,' I said.

'Can she contribute?' the dragon said.

'Yes, this is unrelated to the management of the Mountain or the Heavens,' Yue Gui said. 'She may contribute.'

'If they're enough untamed demon, he can control them, and occasionally flash his perception into them and see through their eyes,' John said.

'So the King made Freddo? That's a complex scheme just to make a horse,' the dragon said.

'But it was a horse that was acting as a pair of eyes for the King, and was able to carry Simone to him,' John said. 'Toi set you up to adopt him.'

'This whole time Toi's been an agent for the Demon King,' Martin said with venom. 'I should send a squad out to find her and bring her to Celestial justice.'

'Go right ahead,' John said. 'But don't take too much time. After Mid-Autumn Festival I am going to Holy Island to see what's happening there, and I need you here to manage the Heavens.'

'Jie Jie can do it,' Martin said, nodding to Yue Gui.

'I need you both here, but we will discuss this later,' John said.

'Count me in,' Michael said. 'I want to come to Europe and see what's going on.'

'You won't get a chance, man,' Rohan said. 'Dad'll have you running in circles administering the West.'

Michael shrugged. 'Damn. You're right.'

I stroked the horse's nose and scratched behind her ears, but she ignored me, more concerned about all the people around us.

'We need to find out who bred her and what her bloodlines are,' I said, then raised my voice. 'Hold on, we missed that!'

'What, Emma?' John said.

'She's a thoroughbred, and they aren't bred in this part of the world. They're all imported. Bet you anything you like she's a Western demon, and she came from the UK — Ireland or Wales.'

'That would explain it,' the Phoenix said with wonder. 'We're experts at identifying our own. Throw a Western hybrid at us and we're unable to pick it.'

John turned to the Horsemen. 'Can you trace her bloodlines?'

'Easily,' Rohan said. He concentrated for a moment. 'But not right now; I'll have to get back to you on that. My contact at the import registry's off at lunch.'

'We have another petitioner outside the doors,' Yue Gui said. 'You may not wish to see him, Father.'

'Who?'

Yue Gui's expression darkened. 'My son, Sang Shen. I told him not to come. He has come anyway, and brought his little sister, the one that shares his father with a different mother.'

'This is a family matter,' John said. 'You are all dismissed.'

'Do you mind if we have a look around Toi's residence before we go?' Michael said.

'Go right ahead,' John said.

Michael saluted him and the Horsemen disappeared.

'That's a good idea,' the Phoenix said. 'I will join them. Golden Dragon?'

'Yeah,' the dragon said. 'By your leave, my Lord.'

John nodded to them and they disappeared.

'Martin, go with them to Toi's residence,' John said. 'Emma, Ling's coming back to take possession of the mare.'

Martin disappeared.

The doors opened and Mr Ling, the owner of Freddo's father, came in. He nodded to me, took the mare's lead rein and led her out. Sang Shen was waiting outside, and he stood back and stared at the horse in wonder as it passed him, then the doors closed.

John dropped his voice. 'I always knew this little asshole would cause the family trouble, Ah Yue.'

'He is an adult, Father. His actions are his own responsibility.' Yue Gui gracefully turned and sat at the table. She waved one hand over the teacups and the used ones disappeared, replaced by clean ones. She poured herself some tea. 'I told him to come in, but I'm not having anything to do with this. This is his own doing.'

The doors opened and Sang Shen strode in, accompanied by his sister, Sang Ye. Both of them had the nut-brown faces of tree spirits; he was tall and solid with a square face, and she was smaller and slimmer with long green and brown hair. Both wore Tang robes of green embroidered with leaves and flowers. They stopped in front of John and fell to one knee, saluting.

'Dai Yeh Yeh,' Sang Shen said, calling John 'Grandfather'.

'Xuan Tian Shang Di,' Sang Ye said.

John leaned on the table behind him and crossed his arms, glowering at them. 'Rise.'

They stood and stared at the floor in a show of humility.

'Well?' John said.

Sang Shen stepped forward, still looking at the floor. 'In three weeks, my sister Sang Ye will be married to a plum tree that lives here in the Northern Heavens. I beg your leave to attend.'

'You tried to kill the woman I love, stupid boy,' John said without emotion. 'Even worse, you did it in the field of honour. You have disgraced yourself and our house.'

'I wish to atone,' Sang Shen said, his expression sincere. 'I wish to confess my transgressions and beg your forgiveness.'

'It is not my forgiveness that you should be begging for,' John said, uncrossing his arms to gesture towards me. 'I'm not the small human mortal that you nearly killed.'

Sang Shen fell to his knees in front of me. 'Lad ... La ... Miss ... I wish I could give you your full title, Miss Donahoe. I sincerely regret my actions. Since knowing you, I have come to realise that you truly have the best interests of the Celestial at heart. I thought you were arrogant and heartless, but recent events have proved that you are of noble intent.'

'Hold on,' I said, raising both hands. 'Are you saying that you hated me up until I made an incredibly stupid mistake that's imprisoned half of the Dark Lord? That doing something as dumb as this has proved that I'm not a bad person?'

He looked confused for a moment, then his expression cleared. 'I suppose I am. I want to serve you to atone.' He turned to John. 'Allow me to take the role of servant to Miss Donahoe. After I have attended my sister's wedding, I will do anything you wish to pay for my crime.'

John waved Sang Shen closer. The tree spirit rose to stand in front of him; he was close on John's height with a heavier build.

John put his finger on Sang Shen's forehead. 'Tell me again why you are here.'

'I wish to atone for my crimes and be released for my sister's wedding.'

'What is your true opinion of Miss Donahoe?'

Sang Shen hesitated for a long time, then dropped his eyes and took a step back so that John was no longer touching his forehead. 'Please release me to attend my sister's wedding.'

'I saw what you were thinking,' John said. 'You still think she's an arrogant upstart who has ideas above her station.'

Sang Shen didn't reply, he just stared at the floor.

'But it's true, I am,' I said.

'You have a point,' John said. He turned back to Sang Shen. 'Your sister's wedding means that much to you?'

Sang Shen nodded without looking up.

'I am giving the victim of your crime the choice,' John said, then spoke into my head. *I know you well enough that you would want him freed, but have a look what I saw in his mind first.*

He transmitted an image to me. Sang Shen had his spear lodged in my back and he was pushing it slowly through me with pleasure.

'What say you, Miss Donahoe?' John said.

'Half of Hell is already after me. The last thing I need is to watch my back in case he's coming as well. Keep him locked up,' I said.

I walked away towards the doors, to the sound of furious protests behind me. I felt rather than heard the running footsteps, summoned my sword and spun to block Sang Shen's spear in front of my face. If I hadn't blocked he would have impaled my head.

He moved closer, our weapons still locked, and snarled into my face, 'You have destroyed my life. You are the reason my father is dead. Now I won't see my beloved sister marry.'

He tried to push the weapon into me, but I kept the block up. My muscles were close to the end of their strength, though, and if he didn't release me soon I would have to yield. As my arms began to tremble, I frantically wondered what had happened to John. Sang Shen's face filled with triumph. He shifted his grip slightly, readying for the kill. I could slip to the side and try to deflect him the way he was already going, but he was faster than me and the move would probably be fatal.

My muscles were at the end of their strength; I readied myself to try the move.

The spear was snatched from behind, the butt whistling past my ear as it was taken from his grasp. The butt hit him sharply on the back of the head and he fell.

'You okay, Emma?' John said, standing over him.

'Yeah.'

'Masterfully done, love. How did you hold him back? He's much stronger than you.'

'The sword helped.'

'Good.' He hit Sang Shen on the side of the face with the butt of the spear. 'You killed your own mother! I cannot believe you would do that.'

'Yue Gui!' I shouted, running towards her. 'No!'

He'd run his spear through her throat and she lay on her back, dead. Her body disappeared and I bent over my knees, gasping with relief, trying to catch my breath. She'd gone to Court Ten.

John was standing over the prone Sang Shen, punctuating his speech with blows from the butt of the spear. 'You are banished from the Celestial. You are to take the form of a tree on the Earthly and stay there until you are pardoned by the Celestial.'

He struck Sang Shen on the side of the face again and Sang Shen raised his hands to protect his head. 'Go meditate upon your faults.' He reached down and put his hand on Sang Shen's throat. 'I disown you. You are no longer any child of mine. Now get the hell out of here.'

Sang Shen vanished as John aimed a kick at the side of his abdomen.

John dropped the spear, strode to me and pulled me into a fierce embrace, burying his face into my hair.

'I wasn't expecting that at all,' he said. 'He moved so fast I nearly didn't make it.'

'You worry me sometimes,' I said into his chest.

'Thanks a lot, bitch,' Sang Ye shouted as she stormed past us towards the door.

I pulled out of John's arms and glared at her. 'You're blaming me for something I didn't do!'

She stopped. 'If you hadn't blinded the Dark Lord with your loose Western ways, our father would still be alive and my brother would be able to attend my wedding.' She waved me down with one hand as she turned away. 'You destroyed our lives.'

'You did that yourselves,' John said.

'You defend her!' Sang Ye rounded on him and her voice rose to a screech. 'How can you defend her after what she did to you? You should lock her up!'

John turned away. 'Leave my dominion and do not return.'

She raised her clenched fists. 'With pleasure.' She spun on her heel and stalked out.

'I cannot believe he would kill his own mother for a chance at you,' John said. 'I'll wager the marriage was an excuse and she won't go ahead with it.'

'They do have a point,' I said. 'Their father is dead because of me.'

'If anyone is to blame, it's Michelle. She started all of this.'

'From what Gold tells me, it was you who pursued Michelle, and she resisted you for a long time,' I said, amused despite myself.

'She wanted nothing to do with me when she found out who I was,' he said, putting his arm around my shoulders and walking with me towards the door.

'And you won her over anyway?'

He dropped his voice. 'I was desperate, and she was ignoring me. Eventually,' his voice became even lower, almost a whisper, 'I was forced to seek assistance from the worst sex fiend on any Plane.'

'Who, the Tiger?'

'No,' he said, amused. 'Gold himself.'

95

8

I left the Residence in some jogging gear for my pre-dinner run and waved to Simone, who was just arriving back from school on a cloud. A couple of students were waiting at the front of the Residence and I stopped to see if they wanted me.

Julie, an American student who was brilliant with bladed weapons, tried to say something and hesitated, bewildered.

'Remember the Jade Emperor's limitation on me,' I said. 'No honorifics, just Emma. What's the problem, guys?'

'If you don't mind, ma ... Emma,' Lai, a phoenix, said, 'Alvin's been severely injured and ...' She shared a look with Julie. 'We know you're a snake, and we were wondering if you could come to the infirmary and help?'

Simone landed behind me and stepped off her cloud. 'Don't you dare, Emma,' she said.

I started moving towards the infirmary and the students walked with me. 'How bad is it?'

'We think he may have a broken spine.'

I stopped. 'Only the Dark Lord's Serpent can fix something as big as that.'

Lai put her hand on my forearm. 'Could you try anyway? Please?'

'Don't you *dare*!' Simone yelled.

Lai glanced at Simone, confused. 'Princess, my Lady, why won't you let her?'

'Because she could take off and merge with Daddy's Serpent if she changes to snake!' Simone shouted.

'Don't be ridiculous. It's in a cage of Celestial Jade and nothing's getting in there,' I said. 'There's no chance. It's always been the Serpent coming to possess me in the past anyway, so if I do this it may even escape and find me.'

'No, don't risk yourself,' Simone said. She raised her voice again. 'I cannot believe you're thinking of doing this! Didn't Dad say you shouldn't take serpent form?'

I ignored her. 'How long ago did this happen, Julie?'

'Only less than half an hour. Dr Edwin said something about it being fixable if you catch it quickly, before his nerves die.'

'Let's go then,' I said, moving off again.

Simone grabbed my arm. 'I am not letting you do this. They don't need you. Meredith's a better energy healer than you.'

'Energy can't do anything for a broken spine, but a serpent healer may be able to, particularly if it's just happened.'

'It's not worth the risk, Emma.'

'I'm the only snake on the Mountain, which means I'm his only chance of being able to walk. I have to try, otherwise I couldn't live with myself.'

She studied my face, then released me.

'Thank you,' I said. 'Let's go.'

We arrived at the infirmary to find Edwin standing over Alvin, checking the drip. Alvin's face was grey and he was on a traction bed, keeping his spine straight. Edwin's expression was grim.

'It's a similar injury to what Lord Leo suffered. The bones of his spine are crushed at T ... about halfway down, and his spine is damaged beyond repair.' He brushed one hand over Alvin's forehead. 'He is in an induced coma to keep him still so that the swelling doesn't cause further damage, but he'll never walk again.'

Lai gave a little cry and ran to kneel next to Alvin. 'It all happened so quickly. If I hadn't swept him down and out of the way like that, he'd be okay.' She rested her head on her arms, leaning on the bed. 'This is all my fault.'

'A routine training day and suddenly it ends up like this,' Julie said, her voice thick with tears. She wiped her eyes. 'I'll never be able to spar with him again.' She turned to me, blinking the tears away. 'Please try, Emma.'

'I'll do my best, let's see what I can manage,' I said, and put my hand on Lai's shoulder. 'Back out of the way, Lai.'

She moved back and I touched my inner serpent. I hadn't changed to snake in a while, but I need not have been concerned; I easily fell into the form.

I raised my head and touched my snout to Alvin, examining him. I moved my healing power through him, doing what I could to reduce the swelling and knit together the damaged nerve fibres and bones, which were in tiny pieces and all jumbled together. It was incredibly fiddly work. If I could reduce the pressure on his spinal column, he might be able to regain a small amount of mobility. But Edwin was right: there was a good chance he would never walk again.

I heard rather than saw John and Simone appear in the doorway.

'Oh, Emma, this is a very bad idea,' John said.

'Quiet, I'm concentrating,' I said through my closed mouth.

He came and knelt next to me and touched the top of my head. 'Magnificent.'

The contact made something dark and primal flare within me, which made me grow and strengthen and fill with power.

He saw what happened. 'Oh, shit, no.'

He removed his hand, but it was too late. His Serpent, the love of my life, was lying at the bottom of the world, alone and in pain, and I went to it.

* * *

Zhenwu

John saw her trail as she spun down to Hell and disappeared into it. Voices swirled around him, loud and demanding.

'Quiet!' he roared, and the noise ceased.

'Daddy, I —' Simone began.

John raised his hand to stop her. 'I know. Be quiet. I'm working.'

Number Two, he called. *Number Two!*

Ah Wu? Er Lang said.

This. He shared the information. *Emma knows where my Serpent is! She went to it. I must find it. Check with legal to see if I have the right to go down there and retrieve my wife and Serpent without Celestial permission.*

Give me a moment, Er Lang said.

John used the time to contact Leo and Martin. *Prepare for battle. This happened. We must find them. You two are coming with me. Gather your equipment and meet me on the forecourt.*

John paced the infirmary as he waited for Er Lang to return to him. If he didn't need permission, he could head down immediately and find both her and his Serpent. He deliberately avoided thinking about the possibility that she was in the jade cage with the Serpent . . .

No, Er Lang said. *She's not your wife. Legal says if you'd had a formal betrothal ceremony . . . No, that still would not have been enough. You need permission from the Jade Emperor to go down there and retrieve her.*

When's his next appointment?

He's finished for the day. Just a moment.

John continued pacing.

'Daddy?' Simone said.

He raised his hand. 'Wait.'

Number One, this is most inconvenient, the Jade Emperor said. *I have retired for the evening and I will take no more appointments this day. I will see you in the morning; talk to my secretary. You will have priority and be the first I see.*

Majesty, I implore you, my wife —

She is not your wife and she is not in danger. It can wait. Now if you do not mind, I am fatigued. Good evening to you, Number One.

The Jade Emperor shut off communication.

The old bastard won't see me until the morning! John said to Er Lang. *What the hell? They could do anything to my wife —*

She's not your wife.

Beside the point! The demons could have her and he won't give permission until tomorrow morning? Realisation dawned. *He knows something.*

Ah Wu, he knows everything. So when will he see you?

First thing tomorrow.

I'll speak to you then. Do you want the paperwork drawn up for an approved sortie into hell?

Of course I do! What a stupid —

Good night, Ah Wu.

Er Lang shut him off as well.

John snapped back to see Simone and Edwin glaring at him, a couple of bewildered students behind them.

'I need permission from the Jade Emperor before I can go down,' he said. 'He won't see me until first thing tomorrow morning.'

'I'm going down myself right now,' Simone said. She held out her hand. 'Give me my yin back.'

'Try,' John said. 'Try heading to Hell. The Jade Emperor knows and he's blocked you.'

Her face filled with concentration, then frustration. 'How can he block me like this?'

'He is who he is,' John said. 'I'll be staying in the Celestial Palace tonight and heading directly out after I've spoken to him tomorrow morning. Leo and Martin will be with me. Stay here where you are safe.'

Simone opened her mouth and closed it again. 'I'd just be in the way in the Celestial Palace, wouldn't I?'

'That's why I'm asking you to stay here,' John said. He nodded to Edwin. 'Look after the boy.'

He patted Simone on the shoulder and went out of the infirmary towards the central court. Leo and Martin were standing on the edge of the square together, fully armed and in their black livery. Leo had his sword, the Black Lion, at his side; Martin wore his black enamel armour and carried the Silver Serpent in its scabbard in his right hand. They saluted John when he arrived.

'The Jade Emperor is being a shit and won't see me until tomorrow morning,' he said.

'Go now,' Leo said.

'I'm blocked. I need permission.'

Leo concentrated and his expression filled with a frustration similar to Simone's. 'I see.'

'Gather what you need and we'll spend the night in the Celestial Palace. We can head out the minute I have permission from the Jade Emperor in the morning.'

Both of them nodded, and called clouds to take them to the Celestial Palace. John summoned Seven Stars and his battledress and called a cloud to carry him as well. He checked his watch: 7 pm. He had at least twelve hours before he could see the JE. The wait would kill him.

* * *

Emma

The room containing the jade cage was dark and fearsomely hot. The tiles beneath my coils were scorching, and the heat shot through my scales into my flesh. The Serpent lay coiled in the centre of the cage, in as small a space as possible. It was covered with open wounds from the acid and its black scales were dull and white around the edges.

I slid over the burning tiles as quietly as I could to the cage and raised my head to see it. 'John.'

It moved and lifted its own head to see me, and kept its warm, female voice as quiet as I had. 'Emma! Emma, my beautiful Emma. What are you doing here? You need to go. Now.'

'I saw you here. I have to get you out.'

I pressed my nose to the latch on the cage door and pushed it. My nose was too big to move it easily and the bar caught on the edge of the latch so it wouldn't move. My tongue didn't have the strength and my tail didn't have the finesse; it had to be my nose. I slid it across the end of the bar repeatedly, trying to shift it. It moved slightly and I felt a jolt of excitement.

The Serpent moved so it was on the other side of the cage door. 'Stop, Emma. I may possess you if I'm released. I can't do that to you.' It dropped its head with frustration and lowered its voice to a barely discernible hiss. 'Quickly, go before they come. If you free me, I could drain and destroy you.' It tapped its nose on the bars with frustration. 'Just go!'

'I want to be one with you. I want to be possessed by you and absorbed by you,' I said, still fiddling with the latch. Then I stopped attacking the latch and raised my head to look straight into its wonderful wise eyes. 'Hold on, no, I don't.' I backed away from the door. 'Screw that, I want to keep my individuality. Are you sure you'll absorb me if I let you out?'

'It's not worth the risk.'

I made a quick decision. 'Yes, it is. The world needs you whole to protect it.'

I pressed my nose against the latch again, but pushed the bar flush with the wall of the cage instead of away from it.

'I have to do this human,' I said.

'Then go. You can't teleport human, and they're probably on their way. Just leave!'

I tried to change to human, but the form wouldn't come. I hit the latch again, cursing the lack of sensitivity in my nose. 'It's so damn fat!'

'Emma, run,' the Serpent said, moving closer to me. 'Get out now!'

'What?' I said, but it was too late. Something grabbed me around the neck in a double-handed hold and I couldn't move. I tried to lash my tail but someone was standing on it.

'Got you,' the Demon King said. He held me so tight I couldn't turn to see him.

'Ready,' someone else said.

'Over her head then,' the King said.

A noose was dropped over my head and pulled tight around my neck.

'Teleport out, love,' the Serpent said.

The King sent a blast of black energy into the cage, knocking the Serpent backwards. 'You shut the fuck up.'

I turned to attack him, but he'd stepped out of reach. A huge bull-head demon was holding me with a snake noose on the end of a pole. The pole was so long that they could stand well away from me and I couldn't touch them. I raised and lowered my head, trying to free it, but the noose held me firmly.

The King put his hands on his hips. 'Take her to a cell on level six and leave her there.'

'Are you sure that's wise, Dad? Wouldn't you like her closer to your own quarters?' the bull-head said.

The King glared at him. 'You question me?'

The bull-head dropped his snout. 'No way, Dad, I just want to be sure about her. I know how much ...' he shook the pole, making me hiss with pain, 'misery she's caused you.'

'I'm going to kill you,' I said to the King.

He turned to me. 'Are you now?'

I stopped fighting the noose and stared into his eyes. 'You raped my nephews.'

He waved me down. 'They would have passed the time jerking off anyway. Males can't be raped.'

'What you did to them was *rape*, George. You hurt my family and my little girl. You've caused so much misery to everybody I love ...' My voice cracked, and I took a deep breath. 'So many innocents. I can't see my family any more because of you. Watch your back, Kitty Kwok, because one day there will be a snake behind you with her fangs out.' I felt ice-cold and full of purpose. 'And I will take a great deal of pleasure in squeezing the life out of your ugly throat.'

'You can't throttle me, I don't breathe,' he said.

'Then I will crush your bones within my coils.'

He took True Form: a snake back end and a male human front end with no skin. Where the Mothers were black, he was the colour of blood. He towered over me, close on five metres, even bigger than the last time I'd seen his True Form. His voice changed to a deep hiss. 'Try me.' He slithered closer. 'I won't force myself on you, but with the right tools your human form could still be very useful. You may even come to like me.'

He changed back to his human form, still smiling. 'Hopefully I'll have the opportunity, but there's something that needs to be done first.' He spoke to the bull-head without looking away from me. 'He made an oath to her that he would find her. They probably don't know that I'm aware of it. Before I can do anything with her, I have to get this oath out of the way.'

He bent to see me more closely, and I spat poison at him. It landed on his face and hair and he jerked back. He pulled an ordinary packet of Hong Kong tissues out of his pocket and wiped his face.

'Demons thrive on poison, Emma, don't waste your spit,' he said.

He threw the dirty tissue onto the floor and put the packet back in his pocket. He took his blood-red hair out of its short ponytail, swept his hands through it and retied it.

'Put her somewhere where it'll take a while for him to find her, but he will find her in the end,' he said. 'Let him find her and take her, and then we'll take her back and she'll be *ours*.' He straightened. 'You hear me, Emma? We will have you.'

'I will kill you with the sword you gave me,' I said.

'Not today, sweetie.'

'So, level six?' the bull-head said.

'Put her in a cell right up the back where it'll take them a while to find her. Make sure she's fed and watered and kept reasonably clean. If she changes to human, let me know immediately; I have some plans for her in that form.' He turned back to me. 'If he comes for her, make sure it's him, that he finds her and that he gets her out. One of his oaths is a very powerful thing and we can't do anything with her as long as it's over our heads.'

The bull-head bowed slightly. 'Majesty.'

The King nodded to him with approval. 'Show some more respect like this, son, and you may find yourself promoted.'

The bull-head grinned, revealing even cow's teeth. 'How about I clear a spot for myself?'

'After she's been taken home, you can challenge anyone you like for their spot. Go for it.'

The bull-head's grin widened. 'You're a prince, Dad.'

'Do a good job and you may be one as well,' the Demon King said. He glanced back at me. 'Off you go.'

The bull-head raised the pole and took me with it. I tried to see behind me for a last look at John's Serpent, but I couldn't.

9

Zhenwu

John, Leo and Martin landed their clouds outside the North
Gate of the Celestial Palace. It was embossed in black and silver
with a ten-metre-tall motif of the Xuan Wu in True Form. John
walked towards it and it swung open for them. He stormed
through the breezeway under the red-gold trees towards
his apartments, unable to control his frustration. The Jade
Emperor's quarters and casual hearing rooms were less than
two hundred metres away on his left, but he was unable to do
anything until the next morning. He wound his way through
the corridors, distantly aware of voices nagging at him.

'John!' someone said loudly, and he stopped and turned.

Leo's jaw was set, ready to face the consequences of
calling him by his first name.

Then John saw the problem. Yin was following him in
a trail of destruction; the walls and floor of the corridor
had been stripped down to the wooden framework. A
Celestial Palace fairy floated five metres away between Leo
and Martin, out of range of the cloud of yin, wearing an
expression of mild exasperation.

John called the yin back and bowed to the fairy. 'My
apologies. Do not spend your own energy repairing this.
Have it repaired by hand and pass the cost on to me.'

She quickly shook her head and floated past him towards his apartments, nodding to him as she passed.

'Looks like you're forgiven,' Martin said with amusement.

'I guess the Palace is becoming accustomed to me,' John said, continuing towards his apartments, this time keeping his anger in check.

The fairies had prepared a meal for them and waited in the dining room to serve them.

'Eat,' he said to Leo and Martin, and went into the courtyard.

He sat cross-legged on the grass under the tree in the clear, cool evening. He wished he could return to the sea for the night, but he wouldn't risk being late to see the Jade Emperor in the morning. He and Emma had sat under this very tree, making plans for their future together, and the pain of missing her pierced him.

He wound down completely, stowing his intelligence away and becoming nothing, unaware of his transformation into a small tortoise sitting on the grass.

Martin and Leo came into the courtyard.

'We should make him eat something,' Leo said. 'They must have some lettuce or grapes or cat food around here.'

'He doesn't need to eat. He's gone,' Martin said. 'He's completely insensible.'

'What if something happens?'

'He's relying on us to tell him. Come on, even if he won't eat, we should. We have a long night ahead of us and we need to be strong. We can do this.'

'As long as we have each other we can do anything,' Leo said.

* * *

Emma

The bull-head demon led me through corridors of rough-hewn black stone that glittered with hidden jewels. Other demons, mostly humanoid guards, passed us. Some stopped to study me curiously, then saw the bull-head's sneer and quickly moved on. We dropped down a ten-metre-wide hole, and I could taste and smell the decay from below as we fell. We landed on a platform that edged the hole, and he pulled me through an opening into a black tunnel. Screams could be heard coming from the other end, and the bull-head grinned.

He turned right before the end, into a tunnel flanked by stone chambers, each with a barred front and door. Some held sleeping serpent-type demons; others were empty. He took me down the corridor to the very end and into a cell, the screams of the tormented drifting all the way into this part of the complex.

He led me into the cell, which although black stone was warm and dry. He poked the end of the pole out through the bars, went out and closed the door. Then he released the noose around my neck and pulled the pole quickly out.

'Just sit tight and your boyfriend will be along shortly,' he said. 'Anything you need, give the guards a yell. It'd be sort of pointless to try to escape since we plan to let you go anyway.' He shook his head, flicking his ears. 'Try to see it as a research trip. I don't think you've been this far into the demonic side of Hell before. If you're lucky, you might see some of the poor wretches that we play with on this level. We love it when we get one with a snake phobia; we see how long we can play before they go mad.'

He nodded to me and walked away.

I slithered around the perimeter of the cell. Three of the cell walls were rough-hewn black rock and the fourth was the cell door set into the bars. I was trapped.

For a human, the cell would be unpleasant, but for a snake it was a cosy habitat. The black stone was warm and dry, and there was a pile of soft rubber foam chips in one corner under a rocky overhang, perfect for making a nest. Next to it stood a small cage containing a live rat. All I had to do was bang the push-button door with my nose and the rat would be released: dinner. A rodent-type drip water feeder was clipped to the bars of the cell.

You there? I asked the stone.

I'm underground, I can't contact anybody, it said.

I'm well aware of that.

A series of screams drifted down the hallway, then abruptly stopped.

I hope he comes soon, I said.

I curled up in the nest of foam chips and moved my chi through my serpent body, cycling down to meditate and trying to ignore fresh wails of terror.

Don't attempt to change to human, the stone said. *You heard what the Demon King said.*

He wanted to do things to my human form, and I had a good idea what they involved. What my nephews had suffered would be nothing in comparison. *I know.*

I'm here. You're not alone.

I was silent for a moment, trying to think of a way to express exactly how much I appreciated it, and found myself lost for words.

Thanks, was all I could manage.

* * *

Emma, quick! the stone roared telepathically, so loudly that I banged my head on the overhanging stone ledge. *Lock your door!*

I can't lock the door, I'm on the inside.

110

They lock on the inside. They're to keep things out not in. Now hurry!

I slithered up to the cell door. The stone was right. The door was closed and the latch was on the inside; a large wide ring that was easily manageable by my serpent nose. Screams and the sound of scuffling echoed down the hall as I pushed the latch across.

All the way into the cover, the stone said. *That way they can't open it from the outside.*

What's out there? I said as I pushed the ring into the metal cover, then saw what was coming down the corridor towards my cell and quickly backed away. It was a level seventy-five Mother in True Form, holding a writhing snake demon in each hand.

Her skinless head brushed the ceiling of the hallway as she stopped and stared at me. 'What the hell are you?'

'I'm just a little snake,' I said. 'Nothing important.'

She moved closer to the bars and flicked her forked tongue. 'You smell different, and different is important.' She raised the serpent demon in her right hand and spoke to it. 'Tell me what she is and I won't eat you.'

'That's the Dark Lady, the Xuan Wu's promised,' the snake demon said. 'Let me go!'

'Really?' The Mother grinned at me through the bars, and absent-mindedly bit off the snake demon's head. 'Fascinating.'

'You promised you wouldn't eat her,' the other snake demon said.

The Snake Mother spun and smashed the living demon against the wall of the corridor, making it explode. 'I know. I forgot. I'll remember next time.' She took another bite out of the dead demon's corpse, licking at the demon essence. 'What are you doing here, Emma?'

'Oh, you know, the usual,' I said. 'Beautiful princess held in the gleaming tower waiting for her handsome prince to come and rescue her.'

The Mother guffawed. 'I like that. I heard you're an ugly bitch, but that he's an uglier one.' She took another bite of the snake demon, then popped the end of its tail into her mouth and wiped it with the back of her hand. Her voice went sly. 'He's not here right now, though, and you look like you'd taste different.' She leaned towards the bars and flicked her tongue again. 'I haven't eaten Western in a long time.'

She took hold of one of the bars and pulled at it. When it didn't give, she yanked harder on it, making the door rattle. The bar bent in her hand. She stopped.

'You don't seem that big. I wonder if you have to do what I tell you?'

'The King's holding me here at his pleasure. Do anything to me and he'll be pissed,' I said. 'Really, really pissed.'

'You sure about that?'

She raised her other hand, summoned a mobile phone and texted someone. She waited for a moment, then a jangling Chinese pop ringtone went off. She checked the message.

'Damn, he says to leave you alone.'

The phone disappeared and she turned to look back up the hallway. 'I'm still hungry. See ya.'

She slithered away, leaving a trail of toxic slime behind her. I went back to the bedding and hid underneath the foam chips as much as I could. I curled myself into the tiniest ball possible and watched the door of the cage.

How long was I asleep? I asked the stone.

About four hours. It's midnight. I think she sneaked in for a snack while the guards aren't alert.

How long have I been here? I'm losing track of time.

Six hours.

He should be here by now!

He has to gain permission, Emma, and he won't be able to do that until court is in session at the Celestial Palace.

You'll be here at least another six to eight hours, and possibly longer if the Jade Emperor delays granting access to Hell.

What about the Demon King granting access?

The stone hesitated, then said, *I know. He's supposed to ask the Demon King for permission, but the King knows that the Dark Lord has to find you for the oath to be fulfilled.* Its voice changed slightly. *Hold tight, dear one, look after yourself. This may take a while.*

I buried myself deeper under the chips.

When I woke again there were quiet discussions and the sound of movement down the hall, but no screams. I crept out from under the rock ledge and studied the rat in its cage. Maybe later. I sipped at the water bottle and it worked surprisingly well for my serpent form.

What time is it?

The stone was silent.

I'm losing track. I feel like I've been here a couple of days already. Tell me it's morning and he's coming for me.

It's only 2 am. The stone's voice grew more affectionate. *Go back to sleep, Emma, there's nothing you can do. He will find you, remember that. Once that is done, he can Raise and marry you, and you can live on his Mountain and you will be together. That's the whole oath, and it will happen.*

I didn't reply; I just crawled under the stone ledge and buried myself in the foam again.

If you're bored and can't sleep, I can play you a recording of something pleasant, the stone said. *Pick a place and I can put you there.*

Thanks for the offer, but I want to be fully aware when he comes.

I understand.

There was a disturbance outside my cell. I poked my head out from under the rocky overhang to find a group of demons standing at the door of the cage.

'Look! She stuck her head out,' one said. 'The Mother was right.'

I moved further out to see better. There were two guard demons with a serpent-type demon. One of the guards held a small human male by the scruff of the neck. The man was wearing nothing but a stained loincloth and hung dully in the demon's grasp, his mouth open and saliva dribbling from one corner.

The serpent demon raised its head and moved it from side to side. 'What is it? I've never seen anything like it before.'

'It's the Dark Lady,' one of the guards said in awe. 'The real deal. That's her.'

'But what is she?'

'Some sort of Western snake Shen hybrid thing,' the other demon guard said. 'Apparently if they breed two of these things together, you get a powerful snake like her, and the King did it.'

I waited silently, watching them.

'Does she talk?' the serpent demon said.

'Should do, supposed to be a major brain.' The guard grinned, revealing four tusks in the corners of his mouth. 'For a female, anyway.'

The snake demon glared at him. 'I'll tell the Mothers you said that.'

His grin was quickly replaced by a look of concern. 'Hey, no, I didn't mean that. You girls can be brighter than us men sometimes. Really.' He moved back so that the snake demon could see better. 'See if you can get her to talk.'

The human prisoner wailed quietly, gradually rising in pitch and volume to a scream. He didn't move or change his expression otherwise.

'Ah, shit, better get this one back to the prison section,' one of the guards said. 'Oh, he was heard.'

'Da Shih Yeh,' the demons said in unison with reverence.

A tiny, white-skinned elderly man wearing a simple ragged tunic down to his knees and leaning on a twisted wooden staff hobbled up to the group. His beard nearly touched the floor and his eyes glittered with intelligence under his bushy brows.

'Is this the one making that racket?' he said.

Don't say a word, Emma, the stone said urgently.

The demon guard pushed the human victim towards the old man. 'Can you shut him up for us, Da Shih Yeh?'

Da Shih Yeh held out one bony hand and put it square over the prisoner's face. The man's eyes went wide and he stared into Da Shih Yeh's eyes, then completely relaxed. His eyes half-closed and he almost smiled.

'That will keep him quiet for a while,' Da Shih Yeh said. He swivelled on his staff to look inside my cell. 'And what is this? I've never seen anything like this before.' He shuffled closer. 'A human serpent thing?' He chuckled with delight. 'I love to see new things, don't you?' He spoke over his shoulder to the guards. 'You'd better put that human back where it belongs before someone realises he's not where he's supposed to be.'

'Uh, yeah,' one of the guards said. 'Come on, guys, let's get out of here. The boss'll be down on us hard if she finds us slacking around here.'

I waited until they were out of earshot, then quickly slithered to the bars of the cage. 'You need to get out of here right now. He knows who you are and if he finds you he'll have you. Go now.'

'They all know who I am, little one,' the Grandfather said, leaning on his staff. 'I just move faster than they do.'

'Those guards will be running to tell the King!'

He glanced back down the corridor. 'I've done all of those ones a favour in the past. None of them would exist without me and they know it. They won't do anything.'

'What if he ordered them to tell him if you showed up?'

'They would tell him; they have to. But they can take a couple of days thinking about whether or not it was really me.' He reached through the bars to touch my nose and the warm feeling of comfort spread through me. 'I am here if you need me, but sometimes I need to move away quickly.' He raised his head. 'Now is one of those times, I am sorry. I will return later if you are still here.' He took his hand from my nose. 'I will tell those who need to know what they need to know.'

'No!' I said urgently. 'Don't tell him where I am. He needs to find me —'

Da Shih Yeh disappeared.

'— himself.'

* * *

Zhenwu

There were sounds above him, but they didn't break into his reverie. Then one loud noise did. Someone was calling 'Father'. Simone?

'Ah Ba!'

He opened his eyes and saw the huge humans. They needed him. He pulled himself back into his shell and took human form.

'Is it time to go?' he said.

'No, there's a message for you. The fairy won't give it to anyone else,' Martin said.

The fairy floated to John and held out a piece of paper, carefully folded into four. He took the paper and opened it, then shot to his feet.

'Who gave you this?' he asked the fairy, and his tone made her flit backwards with fright. He waved the paper in front of her face. 'Who has done this? Where did this come from?'

The fairy's face went serene and a voice echoed around the courtyard, whispering with the sound of trees and water, 'Buddha.'

'Which Buddha?'

The fairy shook her head.

'I suppose we all look the same to you. What did the Buddha look like?'

The fairy gestured towards the pond and an image of Kwan Yin appeared in the water.

John dropped his arm, suddenly limp. 'I cannot believe she would do this to me.'

'What does it say?' Martin said.

John handed him the note and Martin glanced at it, then smiled broadly. 'This is marvellous. It will mean much less searching.' He glanced up at John. 'Why are you unhappy? This is good news.'

The fairy had disappeared. John fell to sit cross-legged on the grass again and checked his watch: 3 am. Still hours before he could see the Jade Emperor, and Kwan Yin had ruined it.

Leo glanced at the note. 'Oh, that was a rotten thing to do. I understand how you feel.'

'What?' Martin said. 'What am I missing?'

Leo gestured towards John. 'He vowed to find her, Raise her and marry her. She's lost in Hell, so if he finds her now it's one of three, and they can stop worrying about being separated. It's been driving both of them nuts.'

'I don't see what this has to do with it,' Martin said.

Leo tapped the paper in Martin's hand. 'Kwan Yin found Emma first. And this tells him where Emma is; she's not lost any more.'

'If you go through that maze in level six to find Emma, you are still finding her,' Martin said, confident. 'Don't be concerned, Father, this is nothing. I'm sure that finding her in Hell will fulfil your oath.'

John leaned the back of his head against the tree. 'I sincerely hope so.' He pulled himself to his feet. 'I suppose I should try to sleep until we see the Jade Emperor. I suggest you two return to bed as well.'

Martin and Leo nodded and turned away. When they reached the doorway into their quarters, Martin stopped and turned back. 'Do not be concerned, Father. You will find her.'

'Thank you,' John said.

He walked around the courtyard to his own bedroom, stripped off and fell onto the black silk sheets naked, too emotionally drained to change into sleep clothes. The fairies would just have to put up with him.

* * *

Emma

Later that night, it became quiet. The other residents of the cells were parked in the demon equivalent of sleep. I couldn't sleep, so the stone retrieved the Archivist's files and projected them into the air in front of the rocky overhang.

'There's so little to go on,' I said, frustrated.

'Serves them right for not writing anything down,' the stone said. 'Oral tradition. That's nearly as bad as the way kids learn by recitation rather than understanding.'

'I didn't know you were pro education reform,' I said. 'I would have thought you'd support the way it's always been done.'

'One of my children helped start the Native English Teacher Scheme,' the stone said with pride. 'Look how that's improved the standard of English in the Territory. When they made all the schooling in native language, he said —'

'Psst! Snake lady!' someone hissed at the door of the cage.

The stone blinked the projections off and I poked my head out of the overhang. It was a snake demon; a small one, about level thirty.

'What do you want?' I said.

He dropped his head. He had many similarities to a natural snake, but his scales jutted out in spiked disarray, his head had horns and there were pointed projections under his chin.

'Can I ask you something?' he said.

'What?'

He looked around furtively, then back to me. 'Come closer. I don't want anybody to hear.'

Are there any other demons close by?

No.

I slithered out of my alcove and approached the bars, but stayed well back.

'Go ahead,' I said from two metres away.

'You have a crown,' he said in awe.

'It's to hold my engagement stone. It's pretty, isn't it? The Tiger made it for me.'

'Is it silver?'

'Platinum.'

'I love the work they put into it,' he said. 'It's all twisted wires, so lovely.'

I dropped my head slightly. 'Thank you. Is that what you wanted to ask?'

He looked around again, then moved closer to the bars. 'Can you give me a lesson?'

'A lesson in what?'

He dropped his voice to a whisper. 'Kung fu.'

'Why do you want to learn?' I said with interest.

'You must have seen what happened earlier. That Mother grabbed my sister and ate her. I don't want that to happen to me.' He raised his head and spoke with dignity. 'I want to be a Mother too one day. There has to be more to life than torturing adulterers.'

'You torture adulterers?'

Don't ask, Emma, you really don't want to know, the stone said.

'Not all of them,' the demon said. 'Just the ones the judges send here, which is only a small fraction of them. The boss keeps complaining that the judges are too lenient, whatever that means. We only get the really bad ones — you know, the ones who messed with little kids, or hurt other people physically or mentally. Some of the people we get down here are really nasty pieces of work.' He dropped his head. 'I can't believe how cruel humans are sometimes. They put our efforts to shame.' He looked back down the hallway. 'Had one evil bastard here for close on ten years and every day we made him scream. I enjoyed every second of that, until they took him to the Hell of Red-Hot Grates next level down.' He cocked his head at me. 'So will you teach me? I don't want to die like my sister did.'

'I can't teach you,' I said.

'Could you just tell me what to do?'

'No. The Jade Emperor's locked me out from teaching as punishment. I can't teach anyone.'

'He has no jurisdiction down here,' he said.

'His Edict applies to me wherever I am.'

'Okay.' He sounded disappointed. 'Hey, it's been nice talking to you anyway, Emma. I hope we never meet again.'

'Thanks. So do I. What's your name?'

'Rocky.' He took human form: a young, round-faced Chinese boy with dyed blond hair, wearing the white shirt and pants that served as a school uniform in China. 'What do you think of my human form? I've been working on it for a while.'

'You need to either make your head smaller or the rest

of you taller,' I said. 'Your head's slightly too big so it looks a little strange. Apart from that, it's very fetching.'

'Thank you,' he said shyly.

There was a loud hiss down the corridor. He looked and his face filled with terror. He backed towards the wall. 'Oh shit, no, a Mother. No, no, no.'

He spun towards the cell across from me, which was empty, and frantically worked at the door. 'Let me in! Let me in!'

The door wouldn't open and he huddled against the wall.

I went to the door of my cell and opened it. 'Come in here. Quickly! You'll be safe.'

No, Emma! the stone said, but I ignored it.

Rocky raced into my cell and I slammed the door shut, flipping the latch across just as the Mother appeared on the other side of it. She was in True Form: massive snake back end with human front end.

'You two having some sexy times?' she said. 'Don't stop on my account.'

I backed away from the door. 'We were just talking.'

'What the hell sort of accent is that?' She moved closer to me and I backed further away. 'You don't belong here. What are you?'

Rocky changed back to snake and moved next to me; we were of a similar size.

'This is the Dark Lady herself, Ninety-Four, so piss off. We were just talking, and if you hurt her the King will rip your scales off.'

'So this is her. She smells delicious,' the Mother said, then focused on Rocky. 'So do you.'

Rocky's voice squeaked with effort. 'You can't hurt us.'

'I'm bigger than you,' she said, her voice silky. 'Come to me, my darling.'

Rocky swayed as if mesmerised, then slithered towards the door.

The Mother pulled at the door and grimaced with frustration when it didn't open. 'Oh, it's locked on the inside. Open the door for me, honey.'

There's nothing you can do for him, Emma, back up! the stone said.

I slithered under the stone ledge as Rocky pulled the latch across and opened the door. I poked my head out and watched with frustration as the Mother reached in and picked him up by the base of his neck. She opened her mouth impossibly wide and shoved his head in, biting it off and sucking the demon essence out of him.

When she was done, she dropped on her coils and leered at me. 'Your turn.'

She came into the cell and grabbed me with one hand, dragging me out from under the overhang. She held me around the throat hard enough to cut off my air and I thrashed against her, trying to suck in enough to breathe. She raised me to her face and dropped me. The cell walls spun around me in a dizzying spiral and the floor slammed into my head.

When I came around, it was to a jumbled vision of blackness and a shiny silver needle, different in each eye. I lurched up to see what was happening, hitting whatever was standing over me.

'I told you she was coming round,' a woman said.

A group of demons were crowded into my cell: a small black-skinned one with a bulbous head and impossibly skinny body and limbs, holding a syringe; and a humanoid guard carrying weapons, with two similar guards behind it.

The small black demon put its hands up. 'I was just treating you. I'm not here to do any damage.' It sounded like a middle-aged man.

I hesitated, swaying my head in front of them.

It's speaking the truth, the stone said. *They destroyed*

the Mother before she could eat you, then they called a doctor. They were worried you were poisoned.

The skinny demon spoke to the guards without looking away from me. 'I'd say she'll be fine, but I really have no idea. I've never seen anything like her before. Keep an eye on her, and if she complains about anything at all let me know.'

He tossed the syringe into a physician's bag sitting next to him, then nodded to me. 'Dark Lady. It has been an honour to meet you. I hope you survive whatever it is that His Loathsome Majesty has in store for you.'

'I apologise for hitting you,' I said. 'A disadvantage of having no eyelids is that when I wake up I see everything right in front of my face.'

'You aren't the first,' he said.

The guards parted and allowed him to walk out of the cell, lugging the big bag with him.

The head guard turned back to me and spoke in a gruff woman's voice. 'The King's put us here to guard you. Apparently the Mothers know about you and they all want to see you.' She looked down the hallway. 'Three of us should be able to handle any of them.' She turned back to me and raised her axe in front of her gleaming, black-scaled face. 'I hear the Dark Lord is coming for you. I hope he'll do me the honour of letting me take a swing at him before he destroys me.'

She nodded over her shoulder to the other two humanoids, and the three of them took up position outside my cage.

'Turn and he won't destroy you,' I said. 'Pledge to me and I'll make sure you're treated well.'

She gestured with her chin towards the ceiling. 'Can't turn while Grandad's watching us.'

I moved closer to the bars and looked where she'd indicated. A slime demon, more than a metre across, was

123

stuck to the ceiling. It was made of bright orange and green filaments that writhed over each other, and was completely covered in glassy opaque eyes of all sizes, blinking and moving over its liquid surface. When it saw me looking, it made some sticky hissing noises.

'Grandad says hi, and sorry about the Mothers,' the guard demon translated for me. 'He says, how do you like the security camera? Oh, he wants me to tell you how he made it.' She grinned, revealing gleaming white tusks. 'He grabs the eyes out of any demon that has displeased him, and holds them in shape while the rest of the demon explodes. Then he pokes the eyes into that thing so it can keep watch for him.'

'Charming.'

10

Zhenwu

John stormed into the Gold Spirit Audience Chamber and roughly fell to one knee, glaring at the floor. 'Ten thousand years.'

'Ah Wu,' the Jade Emperor said.

'Majesty.'

'I suggest you take a deep breath, reach into the Tao and control your temper before we take this further. Your conduct is unbecoming of a Celestial Immortal.'

John didn't look up from the floor.

The Jade Emperor's voice was mildly exasperated. 'Very well. Rise and sit with me, Number One, and we will see what we can do.'

John stood, flicked his black robe into place, and sat on a chair side-on to the Jade Emperor. One of the fairies poured tea and he nodded to her.

'I understand that Miss Donahoe travelled to Hell under her own power and without being coerced,' the Jade Emperor said.

'Just give me permission to go down and get her out.'

'Do you have any idea where she is?'

John studied the Jade Emperor. Nobody was really sure exactly how omniscient he was, but the consensus was that he knew everything that happened.

'I know exactly where she is. I just need your permission to go.'

The Jade Emperor waved one of the fairies over. She placed a scroll on the tea table next to him. Another fairy placed the Great Imperial Seal, a block ten centimetres each side and twenty high, on its own small tray next to the seal. John tried not to fidget with impatience as the Jade Emperor carefully inked the seal and stamped it onto the scroll. The Emperor picked up the scroll, waved it around a few times to dry the ink, then rolled it up.

'It is the nature of the Tao to act without acting, and to act only when there is no other choice,' the Jade Emperor said. 'You have been too impatient to act in this case.'

'I have no other choice. I must find her; she is in danger. I do not need a lecture in the nature of the Tao.'

'Your impatience and frustration indicates that you do. Your impudence suggests other actions may be appropriate, Number One.'

John deliberately calmed himself, touching the spinning yin-yang deep inside him. A feeling of serenity filled him.

'Good,' the Jade Emperor said. He gave the scroll to the fairy standing next to him. 'You do not need to ask permission from the Demon King because he has already given it. Proceed to Hell and find your lady. Then please, if you would, Raise and marry her and stop letting this emotional nonsense interfere with your duties as First Heavenly General. You are acting with selfish intention, seeking pleasure in the company of this woman when you should be focused only on protecting our realm. Like it or not, Ah Wu, many people rely on you to keep them safe. You are too necessary to the security of the realm to waste your time pursuing romantic liaisons with human liabilities.'

'Once she is Raised and we are wed, she will not be a liability,' John said, 'she will be an asset.'

'We shall see.' The Jade Emperor picked up his cup and sipped the tea. 'Go and find your lady, Ah Wu. She is safe and waiting for you.'

John rose from his chair and knelt to the Jade Emperor. He stood, accepted the scroll from the fairy and did his best to leave the audience chamber without breaking into a run.

* * *

Emma

A few hours later the demon guards were sitting cross-legged on the other side of the bars, telling me stories about their lives.

'And so when we hatched, we were all big humanoids, so they put us in the army,' the leader, Three Four One, said. She gestured towards the other two. 'These two are from a different clutch, same father, different Mother. Our father's a minor horse-head duke. They're slightly smaller than me.'

'And we're both male,' one of the other guards said.

'Can you take human form?' I said.

They all shook their heads.

'Stuck like this,' Three Four One said.

'How old are you?'

'I'm four years old,' Three Four One said with obvious pride. 'My little brothers here are about six months old. Same clutch.'

'I hope you all go on to live long happy lives,' I said.

'You're so caring,' the smaller demon said with awe.

'Listen,' I said, lowering my voice, 'after you're done here, and the King can't see you any more, try to find me. I'll look after you.'

The air temperature plummeted to nearly freezing and the guards all jumped to their feet.

'He's here,' Three Four One said.

The slime demon on the ceiling made a series of hissing, gargling sounds.

'No,' one of the smaller demons said.

'You heard him,' Three Four One said. 'If you can't do it yourself, kneel down and I'll do it for you. I promise it'll be quick.'

'We did what you told us to!' the smaller demons wailed at the slime demon's many eyes. 'We obeyed your orders! Why?'

'You know damn well why, stupid,' Three Four One said. 'He knows that the minute he can't see us we'll all make a run for it, try to find her and turn.'

The slime demon's gurgles rose in pitch. It sounded like it was drowning. The two smaller guards exploded, dissipating into streamers of black demon essence that sank slowly through the air.

'I have a favour to ask you,' Three Four One said.

'Anything.'

'Oh, don't say that,' she said with humour. 'Do you know what I'd gain if I gave Grandad your human form?'

'So what do you want?' I said.

The temperature was still dropping and terrified screams resounded through the hallways. The ground shook beneath us, then shook again with a low rumble that I felt more than heard.

'If for some reason the Dark Lord spares me, the King will throw me to the Mothers,' Three Four One said. 'I make this request of you: please ensure that I am not spared, and that when he does it, it is quick.'

'I wish there could be another way, but if that is the only way then I will do my best to make it quick for you.'

She bowed her head slightly. 'Thank you.'

A flurry of stinging snowflakes blew down the corridor and a low strumming bass sound made the floor reverberate.

Screams resounded off the black stone walls. Three Four One took a couple of steps back until she was against the wall, staring grimly in front of her. The slime demon on the ceiling made slurping sounds and dripped globules of ooze with each shock of vibration.

John strode down the corridor in Celestial Form, a dark aura of blue-black energy floating around him. He held Seven Stars, its blade loaded with his glowing chakras. Martin was at his right hand and Leo was on his left, both of them in Celestial Form.

John stopped in front of my cell, ignoring Three Four One completely. 'Found you,' he said in his normal voice.

'She was right about level six,' Leo said. He raised his sword to destroy Three Four One.

'Don't hurt the demon!' I said. 'It's guarding me.'

Leo lowered the sword and stared at her. 'Still a demon, Emma, and it hasn't been tamed. It could go for us any time.'

Three Four One raised her axe and saluted Leo. 'That's right.'

She swung the axe and he blocked it with his sword.

'Don't hurt her!' I said.

Leo put one massive hand around her throat and lifted her, taking the axe from her and dropping it on the floor with his other hand. 'You sure? It seems pretty nasty to me.'

'I'm sure.'

'Back up, Emma,' John said.

He raised one hand towards the bars and they froze with an audible crack, then instantly covered with frost. He leaned forward and tapped one and it shattered. He tapped each of the bars in turn, destroying them and sending shards of metal glittering to the floor.

He strode into the cage, ducking to fit under the low ceiling. 'Touch my hand and I'll take you home.'

'Before you do, destroy that slime demon on the ceiling,' I said.

John didn't turn away from me. 'Ming Gui.'

Martin generated a ball of shen energy and blew up the demon.

'You can turn now, Three Four One,' I said. 'Come with us.'

'If it's all the same to you,' the demon said, her voice muffled by Leo's hold, 'I'd prefer to go by the Dark Lord's own hand. My nest mates will honour my number for a long time if I do.'

'You could come live in Heaven with us and try to attain humanity,' I said.

'I have no human form,' the demon said. 'I cannot exist in Heaven or the Earthly. I can only live here, and my life here is over. I have no hope, no chance, no future. The King has ordered me dead.' She tapped Leo's hand around her throat. 'I beg this kindness, that it be the Dark Lord himself.'

John turned. 'Put her down, Leo.'

'I thank you, Lord,' Three Four One said with obvious emotion.

John gestured a come-on. 'Pick up your axe, little one. Let's see how much you have learned.'

Three Four One grabbed her axe from the floor and with one fluid movement swung it at John. He blocked with Seven Stars, twisted the sword down and sliced her from shoulder to hip. She dissipated with a wide-tusked grin on her face.

'Very underskilled,' he said with interest.

'You could have at least given it a couple of strikes at you,' Leo said.

'That would be unfair to it. It would not appreciate me using anything less than my full abilities.' He turned back to me and held his hand out. 'Touch your nose to my hand.'

I touched his hand and the cells around me disappeared. We arrived outside the infirmary next to the Japanese maple tree. The sun was rising through a fine, cold, misting rain that covered the Mountain with grey clouds. I tried to change back but couldn't find the human form. John watched me, his face full of concern.

'I can't find it,' I said. 'I'm stuck as snake.'

'Touch the earth. Touch the sky,' he said.

I cycled my energy through my serpent form, touched the earth and sky and relaxed into it.

'Now find where your arms and legs have gone.'

I found them and they returned to me.

'Good,' he said, and caught me as I fell into his arms. 'What did they do to you? Did they hurt you?'

'They didn't do anything to her,' the stone said.

'Thank the Heavens.' John lifted me and carried me into the infirmary. 'Emma, do you know where my Serpent is?'

'Yes, it's ...' My voice trailed off. 'It's just ...'

He gently placed me onto one of the beds and put his index finger on my forehead. 'Think where it is.'

I tried to capture the memory. 'Dammit, my serpent knew exactly where it was ...'

I tried to change back to snake and felt a moment of dizziness.

'Don't try to change,' the stone said. 'You'll head straight back down there looking for it.'

'What about you, stone?'

'I don't know, my Lord. One part of the demonic side of Hell looks much like another.'

'But my snake knows where it is!' I said. I struggled to sit up and failed. 'Let me change and I'll lead you down there.'

The stone broke in. 'The Demon King knows about your oath, my Lord. He said that he would wait until you'd found her, then he plans to take and use her.'

'But he doesn't know the other parts of the oath,' I said.

'I hope —' John began.

Edwin pushed him out of the way and put a stethoscope on my chest. 'Stop talking. Cough.'

I coughed for him and he moved the stethoscope. 'Again.'

'You can move me out of her back now and return me to my ring,' the stone said. 'You've found her. One out of three. The rest will happen.'

Edwin shone a light in my eyes, checking my pupils. 'You seem to be completely uninjured,' he said. 'Slightly dehydrated, but otherwise fine.'

'We have to go get your Serpent out, I know where it is,' I said to John.

'When you've recovered, we will. We'll set up a diversion, and at the same time you can lead me down to the Serpent's cage. For now, rest.' He turned to Edwin. 'Can I take her home?'

'Put her to bed and make her sleep.'

'Come on, Emma,' John said, taking my hand and helping me up. 'Let's go home.'

'Sometimes, my Lord, you say the greatest things ever in the history of the world.'

'I thank you, my Lady.'

'You two are extremely cute sometimes,' Edwin said, grinning.

'I am not cute,' John said, glowering, and led me out.

* * *

I woke to grey light shining through gaps in the window screens. I appeared to have slept most of the day away. John was lying next to me, holding me close and waiting for me to wake up.

'Welcome back,' he said.

I sighed. 'I am so glad to be home.'

'So am I.'

'Do you think that was it? You actually found me?' I said.

'I travelled down to where you were held and searched until I found you.'

'But you knew where I was.'

He was silent for a long moment, then said, 'I know.'

'Stone, do you think he fulfilled his oath?'

'I'd very much like to believe so, so I can be freed from this fleshy —'

'Stone!' I said, shocked.

'— prison,' the stone finished. 'Fleshy prison! It is very uncomfortable being stuck in here and only seeing things second-hand. I need air on my surface, I am losing my lustre.'

'I'll have you removed tomorrow,' I said.

'Emma,' John said, 'it might be better —'

'The stone has suffered enough. We've all suffered enough,' I said. 'You found me and that's that. Now all you have to do is Raise and marry me.'

'The Jade Emperor said something while I was talking to him today — he said I am selfishly enjoying having a relationship with you and not considering the needs of others. Is he right? Are you sure you still want to be with me? It's been a long time since I asked you, and so many things have happened ... Is this still what you want?'

I was silent for a moment, then chose my words carefully. 'This is what I want more than anything. I have no hesitation about marrying you and joining you here on the Mountain. It's what I want most in the world.'

He squeezed me and pulled me into him, and his unbound hair fell over both of us.

'I hesitate to ask you to show me where my Serpent is,' he said. 'It will lead you into danger.'

'We have to go as soon as possible before they move it.'

'Can you show me where it is and then head back here immediately?'

'Yes. But if there's any chance you'll be trapped, you get the hell out of there.'

'I'll be in and out so quickly the King won't know what happened. Europe, on the other hand, is an unknown quantity. I should tell the Jade Emperor to wait until this situation is settled and you are safely Raised before we start the search for Western Shen. This is too dangerous.'

'Has the Jade Emperor ever rescinded a command, Turtle?' the stone said.

'You know he hasn't. But I am beginning to doubt his intentions when it comes to Emma.'

'You have your oath. You will Raise and marry her. He cannot interfere with that.'

'I should leave you here on the Mountain where you are guarded while I go to Britain,' John said.

'Are you sure about that?' I said.

He was silent for a moment, then, 'No. You're safer with me. Both of you are always safer with me. I wish that the Elixir was ready now.'

'I can wait.'

'I can't,' he said. 'I hate seeing you in the black and white of a servant. I want you to be my Empress, in silk of black and gold on a throne beside me.'

I pretended to pull away. 'I changed my mind. I'd rather lounge around in the servant's uniform doing mundane stuff than sit on any sort of throne.'

He buried his face in my hair. 'That's what makes you so ideal for the job.'

I couldn't keep the exasperation from my voice. 'All that responsibility!'

'We can share it.' He pulled back to look at me, his face a silhouette in the light shining through the closed screens. 'When we marry, you must be the Empress with all that it entails; there is no avoiding it. If you really do not want to rule beside me, you can do what your family has done and seek anonymity and seclusion on the Earthly, living a normal life.'

'A normal life, without you and Simone and my sword and the Mountain? I could never be happy living like that.'

'Are you sure?'

The uncertainty in his voice saddened me. I ran one hand down the side of his face.

'Know this, Xuan Wu: I love you, and I always will. Not because of some demonic intervention, or some silly romantic ideal, but because you are who you are. You're a kind, generous, noble and sometimes ridiculously idiotic man who I love with all my heart. And I will be proud and honoured to help you rule your domain.'

'The King doesn't know what a favour he did me when he drew us together. You were already something that I would love — you are something that I love — without his intervention. You brought me back from my grief, brought me closer to my daughter, and managed things,' his voice filled with humour, 'almost acceptably well in my absence. I owe you — and, in a way, him — a great debt.'

'And?'

'And what?'

'Oh, you *guy*,' I said, poking him in the ribs, making him jump and grunt.

He changed against me, becoming a woman.

'You're still a guy,' I said, gently brushing my hand over one of her breasts, making her gasp.

'And I love you,' she said, and kissed me. She pulled back. 'I'll stay female now, just so I can say it again.'

I pushed myself closer into her and spoke into her neck. 'Nope, I want you male, and I want to hear you say it.'

He changed back to male. 'Do I have to?'

'Sometimes I think you and the Tiger *are* brothers.'

'I love you,' he whispered, and we both sighed with bliss.

11

First thing the next day, we rallied at the Mountain's main forecourt outside Purple Mist and prepared to sortie into Hell.

Two of the biggest Generals were leading the diversion: Zhou Gong Ming and Ma Hua Guang. Their two companies of demons, each a hundred and twenty soldiers, in neat ranks, made an impressive sight. Zhou wore a tiger's skin draped over him, his fierce dark face glaring out from between the tiger's jaws. Ma was in full Celestial Form, as tall as John, his red robes with burning flames around the edges.

John was also in Celestial Form, in his black battledress, with Seven Stars strapped to his back. I had taken serpent form, and made it as big as I could to avoid being stepped on. None of the soldiers going with us were less than three metres tall.

A large group of enthralled students stood to the side of the square, watching and discussing the group.

Ma and John were in the final stages of arranging the diversion. Ma waved Zhou and the company leaders to him, and they stood in front of a map of Hell made of a tracery of flames floating in the air. Hell's wheel shape was obvious, with the Celestial side in the middle, surrounded by a huge lake, and the demonic side joined to it by causeways that formed the spokes of the wheel.

Ma pointed at the map, sticking his finger into the flames. 'This is where Emma said the Serpent's being held: level one, demonic side. We'll gather outside Death's house on the Celestial side first. My group will go to level four and cause some trouble, while Ah Wu and Emma free the Serpent. Listen for Ah Wu's signal. We'll throw ourselves at them and redouble while he's pulling the Serpent out.'

The Zhu sisters appeared on the other side of the square and strode towards us. Both were in battle armour and had swords strapped to their backs. The elder sister, Bei Niang's sword, the Shadow Sword, was a grey shifting shape that was impossible to focus on.

A couple of the soldiers broke ranks and ran to them. The sisters stopped and the demons fell to one knee in front of them.

'Oh, that's cute,' Ma said.

'They should be put on report,' Zhou said, gruff.

'Lady, please return and lead us,' one of the demons said.

'Return to your ranks immediately,' Zhu Bo Niang said.

'We will,' the other demon said. 'But please return to us, we need you.'

'Back in line, soldier,' Bei Niang said.

The two demons rose, bowed to the sisters and ran back to take their places in the demon cohort.

Bei Niang strode up to us and put her hands on her hips. 'You're not going without us.'

'You want to come?' John said.

'We *are* coming,' Bo Niang said.

'Only if you take up your commissions again,' John said.

The Zhu sisters hesitated for a moment.

Bo Niang put her hand out. 'Deal.'

Bei Niang put her hand out as well and John clasped each of their hands.

Half a dozen demons in the ranks went wild, jumping up and down with joy and hugging each other.

'Attention!' Zhou snapped at them and they quickly sobered.

'Good,' John said. 'We just need someone to cause havoc on level four while we find the Serpent.'

Bo Niang smiled tightly. 'Havoc is what we're good at. We don't have time to restore our regiments, so we'll come as we are and help out.'

'Excellent.' Ma made the map disappear. He turned to the others. 'We ready?'

'Emma?' John said.

'I'm good. Let's go.'

'Bring my daddy home!' Simone shouted from the other side of the forecourt.

John touched his hand to my nose and the Mountain disappeared.

We arrived outside the modern concrete bunker that was the office of the god of death, Yanluo Wang. It stood on the edge of the lake that separated Celestial Hell from demonic Hell. The lake seemed to stretch forever with a couple of the causeways visible, spreading from the central island. The sky was light without being blue and there was no breeze.

'Keep your hand on my head,' I said. I looked for the room that held his Serpent. 'Found it.'

John released my head. 'Ma.'

'Death's coming,' Ma said.

The group separated to let John step forward to face Yanluo Wang. He was in red robes embroidered all over with the character of death, and wore a high red hat with extensions each side that wobbled as he walked.

'This is serious,' Ma said, his voice low. 'He hates uniform and avoids it whenever he can.'

Yanluo Wang stopped in front of John and saluted him. 'Dark Lord.' He nodded around to the group. 'Generals.'

There was a polite sequence of small bows and salutes.

Yanluo Wang put one red-robed arm out towards me.

'You brought a human mortal here in breach of every single protocol. She will remain here until her time has been allocated, and then she will be Judged.'

'Oh, shit,' Ma said softly.

'She has permission to be here and permission to leave,' John said.

He raised one hand and a scroll appeared in it. He passed the scroll to Yanluo Wang.

'Is that the same one?' Ma asked me.

'It's still valid,' I said, then dropped my voice. 'I hope.'

Yanluo Wang obviously agreed with me. He opened the scroll, perused it, then handed it back to John with both hands and a small bow. 'The human is permitted. She is to complete her task and return as soon as it is done.'

John bowed formally and stiffly to Yanluo Wang, then they relaxed.

Yanluo Wang eyed me. 'Nice snake, Emma. You'll be a great match when you free his. I heard you spent some time on level six and fitted right in.'

'We're ready to go,' Ma said.

Yanluo Wang slapped John on the shoulder. 'Go find your better half, and give the Demon King a good swift kick in the ass for all of us.'

'I plan to,' John said. He raised his head to speak to Ma. 'Whenever you're ready.'

'Going now,' Ma said, and the diversion group disappeared.

John put his hand back on my snout. 'Show me.'

'I'm not wishing you good luck because you don't need it,' Death said.

* * *

I showed John where the Serpent's cage was, and felt the heat immediately as he transported us to the hall. The

139

walls and floor were beige tiles, carved with serpents and scalding hot. The room was oval, twenty metres across, with tall windows on the wall leading up to a domed roof, all covered in the shining tiles.

The cage was gone; there wasn't even a mark on the floor where it had stood.

I slithered around the area, but all I found was a screwed-up tissue. I picked it up in my mouth and returned to John.

'This is where it was. I remember this place.' I looked around. 'I saw it here just before. Where's it gone?'

'Concentrate and try to find it.'

Before I could focus, the clamour of sirens filled the cavern and I dropped the tissue.

'They've attacked,' John said. 'Concentrate. Where is the rest of me?'

'Put your hand on my head again.'

I dropped my head slightly, feeling his hand on me, and tried to contact John's Serpent. There was nothing there. I relaxed, cycled the energy through myself and concentrated on the Serpent's nature. John glowed with blue-black darkness in front of me, but the Serpent wasn't there.

I pulled the energy back. 'Give me a moment ... I can't see it. Can you?'

'I don't want to risk it.'

I slithered around the room, feeling for it. I thought I sensed a reflection of it and stopped. I relaxed and concentrated again, and saw it.

'John, here,' I said. 'I've located it.'

John came to me and put his hand on my head. 'I see, not too far. Let's go.'

He disappeared. He'd completely forgotten me in the excitement of the moment.

I thought hard about where the Serpent was and envisaged myself there. My surroundings shifted and merged into what I wanted — I'd done it. I felt a surge of satisfaction, until I saw the large number of demons, all bristling with weapons, between us and the Serpent. There were more than two hundred of them, filling the huge hall. That was why they'd moved the Serpent — this larger area could hold an army. So much for our stealth mission.

'Behind me, and head straight home,' John said, putting one hand on the back of my neck to manoeuvre me into his protection.

A volley of arrows arched from behind the demon warriors standing before us. The arrows disintegrated before they reached us. I tried to envisage the Mountain, but a shout distracted me and the demons ran towards us. John glowed purple-black and their front row disappeared. The rest of the demons stopped in alarm, and more of those in the front ranks disappeared.

John's energy aura shrank into him and he grew slightly smaller. 'Emma, go,' he said.

'I'm trying,' I said.

The demons rushed him again and he pulled out Seven Stars. He loaded the blade with his internal energy and swung it at the demons. He fought faster than I'd ever seen him fight before. The placement of my serpent eyes on the sides of my head meant that my vision encompassed nearly a complete circle and I saw his battle fury in majestic detail.

The demons surrounded us and the need to fight them sang through me. This was what I lived for. To hell with going back to the Mountain. I stood back to back with the God of War and fought the demons with him. I couldn't take human form and summon a weapon, but in serpent form I was deadly and filled with fierce joy at the amount of destruction we could wreak together. I took out those behind him that he couldn't see, biting their heads off and crushing them.

He destroyed ten for every two of mine. His blade sang with his energy and he occasionally used it to launch balls of shen into the demon ranks to thin them. I was drawn back to cold reality as I realised he was breathing heavily. He still had burns and cuts and wasn't at full strength.

There are too many of them, the Serpent said. *I can't do it!*

'But I have to do it,' John said. 'I can't give up now I'm this close. Dammit, why won't they answer? We need backup!'

I heard the whistling thump of arrows. Something slapped into me, then something else, then pain flattened me — I'd been hit. I rolled over, which pushed the shafts of the arrows deeper into me, but I needed to see John. He was facing me as he fell, four arrow shafts sticking out of his shoulders and one in his neck, its wound pumping with blood. He landed on top of me, his huge Celestial Form crushing my midsection. Blood — his blood — flooded over my face, threatening to choke me.

Get out! Get out! the Serpent shouted into my head. *Turtle, take her out!*

I was crippled with pain, unable to move; red spots swam over my vision. I hoped he was conscious enough to get us out because I wasn't taking myself anywhere.

One of the demons grinned, revealing jagged uneven teeth, and pointed the tip of its spear at John's face. 'Now we have you.'

John raised one arm, crying out with pain at the effort, and slammed it into me. The ground changed. I saw feet in front of my face and had the incongruous thought that Shaolin monks' shoes were nearly the same colour as their robes ... then everything faded away.

* * *

142

'We need them in human form!' Edwin said, frantic. 'Lord Xuan ... Lord Xuan!'

Leo's tone was demanding. 'Emma, can you hear me?'

'Huh?'

'She spoke. Edwin, she said something.'

'Emma, take human form,' Edwin said. 'I can't work on you like this!'

It all faded away again, then their shouting roared back to me.

'Lord Xuan. Lord Xuan! John. You have to listen to me,' Edwin said.

John made some guttural noises.

'You must take human form,' Edwin said. 'I can't work on you while you're this big.'

'Hey! Emma moved,' someone said.

Edwin's voice moved closer, but I couldn't see anything. 'Emma, take human form. I can't anaesthetise you as a snake.'

'The vet's on his way,' Simone said from the other side of the room.

'Emma, these arrows need to come out and I can't do it while you're a snake,' Edwin said again. 'For god's sake, woman, change to human!'

I needed Meredith to help me. I struggled with the name. I shouted it inside my head at them. *Meredith!*

I'm on my way, Meredith said.

I relaxed and blacked out again.

* * *

'I'll just have to sew him up on the floor,' Edwin was saying. 'Damn, he's lost a lot of blood — we need to do a transfusion. What blood type is he?'

'Non-human,' John said. 'Wait, I'll change.'

'Well, thank the Heavens for that,' Edwin said. 'Get him on a gurney and clean this up.'

'Keep the ...' John began, but couldn't go on.

'Keep the blood if you can,' Meredith said for him. 'It's a potent healing agent.' I heard her voice come closer. 'Now, madam, let's get you human.' Her cool hands touched either side of my head. 'Are you conscious? Think the answer — I'll hear you.'

Yes.

'Good. Let's work together on this.' She raised her voice. 'Nobody touch either of us, and a bit of hush would work wonders.' She dropped her voice again. 'Ready? One ... two ... three!'

I helped her as she shrank me into human form, then shrieked as the change made the arrows plunge deeper into me. She stopped, horrified at the damage she was doing, and I was stuck poised between human and snake.

'Dear god,' Edwin said.

'Don't leave her like that!' Simone said, distraught.

'If I push her into human form, the arrows will do more damage,' Meredith said.

'I can't work on her like that. Not even a vet could work on her like that,' Edwin said. 'We'll handle the injuries. Do it.'

'Sorry, Emma,' Meredith whispered, and slapped the inside of my head.

I fell into human form, and the arrows burrowed deeper into my back. Thankfully they'd put me on my stomach so I wasn't lying on them.

'All yours, Edwin,' Meredith said, her voice full of regret.

'Stitch the rest of this up while I do these arrows,' Edwin said.

He stabbed me next to one of the arrow injuries and I made a clipped sound of pain.

'Local anaesthetic,' Edwin said, putting his other hand on my shoulder. 'The pain will ease now.' His voice became more urgent. 'Forget that, get the gas. I need to operate. Find the anaesthetic trolley, we have to put her under *now*. This damn arrow's gone into her liver.' He started yelling. 'Prep the room! Get me the trolley! Leo, are you okay to finish there?'

'I'm good,' Leo said from the other side of the room. 'Two more.'

'When you finish with him, hand him off and come help me in theatre,' Edwin said. 'She's bleeding out from the other arrow; it looks like it's clipped her aorta. Forget the trolley. Meredith, put her under and help me.'

'Done.'

* * *

The room was too bright and I winced.

'Emma, thank the Heavens,' Simone said.

I tried to say something but my throat was too dry.

'Do you think you'd be more comfortable lying on your back?' Edwin said next to my head.

I raised my head slightly and pain shot down my back. I dropped my head again, then shook it in a reply.

'Do you need anything?' Simone said.

I tried to croak out 'Water' but nothing happened.

'She's trying to say something,' Simone said.

I tried again.

'I think it's water.'

'Give her some ice to suck,' Edwin said.

I winced at that; I was dying of thirst. Simone slipped some ice into my mouth and I worked around the cold to try to get as much of it down me as I could.

I tried to speak again. 'John?'

'He lost a lot of blood,' Edwin said, 'but Meredith said it was important to keep him alive after he'd been so close to the Serpent. We stitched him up and he's in better shape than you. He'll be up and around in twenty-four hours. You look like you'll need a few days.'

'Damage?'

'Pierced liver and clipped aorta. We need to keep an eye on you to make sure that the stitches in the blood vessel aren't leaking.'

I let my breath out in a huge sigh. 'Okay.'

I raised my head slightly and winced at the pain it caused down my back. I considered asking them to turn me over, but the idea of the pain it would cause made me decide against it.

'More ice,' I croaked. 'So thirsty.'

Simone slipped another cube into my mouth and I nodded my thanks with minimal movement.

'Let me know if the pain is too strong and I'll top up the painkillers,' Edwin said.

'Others?' I said.

'What others?' Simone said. 'Oh, Ma and Zhou. They lost nearly their entire hosts of demons, and one of the Zhu sisters was killed as well. The demons were waiting for them.'

The ice soothed my dry throat and it was easier to speak. 'Waiting for us as well.'

'Daddy said there were hundreds of them.'

I smiled grimly. 'We took a great many of them down before we fell.'

'That's exactly what he said,' Edwin said. 'Wait — that's *exactly* what he said.'

'I wish you wouldn't do that,' Simone said.

'Is he in this room?' I said. I wanted to turn my head to the other side to see him, but it would probably hurt too much.

'No, you're in here by yourself. You need to rest in quiet,' Edwin said. 'He'll be in as soon as he's walking around. For now, just rest. Get some sleep, and heal. Meredith will be back later to block your meridians again and give you some energy healing.'

'Thanks.'

'Leo's with Daddy. I'll stay here,' Simone said.

I closed my eyes. 'Thanks, sweetheart.' I opened them again. 'Sorry.'

She patted my hand. 'I don't mind.'

* * *

A couple of days later, I was up and sitting with John under a tree in the cool autumn sunshine. The flow of staff and students checking up on us had stopped, and we sat in companionable silence, enjoying the fresh air.

Meredith walked over one of the arched bridges from the training area and sat on a bench across from us. 'How's the pain, Emma?'

'I'm managing on minor painkillers. I don't need your help any more.'

'Good. You'll both be well enough to travel after Mid-Autumn Festival.'

John didn't reply, brooding.

'I hope we find what we're looking for in less than a month,' I said. 'Being away for so long will be tough.'

'It's strange,' she said, leaning back, 'I'm originally from the UK and I feel the same way. Are you ever homesick for Australia?'

'No, not really.' I put my hand on John's thigh and he covered it with his. 'Everything I love is here.'

'How about the place in your dreams?' Meredith said.

I didn't reply. Something inside me would throw away everything to be there. John squeezed my hand and I squeezed it back.

147

'Don't forget that you're nearly there,' Meredith said. 'The Elixir will be ready soon and neither of you will need to worry any more. It'll be two out of three, found and Raised, and the third is just a formality.'

'I know,' I said.

'And it's a huge relief to be out of her back,' the stone said.

Meredith rose gracefully. 'I have students to harass. Don't overdo it.'

We both waved her goodbye as she headed back over the bridge.

'Someone told the Demon King,' I said.

'Possible.' John shifted slightly, making himself more comfortable. 'But it would not have been hard to work out what we had planned. I should have taken a larger force with us, and not relied on stealth.'

'We were so close,' I said with a sigh.

He gripped my hand. 'To losing you. I won't try again until after you're safely Raised.'

'I'll drink that Elixir as fast as I can, and we'll go straight down to bring you back.'

He released my hand and put his arm around my shoulders. 'It doesn't work like that,' he said.

'I remember … Leo was carried away on a cloud.' I straightened slightly. 'And everyone was concerned that he might not return.'

'It's always a possibility when the new Immortal is particularly enlightened,' John said. 'Frankly, I'm surprised that he returned so quickly.'

'You'll have nothing to worry about with me then.'

He kissed the top of my head. 'I wish.'

12

Two weeks later, I was doing a Tai Chi set under the tree outside what used to be my office when John sent a broadcast message to the entire Mountain.

I'm closing the pool. I believe some of you wanted to see this. If so, come now.

There were shouts and a rush of people coming out of training rooms and residences. I joined the crowd heading towards the eastern wall. As we went, students called to each other to let those who'd missed the broadcast know, and the group became even larger. Eventually, there were nearly a hundred students crowded around the pool.

Simone saw me and waved. She was standing next to Michael, and the students had left a respectful space around her.

'How are you feeling?' she said when I joined them.

'Nearly back to a hundred per cent,' I said. 'Everything's healed up nicely.'

'That's good to hear,' Michael said. He glanced up at the pool. 'This is very impressive. I'd like to know how he does it.'

The pool was a block of water fifty metres long, twenty wide and five deep, standing on four slender pillars of what appeared to be ice that thrust from the base of the gorge on the eastern side of the Mountain. Crystalline stairs led from the wall to the top of the block of water, but there were no other barriers around the pool.

'The bottom and sides are solid, but you can't see it,' Simone said.

'What, they're ice?' Michael said. 'Doesn't that make the water cold?'

'Not ice, solid water. It's like ice, but at room temperature,' Simone said. 'Most frightening thing I've ever seen in my entire life. He's the only one in the whole Celestial Plane — which basically means anywhere — who can make it. He's teaching me how to do it.'

'Why's it scary?' Michael said, then dropped his voice. 'Holy shit.'

'Exactly,' Simone said. 'If he were to change the water in your body to a solid, your blood would stop flowing and you're dead. If all the world's water was changed to this, every living thing would die.'

Michael floated into the air to hover above the wall, then went to one side of the pool and touched it. He ran his hand over its surface, then shook his head and returned to us.

'This puts my abilities with metal firmly in their place.'

'Which is an exceptional place,' Simone said. 'I've heard what your dad says about you.'

Michael shrugged. 'This is the first time since I was made Number One that I've gone for more than a week without losing a duel.'

'Judge Pao must be sick of the sight of you,' I said.

'Every time I go down there, he makes my court hearing exactly one minute longer than the last one,' Michael said. 'I didn't realise at first, it's so subtle. The guy's OCD in the way he makes me suffer.'

'Sounds about right,' Simone said. 'One of the advantages of being mortal is that I don't have to deal with him.'

He gazed down at her. 'Hurry up and learn to dance the stars and ride the wind, Simone. I worry about you.'

Their eyes locked for a long moment.

I shuffled my feet and coughed, but didn't need to interrupt. John floated up to the top of the wall, his long hair twining around him. The students all went silent and fell to one knee in unison.

'Show-off,' Simone said softly.

'It's not showing off if you're just being your awesome self,' Michael said with quiet amusement.

Simone gave a soft sigh of pleasure. 'I am so glad to have him back with us.'

'All of Heaven is,' Michael said.

John changed into a giant black sea turtle swimming through the air, and the students made chorusing sounds of wonder. He soared over us and dived into the swimming pool. He was a dark shape in the water for a long moment, then the block of water collapsed and fell into the gorge, the Turtle falling above it.

'Is he supposed —' I began, but Simone was ahead of me.

'Daddy!' she screamed, and jumped off the wall after him.

He tumbled through the air, his eyes half-open. Simone hit the water at the same time he did and they disappeared into it.

Michael peered over the edge of the wall, moving left and right to try to get a better view. 'I can't breathe underwater,' he said. 'Damn, it's a long way down!'

He climbed onto the wall and jumped off. There was a long, horrified silence, then Simone and Michael floated back up out of the gorge and landed on the wall. She fell into his arms and sobbed.

'He's dead; he hit the bottom,' Michael said to me. He spoke to the top of Simone's head. 'Come on, we need to check what happened to him. I'm sure he'll be fine, Simone. He took the body with him, so that probably means he knew where he was going.'

Simone nodded into his chest. They turned and jumped off the wall into the compound, still with their arms around each other's shoulders, and headed for the administration section.

I couldn't order the students to return to their quarters, so I just followed Simone and Michael on foot, full of dread. If John had been unaware of his surroundings when he hit, he could have rejoined the Serpent and the Demon King could have both of them.

When I arrived at John's office, Meredith and Liu were there too, with Michael and Simone, all looking concerned. Zara had taken the androgynous human form that she normally used when working as John's assistant. Her face was full of concentration, and then she came back, smiling broadly. 'He's in Court Ten. He didn't rejoin.'

'Oh, thank god,' Simone said, and leaned on John's desk. 'How long do you think ... Never mind, I know the answer to that.'

'Leave it to us,' Meredith said. 'We can manage things for a few days while he's away.' She nodded to Zara. 'Was he lined up for anything urgent?'

'There's a court session in the Northern Heavens tomorrow, but Ming Gui and Yue Gui can handle that,' Zara said. She shrugged. 'Apart from that, nothing terribly urgent.'

'We had a charity thing tonight. He was planning to introduce his new persona to everybody in Hong Kong,' I said.

'That's right. He's using his old identity papers, which means he has to pretend to be my grandfather,' Simone said.

'We had David Hawkes lined up to be there and confirm his legitimacy,' I said. 'We'll just have to do it another day.'

* * *

Michael stopped me as we left the office. 'When you have a moment, Emma, could you come to the Western Palace and talk to Clarissa for me? We'd both appreciate it.'

From the corner of my eye, I saw Simone scowl; then just as quickly the expression was gone and she composed her face.

'Go, Emma,' she said. 'See if you can bring Clarissa out of it. I really hate to hear about her like this.'

'Now is good,' I said. 'I have nothing on right now. I'll pop back to the Residence and get some better shoes,' I indicated my canvas boat shoes, 'and meet you back here, okay?'

'Those shoes are fine, Emma,' Simone said.

'Last time I wore them to the Western Palace, the Tiger called me so many offensive terms for low-grade workers that I vowed to wear stilettos every time after that,' I said. 'Shame I don't own any.'

I headed back to the Residence, pulled off the boat shoes and opened the shoe cupboard. 'Er Hao!' I yelled, staring at the shoes with shock.

'Yes, Miss Emma?' Er Hao said, coming out of the kitchen. She stopped when she saw the shoes. 'You bought new shoes?'

I pulled out my loafers; they'd been changed from dark brown to brilliant violet. Leo had changed all my shoes and arranged them in colour order so that they formed a rainbow along the cupboard shelves. I pulled out my pumps; he'd changed them from tan to fluorescent orange. My kung fu shoes were no longer black, they were lime green.

I sighed. 'Never mind. It's good to know Leo's back to his old self.'

I pulled on the violet loafers, which clashed with my jeans and black T-shirt.

'It's very pretty,' Er Hao said diplomatically. 'Maybe he can do your clothes to match?'

I shut the cupboard door. 'That man is not to get anywhere near my clothes, do you understand? If he comes in here again when I'm not around, let me know.'

'I didn't know he was here when he did these shoes,' Er Hao said. 'I'm sorry, Miss.'

'Then he had help from Martin,' I said under my breath, and stormed back to meet Michael.

* * *

Simone came with us to the Western Palace; she wanted to pass on her good wishes to Clarissa as well. She and Michael waited outside Clarissa's private room in the Tiger's medical centre while I went in.

Clarissa was sitting up in bed reading an ebook. The television was running softly in the corner, showing one of the news channels. She smiled when she saw me and turned the television off with the remote. Her hands were no longer rigid claws, but she obviously had some difficulty closing the cover of the ereader and placing it beside her.

I sat next to the bed. 'You're looking way better, Clarissa.'

She smiled gently and brushed one hand over her thin hair. She hadn't put on much weight and her skin was sallow and transparent. 'I know I still look awful.'

'At least you look halfway alive,' I said.

She touched my hand. 'That's what I always liked about you, Emma, you tell the truth when it's needed.'

'And sometimes when it's not,' I said. 'Have you decided what you want to do with yourself? The doctors told me that with physical therapy you can probably regain the use of your hands, and might even be able to run and ride your bike again.'

'Did you ask the psychiatrist about the ongoing mental damage?' she said, curious.

'No, your mental health is your own business.' I paused, and shrugged. 'Funny, isn't it? I didn't hesitate to ask about your physical state, but your mental state is hands-off.'

'You probably have more of an idea of what I'm going through than anybody else around here,' she said. 'I hear you have some problems of your own.'

I nodded. 'Flashbacks, mostly.'

'I understand.' She looked down at her hands. 'That's why I wanted to talk to you — you're always willing to tell the truth, however painful it might be.' She looked up into my eyes. 'Michael and I have been talking. After everything we've been through, we still feel the same way about each other. Stronger, if anything. I think we can build a future together, but there's some things I need to know. If I ask you a couple of questions, will you answer them truthfully for me?'

I didn't shift my gaze from hers. 'I promise.'

She looked down again. 'First question is: How does Michael feel about Simone? What do those two have together? Tell me the truth.'

'That's two questions, and I'll answer them both truthfully for you,' I said. I took a deep breath and she winced. 'Don't worry, Clarissa, Michael sees Simone as a little sister. Nothing more.'

'And Simone?'

'She has the biggest schoolgirl crush in the world on him. She's madly in love with him.'

'Does he know?'

'Yes, he does.'

'And?'

'He thinks it's adorable.'

'What, like little sister adorable?'

'Precisely. She's a lot younger than him, and although she's experienced more of life than any girl her age should, he still sees her as a little girl.'

She frowned. 'I should let them be together. They're Immortal, I'm not. They have more in common than I do.'

'Simone's not Immortal, Clarissa. And you have more in common with Michael than she does.'

She glanced up, full of hope. 'Really? She's not Immortal? I thought it came with the territory.'

'Nope, and it'll probably take her a while to get there as well.'

'Okay, that's a relief.' She raised her face slightly and closed her eyes. 'If that's the case, then I don't have anything to worry about, do I?'

'I sincerely believe that you don't. Simone loves you like a sister; she honestly wants you and Michael to be happy together.'

'Really?'

'Really.'

She took a deep breath and gazed into my eyes again. 'Next question. This one's very personal, but I have to know.'

'Oh dear,' I said.

'You've made love with Lord Xuan, haven't you, even though you're not married?'

'Uh ... yeah,' I said, wondering where this was going. 'Animal spirits like Lord Xuan — and Michael's father — tend to think human social rules don't apply to them.'

'Michael changes to a tiger when he's really excited or stressed. When you're together, and things get ... that way, does Lord Xuan ... Does he ... change?' Her voice petered out.

I couldn't help myself; I laughed. 'Absolutely not.' I bent closer to speak conspiratorially to her. 'I don't know how I'd do it with the Turtle form anyway; that thing is *massive*. He'd probably squash me flat.'

She giggled, her hand over her mouth, and shook her head. 'I heard stories about the Tiger's wives — apparently some of them like it.'

'If they don't like it, he definitely doesn't force them,' I said.

She stared at me for a moment, then said, 'Uh ... how do you know that?'

'One of my best friends is wife number ninety-seven. She's never been backward about boasting. I think she's as bad as he is.'

She nodded once, her dark hair bobbing with the movement. 'Thanks, Emma. Can you send Michael in?'

I quickly hugged her and kissed her on the cheek. 'Simone is here too. She'd love to say hello.'

She hesitated for a moment, then said, 'I don't think so. That would just be rubbing it in. It might be kindest to let it be for now, and talk to her later.'

'That makes sense.'

'And can you ask the doctor to contact my parents? I think I'll be wanting to talk to them soon as well.'

I took her hand and squeezed it. 'I can't tell you how glad I am to hear that.'

'Oh, and Emma?' she said as I was halfway to the door. 'Thanks.'

I nodded to her and went out.

Michael was sitting alone in the waiting room, elbows resting on his knees, his expression grim.

'Clarissa would like to speak to you,' I said.

He took a deep breath and stood. 'Time to face the music.'

I touched his arm. 'Don't worry, the news is good.' I looked around. 'Is Simone still here? I need a lift home.'

'She's outside somewhere, chasing butterflies or dragons or something.' He concentrated for a moment. 'She's on her way to take you home.'

'Do you know what Clarissa's going to do?' Simone asked as we rode her cloud back to the Mountain.

'She's much better, and feeling confident about her relationship with Michael. I think she wants to get back together with him.'

'That's great,' she said, sounding distracted. 'Michael talked to me while we were waiting for you two. He has big plans if they get back together. He wants to nurse Clarissa back to health so they can buy a house on the Earthly Plane together, settle down and have lots of *babies*.'

She said the last word with so much distaste that I had to laugh.

'What?' she said.

'When you see the babies, you'll change your mind.'

'Ew.' She shuddered. 'Milk-puking poo machines. I am so glad that Little Jade and Richie are out of nappies. Have you ever changed a nappy? Oh. My. God.'

I looked for the Mountain to appear in the distance. 'You say that now, but wait until it's your turn.'

'Not for a long time,' she said with emphasis.

'Good.'

'I took Emma to see Clarissa,' she said.

'What?'

'Sorry, spoke out loud. Daddy's back already; he's in the mess with Master Liu.'

'Already? That was quick. Wait — Master Liu? Which Master Liu?'

'Cheng Rong.'

'Oh, no.'

The cloud rose in the air slightly and picked up speed.

13

Both of us stormed straight into the mess, which was deserted apart from John and Liu sitting at one of the tables in the corner. The table was covered in beer bottles, some of them on their sides and all of them empty.

'Your beard,' John said to Liu, obviously the worse for wear, 'looks like pubic hair on the front of your face. And it's not even yours!'

'Ew!' Simone said. She spun on her heel and went out.

'Thank you!' Liu yelled, and raised his bottle.

'Damn,' John said, and drank.

I stood next to the table and put my hands on my hips. 'It's three o'clock in the afternoon.'

'Not in …' John tried to focus on me and failed. 'Somewhere else.'

'Your wife', Liu said, waving his bottle unsteadily at me, 'is the ugliest damn bitch I have ever seen in my entire life.'

'I know!' John said, and raised his bottle towards Liu.

Liu took a large swig, finished the bottle and peered down the neck. He dropped the empty into the case next to him, grabbed a full one and twisted the top off.

'Go for your life, oh Mighty Emperor of the Northern Heavens,' he said.

'We're onto wives, eh? Now it's getting serious,' John said. He winked at me. 'Your wife came to me asking if all Chinese men were as poorly endowed as you are.'

Liu shot to his feet and waved his clenched fist in John's face. 'I'm a fucking Immortal, you moron! I can make my dick as big as I want, and I've *never* had a problem satisfying a ...' His voice petered out as he saw John's triumphant face. He swung his hand out and they slapped palms. 'You win, as always, you ugly bastard.' He took a huge swig from the bottle, spilling beer into his beard. 'I'm going to pass out in my bed. And probably throw up a bit first.'

He peered blearily at me. 'Is that you, love?'

'No.'

'Oh, Emma.' He turned groggily to John. 'You're in serious trouble, my friend.'

John gestured towards the door. 'Not as much trouble as you are.'

Liu managed to turn without falling over and saw Meredith, who'd just arrived.

'Love of my life, passion of my strawberry, butterfly of my ... something or other, he won again.'

Meredith came and stood next to me. 'You know the Dark Lord was returned faster because Pao realises just how much the Celestial needs him?'

John jabbed his finger at Liu. 'It was his idea!'

Liu staggered to face John. 'Liar, it was all your idea!'

'The Celestial needs me,' John said. 'You are an agent of Hell sent to get me drunk and make me useless.'

'Once I'm finished with him, he'll think that I'm an agent of Hell,' Meredith said. She linked arms with Liu and turned him towards the door. 'Take your Turtle home and let him sober up, Emma. And I suggest you provide him with a bucket. If you're lucky, he'll make it home without puking on you.'

'This wasn't nearly as much fun without the Tiger,' John said as he leaned heavily on the back of the chair to stand. 'He loses his temper straight away and becomes most comical. But it was worth it to see his face when Pao let me out of Court Ten first.'

Meredith met up with me later, after we'd left both of them in their beds with buckets alongside.

'Don't be too mad with him — they needed that,' she said.

'I know. I've seen what this is doing to him. Both of them needed to blow off some steam.'

'Did he tell you what caused him to fall like that?'

'They hit the Serpent in the face with the carbon dioxide from a fire extinguisher and suffocated it until they both passed out. They can knock him unconscious any time they like without killing him.' I hesitated. 'The timing was too perfect.'

'Could have been a coincidence,' she said thoughtfully. 'They've been randomly playing with him for a while. This isn't the first time he's fallen out of the sky.'

'He should have looked for a spy before he went on the piss with your husband.'

Her expression sobered. 'He did, Emma. That's why they pulled out the beer — they couldn't find anything. It may have been just a coincidence.'

'What are the students saying?'

'Most of them are in awe of how much alcohol the two of them consumed without passing out. That was the third crate of beer.'

'I'm planning to be a long way away when they wake up,' I said.

'Good idea.'

She patted me on the shoulder and went back to the training section.

* * *

'John.' I pushed him gently as he lay on the bed. 'Geez, you stink of alcohol. John!'

'What?' he said. He raised his head and groaned, then covered his eyes with his forearm. 'Oh shit, my head.' He peered at me. 'Can't you just leave me alone, woman? I'm dying here.'

'I'd love to, but we're supposed to go to a charity thing tonight, for the introduction of your new persona on the Earthly. It's all set up, so you have to sober up and come.'

'I don't want to,' he said, rolling away from me. 'Let me die in peace.'

'If you do not sober up now, the next time you're unconscious I will leave you in the middle of the main square wearing nothing but your black boxers where all the students can see you.'

He rolled back and glared at me from under his arm. 'You wouldn't dare.'

I crossed my arms and matched his stare.

He smiled slightly and shook his head. 'You would too, wouldn't you?'

'Damn straight.'

'Okay.' He groaned as he pulled himself upright, and waved one hand at me. 'Move back. If I'm going to sober up, I need to sit.'

I shifted back so that he could sit cross-legged on the bed. He put his elbows on his knees and cupped one hand in the other, then closed his eyes. His hair floated around him and steam rose from his head and shoulders. I coughed and moved further back; the steam was almost pure alcohol.

The steam stopped, his hair dropped and he opened his eyes. He put his hands on his knees and shook out his shoulders. 'What a waste. Oh well, it was cheap beer anyway.' He brushed one hand over his forehead. 'How long until we have to go? I need a shower.'

'You have half an hour. Do you have clothes that will fit?'

'I'll summon something, don't worry.' He smiled slightly. 'I need someone to scrub my back.'

'You have thirty minutes,' I said, rising. 'You do not have time for back rubs. Oh,' I pointed at his crotch, 'next time remember to button your boxers, okay? The servants would have a heart attack if they saw that.'

He glanced down at himself. 'Only because of my magnificence.'

'Oh, go take a shower,' I said, and went out.

I tapped on the door of Simone's room. 'I made him get up, he's taking a shower.'

She opened her door a crack; she was in a bathrobe with a towel around her hair. 'Did he sober up?'

'Yes.'

'Wait — he needs to take a shower?'

'I'm afraid so.'

'God.' She dropped her voice. 'I didn't know he was that bad. Just the idea of him needing to take a shower is so scary.'

'Neither did I. Don't mention it to anyone, okay? Pretend he's as strong as he always was.'

She nodded. 'Okay. There's a good chance there'll be demons there tonight; we have to make it look good.'

* * *

'Simone's driving,' John said when we arrived at the car park near the old Star Ferry terminal in Hong Kong.

Simone stopped next to the car. 'I am not driving this.'

'You have to,' John said. 'I need to fix myself up for my new identity. Emma, love, sit in the back and help me? I need to get it right.'

Simone pointed at the car. 'I am *not* driving this. It's freaking enormous. Jade, you drive.'

Jade raised her hands. 'I'm sorry, my Lady, I can't drive.'

Simone put her hands on her hips and glared at her. 'Lies!'

'The honest truth, ma'am. Before I joined the household I never needed to drive, and after I joined we already had Leo to drive for us. I've never learnt.'

'Can't you just sit behind the wheel and make it move or something?'

Jade bowed slightly. 'Forgive me, my Lady, I am a very small Shen.'

'Well, if I run into someone it's your fault,' Simone said to John.

'You won't,' John said, and got into the back seat.

I pulled myself in to sit next to him and Simone sat behind the wheel.

She inspected the controls. 'What the hell is all this? This isn't a car, it's a spaceship.'

'The usual controls are in the usual places,' John said. 'Stop complaining and hurry up. We'll be late.'

'Keys?' Simone said, reaching behind her.

'Doesn't need any; keyless start,' I said. 'Press the red button.'

Simone made small grumbling noises as she jerkily drove the car out of its spot and headed towards the car park exit. The gate opened by itself and she slowly eased the car up the ramp and out onto Connaught Road, one of the busiest in Hong Kong: six lanes each way and packed with fast-moving traffic. She did the Hong Kong thing of rushing into the lane when there was a tiny gap available, and the traffic slowed to let her in. Then she was obviously frustrated as she had to merge from the left all the way to the right to make a U-turn back towards Pacific Place where the movie premiere was being held.

As we travelled through the stop-start traffic, I pulled a photograph and mirror out of my clutch purse and held them up for John to see while he changed his appearance. He left his hair long, but aged until he looked eighty years old. He held his hands out in front of him; his right arm was slightly longer than his left. He shortened it, then nodded with satisfaction and grinned at me, his face a network of lines.

'How's this?'

I turned the photo around and held it next to his head to inspect the similarity. 'Your face needs to be slightly longer and narrower.'

He changed and I nodded. 'Perfect.'

'Give me a couple of minutes to focus the form,' he said, and went completely still, gazing blindly in front of him.

'Oh, for fffsss …' Simone didn't finish it. 'Let me in, asshole, I need to go up the hill!'

The other car blew its horn at her and she roughly spun the wheel to merge into the lane, cutting it off. She slowed to enter the car park at Pacific Place, turned and then stopped. She had misjudged the angle and the car was in danger of hitting the wall.

'Just move it,' John said. 'Nobody's around.'

Simone took a deep breath and the car lifted slightly above the ground, moved to the left and dropped again, bouncing on its springs. She revved the engine a little too hard and jerked the car forward, but missed the wall and headed down the ramp.

'Excellent job, Simone, I knew you could do it,' John said.

'I hate this car,' she said through her teeth. 'No wonder you made him buy you a smaller one, Emma.'

'I wanted a blue one, but he wouldn't let me,' I said. 'All the livery in the House of the North has to match.'

'The blue was ugly,' he said. 'And I wouldn't give the Dragon the satisfaction.'

Simone glanced at her father in the rear-view mirror. 'You forgot your voice.'

'Whoops,' he said, suddenly sounding much older.

'I have the story memorised,' Jade said. 'If you forget any details let me know and I'll fill you in.'

'I don't think that will be necessary,' John said.

'Speak for yourself,' Simone said.

* * *

It was the usual tedious social event: overdressed people standing around criticising each other's appearance and smiling for the benefit of the fawning media. David and Bridget Hawkes were waiting for us when we entered the lobby of the cinema. Part-Chinese, part-Scottish David was the taipan of one of Hong Kong's largest companies, which had a history dating back to the Opium Wars.

'That's not really you, is it?' David said to John.

John changed his voice to his normal one. 'One hundred per cent me.'

'That's astonishing,' Bridget said.

'So you're your own father?' David said. 'Is that right?'

John changed his voice to old again and raised it. 'Yes, I'm John Chen's father. I came over from the village in China to see how well Miss Donahoe here is looking after my granddaughter.' He patted my shoulder, fatherly. 'She's doing a fine job. Soon I'll be able to return to my wife back home, confident that little Simone is receiving the best of care.'

'What?' Simone said, turning to him.

'I can't stay here forever. I have the Mainland side of the business to run, you know that.'

'No, I don't.'

He dropped his voice. 'Well, you do now. I don't have time to come to every charity event. You can represent the House in my place. You're Princess of the House, it's part of your duties.'

'Emma …' Simone pleaded.

'About time you started taking part of the royal workload,' I said.

'Come on, Simone, don't look like that,' Bridget said. She took her arm to lead her away. 'Making a career out of attending events like this isn't so bad — there are plenty of lovely young men here for you to meet. Have you met my son Phillip?'

'Isn't he, like, fifteen?' Simone said.

'Nearly sixteen,' Bridget said, and they were gone in the crush.

'That was totally shameless,' David said with amusement, 'and I apologise on behalf of my wife.'

'No need,' John said. 'I'm sure he's a delightful young man.' He moved closer to David, more serious. 'I understand that you've been to my Mountain. The real one.'

'I knew for a couple of years already, but it didn't really hit home until we actually saw it,' David said. He studied John carefully. 'I could say the idea of you being a god is hard to take, but look at you. You look at least seventy.'

'I'm just me,' John said. He took a couple of mineral waters from a passing tray and handed one to me. 'It's advantageous for us to have liaisons on the Earthly, and I'm pleased that you'll be one of them. It's always been good to work with you.'

David bowed slightly. 'I thank you, Majesty.'

'I'm a Highness,' John said, amused. 'The Jade Emperor's His Majesty.'

David bowed again, sharing the amusement. 'Highness.' He turned to me. 'And you are a —' He choked on the word, tried again and stopped, confused.

'I'm being punished by the Jade Emperor,' I said. 'Nobody can use any sort of title except "Miss" when they talk to me.'

'And that's stopping me?' David said.

'Yep.'

'What did you do, if you don't mind me asking? It must have been serious.'

John and I shared a quick glance and he nodded slightly.

I sighed. 'It's a long story.'

I was about to continue when we were approached by a demon in human form. John stiffened; this was a really big one.

'David, move away and stay away,' John said as the demon drew nearer.

'What?' David said.

'Go!' I said, nudging him.

He had the sense to walk away quickly but casually, although I could tell he was obviously more than a little scared. As the demon drew closer, it became clear that it was the King himself. He was in a human form slightly older than usual, mid-forties, and was shorter than me, slim and elegant. He walked gracefully towards us wearing an expensive made-to-measure maroon suit that complemented the dark red highlights in his gleaming shoulder-length hair.

He bowed slightly to John. 'Xuan Tian.'

John bowed back. 'Wong Mo.'

The King turned to peruse the crowd. 'Lovely group tonight, eh? Should raise quite a sum for the poor orphans.' He saw the look on my face. 'How big a donation would it take for you to come be with me for a while?'

I answered without hesitation. 'Let the Serpent go and swear that you won't harm him or Simone and I'm yours.'

'Oh, that's tempting. I might just say yes to that.'

'No!' John said, glancing wide-eyed from the King to me.

The Demon King grinned. 'Just kidding, Ah Wu, it would take much more than that to free my favourite zoo exhibit.' He eyed me appraisingly. 'Are you seriously open to negotiation?'

'Absolutely.'

'No, Emma!' John said loudly.

'You shut up,' the King said. 'This is between the lady and myself.' He turned back to me. 'Do you still have my phone?'

'Yes.'

'Hold on to it. I'll be in touch.'

He disappeared and nobody around seemed to notice.

John dropped his voice, looking around to ensure he wasn't heard. 'I forbid you from dealing with him. He already has me. I don't want him taking you —'

'I'm sorry, you what?' I said sharply.

He closed his mouth with a snap and took a deep breath. 'Don't deal with him; you don't need to. He won't kill my Serpent, he has to keep it alive. I can handle what he's doing to me.' He moved closer to me. 'Trust me. We'll find a way to pull the Serpent out without sacrificing anything. We can do this.'

'I know. Same as last time: it's a last resort if there are no other options. It won't happen.'

He ran his hand over his forehead and took a deep breath. 'Last time it did happen.'

'This time it won't.'

'Then you don't need to negotiate with him.'

'Trying to work something out will keep him occupied,' I said. 'Here comes David again. Game faces.'

'Game faces? What does that mean?'

'Never mind.'

'Who the hell was that?' David asked roughly under his breath. 'He scared the living daylights out of me.'

'That was Kitty Kwok,' I said.

He stared at me.

'Remember her? Ran a string of kindergartens? Had some serious Triad connections until the police shut it all down?'

'I do, she was a nasty piece of work. But how could that man …' He inhaled sharply. 'She was a demon?'

'That was the King of all the Demons,' John said.

'No way. Wait … Kitty Kwok was the Demon King? I sent my boys to one of her kindergartens. What if he did something to them?'

'He took blood and tissue samples from them, but they won't remember it,' I said. 'He used the children as donors to build all sorts of very nasty things out of demon essence. But he wouldn't have hurt them otherwise.'

David's face went very grim. 'I hope you track him down and do what needs to be done, John.'

'It is possible that things will be worse before they are better,' John said, looking around. He focused back on David. 'I may have some of my people pay you a visit later and start a closer Earthly liaison.'

David blanched. 'We're not in any danger here, are we?'

'I protect you. I protect all of you,' John said. 'But while I was gone, the King worked hard to make himself very strong.'

'Stronger than you?' David said.

'I am the force of yin, the essence of weak and soft,' John said. 'Yes, he is stronger than me. But I am the darkness that swallows all.'

Threads of yin appeared in John's hair and the air around him turned cold. David took a step back.

'John, call that yin in,' I said softly.

The yin disappeared and John was a harmless old man again. He grinned ruefully. 'Sorry. The presence of the King has made me a little uneasy.'

'You protect all of us? Exactly how big a threat are they?' John didn't reply.

I answered for him. 'The truth is that they would like to enslave all of humanity and conquer the Earth. Then they'd use us as an army and make a try for Heaven.'

'You're kidding,' David said.

'He will never succeed as long as I am here to protect you,' John said. 'I drove the demons off the face of the Earth once before, and if I must I will not hesitate to do it again.' He sighed. 'Ah, little Emma, always bringing things out into the open when there's absolutely no need. You should not have told him that.'

'Call me little again, old man, and I'll call you out.'

'Try me, little one. Your skills are as lacking as your ability to keep your silence.'

'I'll say what I want when I want, and when we get home it's you and me, your choice of weapons.'

'Deal.'

'I appreciate the truth about the situation,' David said. 'And you two are standing here joking about it.'

'Not a word of jest from either of us,' John said.

'Deadly serious,' I said.

'You challenge him to duels?'

'All the time.'

The bell rang for the movie to start.

'We're up,' David said. He shook John's hand, then kissed me on the cheek. 'Talk to you later, okay? I like the idea of being a liaison for you; it would make my life way more interesting.'

'You are a complete idiot,' John said with wonder.

'I know,' David said, spreading his hands. 'Isn't it great?'

John shook his head and clapped David on the shoulder. 'Actually, yes it is. I'll have our PR director contact you; she can set up the liaison for us. She's around here somewhere, probably collecting business cards and ... what's the word?'

'Schmoozing,' I said.

'That's it.'

'A god with a PR director,' David said.

'It was her idea, and she's doing a great job,' I said. 'You may have seen the story about the local kids killed in the earthquake in China? That was us.'

'Children were killed?' David said, wide-eyed.

'By kids she means young adults, students of the Mountain,' John said. 'Jade will explain.'

'Your students die?'

'Not if I can help it, but they're an army, and it's part of what they do,' John said. 'There's Bridget and Simone, let's go in.'

14

The movie was a romantic comedy. Simone and Jade seemed to enjoy it, but John and I dozed on each other's shoulder, bored to death.

About halfway through the film, John had a massive coughing fit, wheezing as if he couldn't breathe. People around us asked about him, concerned. He pulled himself out of his seat, still coughing, and headed for the door. Once we were all in the lobby, he raced to the bar and I ordered a glass of water for him. It seemed to settle when he had something to drink. As soon as the bartender had moved away, John stopped wheezing and put the glass down.

'Thanks, Daddy,' Simone said, grabbing his arm and leaning into him. 'I appreciate it.'

'I was enjoying it,' Jade said, disappointed.

'Oh, come on, Jade, it was boring,' Simone said. She saw my face. 'Sorry, Emma, I didn't think you'd hear me talking over the coughing.' She nudged John. 'Let's go buy some lanterns up at the market.'

My phone went off with a text message. It was from David. *Is he all right?*

I replied. *He's fine, it was a sham. They were bored.*

The phone dinged again. *Damn, should have told us, we could have escaped with you.*

Catch you later, we'll be in touch, I replied.

Gotcha.

'David wanted to come with us,' I said.

'Half the cinema wanted to come with us,' Simone said. 'Haven't we seen that plot in another movie not long ago?'

'It's a good story!' Jade said. 'And that actor is so cute.'

'You can go back in if you like,' I said.

'No, I want to come to the market with you,' Jade said. 'I'll come back with Winnie to see it another time.'

'You okay, Daddy?' Simone said. 'You can go young again now.'

'Wait until we're further away,' John said. 'How about we leave the car here and walk down to the market? It's not far and there's no parking down there.'

We walked the couple of kilometres along the main road, which was still busy with pedestrians and shoppers even though it was late. Autumn had started, but the weather was still warm and humid with no hint of the coolness to come. The air was thick with exhaust fumes from the diesel taxis and trucks; many of them used cheap contaminated fuel from across the border.

John grew younger as we approached the market, gradually changing his Western suit to a pair of black jeans and a black T-shirt, but leaving his hair long and in a topknot.

We reached the market behind the hospital: a maze of narrow streets, with shopfronts on either side selling brightly coloured fruit and vegetables that shone under the harsh hanging bulbs with their transparent red plastic shades. Plastic buckets and basins hung from hooks on the awning of a kitchenware shop, and fresh fish, still flapping, lay on the ice-covered foam trays of a fishmonger.

We passed a butcher, where glistening arms hung from the vicious hooks, the hands dangling, their fingernails blackened with dried blood. The world lurched around me and I gripped John's arm to hold me up.

He looked down at me, concerned. 'Are you all right? Did you see something?'

Simone came around her father to stand next to me and Jade moved to cover our backs.

'You look like you saw a ghost, Emma.' Simone glanced around. 'I don't see anything.'

'It's nothing.' I released John's arm and straightened; I wouldn't let this spoil our evening. I took deep breaths and didn't look at the butcher stall. 'I'm fine.'

You will tell me later, John said.

I nodded.

We worked our way around a group of people in front of a shop that sold medicinal soup. A metre-and-a-half tall urn and ceramic bowls stood on a table; each bowl had a plastic cover. Patrons paid for the bowl, drank the bitter, medicinal soup to ward off chills, then returned the bowl to be washed. A sugar-cane drink vendor nearby was grinding cane stalks in his machine to make the hot juice, and Jade quickly pounced on a paper cup. She sipped the sweet juice with pleasure as we walked.

Simone stopped us at a toy shop that was swathed in lanterns, hundreds of them, hanging from the awning in front of the shop as well as stands set up around the entrance. Most were made of inflatable plastic, with a small electric light at the top illuminating them from inside, and a cord leading from the globe to a battery-powered handle that sometimes played a tinny, annoying tune. Others were traditional style: bamboo frames covered in cellophane with simple designs of good-luck fish and animals. Boxes of cheap red candles to go inside the traditional lanterns were stacked around the front door, with a government sign pasted above them warning people about the illegality of burning wax. During the Mid-Autumn Festival, people would stand a whole box of candles in a bunch on the ground and light them all at once so the wax itself caught alight, causing a mini fireball that left a huge molten blob of solidified wax on the ground that was impossible to clean away.

Simone stopped perusing the lanterns and moved her head from side to side. 'Heads up, demons just up the street,' she said. She turned to look. 'The lolis?'

'They're ours,' I said. 'They live in our building in Spring Garden Lane.'

'Oh,' John said, understanding.

'I've never seen them before; I didn't even know we owned a building there,' Simone said. 'They are so cute! I wish I had the nerve to dress up like that. Ha! They're stopping traffic.'

The demons were two girls in their late teens or early twenties, both wearing knee-length dresses with so many petticoats underneath that they looked like Little Bo Peep. One had on a bright pink curled wig, and her dress was cream with small strawberries all over it and a multitude of pink petticoats underneath. The look was finished off with a long hot pink pair of Doc Martens boots. The other loli was full-on goth: she wore a black wig with a tiny top hat perched on top of it, a black lacy ruffled dress with black lacy petticoats, thigh-high purple and black stockings and chunky platform mary janes.

The lolis really had stopped traffic. The narrow street allowed parking on one side and was blanketed with cars, leaving only one lane for the taxis and trucks to creep through. An old woman had stopped to berate the lolis; she was wagging her finger at them, unaware that she was blocking a taxi from passing by. Eventually one of the lolis pulled her gently to the side and waved to the taxi driver, who cheerfully waved back.

The pink loli saw us and hesitated, then she nodded and both of them turned and smartly walked away from us, their full skirts swinging.

'Oh, I wanted to say hello, and ask where they bought their dresses,' Simone said, disappointed.

John made a show of looking at the lanterns. 'We should buy some for Amy and Gold's children, and your children too, Jade.'

'My children are spending the festival with their father, so you don't need to buy them any,' Jade said.

'Are you going too?' I said.

'No,' Jade said, studying the lanterns.

'It's a holiday, there's nothing to stop you from spending the time with the father of your children.'

She frowned. 'I wish everybody would stop trying to throw us together. It will never happen and he knows it.'

'What, you and Qing Long?' Simone said with horrified fascination. 'How could you even think of having anything with him? He's so ...' She searched for the words. 'I don't know how you can have kids with him in the first place, Jade.'

Jade raised her eyebrows at me and I shook my head slightly. Simone didn't know about the Blue Dragon's true nature; that the self-serving asshole thing was just an act.

'That's right, Simone, not happening,' Jade said, turning back to the lanterns. 'My children don't need any, but Gold's little ones are just old enough to understand, and they should enjoy it.'

'What do you think they'd like?' John pulled one out. 'That's boring, it's just a yellow rectangle with a big face.'

'Spongebob, little Richie loves him, we should get it,' Simone said.

'The demons are coming back,' Jade said. Her voice became more urgent. 'They can't run in those shoes!'

She was right, the lolis were tearing down the street towards us, the one in the mary-janes having some difficulty with her platform shoes. We moved into the street to see what was chasing them. The demons reached us and both hid behind me, one on either side. I put my hands on their waists to steady them and they grabbed my shoulders.

A couple of beautiful tall women in designer suits strolled down the street, pointedly ignoring everyone. The crowd parted around them, people grimacing with discomfort if they got too close. The women stopped when they saw us, and looked the lolis up and down.

'We'll find you later,' one of them said. She grinned with menace. 'You look like strawberry candy.'

The lolis crowded closer to me, wide-eyed.

'Find them and I will find you,' John said.

The Mother glanced from the lolis to John. Her eyes widened as she realised who he was and she stepped back.

The other Mother wasn't as intimidated. 'You can't be there all the time.'

'Beside the point,' John said. 'If you hurt them, I will find you and destroy you. They are not worth the price. Go find something easier to kill. The soccer pitch at Southorn Playground is full of small demons.'

The Mothers shared a look, and one of them shrugged. They stuck their noses in the air and sauntered away, heading towards the Southorn sports centre in the centre of busy Wan Chai.

'Don't worry, we'll protect you,' I said.

John was gruff. 'Return to the house in the lane, you'll be safe there.'

The two demons were obviously still frightened, but they moved away from me and pulled themselves together.

One of them nodded to John. 'It was a bad idea to dress up and come out. We thought it would be fun.'

'If you want to do it again, let me know and I'll come with you,' Simone said, patting one of them on the shoulder. 'I'll look after you, and I think you look so cute!'

'Really?' the strawberry loli said, smiling shyly and tilting her head to one side. 'You would do that for us?'

Simone leaned in close. 'Only if I can find a dress too. Where did you buy them?'

'I make them,' the goth loli said.

'That is not going to happen, Simone,' John said, his voice stern. He spoke to the demons. 'Bring a guard next time if you must do this stupid thing. Jade, escort them back to the house.' He gestured towards the lolis. 'Go.'

'Hey, I was talking to them,' Simone said.

'No, the Lord is right,' the strawberry loli said. 'You shouldn't be seen with people like us. You're a Princess.' She nodded to John. 'We'll return to our shop. Our apologies, my Lord.'

'What?' Simone said, confused. She glared at her father. 'If I want to spend some time with them, that's my choice, Daddy. They're just tame demons. It's not as if they're bad or anything.'

'Jade,' John said.

'My Lord,' Jade said with obvious distaste as she guided the girls away.

They held hands and walked with her, looking behind them as they went, then they turned into a side alley, heading towards Spring Garden Lane.

'You will not seek them out again,' John said.

Simone put her hands on her hips. 'Why not?'

'We will explain later.' He turned to the lanterns. 'So the rectangular yellow person for Richie?'

Simone spun and headed up the street, in the same direction as Jade and the demons. She stopped and shook her head — John was obviously talking to her — then headed off again. He must have finally told her what they were, because she stopped dead about ten metres away, stood for a long moment looking after them, then returned to us, her face expressionless.

'Why do we have tame demons working as hookers in the House of the North?' she said softly and fiercely.

'We will discuss this later,' he said.

'No, we'll discuss it *now*,' Simone said.

Everything around us went still. There was complete silence.

'Impressive. I didn't know you could do that,' he said.

'I didn't either.' She poked him on the arm. 'You have *prostitutes* making money for you? I cannot believe this.'

He stood silently and I could see his mind working furiously.

'It's their choice, Simone. It's what they did before they were tamed,' I said. 'They like having plenty of money to buy cute stuff, and doing what they're doing is about as lucrative as you can get.'

'Convert it to a hostess bar, something less demeaning for them,' Simone said.

John spread his hands. 'That's the same thing. Everybody just pretends it isn't.'

Simone rounded on me. 'And you're in on this?'

'If the demons want to do it, then having us protect them is way better than working any other way,' I said. 'They're actually all very happy doing it, and they keep most of the proceeds. Some of them will retire before they're thirty years old.'

'That's very young for a demon,' she said more softly.

'Most of them tire of the work and come to the Mountain. Many of the nuns in the temple used to work here,' John said.

'There aren't any *humans*, are there?' Simone said.

I didn't reply.

'That's just wrong.'

'Same thing: they want to do it,' I said.

'Then they're stupid,' Simone said, and disappeared.

The market came back to life around us.

'Why does she have this big thing about sex?' John said, confused. 'Just the mention of it sets her completely off. She's old enough to be interested, not afraid.'

'You are so strange sometimes,' I said. 'It's because of what happened on that boat.'

'Which boat?'

'The one where a kid from her school before CH tried to drug and rape her, and she blew the boat up, killing him.'

'It affected her that badly?'

'You really have no idea sometimes.'

He took his hair out of its tie and retied it, exasperated. 'I know. She's my first human child. Help me.'

'I'm doing my best.'

* * *

John and I stayed at the market and bought two of every lantern. It was quite common for cheap novelties like this to have faulty parts, and even buying two was sometimes insufficient insurance to ensure a working set. It was a waste of time taking them back if they didn't work; the stallholder would accuse us of breaking them and trying to cheat her.

It was late evening when we returned to the Mountain. We retreated to one of the pagodas high on a peak with a pot of tea. It was much cooler on the Mountain. The lights of the Academy below us shone from the doors and windows, lighting up the ground and trees with a golden glow; and the stars above blazed in the clear autumn sky. The constellations were the same as on the Earthly; they just seemed bigger, magnified by the clarity. John's symbol of power, the Big Dipper, was particularly magnificent in the centre of the sky.

For the hundredth time I made a quiet vow to myself to ask an expert about the physics of the Celestial Plane, and then realised that, once again, I would probably never get around to it.

'What?' John said, seeing me smile and shake my head.

I gestured towards the Big Dipper. 'That constellation never moves.'

'Don't ask me, I don't know how it works,' he said, wiggling down into his chair to sit more comfortably and hanging one arm over the side. 'I'm just here and the stars do their stuff.' He gazed into the sky. 'Isn't that the essence of being alive?'

'I guess it is.'

'What happened in the market?'

'Just a flashback,' I said. 'I saw arms instead of pork hanging from the hooks.'

He was silent for a long moment, looking at the sky. 'You are too small to be forced to deal with this.'

'I'm ten metres long.'

He shook his head and gazed at me over the rim of his teacup. 'Very small.'

'Screw you.'

He smiled slightly. 'What, up here? Isn't it a little cold?'

'Yeah, let's wait till we're back home.'

He sighed gently. 'Thank you.'

'What for?'

He poured both of us more tea. 'You and Simone have brought me so much joy. The past twenty years have been full of more happiness for me than the previous four thousand.' He raised his cup to me. 'Thank you.'

* * *

He put his arm around my shoulders as we walked through the garden on the ground floor back at the Imperial Residence, then stopped. 'Simone isn't home,' he said. 'It's nearly midnight, she should be here.' He went completely still for a moment, and when he spoke again his voice had an edge of urgency. 'She's not answering!'

He released me and turned to run out of the Residence.

I put my hand on his arm to stop him. 'Before you panic, let's try something low-tech.' I pulled my mobile out of my pocket and texted her. *You okay? You're not home and your father is frantic.*

John paced in small circles. 'Those Mothers have her. She has no yin because I took it from her, she won't let me make a weapon for her, her skills are horribly rusty because she refuses to train … I knew this would happen!' He stopped and concentrated. 'I'm pulling in Leo and Ming, they can start searching for her.' He paced in circles again. 'A geomancer may be able to find her, but it could take *hours*. Where's my copy of the I Ching? I can use that … I cannot believe she went off by herself like this.' He spun to stare at me, horrified. 'What if she went down to Hell to face the King?' He shook his head and paced again. 'Without her yin she doesn't have a chance. I should have given it back to her when she asked for it … Where the hell are Leo and Martin?'

My mobile pinged and I checked it. 'It's a message from her.'

He ran to my side and watched the phone as I brought the message up.

I'm fine. Tell him not to worry, and they're not prostitutes, they run the tea house on the ground floor! They're so sweet. I'll be home in half an hour or so, I'm helping them to close up.

'She's working at the building in Spring Garden Lane?' John said. 'I don't know which is a worse idea.'

'What, that or her going to Hell?' I said, amused, as I put the phone away.

Leo and Martin appeared next to the turtle fountain and ran to us.

'Where do you want us to start looking?' Leo said.

'We found her,' I said. 'False alarm.'

'Go down to Eighty-Eight Spring Garden Lane and escort her home,' John said.

'What the hell is she doing *there*?' Martin said.

'Helping the two demons who run the tea shop on the ground floor to close up,' I said.

'Why?' Leo said. 'Is this some sort of "I want to be normal so I'll take a part-time job" thing?'

John focused on Martin, who nodded. 'I'll explain on the way,' he said, and took Leo's hand. Both of them disappeared.

'Come sit with me,' John said, leading me to the ceramic outdoor table and stools next to the fountain. 'I won't be able to sleep until I'm sure she's home and safe.'

'What will you do when she goes to university?'

He put his head in his hand. 'I don't know.'

'I'd better find something to distract you with, then.'

'I don't think anything will stop me from worrying about her.'

'Oh,' I said, raising my teacup, 'I'll think of something.'

He glanced at me, his expression full of hope. 'Are you ...?'

I shook my head and touched his arm. 'No. But it's just a matter of time. I started a course of fertility drugs.'

'Then I'll have two of them to worry about,' he said.

'Michael's right. Teach her to dance the stars and ride the wind. If she can reach Immortality on her own through internal alchemy, you won't have to worry about her.'

'I've been trying, but she doesn't have the patience to learn,' he said. 'I'd give her the Elixir, but only enough for one person can be made at one time.'

'Make hers first,' I said.

'You're older and more fragile.' His voice dropped with misery. 'Humans age so quickly.'

'Is my life speeding past while you watch?'

He nodded. 'It's like that for all of you.' He glanced at me. 'You should be offended at me calling you old.'

'Sometimes I feel old.'

'Your mastery of energy makes you look much younger than you are, believe me.'

'How much longer before the Elixir is ready?'

'We finally found enough cinnabar to make the recipe. The Dragon had it in his strongroom, and was mortified that he'd been slowing things down by not offering it.' He spoke with more enthusiasm. 'We'll be in Britain when it's ready. I'd give it to you there, but it's impossible to drink the Elixir outside the Centre it's made in. We'll have to wait until we've returned. I can hardly wait to see the effect it will have on you. After you've taken it, your serpent nature will emerge more strongly and you will be able to work with shen and learn some really advanced stuff.'

'I'm reminded of what happened to Rhonda ...' I said, my voice trailing off.

'You're worried that the Elixir might destroy you like it did her.'

'It's just that Rhonda ... her last name was MacLaren, John. The judge who exiled my ancestors from Wales was called MacLaren.'

'You are linked. I wonder if she was something similar to you.'

'Whatever she was, drinking the Elixir killed her.'

'Did it smell good or bad to her?'

'Oh, I remember that very clearly. It obviously smelled bad: she made a face before she drank it.'

'Very interesting. The judge, MacLaren, was somehow demonkind and able to sentence the serpent people to exile in Australia. And Rhonda was descended from this judge, as you are descended from the serpent people. I wonder what else we will find there.'

I took a deep breath. 'Kwan Yin said I was like Rhonda — an example of overcoming my nature.'

'I know about that,' he said with amusement.

'She also said that if the demon essence was removed, the Elixir wouldn't kill me. Are you sure she'd never lie?'

'Then we have nothing to worry about. She will always tell the truth.'

I sighed with feeling. 'Okay.'

Simone appeared on the other side of the courtyard and stormed up to us. She leaned over her father, furious. 'You sent Leo and Martin to bring me home? I am not a child!'

'You're behaving like one,' he said, perfectly calm. 'You have duties and a standard of behaviour to uphold as Princess of the House, Xuan Si Min. You will not consort with prostitutes, you will not be seen in public in ridiculous costumes, and you will on no account *ever* work in a tea house for demons. All of this is totally unacceptable.'

'You know what? I'm nearly eighteen, and when I turn eighteen I'm an adult and I can do what I like,' she said. 'They aren't prostitutes. If they were, they wouldn't dress like that. Lolis get enough shit from people who think they're dressed up as sex dolls, when they really dress that way to make themselves feel pretty and special. God.' She rolled her eyes. 'A girl dresses up and all the men think it's about sex. It's *not*; it's about being pretty!'

'It doesn't matter what it's about, it's not appropriate for *you*.'

She swiped one hand through the air. 'I know that, I know what's expected of me. I understand my position. I know I have to set an example. But they're not prostitutes! Is there *any* way we could work around this so that I can spend time with them? I won't wear a costume, I understand about that. I just think they're sweet.'

John thought about it for a moment. 'As long as it's in Number Eighty-Eight, I don't think so.'

'Can we move the tea house to another of our buildings?'

186

'Of course.'

'Could I visit with them then?'

'Yes.'

'Emma?'

'They may not want to move,' I said. 'They might be friends with the other girls and boys there.'

Simone thought for a moment. 'If that's the case, it would be unfair for me to ask them to move away from their friends just so I can see them.' She took a step back. 'Could you ask them if they'd move?'

I shrugged. 'They'd immediately say yes, they're demons.'

'Don't tell them it's for me. Just ask them if they'd like to move from Eighty-Eight.'

'Deal.'

'Thanks.' She turned to head up the stairs.

'Simone?' John said.

She stopped and turned back to us. 'Hmm?'

'The other Winds have an abundance of children to help manage their realms. I don't, and I appreciate your ...' he searched for the word, 'willingness to be what the North needs you to be. It's a big responsibility for one so young, and you've taken it on without complaint.'

She gestured towards me. 'All my life, Emma's explained what it means to be born into royalty. It's not a privilege, it's a lifetime job that you don't have a choice about. A lot of people need us to be strong and set an example.' She straightened. 'And I intend to help those people as much as I can.'

'You are a credit to both of us,' he said.

She bowed slightly. 'I thank you, Highness. Now if you don't mind, I'm going to bed.'

Her huge grin of delight was visible as she turned away and trotted up the stairs.

I yawned and stretched. 'Me too.'

'You go,' he said. 'I'll be along after I've walked the battlements.'

I patted him on the shoulder and followed Simone up the stairs. As I went around the balcony towards our bedroom, I saw him sitting in the garden, still drinking his tea.

15

Mid-Autumn Festival was celebrated on the day of the largest full moon in autumn, when the sky was at its clearest. The Mountain's staff and students all gathered on the large forecourt in front of the Hall of Purple Mist. The demon staff laid picnic blankets and silk brocade cushions on the ground, and provided the groups with tea and moon cakes.

The sun set in an autumnal flare of orange, pink and purple through the few horizontal banner-like clouds. As dusk fell, the children lit their lanterns and ran around the groups of adults, laughing. People used hot wax to attach candles to the lids of their moon cake tins and lit them, making the square merry with lights.

As the sun dropped below the tops of the western mountains, its last rays lit up the clouds, then gradually faded to blue then lilac, and the stars began to appear. Everybody turned towards the east, where the moon behind the mountains made the peaks shine with a halo of burning silver.

John rose to his feet from the blanket our family was sharing. A silver light shone from him, mirroring the light on the mountains. He raised his hands and dropped his head, concentrating, and his hair rose around him, lit with individual strands of silver. His black Mountain uniform was edged with the silver of the moonlight.

The students watched him, discussing his appearance.

Don't look at me, he said. *Look at ... that.*

The top of the moon appeared above the horizon and everybody made loud sounds of wonder. Even the children stopped running around and shouted, 'Wah!'

John had made the moon so large it filled half the sky, even though only a quarter of it was above the horizon. It was like looking at it through a telescope; every crater was clearly visible. Silence fell over the Mountain as everybody watched the rising moon with awe. It hung in the sky above us like a twin planet.

The moon shines with reflected light, John said.
All watch its stolen finery, captivated,
But its true beauty is held unseen.
It searches for one with the vision
To go beyond the silver glory
To love the noble heart within.

There was a smattering of applause and a few cheers.

John sat back down and leaned into me. 'It seems like forever since I've done that.'

'How long did you work on the poem?' Leo said.

'I made it up on the spot,' John said. 'I don't have the patience to spend time agonising over forms of words.'

'It shows,' Martin said. 'Even in Chinese it's awful.'

'I know. Fortunately, the students don't,' John said. He leaned forward and studied the moon cakes on the tray. Each cake was ten centimetres across with a flaky pastry holding a sweet paste mixed with a large amount of sugar and fat. 'White lotus, red bean ... what is this, chocolate?' He touched one. 'Ice-cream? Wait, Hello Kitty moon cakes?'

'They're for Little Jade and Richie,' Simone said.

'Where are they?' I said.

'Running around with BJ,' Simone said.

'I thought its name was Darcy,' John said.

Simone shrugged. 'BJ stuck.'

John selected a quarter from a white lotus cake without the egg yolk and leaned back into me. I poured him some tea and he nodded his thanks.

'Still can't see them,' John said, looking up at the moon. 'I thought I made it big enough this time. I'll have to arrange for a stone to do the calculations for me.'

'See what?' Simone said.

'The locations of the moon landings. I thought if I magnified it enough you'd be able to see the footprints and the landing modules.'

'I must go up and have a look,' Simone said. 'Will you take me, Daddy?'

He was silent for a long moment, obviously thinking about what to say.

'I see,' she said.

'I really would love to, Simone, and I hope to one day soon.'

'No, it's okay, I understand.' She lay on her back, propped up on her elbows, and pulled a cushion behind her head. 'Uncle Bai can always take me.'

'Is he still dead?' I said.

'Yes,' John said.

'Michael's been complaining on Facebook,' Simone said.

John lowered himself so his head was in my lap and I stroked his hair. I ran my hand down over his shoulder and stopped when I felt a gauze pad under the fabric. He took my hand gently away and returned it to his hair.

'When?' I said softly.

'Today,' he replied, just as softly.

I stroked his hair. 'The other ones were nearly gone.'

He rubbed my knee. 'I know. I'll live.'

'I'm going to find Jade and Richie,' Simone said too loudly, dropped her piece of moon cake onto the tray and stomped away.

There was a commotion to one side of the square and John pulled himself to sit upright to see what was going on. When we saw Kwan Yin drifting across the square towards us in Celestial Form, both of us joined the students in standing. She was sitting cross-legged on a lotus flower floating on a cloud. Her shining hair was piled on top of her head, she wore a white robe, and her eyes were half-closed with contentment. She glowed from within with shen energy that radiated in visible rays from her.

She stopped two metres in front of us, suspended on the cloud, and the students scrambled to make way for her. She dismissed the cloud and stepped down onto the stone barefoot. Her Celestial Form was more than three metres tall. When she spoke to us, her voice was soothing and calm, full of the vibrations of heavenly bliss.

'Lord Xuan Wu. Emma, dearest. Walk with me.'

She turned without waiting for us and drifted up towards one of the pagodas. John took my hand and we followed her. As we flew into the sky behind the glowing Bodhisattva, the moon huge above us, the students below went mad with joy, applauding and cheering. John squeezed my hand.

When we reached the pagoda, Kwan Yin changed to her ordinary human form, wearing a white silk pantsuit. She landed to sit at the table and conjured some tea and moon cakes for us. We joined her, and I poured the tea before she could.

'I appreciate your help,' I said. I knew better than to say more.

'I cannot help as much as I wish.' She sipped her tea. 'When do you depart?'

'Tomorrow,' John said.

She nodded and turned her teacup in her hand. I glanced at John; I'd never seen her so agitated. He matched my look and made the tiniest of shrugs.

'My house in Paris is there if you have need of it,' she said.

'I've been ordered to the UK only ...' John said, then stopped. He dropped his voice. 'Thank you. What can you tell us?'

'Jade Building Block,' Kwan Yin said.

'My Lady,' the stone said.

'Stay with them.'

'It's hard,' the stone said.

'I know.'

She reached out and touched the stone in my ring and it glowed with shen energy.

'Thank you,' the stone said.

'My pleasure.' She sighed gently and removed her hand from it. 'Do not hesitate to call on help from any quarter, Ah Wu.'

'*Any* quarter?' John said.

'But do not negotiate with the forces of Hell.'

'I understand.'

'Wow, how bad is this?' I said.

Kwan Yin held her hand out, palm up, towards John. 'You are severed, weakened and in pain.' She nodded to me. 'You are small and vulnerable.'

'Now it's beginning to sound like a "what could possibly go wrong" situation,' I said.

'Could you petition the Jade Emperor to allow Emma to gain Immortality before we go?' John said. 'He hasn't replied to me.'

'No. It is not my place.'

'Just do one thing for me, Ms Kwan,' I said.

'The answer is yes,' she said.

I put my teacup down and saluted her. 'Thank you.'

'Is the Celestial doing the right thing?' John said.

'Of course he is,' she said. 'Bend. Do not break.'

'I will not break. I know the Way.'

'You may know the Way, but you have still a great distance to go.'

John took my hand. 'I do not strive for perfection and enlightenment. I have joy and love where I am.'

'I know. But love brings misery and pain.'

'And more joy,' John said.

'Yang and yin,' Kwan Yin said. 'Always cycling, one turning into the other. The darkness becomes the light. Joy becomes pain.' She reached out and touched our hands. 'Be strong when it is needed. Be weak when it is needed. Bend. Do not break.' She disappeared.

I shifted my chair so that I could lean into John. 'That sounded very, very bad.'

He put his arm around my shoulders. 'Nothing we didn't know already. What did you ask her?'

'If it would work out okay in the end.'

He squeezed me. 'Of course it will. I will Raise and marry you.'

'We should go back down,' I said.

'They'll want a full account of everything we said.'

'Tell them we played Uno and had jelly shots with her.'

'We played what and had what?'

'Oh, this is good. Tell Simone you've never played Uno.'

He was silent for a moment, then stiffened slightly. 'Suddenly she's completely overjoyed. She says she's finding her cards and we are playing it on the rug right now or else. She says Leo and Martin want to join in, and even the small children will play.'

'I wonder if Leo can arrange the jelly shots for later,' I said as he took my hand to carry me back down.

* * *

Little Jade sat in Leo's lap and they shared a hand of cards. Richie and Simone sat next to each other and she helped him.

Little Jade's tiny face was full of triumph as she placed the black card on the stack. 'Take five, Uncle Martin.'

'Four,' Leo said to the top of her head. 'You'll make him cry.'

Her eyes widened. 'Really?'

Martin picked up four cards and nodded. 'You are very mean.' He pretended to wipe his eyes. 'I'll lose now.'

'Don't make Uncle Martin cry,' Richie said.

Little Jade studied him for a long moment, concentrating, then poked him with the hand of cards. 'You're only pretending,' she said fiercely.

'He can see your cards,' Leo said, pulling her hand back.

'He's letting us win anyway,' BJ said. 'Stop doing that. It's not as fun.'

'You are?' Little Jade said. She poked him with the cards again, and this time she dropped them. 'That's not fair!'

Leo scooped the cards up off the rug. 'Lord Xuan's turn.'

'What colour is it?' John said.

'You have to choose, Little Jade,' Leo said.

'Purple!' she said with triumph.

'Purple it is,' John said, and laid a card on the pile.

'Wait,' Simone said, peering at the purple number ten. 'This game doesn't have purple cards.'

'It does now, right, Jade?' John said.

Jade held her hand out palm forward and John high-fived her. 'Yeah!'

'Don't worry, I'll change it back.' Simone touched the card, making it blue. 'Okay, back to normal.'

'These rules are not in the rule book,' Leo said.

Jade glanced up at him from his lap. 'Is that special stuff, changing the colours?'

'Yes,' BJ said. 'You won't be able to do stuff like that when you're down there.'

'Down where?' Martin said.

Jade raised both her little hands. 'We're going to the Earfly!'

'Earthly,' BJ said. 'Mom will be studying law in Hong Kong, so we'll be living down there for a while.'

'Amy's studying law; Gold will be a full-time parent,' I said.

'And you permit this?' Martin asked John.

'I can't see why not,' John said. 'Amy hates being a full-time mother; Gold loves it. She wants to take over his duties, so I'm encouraging them to follow their desires.'

'Daddy says he can stay home with us just as good as Mummy can,' Richie said, serious. 'He's better 'cause she gets cranky. They say being a girl or a boy makes no difference to being a good mum or dad.'

'Yeah,' Little Jade said. 'We'll live on the Earthly and Daddy will look after us.'

'I'll help,' BJ said.

Little Jade waved her cards in BJ's direction. 'You're going to school.'

'Yeah,' BJ said ruefully. 'What a hike up to CH every day. I may enrol in an Earthly school.'

'CH is way better,' Simone said. 'You should stay up here.'

BJ shrugged. 'I don't have any family up here.'

'You have us,' Leo said. 'There's a spare room in Persimmon Tree. Martin's over at the Northern Heavens all the time, and since I stopped recruiting I'm spending most of my time on the Earthly helping Chang with the orphanages. How about you take it?'

'Can I?' BJ said, full of hope. 'I'd like to stay up here.'

'Talk to your father about it first,' John said.

'I will,' BJ said, determined. She looked down at her card. 'Oh. Uno.'

Simone raised her hand. 'Wait, I have Uno too.'

I looked down at my hand, then around at the group. Everybody was left with one card.

'Hold on, we had five cards a minute ago,' Leo said. 'What's going on?'

'Oh,' John said. He raised his hand, holding one card. 'Sorry.'

'You gave everybody one card?' Simone said.

'It wasn't deliberate,' John said. 'It just happened.'

'Why did that happen?' Little Jade said, turning her card to examine the front and back. 'Where are the other cards?'

'Put them all back in the box, and when you take them home the lost ones will probably return,' John said, handing Simone his card. 'If they don't, I'll buy you a new box.'

'But why did it happen?' BJ said.

'His number is one,' I said. 'I think he somehow just changed reality around him.'

'You *warped reality*?' BJ said.

John tried to shrug it off. 'Things like that happen sometimes. Just be glad I haven't brought winter on early.'

Jade waved her card at him. 'You are so weird, Uncle John.'

'Our daddy's weirder!' Richie said triumphantly.

Jade pursed her lips for a moment, thinking, then nodded. 'Yes, you're right, Daddy is really weird sometimes.'

'Is that a good or a bad thing?' Gold said, appearing behind them.

'Good!' Little Jade said.

'Yeah!' Richie said.

'Bedtime,' Gold said. 'But BJ can stay for a while if he likes.'

'BJ's a she right now,' Little Jade said.

Leo hoisted Little Jade off his lap and handed her to Gold, who rested her on his hip. He held his hand out to Richie, who rose and took it.

'Say goodnight to everybody,' Gold said.

'I'll come too, Dad,' BJ said. 'I want to talk to you about Leo's idea.' She waved one hand at us. 'Night, everybody.'

'Goodnight!' Little Jade yelled, waving.

'Night, everybody. Let's play that again soon, it was fun!' Richie said.

'But Uncle John has to promise not to do that again,' Little Jade said as Gold turned to go.

Richie took BJ's hand in his other hand. 'Yeah, 'cause I would have won.'

'I would have,' Jade said.

'No way, I only had two cards left.'

'But I had more! That means I was winning, right?'

They continued arguing as Gold led them away.

'Will the cards really come back, Daddy?' Simone said as we folded the rug. 'What happened last time you did this?'

'I haven't done it in a very long time.' He patted her shoulder. 'I'm sorry. I'll buy you a new deck.'

Leo threw the rug over his arm. 'It's late and we have an early flight tomorrow.'

'Night, Leo,' Simone said, and hugged and kissed him and Martin.

She watched them walk away to put the blanket into a hamper the demons had placed at the side of the square.

'This will be the first time they've really been apart in forever,' she said.

'They'll be able to talk to each other,' John said. 'Good for them to spend some time apart; I think it will make them appreciate each other even more.'

'Yeah,' I said, putting my arm around his waist and leaning into him. 'Worked for us.'

'If I'd had a choice, I would not have been away for quite so long,' John said, wrapping his arms around Simone's and my shoulders. 'Leo's right: we should all go to bed.'

Simone looked up at the moon. 'I'll have trouble sleeping with that; it's very bright.'

'I'll fix it,' John said.

As we walked back to the Residence, our arms wrapped around each other, the moon shrank back to its normal size and the sky filled with brilliant stars.

16

Simone slumped in the uncomfortable hard chair at the airport gate. 'It's so full here that we're taking seats from people, these chairs are stupid and my bum hurts. We should go to the lounge.'

John was sitting upright and glancing around, alert. 'I'm not having this argument again. The business-class lounge has only one exit and it's harder to defend.'

'Is that a real concern?' Ben said. He and Tom were accompanying us to the UK to investigate Tom's demon nature and Ben's Welsh heritage that was somehow linked with my own.

'Not really, but he's being extra careful,' I said.

'This is torture,' Simone said. 'Are you *sure* there were no first-class seats?'

'It's for your own safety. There'll be nobody in business except us,' John said.

'You're taking this safety thing way over the top, Dad. Give me back my yin and none of them can hurt me, not even the King.' Simone slumped back in her seat again. 'We should just go to the lounge!'

'I was going to give this to you on the airplane, but you can have it now if it'll stop you complaining,' Leo said, handing her a small shopping bag from one of the cheap electronics stores in Tsim Sha Tsui.

She opened it and peered inside, then jiggled with delight. She grinned up at him. 'You are so awesome! Thanks, Leo.'

'What is it?' I said.

She pulled out the handheld game. 'Latest Pokemon. I didn't buy it because of study. Leo, you're the best.' She went to him and gave him a quick hug, then sat back down and opened the console. Her face dropped with disappointment. 'There are no outlets here to charge it up, and none of us is good with metal.' She brightened. 'We *have* to go to the lounge now, Daddy.'

John glowered at Leo, who shrugged and smiled slightly. John turned back to Simone. 'Aren't you too old for these games?'

'You're never too old for Pokemon,' Simone said. 'I've heard that even Emma plays an old version of it on her mobile phone.'

I stopped fiddling with my phone and put it into my pocket. 'No idea what you're talking about.'

'Which one is it?' Tom said.

Simone raised the box for the game cartridge.

'If I'd known I would have brought mine,' Tom said. 'We could have swapped Pokemon on the plane.'

Leo reached into his leather attaché case and pulled out another console. 'Here, borrow mine until we get there.'

'You are definitely too old to be playing that,' John said with amusement.

Leo shrugged. 'What Simone said. Never too old.'

'Come on, Daddy,' Simone said. 'Even if it's just you and me, let's go to the lounge so I can charge it up.'

'You'll have a power outlet on the plane,' John said.

'We won't be in the air for another couple of hours.'

'Go, do it, we'll be fine,' I said.

John sighed with resignation. 'We'll all go, and if we're attacked and have to fight in there, Simone will pay any damages out of her allowance.'

'Deal,' Simone said, triumphant. She hopped up and threw her backpack over her shoulder. 'Let's go.'

'What's your favourite?' Tom asked Simone as we walked to the lounge.

'Charmander, of course, he's so *cute*!' Simone said. She stopped and her face went strange for a moment, then she shook her head.

'What?' he said.

'Just someone talking to me,' Simone said. 'And I am ignoring them,' she added with emphasis.

'That must be a damn nuisance,' Tom said.

'Tell me about it,' she said, glaring at John.

* * *

Zhenwu

John shifted uncomfortably on the aircraft seat. He'd refused the attendant's offer to lay it flat so he could sleep; he needed to stay awake. He could deal with the nagging pain from most of the small cuts and burns, but there were a couple at the base of the Serpent's tail and he was forced to sit on them. He either had to use energy to block the pain or put up with the grinding discomfort that made him exhausted and irritable. In the end, he used energy to stop the pain, fully aware that this would slow the healing process. He couldn't control the urge to feel for his other half. A slight echo, a tremor of misery, and that was all. The gulf between them was like a hole right through him.

Simone slept, her face youthful and angelic.

Please, Simone, gain Immortality soon. I live in dread of losing you. Every day you look more like your mother; I wonder where the Wheel took her.

Emma was curled up with her head in his lap. He shifted under her, making himself more comfortable so that she didn't lean on the wounds. She nuzzled into him slightly in her sleep and he brushed one hand over her brown hair. There were strands of grey through it now, much as he had. He studied her face, as complex and intelligent in sleep as when she was awake.

I must Raise you and marry you and enthrone you by my side. The Elixir must be ready for us when we return. I can't continue like this, unable to call upon your intelligence and human compassion when running my realm.

He smiled slightly. Fifty years ago the idea of a lowly human woman contributing to his rule would have been ridiculous, and now he was lost without her advice.

Leo was asleep across the aisle; he was obviously missing Martin and doing his best to be cheerful through the heartsickness. Martin and Yue Gui were doing a fine job of managing the Northern Heavens, and John pondered the option of making Yue Gui Number One as well. It was traditional for the Number One to be male, but Yue Gui was more intelligent than Martin and as good a leader, even if she wasn't as strong in war strategy and tactics. It would be a shocking breach of tradition for him to have not only a female Number One but two joint Number Ones. John smiled slightly as he imagined the reaction. He'd do it when they returned.

He extended his senses around the plane. To be this high, moving this fast, was exhilarating: the intense cold of the thin air and the plane's movement through it affecting the traces of moisture. He couldn't hold a speed like this for long periods, and he took a moment to admire the advances that humans had made with science.

He could see the stars above them and wondered if there was other life — Shen and human — out there. He wondered how the Shen had come to be. Perhaps they would find some answers if they ever found the Shen of the West.

He relaxed, cleared his mind and looked forward. A dark time ahead. Loss and pain — the echoes of the emotions rippled back to the now. They would be visited by more suffering before things improved. It could not be avoided. Then a premonition hit him like a physical force: bringing Emma was the wrong thing to do. The wrongness of it, and the inevitable consequences, rang through him like a deep bell. She wouldn't be safe there.

He couldn't take her home now; they were following the Jade Emperor's orders and had to complete the mission. He would just have to try to minimise the damage.

He resisted the urge to contact the Jade Emperor to seek counsel. The Emperor knew exactly what he was doing in sending them at this time and John simply had to trust him. He called the Lady and received no response, which either meant she was in retreat after her close call in Hell, or she knew all about it and was withholding her counsel until it was really needed. Either option was disturbing.

He couldn't pinpoint the details of what was coming, he could only see the emotional repercussions. He would have to be extra vigilant.

Exhaustion from the pain of the Serpent's wounds overcame his will to stay awake and he dozed, his dreams full of demons, heat and suffering.

* * *

Emma

'Which one's ours?' John said as we walked out of the customs and immigration at Heathrow Airport.

'There he is — Paul!' Simone shouted, and ran to him.

Twenty-five-year-old Paul was short and round, with pale brown hair and terrible acne on his kind face. He wore a well-worn pair of baggy jeans and a faded pink polo shirt.

He hugged Simone and pulled back to grin at her. 'You're taller than me!'

She pushed him, ribbing. 'That's not difficult.' She stepped away from him, more serious. 'Here's Daddy.'

John stopped in front of Paul and studied him, his fierce dark gaze making Paul immediately nervous.

Paul pulled himself upright and stood to attention. 'Uh ...' He took a deep breath. 'Welcome to London, sir. I'm honoured to serve you.'

'Should have been "my Lord",' Leo said softly from behind John.

John relaxed and slapped Paul on the shoulder. 'Never mind that. Emma and Simone have told me how well you've looked after them. Where's the car?'

Paul let out a huge breath of relief and gestured outside. 'In the car park, sir.' He glanced around at everybody. 'I thought there were five passengers for the van? It's only a six-seater.'

'Leo will make his own way,' John said. He nodded to Leo, who strode away to find somewhere private to travel from. 'This is Ben and Tom O'Breen, the gentlemen who'll be staying with us while we're here.'

'Welcome,' Paul said, nodding to Ben and Tom. 'Please follow me — I'll take you to the car.'

'How is your grandfather?' John asked Paul as we walked through the car park.

'He's ...' Paul hesitated. 'He's really not well, sir. The cancer's taken hold and they've given him six months at the most.'

Simone moaned quietly with sympathy.

'I'm sorry to hear that,' John said. 'How is James holding up?'

'You may not see much of him. He's been spending quite a lot of time with my grandfather,' Paul said.

We climbed into the van while he put the bags into the back then went around to the driver's side.

'How's Peta?' Simone said as Paul eased the van out of the car park.

'She's waiting for you back at the house. She's frantically going through the paperwork for His Lordship, convinced that she's missed something,' Paul said with humour. 'If she lets my scones burn there'll be serious trouble.'

'I'm sorry,' Ben said, interrupting. 'Are Paul and Peta staff? Are they Shen?'

'Normal humans, sir,' Paul said, looking at Ben in the rear-view mirror. 'My grandfather was very close with His Lordship's previous butler, James, and when James grew too old to do the job he asked my wife and me if we would be interested. We jumped at the chance — I mean, it's not every day you get to work for a god, is it? My wife, Peta, is His Lordship's previous housekeeper's grand-niece. We met one another at a family function, but I think James arranged to throw us together.'

'Wouldn't put it past him,' Simone said.

'So how long have you been working for Lord Xuan?' Ben said.

Paul was silent for a moment, concentrating on the traffic, then he grinned at the rear-view mirror. 'Four years now. But this is actually the first time I've met His Lordship. Welcome back to your Earthly realm, sir.'

'Thank you,' John said.

Paul's phone rang and he put it on speaker. 'Yes?'

'Paul, it's Franklin.'

'Hello, Franklin!' Simone yelled from the back of the van.

'Is that Simone?' Franklin said, to a backdrop of loud banging. 'They're here already?'

'Yes,' Paul said. 'They're —'

Franklin cut in, his voice becoming frantic. 'My Lord, help me — I think it's vampire hunters, but I'm not sure. All of this recent business on the television has made my —'

There was a huge crash, then the phone went dead.

Simone pulled herself halfway out of her seat. 'Franklin?'

'Something happening at the cemetery,' John said, distracted. 'Paul, you know where it is?'

'I do, sir.'

'Go. Now,' John said. He hesitated a moment. 'Keep me updated. Let me know the situation the minute you're there.'

'Yes, sir,' Paul said.

'He's talking to Leo,' I said.

'Faster, Paul,' John said.

'How much faster, sir? Do you want to risk being pulled over?'

'As fast as is safe. Don't worry about being pulled over, and don't stop for red lights. I'll change them; nobody will see you. Move!' John said.

Paul floored it. 'Working for you was the best idea I've ever had,' he said with grim delight.

'You may not say that when we reach Franklin's place,' John said.

'Who's Franklin?' Tom said.

'My pet vampire,' John said. 'Last one in existence.'

'You're *kidding*,' Ben said.

'Meet you there,' Simone said, and disappeared.

'She'll get lost,' John said.

'No, she won't,' I said. 'She visits Charlie's grave at that cemetery every time we come to London. She knows exactly where it is.'

When we arrived at the cemetery gate, John pulled open the van door. 'Stay here,' he said, stepped out and ran through the gate.

I closed the door and kept a lookout through the van's windows. A group of five young men came striding menacingly down the street towards us. A couple of them were carrying fence pickets like weapons.

'A riot here?' Ben said with disbelief.

207

'Paul, drive in through the cemetery gate and go right,' I said.

Inside, we saw another group of young men vandalising the old tombstones, knocking them over so that they broke on the ground.

'Bastards,' Paul said. 'We should stop and —'

'Keep moving, don't stop,' I said. 'Hurry!'

'I thought the riots were all finished,' Ben said.

'They're demons,' I said. 'I can't be sure what type. Give me a moment.'

I opened my Inner Eye onto the men and they grew and glowed with dark energy. I drew a sharp breath as they became clear: they were more than two metres tall, grey-skinned, and shaped like skinny humans with large oval heads, oversized eyes and minute noses. There was a variety of them; some had bat-like wings and others had mouths that were a mass of misshapen teeth.

'What?' Ben said.

'Western demons,' I said. 'First time I've ever seen them up close. Meredith never mentioned that some of them looked like aliens from B-grade movies.'

As one the demons turned and faced us; they'd felt my Inner Eye on them.

'I shouldn't have done that,' I said, 'they've seen us. Paul — drive!'

Paul floored the accelerator and we shot across the gravel towards Franklin's house. About fifty demons in male human form were gathered around it, and they'd set up some sort of technical apparatus facing the house. John, Simone and Leo were standing side by side in front of Franklin's door, ready to fight if need be. Franklin stood behind them, cowering and tiny in the doorway of his little house.

'Drive through the demons — don't worry about hitting them — and stop next to the house,' I said. 'Then stay in the car.'

Paul didn't hesitate. He barrelled the van through the crowd, knocking over the equipment, and hit the side of the house in his haste.

The demons attacked. Leo and Simone had no difficulty dealing with them: Leo used his sword, Simone used shen energy, and they destroyed the demons almost on touch. John had more trouble; his energy didn't seem to affect the demons the same way it did back home in China. He threw shen energy at them but it passed through them.

Behind me, Tom made a soft growling sound that grew louder and more rasping. Ben tried to hold him back but Tom threw him off and rushed out of the van. Once free of the confinement, he threw his head back, stretched out his arms and changed to a Snake Mother-type demon: four metres long, with the front end of a skinless man and a serpent's tail. He was no longer recognisable as the Tom we knew. He threw himself at the demons and destroyed them with his bare hands. As the demons became aware of his presence, they panicked and ran from him, crashing into the walls of the house in their terror. He cut through them, picking them up in both hands and tearing them apart or ripping their heads off. He greedily shoved their dismembered limbs and heads into his mouth, stretching his jaw impossibly wide to fit them in.

'Oh no,' Ben moaned. 'Will he ever come back?'

A demon fleeing from Tom ran straight into Simone, knocking her into the wall. Franklin changed into something huge, black and ugly, with a skinny body and bat wings like the Western demons, but bulging eyes and tusks like a Chinese demon. He pushed away the demon that had hit Simone and bent to protect her, covering her with one wing.

Tom threw himself at the demon that had hit Simone, crushing its throat with one hand and throwing it aside.

John stopped fighting and knelt to check Simone. Leo's face hardened and he hefted his sword, moving in front of them to protect them.

The demons moved closer, sensing their distraction.

'To hell with this, they need help,' I said.

I summoned the Murasame and jumped out of the van. The demons all had their backs to me, concentrating on John, Simone and Leo and trying to keep clear of Tom's demon form, which was rampaging through them. I readied myself and grinned, feeling the rush as the sword came to me. I ran the sword straight into a demon's back and it dissipated the same way a Chinese demon would. The others didn't notice, so I chased them down and destroyed them as they ran from Tom's clutches and Leo's shen energy.

Leo saw me. 'Watch where you're going — I might hit you with energy!'

'I'll stay put,' I called.

'Get back in the van!' John yelled. 'Lion.'

Leo fought his way towards me.

I jumped over the head of a demon that was running in my direction, landed on the shoulder of one behind it and thrust my sword down the back of its neck. I jumped free as it dissipated, turned in the air and landed between two other demons. They both reached down to grab me and clashed heads. I took advantage of the confusion to cut them both off at the knees. I ducked as a ball of shen energy whizzed right over my head, hitting a demon that had been coming up behind me.

I turned back to Leo and grinned. 'Thanks.'

'Just watch what you're doing,' he said. 'Back to back.'

We stood back to back and a circle of demons surrounded us. There was a commotion among them to my left, and Tom grabbed three in his skinless arms and ripped them to pieces.

'Now,' Leo said.

We took advantage of the demons' distraction and attacked. Tom had reached for another, so I only had four to deal with. The first stood its ground and reached towards me; the second and third held back, obviously intimidated. The one on the right was glancing between Tom and Leo, distracted. I ducked under the first demon's arms, rolled and came up in front of the distracted one on the right. I jumped into the air, sliced down through its head as I passed over the top of it, landed, rolled and faced the remaining three demons. The two middle ones seemed to be frozen with fear. The one that had been on my left was now on my right; it hesitated for a moment, confused, which was its undoing. Tom grabbed it with both hands and ripped its head off.

I generated a large ball of chi, split it into two and directed one each at the hesitating demons. They exploded with a satisfying rush and I staggered backward as their chi returned to me. I fell to sit on the grass, gasping.

Leo destroyed the final two and crouched in front of me. 'What happened?'

I was unable to speak as I sucked in air; I raised my hand to ask him to wait.

'Do you need anything?' he said, taking my wrist. 'You seem okay. Whoa, more than okay — what the hell is this?'

Where we touched, the chi energy had flared to life in my skin. I drew it back in and returned it to my dan tian. I took a few deep breaths and nodded.

'The energy those demons shot into me was like extra-strong alcohol when all you've ever drunk is beer. It was super powerful. Help me up?'

He gave me a hand as I rose and we went to John and Simone. Simone was sitting next to John and rubbing the back of her head.

'Are you okay?' I said.

'Yeah, no major damage. Minor skull fracture, which I've already taken care of,' she said. 'I have the headache from hell.'

'A fractured skull is not minor damage!'

'Pfft.' She pulled herself upright with effort and smiled at Tom. 'Thanks.'

Tom seemed dazed by the whole business. He swayed on his coils, looking around. The van door slammed and he spun to see what the noise was.

Ben was walking towards us. 'You okay, son? Can you change back?'

'Human,' Tom rasped. He moved incredibly fast, grabbed his father by the throat and lifted him.

Ben clawed at Tom's hand. 'Tom ... no ... it's me.'

John raised his hands to bind Tom, but it was too late. There was an audible crack and Ben went limp. Tom opened his mouth wide, visibly fighting the binding as he tried to bring Ben's head up to his face.

'That was your father!' Simone shrieked.

Tom jumped as if struck. He seemed to see Ben for the first time, and changed back to human. He lowered Ben gently to the ground, then fell to his knees and bent over him, one hand touching his father's face. He rocked silently, his face blank with shock.

Leo checked Ben over, then stood and shook his head. 'Broken neck. Killed instantly.'

'I killed him,' Tom moaned.

He rose to his feet, swaying slightly, then he took off, running across the grass.

I went after him and caught up to him. I didn't dare touch him, so I ran beside him, matching his pace.

'At this speed we'll run out of cemetery in no time,' I said, gasping with the effort of keeping up with him. 'You can't run away. Stop and we can help you.'

'Leave me alone!' he wheezed, and put on a spurt of speed.

He tore through the cemetery gate at faster-than-human speed and onto the road, straight into the path of a London taxi. The black cab wasn't going very fast, but it hit him full-on and he was thrown five metres, bouncing bonelessly on the road.

The taxi stopped and the driver jumped out and ran to Tom, obviously horrified.

Simone, Leo and John caught up with me and we checked Tom. He was on his back, his arm bent wrongly behind him, his eyes wide and glazed. Blood streaked his face and ran down his neck.

Simone covered her face and turned away. Leo gathered her into his arms and walked her back towards the cemetery gate.

She shouted 'Let me go!'

John glanced up at me and shook his head, but he didn't need to. Tom's chi was gone. He was just a husk, the breath of life gone from him.

'He just ran out in front of me,' the taxi driver said, staring at Tom. 'There was nothing I could do.'

'I saw what happened,' I said. 'You're absolutely not responsible. He was upset and I was trying to stop him.'

'It wasn't my fault,' the driver said.

I patted his arm. 'That's right, it wasn't.'

I turned to look for Simone. She was leaning on the wall and weeping, Leo standing helpless next to her.

John pulled out his mobile phone and dialled. 'Hello, police?'

17

After the police's questions and the statements and photos, we walked back to Franklin's house. The van was where we'd left it, and Paul was sitting in the front with his legs hanging outside, smoking a cigarette. He quickly extinguished it when he saw us coming. Franklin, dressed in overalls and a fluorescent visibility vest, was filling in the earth of Ben's grave, helped by a couple of men in similar outfits.

'Are you sure this is all right?' Franklin asked when he saw us.

'He'd been living on the Mountain for more than a year. No next of kin,' John said. 'When they move onto the Mountain it's explained.'

'All right then,' Franklin said, and nodded to the men with him. 'This is Vlad and Boris.'

The two men nodded to us, then stared at John.

'This your boss, the big god?' one of them asked, in a strong London accent. 'Are these others vampires too?'

'What?' I said.

Franklin visibly cringed. 'I had to tell them. They were about to call the police on me.'

'Yeah, he had this constant stream of underage girls — sometimes two or three at a time — visiting him in his damn house,' the workman said. 'Now, I'm a dad, and I

214

won't put up with that, so us two,' he glanced at the other man, who nodded, 'we went to sort him out. When we got inside the house, the girls were laughing and he was serving them, would you believe it, fucking tea and biscuits in his demon form, no less. So he had some explaining to do.'

'Craziest thing I ever saw,' the other one said. He sounded Eastern European. He grinned with mischief. 'We got our own sparkly vampire here, all right.'

'Oh, shut up,' Franklin said. 'We shouldn't be joking at a time like this. Look at the little girl's face. You all head back to your house and take it easy.'

'Come and look at this,' Leo shouted to us. He'd gone over to look at the apparatus that the demons had been putting together outside Franklin's house.

'Yes, my Lord, you need to see this,' Franklin said.

It was a powerful spotlight, at least sixty centimetres across. Leo pushed it to the side to reveal a corpse that looked exactly like Franklin's human form.

'Is that a clone, a demon copy, or something else entirely?' I said.

'Copy. I can't get a good feel of its size or type. I suspect that may be because of its Western origins,' John said. He glanced from the copy to Franklin. 'I can't even tell that it's not the real thing.'

Franklin raised his hands. 'I'm the real me, believe me, my Lord. They were going to destroy me with this big light and replace me. I just thank the Heavens you arrived a few days early.'

'We didn't,' John said. 'We just lied to everybody about when we'd be here.'

'That saved my life,' Franklin said.

John's expression was grim. He put his hand out. 'Franklin.'

'My Lord.' Franklin didn't hesitate; he went straight to John and took his hand.

John concentrated for a moment, then nodded. 'You are nearly there, my friend. Well done.'

Franklin sighed with relief. 'Even I was worried for a moment.'

'What do we do with this?' I said, indicating the demon corpse. I glanced around. 'All the others disintegrated.'

John put a hand out over the dead demon and it exploded in a silent blast of demon essence.

'Let's go home,' he said, then turned to speak to Franklin. 'Pack your belongings; you're coming to stay with us. Leo, stay here and bring him when he's ready.'

'There's no need to ruin your seals. I'll be fine here,' Franklin said.

John dropped his head and glowered at Franklin. 'You will come to the house.' He obviously thought of something. 'And you will bring your workmates tomorrow afternoon. They deserve our thanks for putting up with this.'

Franklin's eyes widened. 'Don't wipe their memories, my Lord. I've really enjoyed having friends I can share my true nature with.'

'Bring them around tomorrow afternoon,' John repeated.

'My Lord,' Franklin said, resigned.

John examined the van. The front fender was severely dented, enough to hit the tyre if we tried to drive it. John grabbed it and pulled it off.

'Whoa,' Paul said softly. 'How much can you lift, if you don't mind me asking, sir?'

'In this form I can only bench press eleven hundred kilograms; it's very weak,' John said, tossing the fender into the back of the van. 'Sometimes I wish we still had Michael around. Having someone who can manipulate metal and electricity would be very useful, and he was a loyal member of the household.'

Simone burst into tears and climbed into the van.

'What did I say?' John said.

'Michael's still something of a sore point,' I said. 'But more than that, she just saw two people die in front of her. We've kept her sheltered from the very worst of it, and she just had it right in her face. And then you had to go and remind her that Michael's gone.'

'She's still not pining over him, is she?'

'You tell her to get over it and I will call you out,' I said, jabbing my index finger at him. 'Leave her alone.'

He shrugged. 'Let's go to the house and settle everyone in. She's jetlagged as well, that doesn't help.'

We got into the van, shut the doors and Paul started the engine.

'Not an auspicious start to your visit,' he said. 'I've never seen anything like that before. Does it happen often?'

'Fortunately, no,' I said. 'You're taking it very well. I'm impressed.'

'Thank you, Emma. I think it's largely due to the training you've given us — I was more excited than scared.' He made a soft sound of amusement. 'I think I'm disappointed that I didn't have a chance to contribute. It's a shame you can't teach us any more.'

'How far along are they?' John said.

'Couldn't take down a level one with a weapon,' I said. 'Extremely basic.'

'Good, we'll leave it there.' He spoke to Paul. 'You're safer not knowing anything at all.'

'Emma said they may not respect that any more; that we might be targets even if we're not trained,' Paul said.

John was silent for a long moment. 'Damn, Emma, you have a point. Four thousand years of Chinese civilisation and it has come to this.'

'Where we are right now, Chinese civilisation has nothing to do with anything,' I said.

'That's what concerns me.'

* * *

'Park on the street here, and wait a moment,' John said when we reached the house. He turned back to Simone. 'Come and watch what I do.'

They both got out of the van. John went up to the house, took Simone's hand and put his other hand against the wall. The entire house flared with a brilliant white flash that passed so quickly it was like lightning, accompanied by a deafening snap.

John turned around and indicated that Paul could take the van down into the basement garage. Inside, John went to his vintage sports car and brushed one hand over the top of the door.

'Did you drive it?' he asked me.

'Every time we were here,' I said. 'I took it down to Kent to explore the country lanes. It's gorgeous there.'

'I know.'

He went to the corner of the garage, where his motorbike sat under a dust sheet. He uncovered it and crouched to look at the engine.

'Why is this piece of junk in here?' Simone said. 'Emma wouldn't let me throw it away.'

'That, young lady, is a 1972 Ducati racing bike, one of only eight in the world,' Paul said from behind us. 'It's worth more than the house.'

'I won it in a bet,' John said, tinkering with the engine. 'Prince someone-or-other ... married a movie star. He bet the bike that I couldn't outride him on my Honda.'

'You cheated?' Simone said.

John rose and turned to her. 'Of course not.' He dropped his voice. 'He was carrying some extra weight, and I could hear that the bike wasn't tuned properly. What he didn't know was that my Honda was a racing bike as well. Mr Honda had

218

asked me to bring it over to try it out on the European roads to see how it went before they joined the endurance circuit. Neither of the bikes were road legal.'

He nodded towards the stairs. 'We need to help with the bags. You didn't have to bring every single item of clothing you own, Simone; surely you have a full wardrobe here? I know I do.'

We each grabbed two or three bags and lugged them up the stairs. Simone levitated the couple that were remaining and they floated up the stairs behind us. When we reached the lobby, John put the bags down and went to the hall table, where Peta had laid out all the current business matters that required his attention.

Peta rushed out from the kitchen, wearing a navy skirt suit. She was taller than Paul, slender and bony, with blonde hair tied into a waist-length braid.

She hugged Simone and me. 'Welcome back, Emma.' She patted Simone on the shoulder. 'Paul's made scones if you're hungry.'

'You didn't burn them, did you?' Paul said.

'Just took them out of the oven,' Peta said innocently. 'They're only slightly scorched.'

'I knew I should have made you drive,' Paul grumbled, heading into the kitchen.

Peta stood in front of John and made a clumsy curtsy. 'Uh ... welcome home, my Lord. I've put all the documents out here on the table; I hope that's acceptable.'

John studied the papers without looking at her. 'Yes, most acceptable.'

'That's his way of saying thanks and good job,' I said, and added in a stage whisper, 'You'll get used to him being rude. It's part of the whole god bullshit thing.'

'What she said,' John said, unfazed. Then he looked at Peta and smiled, changing his expression from intimidating to warm and kind. 'Emma's told me you do a good job, and that's good enough for me.' He turned back to the papers. 'Dismissed.'

'That's his way of saying thanks and he doesn't need you any more,' I said.

John glared at me. 'I am speaking in English, aren't I?'

'No,' Simone said. 'You're speaking in Rude To The Staff.'

He shrugged. 'I'm a god. It's allowed.'

'We'll see about that,' I said. I kissed Peta on the cheek. 'Everything's sorted now. It's good to see you again.'

Paul came out of the kitchen. 'Next time you'll be the one to drive the boss around. Those scones are ruined, I'll have to make a new batch. Do you want some of the wrecked ones anyway, Simone?'

'No, thanks,' Simone said. 'I never sleep on airplanes and that flight was awful. I nearly got out and walked, and then all this happened. I need a nap, but keep the scones warm for me, okay?'

'Deal,' Paul said.

'Do you need a hand with your stuff?' Peta said, gesturing towards the bags.

'No need, but you might like to come up with me, I have gifts for you guys,' Simone said. She took her bags up the stairs, Peta accompanying her. 'We have two more coming — Leo and Franklin. We were attacked in the cemetery.'

'Are you all okay?' Peta said.

'No, it was awful,' Simone said, and her voice cracked. 'I'll tell you about it upstairs.'

Paul watched them go. 'Poor kid. Wait a minute — how much can Simone bench press?'

''Bout the same,' John said, flipping through the documents. 'I swear Gold has the worst handwriting of any Shen on any Plane.'

'Only after you,' I said.

'Conceded,' John said. He glanced at Paul. 'Bring a pot of Earl Grey and a bowl of noodles to my study. I take it Leo is in the room next to Simone's?'

'Master Leo and Prince Martin usually share that one,' Paul said.

John nodded. 'Of course. This time it's just Leo.'

'What about Franklin?' I said.

He was studying the documents again and answered without looking up. 'He's going in the basement.'

'The hell he is.'

He still didn't look up. 'I've known Franklin several hundred years longer than you have. He needs to go in the basement.'

'You can't do this to him. Franklin's been a Retainer of the House for centuries. This is wrong.'

John dropped the documents, came to me and put his hands on my shoulders, gazing into my eyes. 'I don't want to do it, but it must be done. And Franklin would not sleep anywhere else even if you ordered him.' He turned to Paul, still with his hands on my shoulders. 'Prepare the basement … room … for him, then give me the keys.'

'So that's what it's for,' Paul said with wonder. 'The first time I saw it, it scared me to death. Now I'm kind of glad it's there.'

'I'm not,' I said, and took my bags upstairs. 'I'm having a nap too. If I'm not awake in a couple of hours, wake me.'

'How much can *she* bench press?' Paul asked John.

'She's very ordinary. Best she can lift is about two hundred and fifty kilograms,' John said.

'Five hundred pounds?' Paul said, astonished.

'Very ordinary.'

* * *

221

After we'd all woken up, Leo and I left John going over the documents with Peta and took Simone for a walk down to Hyde Park. The minute we passed through the gates, Simone took off, running between the trees like a small child, chasing the squirrels.

'One day she'll catch one and she won't know what to do with it,' I said as we strolled under the trees and watched her.

'I'd like to see that,' Leo said, his voice hoarse with emotion.

'Are you okay?' I said.

'More than okay. Here we are.' He raised his hands slightly. 'I can't believe we made it.'

'Not out of the woods yet,' I said, indicating Simone. Then: 'Holy shit, that's a demon.'

It was in the form of a small boy of about ten years, and racing towards her from behind so she hadn't seen it. We ran to cut it off. The demon got to her before we did, but it didn't attack; it fell face down on the grass behind her. Simone jumped, turned and stared down at it. Leo summoned his sword, the Black Lion, and stood over the demon, but Simone put her hand on his arm to stop him.

'Protect me, I am yours,' the child said to Simone.

'Trick,' I said.

'Let's see if it can take the Pill,' Leo said. 'Stand up for her to complete the process,' he ordered the demon.

It rose and stood in front of Simone. Leo cut it in half at waist height, and it exploded into demon essence.

'Geez, Leo, you could have given me some warning,' Simone said. 'I'm covered in demon essence — I need to change my clothes. I'll meet you back at the house.'

She disappeared.

'Maybe Western demons turn differently and can obey more than one person?' Leo said as we walked back to the house.

'I don't really think that's possible,' I said. 'A demon that turns gives itself to an individual and obeys them only.'

Another small boy ran towards us. We readied ourselves, then relaxed when he came closer and we realised he was human.

'I trust that nobody can see your sword,' I said to Leo, watching as the boy's mother caught up with him and scolded him for running away.

She looked up at us and her face filled with concern. She grabbed the child and hurried away.

'Ah, dammit,' Leo said, and dismissed the sword. 'Wonderful. She'll tell the first policeman she sees and they'll be looking for us.'

'They'll never find us in the crowd,' I said. 'She can't possibly give an accurate enough description of the two of us; we're completely inconspicuous.'

'We should have brought Martin, then we'd be totally invisible,' Leo said. He put his hands in his pockets and kicked at the autumn leaves.

I linked my arm in his. 'Buy him something special while you're here. You can look forward to seeing his face when you give it to him.'

Leo stopped for a moment, then raised his face to the red-orange trees and breathed deeply. 'That's an excellent idea.' He started walking again, dragging me by the arm. 'Come on, let's grab some cash and go shopping.'

'I didn't mean right now!' I said as he pulled me back towards the house.

John and Peta were in the study with Simone, and they called us in before Leo could drag me away to the shops.

'Just need your thoughts on the plan,' John said to me. 'And your information on where these big houses are.'

They had a large map of northwest Wales spread out on the desk and I moved closer to see it.

'Daddy says flying would be a waste of time. The airport's so far away we could drive there faster,' Simone said. 'How primitive is that?'

'You've never lived anywhere except Hong Kong,' I said. 'In some places driving is more efficient.'

'Maybe I should do a gap year and spend some time outside Hong Kong,' she said.

'What's a gap year?' John said.

'Never mind, we're discussing this.' I pointed at the map, then looked around for a marker pen and drew a circle around a landmark. 'This is the manor that belonged to the lord of the island of Anglesey, here next to the ocean.' I circled another area. 'And there's another big house up here, near the beaches.'

Simone shivered. 'Beaches in a cold place like this.'

'Many people can't afford to spend their holidays in luxury resorts,' John said, eyeing her sharply. 'Maybe you should spend a year between high school and university trying to survive and travel on your own income.'

'That's what a gap year is,' Simone said, amused. 'Are those the only two big houses?'

I shrugged. 'Seem to be.'

'We will pay them a small, quiet visit,' John said. He studied the map, then pointed. 'It says this is a castle?'

'Ruined,' I said. 'I did some research on that one: it's uninhabitable. All that remains is the shell of the stone walls; the roof's gone.'

'We will go there anyway.' He rolled the map up. 'We'll leave the day after tomorrow; I'll drive us up in the van. It's a shame we've lost Ben and Tom ...'

Simone dropped her head and gasped.

'People die, Simone,' he said, 'even though we do our best to defend them.'

'I know,' she said, her voice thick. 'I just really liked Tom.'

'How much?' he said sharply.

She looked up to glare at him. 'Well, I wasn't madly in love with him, if that's what you're thinking,' she said defiantly, 'but I really liked talking to him. We had a lot in common.' She wiped her eyes. 'He died, and he was only a year older than me.'

'You have the opportunity to learn the secrets of Immortality, See Mun, take it,' John said, his tone gentle. 'Learn from me.'

'And watch people around me die for the rest of my long existence?' she said sadly. 'Maybe I don't want that.'

'Of course you do,' he said, slipping a rubber band around the map. 'Peta, would you want Immortality?'

'Only if Paul achieved it as well,' Peta said without hesitation.

'See?' Simone said.

Leo tapped on the open door. 'Are you all done? Because I want to borrow Emma.'

'Go with them and help Leo buy something for your brother,' John said to Simone.

He focused on her for a moment and she concentrated back, then nodded.

'Not allowed,' I said. 'Talk out loud.'

'I just asked her to keep an eye on you, Emma,' John said. 'And you please keep an eye on her. I have paperwork to attend to — Leonard is coming to sort out the deeds with me.' He nodded to Leo. 'Lion.'

'My Lord,' Leo said, then grinned at us. 'Put some walking shoes on, ladies, we're going to White City.'

'Oh geez,' I said softly as I followed him down the stairs.

* * *

We were laughing as we climbed the stairs from the basement carrying all the shopping bags. Simone stopped and concentrated. 'Dinner's ready, we should go straight there.'

'Good, I'm starving,' Leo said.

We stacked the shopping bags against the wall and headed to the dining room. John and Franklin were seated at the table, along with my sister's ex-husband, Leonard, who acted as our UK lawyer.

'Good, you're here,' John said. 'Someone make Paul and Peta sit with us. They seem to think they're not part of the family.'

Peta came in and placed a dish covered with a warming lid on the table. 'And I've kept saying that it's not because of that; it's because the princesses were late and we had to keep their food warm for them.'

Simone put her hands on her hips. 'And what's wrong with being a princess?'

'Nothing,' Leo said. 'I'm Princess Leo for the rest of the night. I deserve a promotion.'

'Exactly,' Peta said.

'Come and sit with us and I'll tell you what I bought, Princess Peta,' Simone said.

'As soon as we bring the rest of your food up,' Peta said, and went out.

'Leonard, do you know Franklin?' I said as I filled my bowl.

'My family have known about Franklin since we were first retained. I think it's close on three hundred years,' Leonard said.

'They've been a huge help in my dealings with the local council,' Franklin said. 'The number of times they've stopped my house from being torn down and the cemetery redeveloped — well.' He raised his glass of water to Leonard. 'I appreciate it. Thank you.'

'Still couldn't get around the compulsory visibility vest and OH&S nonsense,' Leonard said. 'If we could get you out of that, it would be a miracle worthy of His Lordship here.'

'Not even I can overcome the dark forces of Occupational Health and Safety,' John said, his voice deep and powerful.

Leo gaped at him.

'What?' John said.

'I don't know which is more scary,' Simone said. 'Him having a sense of humour or him being dark and grim all the time.'

'I like to think I'm scary either way,' John said with satisfaction.

After dinner, we went down to the basement to sort out Franklin's sleeping arrangements.

Franklin studied the MG with interest. 'I hope you've been taking that out for runs. It's far too special to be left locked up down here.'

'So are you,' I said.

Franklin smiled. 'It's for the best, believe me, Miss Emma.'

He followed John to the corner, where a three-metre-square cell had been constructed. Three of the walls were brick and concrete, the fourth was iron bars from floor to ceiling. It looked like a medieval dungeon, complete with manacles chained to the wall.

I pointed at the chains. 'You do not need to use those.'

'No, I don't,' John said, and unlocked the door.

Franklin bobbed his head, went inside and looked around with satisfaction. 'Hasn't changed at all, and thank your manservant for bringing my little bag in here.' His expression changed. 'Um ... have you had a power point fitted? I need to plug in my laptop to check my email. Does the house have wi-fi?'

'I'll find you an extension cable and give you the password for the wi-fi,' John said. 'Use it as much as you like. How's the phone signal down here?'

Franklin pulled a mobile phone out of his pocket. 'One bar.' He touched the phone to the bars of the cell. 'Ah, there we go, two bars … plenty.'

'You are far too intelligent and self-controlled to need this,' I said.

Franklin moved closer to the bars and fixed his dark eyes on me. 'You say that now, madam, but you are powerful and smell fresh and full of life. And in the middle of the night, if I was in a guest room, I don't think I would be able to resist you.'

I gestured towards John. 'He would destroy you in his sleep.'

John closed the door of the cell and turned the key. 'That is why he's in here.'

Franklin bowed slightly to him. 'I thank you, my Lord. Now, if you don't mind, I think I'll get some sleep.' He changed to True Form and flopped to lie on the bed. 'And please don't forget that extension cord — I have a lovely little thing in Russia that I email all the time. She thinks I will send her a lot of money so she can come here.'

'She's a fifty-year-old man,' I said.

He chuckled. 'My favourite flavour.'

Upstairs, John went to find an extension cable. Leonard was still sorting through the documents in the office, chatting with Leo and Simone.

'You should be gone already,' I said.

'Having too much fun here,' he said. 'Actually, I was wondering if you'd like to walk down the street for a pint and share family stories? I know a fabulous little pub just two blocks away — how about it?'

'I'd love to,' I said. 'Just let me get a jacket. Leo? Simone?'

'I'll come too, just to keep an eye on you,' Leo said.

'If you don't mind, I'll skip it,' Simone said. 'I hate the taste of beer. I'm taking a book to bed.'

'You're too young to be drinking beer!' Leo said, shocked.

'I'm nearly eighteen, that's the drinking age here,' Simone said. She pushed Leo playfully. 'You don't know everything about everything, Mister Immortal.'

'I don't know anything about anything,' Leo said. 'Go to bed, Simone.'

She put her arms up and he bent so she could hug him and kiss him on the cheek. They squeezed each other affectionately, and she went out.

* * *

The cool autumn air on the street was invigorating. The pub was one of Leonard's favourites: a genuinely old establishment, with softly glowing brass and dark wood fittings worn smooth from many years of use. Leo sat at the bar and people-watched while Leonard and I shared a booth. He had beer and I had a mineral water.

'He doesn't need to sit there, you know,' Leonard said, indicating Leo with his glass.

'He knows we have family in common that we want to share,' I said.

Leonard studied his lager. 'That we do.' He looked up at me and his intelligent features were subdued. 'Do you hear much from them?'

'I get an email about once a week. They all seem to be doing well.'

'The boys email me,' Leonard said. He shrugged and turned the glass in his hands. 'Jen doesn't. I guess she's too busy with her new life.'

'Andrew's coming along; it's good to hear he's back at school,' I said. I felt a shot of remorse; everything Andrew had suffered was because of me.

'Don't blame yourself,' Leonard said, seeing my face. 'We had a wonderful time living on the Celestial Plane. It was a perfect life. Things happen. I just …' He ran the back of his hand over his tear-filled eyes. 'I miss the boys, you know?'

'I miss them all.'

He took a big gulp of beer. 'Jen used to drive me nuts. Nothing was ever good enough, everything had to be perfect — *her* version of perfect. And now I don't know what to do without her.' He sniffled, pulled a handkerchief out of his pocket and wiped his nose. 'How am I supposed to compete with a god?'

'Come and live on the Mountain with us,' I said. 'We're losing our legal advisor; Gold's resigned to be a full-time parent. He and his wife are moving to Hong Kong so she can pursue a law degree and take over from him when she's qualified.'

'She wants to do that after seeing what Gold puts up with?'

'She says anything's better than being stuck at home with the twins. She hates it, even with domestic help; and he loves being with the kids, so they decided to swap. It'll take her a few years to attain her degree, so we're without a good full-time lawyer until she does.'

'Thanks for the offer, Emma, but ...' Leonard smiled slightly at his beer. 'It's all a little too Chinese for me up there, you know? No good curries, no good lager, all the buildings are so ... pointy.' He shrugged. 'And I have parents and a sister here who need me. But I really do appreciate the offer.'

'Anyone new in your life?' I said.

He shook his head. 'I've done my dash, I've had my family, that's all for me.' He gulped his beer. 'It was inevitable, really; Jen and I'd been drifting apart for a while. I was wrapped up in my work, she was wrapped up in hers — and then Greg shows up, all glowing and powerful. How am I supposed to compete with that?'

'I hope you find someone, Leonard. You're far too good a person to be left alone and sad like this.'

'Ah, you're very kind, Miss Donahoe,' he said. He checked his watch. 'I promised Mr Chen I wouldn't keep you out too long — oh.'

Leo had come to the booth. I wriggled over to let him sit next to me.

'John says we should be getting back, Emma.' He nodded to Leonard. 'Sorry, man.'

'What?' I said. 'Since when did he think he could order me home like a teenager?'

'Something has him seriously spooked,' Leo said. 'He's been checking with me constantly the whole time we've been here. He's been driving me nuts. It's all I can do to stop him from coming down here and guarding you himself.' He tapped the table with the bottom of his glass. 'He was doing it while we were out shopping, but now it's dark he's ten times worse. He ordered me to tell you to come home.' He turned to Leonard. 'As a sworn Retainer, if he orders me to do something, I have no choice but to obey.' He ran one hand over his bald head. 'It's not like him to pull rank on me like this though. I have to wonder what the hell's going on?'

'Has anything happened back at the house?' I said.

Leo silently contacted John, then shook his head.

'That telepathy business is so useful,' Leonard said.

'Mobile phones do exactly the same thing without the invasion of privacy,' Leo said. He stiffened. 'He's doing it again!'

'Can't you block him?' Leonard said.

'Not as long as I'm a Retainer.' He nudged me with his elbow. 'Save me, Miss Donahoe. Please rescue me from the big bad man.'

'I will,' I said grimly. 'Tell him he's getting an earful when I get home.'

Leo concentrated, then grinned broadly. 'Oh, now he shuts up.'

'Go home to your man, Emma,' Leonard said. 'Treasure what you have with him.'

'Don't worry, I do.'

We all rose, and Leonard shook Leo's hand.

'Remember, I want an invitation to your wedding, sir. The two of you are an example of devotion that many of us should strive to emulate, and I want to be part of the celebration.'

'I'll make sure of it,' Leo said. 'But unless the Jade Emperor changes his mind, the best we'll ever have is a half-assed piece of paper saying we're in a relationship.'

Outside the pub, Leonard hailed a passing cab. He waved goodbye as it drove off.

Leo linked his arm in mine and we walked through the cool autumn evening.

'Thinks he can order me home, does he?' I grumbled under my breath.

'Let him have it,' Leo said, amused.

We passed an all-night pharmacy, its lights still bright.

'I need to get something really quickly,' I said. 'Can you wait out here for me?'

'Sure,' Leo said, and leaned on the window, sticking his hands in his pockets. He hadn't moved when I came back out a few minutes later.

'Got everything you need?' he said.

I nodded. 'Let's go home. It's been a very long day.'

'That it has.'

* * *

John was waiting for us in the entrance, his hair a bedraggled mess. He looked like he'd been pacing in circles. I glared up at him.

He shrugged. 'There's something I need to tell you.'

My heart fell. 'What's happened?'

'Nothing. Nothing's happened.' He gestured helplessly. 'Come upstairs, we need to talk.'

'Do you need me any more?' Leo said.

'Dismissed,' John said, and turned to go up the stairs, his shoulders hunched.

Tell me later if you can, Leo said.

I nodded and followed John.

18

'How definite is it?' I said, sitting on the bed as John paced the room.

'Absolutely,' he said. 'You've had them too, you know what it's like. Bringing you here was a horrible mistake.'

'I should go back.'

'Not alone. I can't come with you; the mission's started, I'm committed.'

'Leo can guard me.'

He made a soft noise of dismissal and began pacing again.

'He's the finest human warrior of his generation, you said it yourself.'

'He's just one man, Immortal or not. I'll arrange for a squad to come over here and escort you home.' He stopped and unfocused. 'We're already too far. This cannot be avoided. I will ask them to come anyway; we can't give in to this.'

He smoothed his hair into a ponytail, felt for the hair tie, then realised it was gone. 'Stupid hair.' He plonked to sit on the bed next to me. 'If I didn't have my oath laid out before us, I don't know what I'd do. As it is, something very bad is coming for us and things will be worse before they're better.'

'That's the story of our lives,' I said. I leaned into him and he put his arm around my shoulders. 'I'll stay close to you and we'll see what we can do about minimising the danger. Is that an option? Are there choices — some better than others?'

He unfocused again, then shook his head. 'You are too close for me to see. All I can see is the huge mistake I've made bringing you here.'

'Gods don't make mistakes.'

He fell backwards to lie on the bed, staring at the ceiling. 'This one makes more than most.'

I fell backwards and lay next to him. 'That's what I love about you. You're so strange and elemental and so human and fallible — all at the same time.'

'I think you're more attracted to the strange and elemental,' he said. 'The human and fallible I can do without.'

I pulled myself on top of him and straddled him. 'Take me swimming when we get to Wales.'

'The place where we're staying doesn't have a pool and it's too cold …'

'No, *swimming*.'

'Oh.' He smiled slightly. 'I didn't think of that. The sea will be cold and clean and full of life.' He breathed deeply and his chest moved underneath me. 'New waters to explore — what a wonderful idea.' He patted my back. 'Thank you. Now, if you don't mind, I'm tired and a good night's sleep would do both of us good.'

I slipped my hands under his T-shirt and his smile disappeared as he watched me. I ran my hands over his chest, then down to trace his ribs and abs, hard under my fingertips. He barely moved at all, hardly breathing. I pushed his shirt up over his chest, bent over him and touched my mouth to him, tasting the freshness of the salt of the sea. I pulled back to see how dark his eyes had gone.

'Don't stop,' he breathed, slipping his hands inside my shirt and onto my waist.

I pulled the T-shirt over his head and he flopped back, his long black hair spreading around him. I straightened on top of him, enjoying his reaction as I ran my fingertips over his golden skin.

I bent over him and put my elbows on either side of his head, my face close to his. 'So many years,' I said. 'So many years I dreamed of doing this. I cannot get enough of you.'

He didn't reply, just lifted my shirt over my head and tossed it aside. His expression became intense as he slipped my bra off and cupped my breasts, running his fingers over my nipples the same way I'd done to him when he was female. I arched my back in response and he went rigid beneath me.

He gently levered me off him and slid me down so we were side by side, and ran his hands across my back as he kissed me. I lost myself in the feeling of his mouth on mine, moving over me. He ran his hand down my back and into my jeans, then grimaced at their tightness. He reached around to undo them, working at the zip, and I pressed myself into him, skin to skin. He pulled back and shook his head, frustrated, as he realised he couldn't pull my jeans off with me lying on them. His jeans were looser than mine and I slipped my hand inside. He shivered and took a quick breath, then stopped moving again, studying my face. He gave up on my zip and put his hands on my behind, pulling me into him. I undid his pants and felt for him. His eyes went wide and his body went rigid.

'This ... is ... not ... fair,' he said through gritted teeth. He pulled at the side of my jeans, trying to work them down and not succeeding. 'Modern fabrics.' He made a soft sound of frustration, then gasped again when I slid my hand over him. 'Unfair!'

He gently thrust into my hand, his eyes unfocused and his hands pulling me into him, running up and down my back. He moved his mouth next to my ear and whispered, 'How much do you like these jeans?'

'Don't you dare, these are my favourites.'

'If you don't have them off in two minutes they'll be your destroyed favourites,' he growled.

I got off the bed and quickly slipped my jeans off while he watched me with appreciation. I took his hand and pulled him towards me, then led him into the bathroom. He kicked his pants off as he followed me.

As we went through the bathroom door, I stopped and turned to admire him. He walked past me and tossed his hair back over his shoulder, knowing what it did for me. I closed the door and started the taps to run a hot bath for us.

'Allow me,' he said.

The muscles rippled over his back as he raised one hand and the bath filled with warm clear water, steam lifting from it into the chilly evening. The water rose in a cube above the edge of the bath and nearly to the ceiling.

He put his hands around my waist, and I held his shoulders to steady myself as he lifted me into the water so I was suspended inside the cube. He released me, but continued to hold my hand as he floated into the water next to me. He pulled me close and buried his face into the side of my throat as I wrapped my legs around him, and his hair floated around us. Millions of tiny bubbles filled the water, brushing over us as we spun slowly in the water, moving together and lost in the blissful sensation of being one.

* * *

The next morning when I woke, the sun was already shining through the curtains and John was gone from the bed beside me. A note was on the pillow in his flowing

237

Chinese script. I smiled slightly and tossed it back onto the pillow — he'd forgotten that on the Earthly I couldn't read most of it. I'd picked out 'I walk' and 'kung fu' in Chinese, then 'Simone' in English among the other characters, so I'd worked out the gist of it.

I went to the dining room, but it was deserted. I headed down into the kitchen and found Leo and Paul sharing a pot of coffee at the four-seater table. I put some bread in the toaster, grabbed a mug out of the cupboard and sat with them.

'Simone and John are out having a run and a training session on the common,' Leo said. 'Little miss is in the middle of the park showing off her martial arts.'

'Good,' I said. 'Anything that makes her practise more.'

'What's the plan for today?' he said.

'I'm going with John to Leonard's office to have the documents signed and witnessed.'

'Good luck with that; sounds *fascinating*.'

I smiled smugly. 'And you're escorting Simone for the morning.'

'No way. She's nearly eighteen years old —'

'Hi Leo, we're back,' Simone said from the doorway. 'I'll have a shower and get cleaned up, and we can go to the Science Museum. Morning, Emma.'

'You want to go there again?' Leo said, incredulous.

'It's just been renovated and reopened,' she said. 'I have to see what they've done. It's a shame none of the little ones can come along, they'd love it.'

'How about we fly across the Channel to France and have a wander around there?' Leo said.

She thought about it for a moment, then brightened. 'After the Science Museum, if we still have time.' She turned and ran up the stairs to her room.

'Want to swap?' Leo said. 'Suddenly a morning in Leonard's office sounds deeply interesting.'

I leaned back with satisfaction. 'Nope, John wants to keep me close.'

'What was that about yesterday? Can you tell me?'

I shrugged and tried to brush it off. 'He just had a bit of a premonition — god stuff. He thinks it's a bad idea for me to be here, and he's bringing a squad over to take me home.'

Leo concentrated for a moment, then let his breath out as if he'd been hit. 'Damn, it was a seriously bad idea bringing you here.' He bent forward and his face screwed up with pain. 'Shee–*it*, that hurts. God*damn*! Ow.' He rubbed his forehead with one hand. 'Every single damn time.'

'Does it hurt the others as much as that?' I said, concerned.

'Martin says the bigger you are the less painful it is.' He massaged his temples. 'Remind me not to do that again. How long before the squad gets here? Something really terrible is going to happen.'

'They couldn't get a flight for a couple of days. They'll meet us in Wales.' I hesitated. 'How terrible?'

'Dunno, just ... bad.' He frowned. 'Sorry.'

'I'll stick close to you or John and keep alert until they take me home.'

'What if this thing we're seeing is *because* you're going home?'

'Yeah, we can second-guess ourselves for hours if we like,' I said. 'All of that is beside the point, because he will Raise and marry me. The rest is detail.'

'You're absolutely right.' He smiled, but was obviously still concerned.

Simone appeared in the doorway and he rose to put his coffee mug in the sink. 'Anything you want from France if we ever get there?'

'Trust me, my friend,' I said, seeing Simone's excited face, 'you won't.'

John and I arrived at Leonard's office and went in to speak to the receptionist sitting behind her big mahogany reception desk.

'John Chen for Leonard,' John said.

The receptionist called it through, then put the phone down. 'Mr Black isn't in yet. Would you like to speak to one of the other partners?'

'Just a sec,' John said.

He pulled his mobile phone out and called Leonard. Leonard didn't answer.

'No reason to panic at this early stage,' I said. 'He could just be stuck in traffic.'

John concentrated, contacting Leonard telepathically, then turned back to the receptionist. 'Which other partners are here?'

'Mr Black's sister, Mrs Gration, is in,' the receptionist said.

'Could I see her?'

'Certainly, sir. Just take a seat and I'll call —'

Leonard's sister, Lindsay, appeared in a doorway and waved us inside. She was much shorter than Leonard, with darker skin and dyed blonde hair. 'I heard you, Mr Chen, come on through.'

'That's extremely rude!' I said to John as he followed Lindsay into her office.

'I don't mind at all, it's all part of the magic,' Lindsay said. 'Leonard seems to have dropped off the face of the planet, but he may just be hungover.' She closed the office door, gestured for us to sit and said softly, 'Since the divorce he's been hungover more and more.'

'That's sad to hear,' I said.

'I am concerned about him,' John said. 'Could you call him again?'

'Certainly,' she said, and picked up the phone. She put it to her ear and looked confused for a moment, then her expression cleared. 'Incoming call,' she said to us. 'Yes, of course I'll take it. Hello, this is Lindsay Gration. Yes, I'm Leonard Black's sister.'

She went blank for a long minute, then dropped the receiver on the desk and put both hands over her mouth, wide-eyed and silent.

John jumped up, reached over the desk and picked up the receiver. 'Hello?' he said. 'You said that Mr Black was in an accident?' He listened. 'Which hospital is he in?' He scribbled the address on a piece of paper. 'We're on our way.'

Lindsay broke down into heaving sobs. She went to the window and leaned her forehead on the pane, away from us.

'Single vehicle accident. Ran into a tree,' John said. *He was twice the blood alcohol limit.*

'He only had one beer last night, this is not possible,' I said, numb with shock.

'He may have stopped somewhere on the way home,' John said.

Lindsay tapped her forehead on the window in time with her words. 'Stupid, stupid man,' she said through the sobs. 'Stupid man.'

'Is he dead?' I mouthed.

John shook his head. *Coma. Looks bad.*

* * *

Lindsay's husband met us at the hospital. John and I weren't permitted to join them in the intensive care ward — it was close family only.

'Did they tell you where the accident occurred?' I asked John as we headed back to the car.

'I was about to ask you if you were willing to come with me to the scene,' he said.

'Let's go.'

The accident site was on a quiet stretch of road between two steep banks. There was an oil slick covered in sawdust, a long pair of skid marks, torn-up grass in two long tracks, and a splintered tree. We pulled over next to the tree and got out. John walked up and down the road, carefully avoiding the passing traffic. He touched the oil slick, then brought his fingers to his face and rubbed them together. His expression went grim.

'As I suspected,' he said, holding up his black-stained fingers.

'Demons tried to kill him?'

John wiped his hand on his pants and nodded. 'They destroyed a couple of demons on the road and the essence worked like an oil slick. He didn't have a chance, even if he was doing the speed limit.'

I took his arm. 'You have to tell Greg right now. The rest of the family might be in danger.'

He shook his head. 'I told Greg back at Leonard's office. That was the first thing I did.'

My breath came out of me in a long gasp. 'Oh, dear Lord, poor Andrew — after all he's been through, now his father's in a coma. He and Colin have to be told.'

'They've already been told,' John said. He dropped his head and walked back to the car. 'They don't know that demons did it.'

'Don't tell them,' I said.

'Don't worry, I won't.'

A cargo net of thick rope fell over John, the heavy weights at its edges rattling as they hit the road. He was too strong to be stunned by the impact, but he fell sideways onto the grass beneath it. A small group of extremely high-level demons in human form, all young, strong,

short-haired British men, landed on grass around us —
six of them, each about level eighty. One of them grew to
its True Form and grabbed me from behind, holding one
clawed hand over my mouth, the tips of its claws piercing
the skin of my cheek.

Don't fight them, I have this, John said.

He struggled ineffectually with the net and the demons
crouched around him, working as a team to pull on a rope
that closed its edges.

'You cannot hold me, you stupid creatures,' he said, still
pushing at the rope net. 'Let me *go!*'

Ruse. Don't move.

The demons closed in on him as he obviously tried to
work his way out of the net and failed. When they were
close enough to touch him, he stopped moving for a second.
A blast of freezing gas burst from him, a sphere of ice-blue
cloud two metres across. The demons closest to him were
covered in ice and exploded into a cloud of grey dust; only
two were out of range.

The demon holding me tightened its grip, pushing its
claws deeper into my face. 'I suggest you stop now, or your
lady here will be sliced.'

John stood and the net disintegrated into grey powder.
The two demons near him hung back, hesitating. He
glowered at the demon holding me.

Energy into it on the count of three, he said. *One,
two ... three.*

He sent a blast of cold air at the demon holding me,
and I injected chi directly into its abdomen where it pressed
against my back. The combination of the cold and the
energy split the demon in half at waist-height and the two
pieces fell onto the grass. I put my hand to my cheek and it
came away covered in blood.

John straightened and took full, huge Celestial Form in
his robes and armour, with his hair writhing around his

head. He summoned Seven Stars and loaded the blade with his chakra energy, taking his time to make each indentation glow separately with its own coloured light as the demons watched with horrified awe. He backed away so both demons were in front of him, raised the sword slightly out to the side and nodded formally to them.

'Good morning, demonkind. You may have heard of me. I am the Dark Emperor of the Northern Heavens, Celestial Master of the Nine Mysteries.'

'Oh shit,' one of the demons said.

'Ah, you have heard of me,' John said. 'Tell me who sent you and why, and I will spare you.'

'Deal,' one of the demons said. 'Lord Semias is our master.'

'No way,' I said softly. They ignored me.

'Why was Leonard attacked?'

'To bring you here so we could capture you and take you to our master. Our master believes you aren't as dangerous as his associate says.'

John smiled slightly and conjured his dark blue-purple aura. Waves of almost invisible colour passed from his head to his feet, making a soft bass thrum each time they touched the ground. The grass died in a perfect circle around him, withering and blowing away to leave bare dirt.

'Am I?' he said.

'Shit, yeah,' the demon said. 'What is that stuff? It's like ... the end of the world.'

'That's because it is,' John said. 'I could lose my temper and destroy everything.' He lowered the sword. 'I gave you my word you would be spared. Go back to your master and tell him to call me.' He told the demon the number. 'Tell him we have much to speak about.'

'You got it,' the demon said, and both of them disappeared.

John dismissed the sword and strode to me. 'Are you all right? Let me heal that.'

'Put the energy away first,' I said, quickly backing away.

He stopped and his face went grim as he dismissed the energy. 'I haven't done that in a very long time.' He took my hand in his and put his other hand on my damaged cheek. 'I am so sorry.'

'Just a flesh wound,' I said, and gasped as his cold healing power ran through the nerves in my cheeks, making them sting. 'That really hurts!'

'Sorry, I'll stop. The healing is more powerful in Celestial Form.' He changed back to human form. 'I'll take it slower. Ready?'

'Give me a moment,' I said, and lit up the pressure points. 'Okay, go.'

He closed his eyes slightly and his expression went serene. The healing energy was cooler and fresher this time, more of a tingling than the painful cold.

He snapped out of it and examined my cheek. 'There's still a mark there, but nothing that won't disappear in a week or so. Nothing else hurt? That demon was a big one.'

'No, it was just holding me. I think they wanted to use me as a hostage and take you.'

'There's obviously some conflict at Demon Headquarters. Who is Lord Semias? You recognised the name.'

'Druid master of a Celestial city. Definitely not someone I expected to be working with demons.'

'You can tell me more about it when we get home. It appears we have the advantage: he didn't know how powerful I am. He's in for an unpleasant lesson if he ever comes to face me himself.'

'You shouldn't have intimidated them like that. It might have been better to pretend to be weak and let them take you,' I said.

'I was going to, but they hurt you. And when that happens ... what's that English expression? All the bets are cancelled?'

'All bets are off?'

'That's the one.' He concentrated for a moment. 'Simone and Leo are fine; the demons targeted you and me. Interesting.'

He pulled me in for a fierce hug, then released me and ran one hand down the side of my face. 'If I did not have the Jade Emperor's Edict hanging over me, I would take you home right now.'

I wrapped my arms around him and put my head on his chest. 'You're the Darkness That Swallows All, the Celestial Master of the Eight Mysteries. I'm safe while I'm with you.'

'Nine Mysteries.'

'Eight. You haven't mastered Simone,' I said as we went back to the car.

'She still confuses the living hell out of me,' he said.

'She's your daughter, that's her job.'

* * *

Simone and Leo came running down the stairs when we walked into the entrance hall.

'Is Leonard really dead?' Simone said, distraught.

'No, he's alive,' John said. 'But the demons here are after us.'

He swayed slightly and put his hand on my shoulder to lean on me.

'Are you okay, Daddy?' Simone said. 'You're as pale as anything.'

'I'm fine,' he said, and toppled, nearly pulling me down with him.

Leo caught him before he hit the floor. He held him prone and turned him face up. I put my hand on John's forehead, then quickly pulled it away. It was freezing cold.

'Can you take him upstairs without getting burnt?' I asked Leo.

'Burnt?' Simone said.

'He's as cold as dry ice,' Leo said. 'If I move fast I'll be okay.'

'Go.'

Leo glanced at me. 'Oh, well done, giving an Immortal an order. Now I can't do it.'

'Leo, take him upstairs,' Simone said.

'Good enough,' Leo said, and he and John disappeared.

I slapped my forehead with my palm. 'I keep forgetting.'

'I never realised how much we relied on you to organise stuff,' Simone said with humour. 'I'll have a serious talk with the Jade Emperor when we're home. We need you to boss us around.'

'You manage,' I said as we went up the stairs to check on John.

Leo was pulling the covers over him when we arrived in the room. John was unconscious, and his skin was so cold that a mist of condensation rose off him.

'Out cold,' Leo said, standing back and studying him. 'In more ways than one. Martin wants to know what happened to get him like this?' He looked sideways at me. 'Or do we want to know?'

'Ew, Leo,' Simone said.

'We were attacked by a group of level eighties and he showed off,' I said. I sat next to him and put my hand on his arm; I could still feel the cold through the blankets. 'He's never been this bad before, I hope he'll be all right.'

'Martin ...' Leo said, and trailed off, obviously listening. He nodded a few times. 'Martin says he should be fine, just leave him. This is what exhaustion looks like.'

'Why is he exhausted?' Simone said, touching his face. She ran her hand down his cheek, obviously not bothered by the cold. 'He hasn't been overdoing it.'

'In his current state,' I said, 'I think he has.'

'What current state?' Leo said sharply. 'Those wounds are healing nicely.'

'His Serpent's half-dead.'

'And this half is feeling it too?'

'Don't let it get around,' I said. 'Nobody needs to know how weak he is.'

'Marvellous,' Leo said. 'Is he as weak now as he was back then?'

'No, not nearly,' Simone said. 'Being able to take True Form makes a huge difference for him.'

'Then why doesn't he do it more often?'

'Because when he does,' I said, moving my hand away from the cold cloud over his blankets, 'he feels exactly what the Serpent's experiencing and has a powerful urge to go to it.'

'That bad?'

'I've seen it,' I said. 'It's in terrible pain, burning hot and suffering horribly.'

Simone made a small choking sound and went out.

* * *

The street market in Wan Chai was blacked out, all of the electric lights that usually made the stalls daytime-bright gone, and people were using torches and Mid-Autumn Festival lanterns to make their wares visible. The ground was slippery with a wash of blood, and the discarded leaves of vegetables and other rubbish added to the smell of putrefaction. I would need to rinse my scales off after slithering through this filth.

The stallholders were all demons; a collection of misshapen faces with bulging eyes followed my progress through the market. A butcher, his apron covered in blood, merrily used his gigantic cleaver to roughly chop a human arm into bite-sized segments. He scooped the meat into a plastic bag, handed it to a Snake Mother, then scraped his wooden chopping block clean with the chopper, adding to the already large depression in the blood-saturated wood.

I wandered through the stalls, looking for John and Simone and the baby. A mobile phone stall was brilliantly lit, its green and blue flashing lights reflecting eerily off the plastic rain-walls around it. I couldn't use a mobile phone as a snake; I didn't have any hands. But I needed to find them, and I needed to find the baby.

I felt the coldness in the air behind me: something really big was approaching. I turned and stopped. A massive dark form, roughly human-shaped, towered over me, at least as tall as the second-storey windows above with their rusting metal signs hanging over the road. I couldn't move backwards as snake, so I turned and ran, but the dark coldness pursued me, passing through the overhanging signs as if they weren't there. I rushed through the slippery streets, the dark cold following me.

I gasped in a huge gulp of air and saw the dark shape hovering over the couch I was lying on. I leaped and landed across the room from it in a defensive stance.

'I'm sorry, I woke you,' John said.

I relaxed and bent to breathe deeply, resting my hands on my knees. 'You scared the living daylights out of me.'

He sat on the arm of the couch and fingered the blankets tossed on the cushions. 'I woke up and you weren't there. Why are you sleeping in here? Is something wrong?'

I crawled onto the couch and sat cross-legged next to him. 'You overdid it with those Western demons and passed out. Your skin was so cold that it burned.'

He raised his hand in front of his face and studied it. 'Really?'

'Yes. I'm surprised the bed isn't saturated from condensation.'

'So that's what that was. I woke and suddenly I was back to the time when Simone used to creep in with us and wet the bed.'

'Us? She never crept in with ...' I understood what he was saying. 'Michelle.'

'Yes. Michelle was horrified and wanted to take her to a doctor. I tried to convince her that Simone would grow out of it, but she didn't believe me. She never saw me proved right.' He put his hand on my shoulder, a light touch. 'The bed's dry and warm now and I'm not cold any more.' He brushed his hand down my arm. 'Will you come back?'

I snuggled into him and he wrapped his arm around me. 'Of course. It's very comforting waking up next to you when I have bad dreams like that.'

He went still. 'Bad dreams like what?'

I made my tone light and careless. 'Oh, the usual thing. Being pursued by demons, being chased.'

'I didn't know. I'm making you do too much.'

'Those sorts of stress dreams are perfectly normal; even people who aren't snakes dealing with demons have them. At least I don't have to put up with "naked in public" dreams; in most of them I'm in snake form and it doesn't matter.'

'Human brains are very strange.'

'Hey,' I said, jabbing him with my finger, 'I'm not the one who soaked the bedclothes. And Simone would kill you if she knew you told me that.'

He squeezed me. 'Only if you tell her. Come back to bed. We have a long trip tomorrow.'

'With pleasure.'

19

I was woken by scrabbling sounds in the ceiling. There was a thump and the light fitting above me rattled, sending a tiny trail of dust onto the bed. I rose, wrapped a robe around me, and trotted up the narrow ladder stairs to the attic. Paul was standing at the door watching as John worked his way through the boxes and suitcases stored there.

'Here are the posters,' John said with satisfaction. 'Where are the …? Never mind, found them.' He flipped a suitcase open and pulled out a pair of jeans. 'I do believe I'm bigger in this form. These may not fit me.'

'You cannot be serious!' Simone said behind me.

John held the jeans up. 'They're still good.'

'They're like a metre wide at the bottom,' she said, horrified. 'What are they, a relic from the sixties or something?'

'Early seventies,' he said. He dropped them and rummaged in the case, then held up a purple and green tie-dyed T-shirt with a large peace symbol on the front. 'How about this?'

'What, you're going to Wales in the guise of an ageing hippie?' she said with scorn.

Paul looked from Simone to John, then leaned on the doorway, crossed his arms and grinned.

Simone glared at him. 'What?'

'Yes,' John said, pulling out some more T-shirts and a brown suede jacket with fringing along the arms. He glanced up at Paul. 'Where's the van? You said it would be here.'

'They promised it would be,' Paul said. 'I told them my job's at stake if they don't have it here today. I'll go check on it.' He went down the stairs.

'Did I really wear anything this bright?' John said, studying a T-shirt in shades of blue and green. 'This looks like something the Dragon would like.' He glanced down at the case. 'Not a single black anything in here. Oh, I remember.' He smiled up at me. 'Black jeans weren't invented yet; I had to make do with blue. I tried dyeing them myself but it just wrecked them. I suppose I can wear the black ones I have now with these T-shirts.'

'Wait,' Simone said, holding a hand out towards him. 'Did you say yes?'

'Yes, I'm going as an ageing hippie. The demons are looking for a Chinese Dark God of War, his black bodyguard, his half-Chinese daughter and his,' he looked at me, 'excuse the term, it's what they see, not me — his plain-looking fiancée. They won't be looking for a white ageing hippie, his white ex-boxer turned Buddhist friend, his half-Vietnamese teenage daughter and a gorgeous redhead, all of whom are in Wales to find a magical location for their folk music festival.'

He changed so that he was European, and for a moment his large eyes and big, protruding nose were so out of place that he looked deformed. Then my perception adjusted and he was John again, slightly different.

'Leo will love being a gorgeous redhead,' I said.

'Not Leo, you ...' He saw my face. 'Very funny.'

'Can Leo change that much?' Simone said.

'He's been practising with Ming's help. He can hold it for hours at a time.' John switched back to his Chinese self. 'Would you like to try male form to add to the camouflage?'

Simone concentrated and changed into a feminine-looking male version of herself with short, full hair.

'That absolutely will not work,' I said. 'You'll have hordes of screaming teenage girls following us if you wander around looking like that.'

Simone laughed so hard she lost the shape. She leaned on the wall, unable to breathe, her hand over her eyes. 'It was the first thing I thought of.'

Paul yelled from downstairs. 'The kombi van is here, sir.'

'Good,' John said. 'I suppose we should have something to eat and then go. We can work on the cover story as we travel.' He let his long hair out and tied a tie-dyed bandana around his forehead, then held up a couple of the T-shirts. 'Pink or purple, Emma? Aren't the flowers great?'

Simone's eyes widened. 'A kombi?'

'Ageing hippie,' he said, patting her on the shoulder as he carried an armful of psychedelic T-shirts through the door.

* * *

John drove us himself. Leo couldn't hold the Caucasian shape, stay out of the wheelchair and concentrate on driving all at the same time, so he sat in the back, stiff with tension and trying to distract himself with the newspaper. He'd deliberately made his Caucasian face as ugly as possible, flattening his already broken nose and thickening his features. He covered his speech impediment by removing half his front teeth to finish off the look.

'The cover story is that we're looking to set up a UK version of the Burning Man festival,' John said. 'We need a large field that's on a ley line, magically positive, good fung shui, all of that. A stone circle would make it even better.'

'What do you know about any of that?' Simone said from the other front seat.

'Fung shui?' John glanced sideways at her. 'You're really asking me that?'

'No. Ley lines. Stone circles. Burning Man. That's Western stuff.'

'When I was here doing my PhD in the seventies,' he said, 'I took a year off and studied the hippie lifestyle. I spent a few months in an ashram in Harrow, then moved to a commune in Dorset.' He smiled slightly. 'That was some of my best time here. I didn't have to be something I'm not, and I learned a great deal about Western energy manipulation. It's very different to the way we work; they only have four elements. I tried casting a Wiccan circle, and the other members of the commune could actually see it. Fortunately, they thought it was because of the funky smoke in the room. Didn't try that again.'

'Oh my god, you really are an ageing hippie,' Simone said with quiet horror.

'Tuned in, turned on and dropped out,' he said with satisfaction. He lowered his voice, becoming serious. 'There is something you should know.'

She heard his tone. 'What?'

'They filled you full of heroin in Angkor.'

She dropped her head. 'It was horrible.'

He didn't look away from the road. 'Because of our nature, we can experiment and control our metabolisms. I'm less worried about you than I would be about an ordinary human.'

'Are you sure you should be saying things like this?' I said.

'Yes. While I was living in the commune, people were experimenting with acid. You know what that is, Simone?'

'LSD. Yes,' she said.

He shrugged. 'I'm so powerful, I thought stuff like that shouldn't have much effect on me. I was wrong.'

'What happened?'

'We were working as waiters in the revolving restaurant in the BT tower. One of the other commune members scored a hit of acid on the way there, and shared it with me in the men's bathroom.'

She glanced sharply at him. 'You tried acid?'

'I've tried many things, Simone. I'm old and strange and sometimes ... bored.'

'I really don't think —' I began.

He interrupted me and continued. 'When I took it, I saw things. I saw demons. I thought Jory was a demon and so I defended myself. I killed him and blew up half the tower.'

'What?' Simone said.

'And I've never tried any mind-altering substances since,' John said. 'They're not worth the risk. I suggest that you stay away from things like that as well, particularly after I return your yin. Your own safety isn't at risk, but those around you could suffer.'

'I wouldn't anyway,' she said, watching the road. 'I saw things in Angkor as well, things I never want to see again.'

He took his hand off the gear stick and placed it over hers. She turned her hand over and squeezed his.

'How many died?' she said softly.

'Just Jory, and I didn't even need to cover it up. The police didn't want to file a missing person report on a hippie who lived in a commune.' He smiled slightly and shook his head. 'The IRA claimed responsibility as soon as they heard about it. Everybody believed them; after all, it was a strategic target.'

'Why were you working as a waiter in BT Tower?' Leo said from behind the newspaper.

'Jory told me a Middle Eastern prince with a bunch of gorgeous wives would be there, and I couldn't miss the chance.' John smiled, smug. 'He had to pull his white furry ass up off his chair, kneel and salute a waiter in front of half a dozen of his most class-conscious wives. Shame I didn't have the Polaroid with me at the time.'

Leo barked a short laugh, then his tone changed to concern. 'A stone circle disappeared.' He turned the newspaper around to show us a large photograph of a circle of holes in the ground. 'This is the third one gone missing this year.'

I tapped the stone. 'Did you hear that?'

The stone didn't reply.

'I swear next time that stone ignores us, I'll freeze it and take it into orbit,' John said. 'It's becoming more worthless every day.'

'Cut it some slack, it's old,' I said.

'So am I. I should give you Zara; she's much more diligent.'

'Don't you dare,' Simone said fiercely.

'I rely on this one,' I said.

'But after it dies —'

'Shut *up*, Daddy! Jory died and now you say this. I do not believe you sometimes!' Simone turned away and leaned her forehead on the passenger side window.

'Sorry.'

She stayed with her forehead on the window.

'Simone?' he said.

She didn't reply.

'I truly am sorry. Help me to be more human.' He dropped his voice. 'I need you.'

'And we need the Jade Building Block,' she said.

'Huh?' the stone said. 'Did someone say my name?'

'You're fading, stone,' John said.

'I know,' the stone said.

'What if you're gone and she needs you?'

'You should replace me, my Lord.'

'Not on my watch,' I said. 'We can find a volunteer to back you up, but I'll always wear you as my engagement ring.'

'I'll start looking for someone to help me now,' the stone said. 'We'll have one ready for you as soon as you get home.'

'How active is the network here?' John said. 'Can you communicate?'

'It lags slightly, but I can talk to everybody.'

'Then start making inquiries, because stone circles here have been kidnapped.'

'What?'

'Stone circles are disappearing,' Leo said. He showed the picture to the stone. 'Find out what you can.'

'Right,' the stone said with renewed purpose. 'Let me link into the stone network here and find out what's going on. I'll report back as soon as I have something for you.'

'Good,' John said.

'Oh, and Emma?' the stone said.

'Hmm?'

Its voice softened and filled with affection. 'Thank you.'

'Heh, I like having you as an engagement ring,' I said. 'People ask me if you're "that" stone.'

'People used to ask the Yellow Empress the same thing.'

* * *

After three and a half hours of travel on the motorway, the traffic had thinned until we were one of the few cars on the road. We passed over a large causeway with flat muddy ocean on either side of us.

'We're arriving on the island of Anglesey,' John said. 'Only about twenty more minutes and we'll be on Holy Island.'

'Good, my bum hurts,' Simone said. 'This van is the most uncomfortable thing ever.'

'One of the large houses we talked about is on the coast near here,' I said, watching the green hills pass by.

257

'We'll settle into the inn first and reconnoitre,' John said. 'Leo?'

'No problem at all holding the shape.'

'Good. Stone? Any word?'

'A moment, my Lord.' The stone was quiet, then, 'I have been given a contact on Holy Island. It will meet us in human form in the centre of town for lunch. I suggest I take human form myself to make communication easier.'

'Good idea. One more person will add to our camouflage, and we have an extra room booked anyway,' John said.

'Is that all right, Emma?' the stone said.

'Of course.'

The stone took human form: a tall, slim European man in his mid-sixties with a shock of white hair. He was wearing a pair of jeans, a green turtleneck and short black leather boots. He took one of the spare seats at the back and buckled up, then briskly rubbed his hands through his hair, making it all stand on end.

'Ageing hippie enough for you, Simone?' he said.

Simone leaned her forehead on the window. 'I'm surrounded by old people.'

'I am not a people,' the stone said with dignity. He leaned his elbow on the windowsill, his chin on his hand. 'I wonder if there's a retirement village on the beach here?'

'What on earth for?' Simone said.

The stone glanced at her, his eyes full of mischief. 'Mature British women are completely wild. Absolute powerhouses.'

'The Tiger said that too,' John said.

Simone covered her ears. 'This conversation is stopping *now*!'

'Suit yourself,' the stone said, and grinned into his hand.

We went over another, shorter bridge fifteen minutes later. The road was almost deserted.

'We're crossing onto Holy Island now,' John said.

'It's all farms and ponies,' Simone said with interest. 'Cute little farmhouses.'

John's phone rang.

'Simone, put that on speaker for me,' he said.

'A "please" now and then wouldn't kill you,' she grumbled as she pressed the button.

'Gods don't beg.' He raised his voice. 'Hello?'

'Lord Xuan. It's Lindsay Gration, Leonard's sister.'

John dropped his voice and spoke kindly to her. 'Good morning, Lindsay. How is Leonard?'

'He's still in a coma.' Her voice brightened. 'The doctors are positive he'll recover. We just have to wait and see.'

'That's good to hear. If there's anything I can do to help, just call me.'

'Thanks. There's something you need to know; it might be important.'

'What?'

'The police came around to my house this morning. They're looking for Emma.'

Simone glanced back at me, her expression unreadable.

'Do they think I did it?' I said loudly enough for the phone to catch it.

Lindsay took an audible deep breath. 'They didn't say as much, but it's obvious that they do. They asked me if you held a grudge against Leonard because he was your sister's ex. They also wanted to know where you'd gone. You all disappeared the day after he ...' Her voice faded, then she rallied. 'After he was attacked.'

'Thanks for warning us, Lindsay, we can handle it,' John said. 'You don't need to worry, we can fix everything up. Liaise with my butler, Peta, and call me any time.'

'Thanks, John,' she said, her voice full of tears, and hung up.

'Stone,' John said. He glanced in the rear-view mirror and his voice sharpened. 'Jade Building Block.'

The stone jerked awake from where he had been drowsing in the back seat. 'My Lord.'

'They think Emma tried to kill Leonard. Contact Gold immediately. Have him arrange for records to show that Emma returned to Hong Kong the night before Leonard was attacked. Also have him arrange an Emma double in Hong Kong ready to be questioned if necessary.'

'My Lord,' the stone said, and his eyes unfocused. 'Oh, to hell with this, it's way too hard,' he added, and changed to True Form: a small green stone sitting on the bus seat.

'It's too hard to hold human form while you talk to him?' Simone said, concerned.

'Well, holding a shape as profoundly charismatic as that does take some energy.'

'Charismatic,' Leo said from behind his newspaper. 'Sure. Let's see you run for Chief Executive.'

'Charisma has nothing to do with winning an election in Hong Kong, you know that.'

'People's Congress, then.'

'As I said,' the stone said with dignity, 'I am not a people. Now be quiet, I'm talking to Gold.'

* * *

As we neared Holyhead, the mountain came into view. The shape of it went through me like a flash and I remembered the dream. I was climbing that mountain in snake form and there was blood on top. I needed that blood, my whole body sang for it. Suddenly I could smell the blood of everybody around me — and I craved it. John was deep and powerful, like a vintage red wine, meaty with hints of spice and fruit. Leo was tainted by the large amount of coffee he drank, but strong and rich. The scent of Simone drove me mad — she was light and fresh, full of clean air and green grass, with an icy powerful fizz that bubbled within her. She was too good just to smell and I nearly couldn't control the need to taste the blood singing within her. I closed my eyes, put my head in my hands and slammed my forehead onto my knees, trying to clear the craving. The mountain's shape throbbed inside me and I took deep breaths. That didn't help because I inhaled even more of their scents.

Someone grabbed me, undid my seatbelt and bundled me out of the van. I leaned against its side and filled my lungs with tasteless air.

'Talk to me,' John said.

'I can smell your blood. It smells so good,' I said between gasps. 'Move well away from me.' I banged the back of my head against the side of the van, trying to distract myself. 'Back off!'

'Touch the earth. Touch the sky. Touch your Buddha nature and what makes you who you are,' John said. 'Feel for your yang and take snake form if you need to. I will hide you.'

I reached down within myself and found Kwan Yin's essence, the purity of compassion that would never harm another living thing, and the need for their blood subsided. A passing car slowed, but then roared away. They'd probably seen John's wild hair and lurid T-shirt and decided not to stop.

I bent over my knees and ran my hand over my forehead. 'Holy shit, I'm a freaking vampire.'

'Nope,' Simone said, 'no fangs, and no sparkle.'

'Don't joke about it,' I said. 'My snake form has very nice fangs.'

'Yep, hottest thing about it,' John said. 'Feeling better?'

'I can't go back in the van with all of you.'

'Try doing it as snake,' John said.

'I can't change to snake right now.'

'Yes, you can. Just concentrate; nobody can see you.'

'No, John, I can't risk it.'

'I'll help you. Do you want me to hold you so you don't run to find my Serpent?' He reached out to me and I quickly backed away. 'It's all right; your snake may not be similarly affected.' I continued to back away from him and he stopped, confused. 'It's all right, Emma, your snake may be able to control it. Just bring it out and have a try. I'll help you.'

I was backed up against a tree and I raised my hands. 'Stop, John.'

He kept moving towards me. 'It's all right, I'm here. I'll help you change.'

'John, stop. I can't change when I might be pregnant!'

He stopped and stared at me.

'The test you bought the other night was positive?' Leo said. He rushed to me and pulled me into a huge hug, dragging me off my feet. 'Damn girl, that's great news!' He put me down gently and backed off, concerned. 'I didn't squeeze you too tight, did I?'

'No, I'm fine. The test was negative, but it might be too early to tell. I have to be careful until I'm sure one way or the other ...'

'And a human baby can't live in your snake body,' John said, understanding. His face went slack. 'A human baby? Another one?' Realisation dawned on him and it was wonderful to see. 'We're going to have a baby?'

He came to me and lifted me the same way Leo had. 'This is wonderful!' He spun me around, then gently lowered me, gazing into my eyes. He brushed one hand over my hair. 'You have to be careful you don't change to snake. And no energy work.'

'Like I said, John, the test was negative, but it might be too early to tell.'

'Can you look inside and see?' Simone said.

'At this stage there isn't anything to see,' he said. 'As Emma said, we'll just have to be careful until we're sure one way or the other.'

Simone hugged me more gently than the men had and spoke with her voice full of tears. 'I hope you are, Emma.'

'Thanks,' I said. 'Just don't get your hopes up too much. I've only been on the fertility treatment for a couple of months and the doctor said it might take a while for it to work.'

'Let's go on to Holyhead,' Leo said.

'I can't go back in the van with all of you. As long as I can see that damn mountain, the bloodlust is too strong.'

'So what do we do?' Simone said.

I had an idea. 'I'll be okay as long as I can't see the mountain. Hide the top of it.'

'Hide it? What, put a really big tablecloth over it?' Simone said.

'Weather. Fog. Clouds. We have a weather god here, don't we?'

'Brilliant,' Leo said.

'I can, but I'll need to take Celestial Form,' John said.

'Will it fit inside the van?' Simone said.

John looked around. 'Pull the bags out and I should just fit.'

I sat on the grass at the side of the road with my back to the damn mountain, but still intensely aware of its dark presence, while all four of them pulled the bags out and stacked them on the roadside. John climbed into the van and sat on the floor, cross-legged. Leo sat on the grass next to me, and Simone and the stone stood beside us to watch.

John changed to Celestial Form. His head was too tall for the roof of the kombi so he placed one hand on the ceiling, and pushed a dent into it with a horrible shriek of distressed metal.

'You're paying for that,' Leo said.

'I can afford it.'

John settled with his head in the dent and put his hands into his lap and closed his eyes. His hair rose around his head, a nimbus of shen energy surrounded him and the air around us grew cold.

'Asian god in a kombi. That is the hippiest thing I have ever seen in my entire life,' Simone said softly.

Quiet, I'm concentrating, he said.

Something in the cold air shifted; it became denser and more humid. Clouds formed around us, then the humidity was gone and the air returned to normal. John dropped back to his normal human shape, ran his hand over the top of his head and smiled at us.

'You're not too drained?' Simone said.

'I'm fine.' He climbed out of the kombi and studied the mountain. 'You won't be seeing that for a while.' He turned to me. 'How's the blood fury?'

I checked the mountain; the clouds completely covered it. 'Still there, but as long as I don't see the mountain I should be okay.'

'Let us know if it starts to come back.'

Leo indicated the roof of the van. 'You hold it from inside, I'll push it from the outside.'

'No need.'

John lightly jumped onto the roof of the van, held one palm against the dent he'd made, hesitated for a second then leaned into it. The dent snapped back into place. He vaulted down off the roof and we put the bags back and headed towards Holyhead.

20

The motorway ended at a train station and Holyhead's Irish ferry terminal. We stopped at the traffic lights in front of the terminal, and John turned left into the village with its narrow cobblestoned streets. Rows of two-storey houses with small windows were built up the steep hillside heading away from the harbour. The base of the mountain was visible behind the town, but the top was covered by John's clouds. I kept myself distracted by concentrating on the scenery around us.

'Jade Building Block,' John said. 'Guide us to the inn, if you will.'

The stone jerked awake again. 'Accessing ... go straight through the lights and around past the old church.'

'That church is extremely ancient and on the site of an old Roman fort,' I said. 'The walls are Roman.'

'Romans. Ugly bastards, very fond of killing,' John said. 'I ran into a few of them when they were expanding; they came as far as China to trade. Considered themselves vastly superior to every other race on the planet.'

'Um ... didn't the Chinese feel that way at the same time?' I said.

'We still do,' the stone said with humour. 'But then again, everybody always does. Turn left here and head up the hill.'

We threaded our way three hundred metres up the hill until we came to a three-storey guesthouse overlooking the bay. A ferry as big as a cruise ship was heading out of the harbour beyond the breakwater. The sky above the sea was a pale watery blue.

John turned to speak to us. 'We probably only have a couple of days at the most before they work out who we are. Let's find out what's happening before they do. When we're inside, assume we're being listened to at all times and stay in character.'

'Report from Gold,' the stone said. 'The alibi's all set up; and the squad will be here day after tomorrow to take Emma home.'

'Good.' John studied the house across the road from us. 'All clear. Let's go.'

The front door opened to a narrow hall with stairs leading up. A door on the right led to the breakfast room, comfortably furnished with three wooden tables. The owner of the inn came out of the back room and welcomed us warmly. She was a motherly Welsh woman in her late fifties named Mabel Defaoite. She glowed in my heightened senses; something about her was rich and cool and much sweeter than the average human.

'We have three rooms,' she said. 'Since there are six of you, you have the whole house.'

'Only five now,' John said. 'One of us couldn't make it.'

'Do you still want all three rooms?'

'Absolutely.'

'Then come on up and choose who sleeps where. It's all completely up to you.'

'Thanks,' I said, immediately liking her.

'Is your hair natural?' she asked me as she led us up the stairs.

It took me a moment to realise she was referring to my redhead camouflage. 'Yes. I get constant grief about it.'

'I can understand why people would be jealous,' she said, smiling. 'These are the blue and yellow rooms, sleep two each.'

We all hesitated for a moment.

Simone, top floor by herself, John said. *Me and Emma in the room at the end of the hall. Leo, take the other room this floor.*

'What about Jay?' I said, indicating the stone.

Mabel looked from me to John, bewildered.

'I'll share with Gerry,' he said, slapping Leo on the shoulder. *I'll go back to the ring at night and help guard.*

'Okay.' I followed John into the double room at the end of the hall.

'Well, you seem to be organised,' Mabel said.

Simone raced up the stairs and shouted down, 'This room is huge!' *Leo, want to share this one? The view is great from up here.*

Leo stays one floor below to guard, John said.

You are so boring, Simone said. *We could have a slumber party.*

Ugh. Me big tough man, no want slumber parties, Leo said.

'Since you have the whole house, breakfast is whenever you want it,' Mabel said.

'Vegetarian for all of us,' John said. 'We are all seeking the truth of eternal enlightenment and harmony, and consuming the flesh of animals dulls our spiritual purity.'

Her smile froze. 'Yes, well ... I'll see what I can do. Settle in, and if you need anything, just give me a shout.'

'We may need you to help us with the locations we're looking for,' John said. He pulled one of his vintage psychedelic posters out of his back pocket and waved it around, enthusiastic. 'This place is perfect for the spiritual gathering we're planning, but we need to check with a druid or local shaman.'

'A spiritual gathering?' she said, eyes wide.

'He means a folk music festival, don't mind him,' Simone said from the landing above us. 'Ignore all the crystal and druid stuff, that's just his way.'

'Do you know something about druids?' John asked Mabel, sounding even more excited.

'No, there's nothing like that around here. Holyhead's a very boring place,' she said. She patted him on the arm. 'Good luck with your festival. It would do the town — and the island — a lot of good to have something like that to rejuvenate the economy.'

'Peace and light,' he said expansively.

The stone leaned on the wall next to her and crossed his arms. 'That's an interesting surname, Defaoite. Is it French?'

'Irish. It sounds fancy but it just means white.'

'So you're Irish?' he said.

'No, no, my people came over from Ireland a long time ago. I'm Welsh from way back; the surname is sort of a legacy.'

'Fascinating,' the stone said. He put on his most charming smile and moved slightly closer to her. 'Do you run this place by yourself?'

'No, my partner helps me,' she said, brushing her hand through her hair.

'What sort of partner?' he said. 'Strictly business?'

'He wouldn't say that.'

'I see,' the stone said, and moved back. 'Shame.'

'You're telling me,' she said under her breath as she headed back down the stairs.

* * *

After we'd sorted out our stuff, we went down to the main street to meet with the stone's contact. To get there, we walked through narrow streets fronted by houses jammed close together with no front gardens. The cobbled main street was divided off with bollards to make a pedestrian mall, but the place was deserted and many of the shops were vacant.

'That one,' the stone said, indicating a café.

We went inside. It had a scarred wooden floor and was furnished with wooden picnic tables and benches down either side. A young waitress stood behind the counter, listlessly flicking through a magazine. The place was completely empty.

We sat at one of the picnic tables and Simone pulled the menu out of its stand. She quickly perused it, then searched the stand. When she didn't find anything else, she turned back to the menu. 'This can't be right; they just have breakfast, baked potatoes, sandwiches and nachos.' She flipped the menu over, then peered at the blackboard over the counter. 'They don't even have a proper coffee machine. And what the hell is a breakfast bap?'

'Welcome to the boonies,' Leo said, reaching for a menu from another table.

The waitress came up to us; she had short blonde hair and a pierced nose. She scowled around at us and pulled out a notepad. 'What can I get you?'

'Salad sandwich,' John said cheerfully. 'Vegetarian if you could.'

'Same here,' Simone said. 'And a Coke.'

'Grilled ham and cheese,' Leo said with relish. 'And a black coffee.'

'I'll have a salad sandwich, same as the other guys,' I said. 'What sort of tea do you have?'

The waitress looked up from her pad, seemed to see me for the first time and froze. She shook herself out of it. 'Uh ... black or white.'

'White then. Jay?'

'Just water for me, if you could,' the stone said, putting on his best Charming British Gentleman.

'Uh. Ok.' The waitress looked completely flustered. 'Um. I'll be right back with that.'

She nearly ran out the back door.

'Heads up,' Leo said, indicating me with a nod.

'I know,' John said.

'Yeah. WTF,' Simone said softly.

'It's here,' the stone said, rising and turning towards the door.

A small, round middle-aged woman with short red hair hurried into the café, smiling broadly. 'About time you people got here, I've been waiting to hear from you.' She hugged and kissed everybody as if they were long-lost relatives, pulling back to smile at Simone. 'You've grown so much!' She squeezed the stone around the shoulders. 'And you, you old ingrate, you don't look a day older.'

'Neither do you, Ruby, you look terrific,' the stone said. 'Everybody shuffle over, make room.'

Ruby sat on the bench and spoke through her huge smile. 'There's no one eavesdropping, but we may be watched, so you can speak freely but mind the special stuff.' She glanced around. 'Where's that little blonde thing that runs the place when her dad's on the piss?'

'She had one look at Emma and took off,' the stone said. 'She obviously saw through her disguise.'

'That's not good,' Ruby said. 'Nice disguise, who did it?'

'Me,' John said.

She studied John carefully. 'Damn, your stone friend here wasn't kidding. May I?'

She held her hand out. John put his hand out across the table and she took it, concentrating. Her expression filled with awe and she pulled her hand back.

'Bloody hell,' she said, then bobbed her head in Simone's direction. 'Sorry, love.' She pointed from John to Simone. 'This your daughter?'

'I'm half-human,' Simone said.

'Nearly as big as he is, too.' She studied Leo. 'And you're another one. I never thought I'd see your kind again.'

'Do you know what happened to them here?' John said.

She shook her head. 'No idea. I'm old enough to remember when they were drifting around causing trouble, and then one day, poof! They were gone as if they'd never existed. We stones spent some time looking for them, and in the end we gave up.' She leaned on the table and put her chin in her hand. 'It would be a hell of a relief to have them back, helping us out when the demons run out of control. Look at that stuff in London back in 2011.'

'That was demons?' Simone said.

'Mostly, yes.'

'Damn,' I said.

'And you,' Ruby said, turning to me. 'Something's not quite right about you, but I don't know what it is. It's times like this I really wish we had them back.' She studied me and I felt more than her eyes on me. 'What's your surname?'

'Stevenson.'

'I see. For a moment ... Never mind.'

'What do you know about the stone circles disappearing?' I said.

She dropped her hand and leaned across the table. 'One of them was my *parent*,' she said with venom. 'When we find out who is doing this ...'

She stopped as the waitress returned with her father. He came to the table and stared around at us, then nodded to the stone. 'Ruby.'

'Jamie,' she said with distaste.

He reeked of alcohol, and was wearing a pair of tattered jeans and a stained grey sweater, ripped around the neckband.

271

He glared at me. 'I don't know what you think you're doing, but it would be best if you cleared out right now.'

'I'm researching my family tree,' I said. 'It led me here.'

'What family tree?' he said, swaying slightly. He peered at me. 'What's your surname?'

Don't tell him, John said.

'Stevenson,' I said.

'Liar.' His face twisted with anger. 'You're a fucking O'Breen.'

'I'm not an O'Breen,' I said.

He jabbed his finger at me. 'You're one of those O'Breens who went to Australia.'

'My last name is Stevenson.'

'What's your mother's maiden name then?' he said.

I took a gamble. 'Donahoe.'

Dammit, Emma, John said.

'Oh shit,' Ruby said.

The breath went out of Jamie in an audible gasp and he took a step back, his eyes wide. 'You get yourself out of town right now. Leave. All of you.' He focused on Ruby. 'I don't know what you're doing consorting with these people, Ruby, but you know damn well what this one is, and she's going to bring trouble to us all if she doesn't leave now.'

'What am I?' I said.

His watery eyes screwed up and he scowled. 'Abomination. Get out of my caff.' He raised his voice and pointed at the door. 'All of you! Out! Now! Before I call the police on you. And *you*!' He rounded on Ruby. 'I don't know what the hell you think you're doing, but it's only a matter of time before everybody knows. We thought we could trust you, Ruby.' He glared around at us again. 'Get out of town before someone gets hurt.'

'Can you explain why you want us to leave?' John said, attempting to placate him. 'We have no idea what you're talking about. What's the problem with my girlfriend?'

'No!' he roared. 'If you don't know, I ain't telling you. Get out of town. Now!'

He spun and headed out the back door, the waitress cowering as he passed her.

Ruby stared at me. 'You're related to a Donahoe?'

I raised my hands. 'It's my last name.'

'Jesus. You're not Australian, are you?'

'I am.'

'Holy shit. We have to get you out of here before he comes back with a gun or something. Do you have transport?'

'We have a kombi outside the B&B at the top of the street,' the stone said.

'We need to talk,' she said. She glanced around. 'Somewhere else. Let's go for a drive.'

* * *

We wound around the base of the mist-covered mountain and arrived at the quarry, now abandoned, where the stone had come from to build the breakwater. It was overgrown with spiny gorse and yellow heather, and fenced to hold the wild ponies that had been released to graze on it. Ruby led us to a park bench near some duck ponds. John gave up on the European look and settled back into his Chinese form with relief, and Leo took his usual African-American shape.

'First of all, I'm only two thousand years old so I don't know most of what happened firsthand,' Ruby said, pacing up and down in front of us. 'Most of the older stones have retired into stone circles, and they're the ones that have been disappearing.'

'How many have gone?' my stone said.

'Nearly a hundred,' she said. 'The humans don't know about every circle that's missing.'

My stone blanched and staggered slightly. He rubbed his hand over his forehead. 'We're facing extinction.'

'Not while the Grandmother lives.' Ruby turned to me. 'Here's what happened. About two hundred years before I was born, the people of Rome turned into a war machine and started conquering everybody around them. They were very, very good at it.'

'A little too good at it,' John said.

'Yeah. So the gods came up here, hid themselves offshore and built a powerful race that would stop the Romans. They mixed demon in as well as god and human, had a bunch of kids, gave them the abilities to really kick the Romans' arses, and settled them in Ireland where they were well hidden. The children of this new race would join with the armies of the indigenous people and help them fight the Romans.'

'Druids,' I said. 'Or Tuatha?'

'The mixed-breed results were the druids. Tuatha are what the druids called the gods.'

'But the druids weren't nice people,' I said.

'Yes, they are, Emma — they're all nature-worshipping hippies who wear white robes and perform silly rituals at Stonehenge,' Simone said.

'They never had anything to do with Stonehenge; that was built thousands of years before any druid,' Ruby said. 'That's the romanticised version of the story, all propaganda. The truth is way uglier.'

'Human sacrifice,' I said. 'Bloodletting.'

'And sacrificial drowning and mass burning,' Ruby said. She sighed with feeling. 'They were losing, so they did the unthinkable to try to win. They used blood and death to enhance their power — and it worked. Each time they fought, it became easier to use blood to win, and eventually it turned into an addiction. They couldn't fight without it, so they sacrificed prisoners.' She nodded towards the mountain, still swathed in mist. 'They'd prepare for battle up there — and that meant someone would die. They helped the Celts fight off the Romans, all right, but they exacted a price — in blood.'

'The weapon they forged turned into a monster greater than the one they wanted to destroy,' John said.

'Exactly,' Ruby said. 'The gods wanted to create a band of noble serpent soldiers, and instead fathered a race of nasty, cruel snake people. They gave up in disgust and pissed off, leaving us all in this mess.'

'And that's me,' I said. 'But you don't hear of them being around any more; all the snake people were driven out of Ireland.'

'That's right, the Irish were so disgusted with them that they ran them off,' Ruby said. 'Right into the sea. Some of them managed to make it across to here, then they were squeezed on both sides — the people of Ireland killed them on sight, and the Romans were moving up through Britain set on destroying every last one of them. They did the only thing they could.'

'Hide?' Leo said.

'Nowhere to hide, and they were just as sickened by themselves as everybody else was. They knew how much they were hated, and they saw how evil they'd become, so they decided to commit racial suicide. As long as they didn't breed pure, their children wouldn't change to snakes and wouldn't crave blood. So they kept a careful lineage register — here in Holyhead — to ensure that they didn't create any more of their kind. The snake lines have particular names, and they're not permitted to have children together. The women keep their surnames after marrying so we know exactly who's who.'

'You mean everyone in Holyhead could be like Emma?' Simone said.

'And other places as well. Some of them left and hid in Scotland and England, and even other parts of Europe, anywhere the Celts were. Emma's two ancestors did the unthinkable on the sly. Everybody hoped that the baby wouldn't be a snake, but it failed the first test they gave it. Even after trying to breed themselves out of existence for two thousand years, first time they cross it comes out again. The townspeople couldn't bring themselves to execute them — they couldn't kill a baby, snake or not — so they were banished to Australia, where there were no snake people at all.'

'They were banished by a MacLaren,' I said.

'That's one of the names. Donahoe, Defaoite, O'Breen, MacLaren, Anathain.' She smiled slightly. '"Before you have your way, remember DDOMA." Jamie's an Anathain.'

'But the MacLarens are demons,' I said.

'Honey, you're *all* demons to some degree or other,' Ruby said. 'Like I said, a mixture.' She studied me. 'That doesn't explain you though. That all happened generations ago; it should be bred out of you.'

John rubbed his eyes. 'I'm a snake, Ruby.'

'No, I can see you; you're a big turtle thing.'

'I'm a snake as well. I'm two animals. The Demon King is holding my snake part hostage.'

She stared at him with disbelief. He met her gaze.

'And how does that work for you?' she said. 'With your girlfriend along here, you're automatically a threesome? Damn, I thought we stones were weird.'

'That's beside the point,' John said. 'Being with me has activated her serpent nature.'

'And of all the places in the world you could have gone, you came here,' Ruby said. She rose and paced again. 'If Jamie spreads the word, there'll be a mob waiting at the guesthouse ready to string the redhead up.'

'Our Eastern Demon King knows all about this,' I said. 'He's been messing around with the bloodlines himself, infusing more demon into them. He crossed Ben O'Breen with a Chinese demon and made a male Snake Mother.'

'What's a Snake Mother?' Ruby said.

'A really big, ugly demon — back end of a snake, front end human with no skin,' John said.

'Lamia,' Ruby said. 'A *male* one? Where is it?'

'He was run over by a London taxi the day before yesterday,' Simone said, her voice thick. 'We were attacked by Western demons and he changed. They're after us too.'

'Is Ben all right? It's been a long time. His father died and his mother took him from Holyhead when he was a baby, before we could tell her what Ben was,' Ruby said. 'We tried to track him down later and talk to him, and couldn't find him.'

'His son killed him. The demon side of him took over and he couldn't control it.'

'So it's happening again. This just gets better and better,' Ruby said. She glared around at us. 'Thanks so much for bringing *your* war to our peaceful island.'

'The Demon King brought it here,' I said. 'We're just following.'

'I'm on a mission,' John said. 'I'm here to find the demons and establish what they're up to. Emma came along to trace her family history.'

'And I found it,' I said. 'This is the source. Can anyone here help me control my destructive nature?'

'Yes,' Ruby said. 'But their solution is a bullet. The best thing to do is get out of town, like Jamie said.'

'She's leaving day after tomorrow,' John said.

'Leave now.'

'She's my fiancée. If the demons hold her, they have power over me, so she has to stay where she's protected,' John said. 'An escort will be here in two days to take her home.'

'If she survives that long,' Ruby said.

'We can camp out on the mountain,' Simone said.

'We may have to,' John said. 'But all our stuff is back at the inn.'

'Let me go talk to them, see what I can do for you,' Ruby said. 'I've been advising them on supernatural matters for a long time and they trust me. It's not the girl's fault she is what she is, and she'll be gone soon. They couldn't kill her ancestors back then, and they may not be able to do it now. I'll be back.' She disappeared.

'Well, you know what you are now,' Leo said to me. 'Congratulations.'

I rose and stalked to the fence that edged the cliff, and leaned on it to watch the long strands of kelp float in the ocean surge. They didn't follow me.

Ruby reappeared five minutes later. 'They will hear you out. Can't promise anything.' She pointed from John to me. 'Stick close to Miss Donahoe.'

'I will.'

'Meet you back at the guesthouse,' she said, and disappeared.

* * *

We parked slightly up the street from the inn. Mabel Defaoite was waiting outside next to Ruby.

'Ruby says you're gods and we should trust you,' Mabel said. 'She's guided us for a long time and it would be a shame if she's wrong.' She gestured with her head. 'This way.'

Ruby and Mabel led us up the hill a little, then took a sharp left into a road that headed down again, almost parallel to the one we'd just come off. Three houses along stood an old church, its walls painted dark grey, its windows boarded up. Cracked concrete and weeds surrounded it; it looked like an abandoned scout hall.

A couple of other people arrived at the same time as we did, and glared suspiciously at us. One, an intelligent-looking middle-aged woman with shoulder-length brown hair, unlocked the padlock that was holding the chain across the hall's double doors and pulled them open. She stood back and gestured for us to go in.

John and I entered the tidy, polished hall. Six people were waiting for us inside. I had a brief moment of recognition before they shot at us. I steeled myself for the bullets to hit, but John jumped in front of me, a dark blur with his hair flying, and took the bullet in the middle of his chest. Leo grabbed me from behind as John fell in front of me.

'Together, take her!' Leo said. Simone grabbed my other arm and everything around us disappeared.

We landed in a ruined cottage in the small village on the hillside above the town. The floor was stone, but there was no roof; the walls were falling down and long weeds had taken over. It was a good spot: we weren't visible from outside.

'What if we hurt the baby?' Simone said.

'You can teleport in the first trimester,' Leo said, checking me for wounds. 'The bullet didn't go through him and hit you, did it?'

'Leo, you're bleeding,' Simone said.

'You've been hit, my friend,' the stone said.

Leo glared into my eyes. 'Were. You. Hit?'

'No,' I said.

'Good,' he said, and fell sideways to sit on the ground. 'Give me a moment and I'll bring the van and we can get out of here.'

I checked him. He'd been hit by a bullet in his abdomen and blood was seeping through his clothes.

'Simone, can you conjure a pad and bandages to put over that?' the stone said.

'I'm an Immortal. I can take it,' Leo said.

'Even an Immortal can die if they lose enough blood,' the stone said. 'Simone?'

'Here,' Simone said.

They took Leo's shirt off and examined him. Simone flopped to sit on the other side of Leo and put her head between her knees.

'I didn't think you'd faint at the sight of a little blood,' the stone said, mopping at Leo's abdomen with the gauze she'd summoned.

'Neither did I,' Simone said from between her knees.

'Don't look if it bothers you, sweetheart,' Leo said. 'Ow. How bad is it?'

'It's just a flesh wound,' the stone said, leaning back on his heels.

'As if hitting me somewhere else would be okay,' Leo said. 'I'm *made* of flesh, and this damn well hurts.'

'Well, it's not mortal, it just grazed your side. You probably don't even need stitches, but we should find some antiseptic to clean it out as soon as possible.'

Everybody was ignoring the most important thing.

'What about John?' I said too loudly.

They were silent; the stone kept working on Leo's injury.

'Dear Lord, he's dead, isn't he?' I said.

'They were aiming for your head. They hit him in the heart,' the stone said, not looking up from Leo's abdomen. He sat back and studied the bandage. 'That should do it until we can find some proper medical attention off this damn island. Then we can head back to London and hope that the squad or the Dark Lord meet us there.'

'Can you tell if he's rejoined, Simone?' I said.

'Not this far from home,' she said, looking up from her knees. 'I'm as worried as you are, Emma.'

'I'll be right back with the van,' Leo said, and disappeared.

While he was gone, I stood up and checked outside. There was nobody nearby. The stone cottage was very high up in the village called Mountain, with a sweeping view of Holyhead and the harbour below. The scenery resonated through me, and I realized — this was the village from my dream. I had come home.

The scent of Leo's blood on the ground wafted to me and I leaned on the broken wall, gasping. I would not change to snake and attack them. I desperately tried to convince myself that this was not what I wanted, closing my eyes and concentrating. There was a reason I couldn't change but it seemed unimportant — what really mattered was the rich scent of Leo's blood. If I changed it could be so good ...

And I could hurt the baby, if I was pregnant. The shock of this knowledge was like ice water splashed over me and I straightened as it subsided. Simone and the stone hadn't even noticed my internal battle. I took a few deep breaths and remembered that a tiny life could be growing inside me, and that was enough. I was in complete control and the village meant nothing.

I turned back to the cottage, then stopped when I saw the sign at the front door.

Simone saw my face as I rejoined them. 'What, Emma? What did you see?'

'There's a nameplate on the front of the house,' I said. 'Iain and Brede Donahoe.'

'Your ancestors?'

'The ones that were sent to Australia.'

'Oh, that's interesting,' she said. 'Wait, this was their house?'

'Yes. After the townspeople sent them to Australia, they must have destroyed it.' I looked around. 'From the marks on the walls, I'd say they tried to burn it to the ground; and when it wouldn't fall, they took sledgehammers to it.'

'Why would they do anything like that?'

'If your home's gone, you have nothing to return to,' I said. 'They really wanted to make sure that Brede and Iain never came back.' I studied the cracked stones beneath my feet; this village was full of hatred and death and no longer felt like any sort of home. We needed to get off this awful island as soon as we could.

21

'Left here and around the corner,' the stone said. We were winding along narrow lanes that were barely wide enough for the kombi, passing fields holding sheep and ponies. 'Nearly there. Three kilometres to the motorway and we're off the island.'

Leo grunted with pain as he shifted gears. 'Couldn't get a modern automatic van, oh no, had to get the ancient hippie wagon,' he grumbled.

'Stone, does the network know anything about Daddy?' Simone said.

'No stones in Court Ten right now,' the stone said. 'Gold is trying to find out the situation.'

'Oh god,' I said softly.

'Turn left here, up the ramp and you're on the motorway,' the stone said. 'Across the bridge and we're out of here, and not before time.'

'The Jade Emperor told him to stay a month,' Simone said. 'Does that mean the JE didn't know this would happen?'

'I share your concern,' the stone said. 'The Jade Emperor is supposed to know all. But maybe this far West is outside his influence.'

'I just want to know about Daddy!' Simone said.

Leo stomped on the clutch and wrenched the gear lever, his face a mask of concentration to combat the pain.

'I'm not hurt, I should drive,' I said.

'As soon we're off this island, I'll let you take over,' Leo said. We approached the bridge that would take us off the island and he slowed. 'What's that?'

Six cars were parked in a group, blocking the bridge, and men with guns were standing in front of them.

Leo braked hard, spinning the wheel to turn the van, but all it managed was a huge clumsy circle, which brought us head-on into the side of the bridge.

The men fired and we all ducked.

Leo did a painfully slow three-point turn as bullets pinged off the outside of the bus. One cracked through the window above our heads and buried itself in the back of Leo's headrest, sending yellowed foam flying around us.

Simone raised herself out of her seat, turned towards the back of the bus and put her hands out. The men shooting at us were knocked over, arms and legs flying.

'We can't ram that many cars, the kombi can't do it,' Leo said. 'Can you move them, Simone?'

'Not that many. They're too heavy.'

'Then we'll have to stash the van somewhere and fly.'

'They're getting in the cars to follow us,' Simone said. 'Move, Leo!'

Leo crunched the gears, revved the engine and we shot off back the way we'd come.

'They're gaining,' Simone said. 'This thing is so slow.' She concentrated and the tyres blew out on the three cars behind us. She pulled herself back into her seat and ran her hand over her forehead. 'I hope there aren't any more,' she said, her voice trembling with effort.

'Stone, find us a place to hide,' I said.

'Accessing,' the stone said. 'This island is tiny, and that bridge is the only way off. Can you lift the van, Simone?'

'No.'

'What about flying Emma off the island?'

'I may not make it, it's too far,' she said. 'Just find us another way out!'

'I hate to suggest it, but you could leave Leo in the van and swim Emma back to the mainland.'

'Good idea, I can catch up later,' Leo said.

'I can do that for a short distance,' Simone said, studying me.

'Go for it,' I said. 'Head for the sea. Just don't forget to keep me warm; I'll die of exposure in no time in water that cold.'

'We can do it,' Simone said.

'Next left,' the stone said. 'Keep heading that way and we'll reach the lighthouse.'

'Do you think they left the other cars on the bridge?' Leo said. 'If they didn't, we can sneak back over.'

'Not worth the risk,' I said.

We drove painfully slowly along the narrow lanes towards the other side of the island. A car approached us from the opposite direction and we slowed even more.

'Pull over to the side. Completely off the road,' Simone said.

Leo eased the van onto the verge, but it was so narrow that some of the van was still on the road.

'Okay, now stay very quiet,' Simone said. 'And hope they don't hit us.'

Leo cut the engine and we all held our breath. The other car didn't see us; Simone had made us invisible. Fortunately, it hugged the other side of the road and missed us entirely. One of the people in the car said something about sheep as they passed.

Simone waited until they'd gone around the bend, and collapsed onto her seat. 'I hope that doesn't happen again, that was really hard.'

'Why did they steer so clear of us?' Leo said. 'If they'd driven in the middle of the road they would have hit us.'

285

'I made us into some stray sheep on the road,' Simone said. 'Quickly, Leo, let's get to the ocean.'

'Dark Lord's in Court Ten,' the stone said.

Everybody let out a huge breath of relief.

The stone's voice filled with amusement. 'Apparently he's done something he very rarely does: he's lost his temper with Judge Pao and is giving him a piece of his mind.'

'Does someone have a video camera down there?' I said.

'Several. Follow this road along the cliff. Past the lighthouse — all the tourists stop there and look at the ancient huts across the road. They never go any further so the road should be empty.'

We headed up a gently sloping road with the cliffs plunging below us on the left and the mountain on the right. I took a deep breath and looked away as I realised that John's weather was breaking apart and the mountain top was becoming visible.

The cliffs on our left became steeper and more jagged, and we were soon more than two hundred metres above the crashing waves. We passed the lighthouse, on its own small island, with a steep, narrow line of stairs leading down onto it. A couple of cars sat in the car park, and a few tourists were on the other side of the road, looking at the ancient huts, but none seemed to be our pursuers.

Another two hundred metres along, the road stopped after a sharp bend. Leo pulled the van over and we all got out. The wind blew up the cliffs and straight through my sweater, biting and cold. We crept to the edge and looked down: the black cliffs were jagged and dangerous, with sharp boulders at the bottom, far below.

'We can do it, Emma,' Simone said.

The stone clapped Leo on the shoulder. 'Let's lead the rest of the village on a chase across the island while the ladies escape.'

'Good idea,' Leo said. He hugged us, kissed me on the

cheek, and headed back to the van. When he reached the door, he stopped and turned. 'Simone.'

'Yeah, Leo?' Simone was distracted by the waves below.

'Keep me updated telepathically, okay?'

She turned to wave him away. 'We'll be fine.'

'I sure hope so,' he said.

He and the stone climbed into the van, but he didn't start it. He sat and watched us.

'Waiting to make sure we're okay,' Simone said. She turned to me. 'Emma, I might have to change form down there. Please don't tell anybody what I look like.'

'Your snake demon form?' I said. 'A few people have seen that.'

'No.' She looked down at the waves again. 'I don't know where this came from, and please don't tell Daddy.' She glanced at me. 'It's a snake. Like a snake. But with four small legs, like a dragon.'

'Then you're a dragon,' I said.

'No,' she said. 'It has the head and body of a snake, it's not like a dragon at all. It's a snake ... kind of with legs.' She shrugged. 'Just hold on tight to me, okay? If I have to change, I'll move you underneath me and hold you with my legs. But they're awfully short.'

'How long have you had this form?'

'It came out when I started working with yin.'

'You should tell your father, Simone.'

'No,' she said firmly. 'Don't tell anybody. It's too weird.'

I raised my hands and was about to reply when Leo spoke into our heads.

I suggest you move. The stone went to reconnoitre and there are cars on the way.

'Hold on tight,' Simone said. She took my hand firmly in hers and nodded to me.

I nodded back and we turned to face the cliff, the fierce cold wind in our faces.

'Leap hard off the edge; I'll have to guide us out so we don't hit the rocks,' she said. 'On the count of three.'

We both jumped as far away from the rocks as we could. The cliff whistled behind us, but the water didn't seem to be rushing up towards us — and then it was. Both of us concentrated to slow our fall, but we still hit the water hard. The cold nearly knocked the wind out of me, but I had no difficulty breathing or staying afloat as long as I held Simone's hand.

'I'll take us under, I can move faster underwater,' Simone said. 'Just keep hold of my hand.'

'Simone!' I said, pulling on her hand as she plunged.

She came back up again. 'What?'

'It's freezing. Can you warm me up?'

'I'm already warming you to about ten degrees higher than the water's natural temperature,' she said.

'It's bloody freezing,' I said, my teeth chattering.

'Let's just get off this damn island and find somewhere to hide from your lunatic relatives,' she said. 'I thought my family were bad. At least they're not paranoid psychopaths.'

'Your nephew is.'

She was preparing to dive and stopped. 'Which nephew?'

'Sang Shen.'

'Oh, you're right; he is. Don't hold your breath,' she said, and dived.

We sped through the water. Simone's control wasn't as strong as John's and the cold and pressure were intense. Each breath was impossibly difficult because of the thickness of the ice-cold fluid. I tried holding my breath, concentrating on holding her hand, but my body wouldn't let me do it. I was exhausting myself just with the effort of breathing, and my arm was in danger of being dislocated from being dragged behind her.

Slowly and with immense effort, I moved my other hand to her wrist, above where our hands were clasped, attempting to solidify my grip, but her hand slipped out of mine. The minute I was released, the cold and pressure bore down on me. Simone's backwash tumbled me through the water and I had no idea which way was up. My ears were bursting and I nearly screamed from the pain. I needed to get to the surface, but we were so far down I probably wouldn't make it.

I opened my eyes, but the water stung them so horribly I closed them again. I thrashed in an awkward breaststroke towards what I hoped was the surface, and willed her to find me. Something grabbed me around the middle, nearly cracking my ribs with the strength of its grip.

Sorry, Simone said. *I have to change and hold you.*

I tried to take a deep breath, but it was too hard, so I gave up and took a few small ones. The difference in temperature was obvious now that she was touching me, but the water was still like liquid ice. I grabbed her hand in both of mine and gestured with one thumb upwards — the standard diving gesture.

Understood.

I took more small breaths as we surged in what seemed to be the wrong direction, and then my head burst above the waves. I opened my mouth to say something and it filled with water.

'Can you lift me slightly so I can talk?' I said.

She picked me up under my arms and raised me above the waves. The wind blew against my sodden clothing, making me even colder.

'I'm having real difficulty breathing,' I said, my voice quivering as I shivered. 'The water's so thick it's like breathing syrup. Can you do something about that?'

Sorry, I'm a little tired. I'll fix it for you. Okay to continue?

'How far?'

We only just started.

'Do you know how your dad does it so I don't feel the pressure or the movement?'

Yes. I'm doing my best, Emma, I'm sorry.

'I understand. Let's get moving.'

She lowered me gently into the water.

Tread for a bit while I change.

She looked like a big black cobra nearly three metres long. She raised the first third of her body above me and I felt a chill as I saw her small legs, incongruous against her huge dark shape. She moved towards me and I had to control the urge to back away. She gently turned me and took my shoulders in her hands; each looked like a human hand, just black and scaly.

Tap my hand if I'm holding you too tight, she said, and the sound of her voice in my head was reassuring.

She was right: this form really was very weird. I felt a rush of sympathy for Leo, who was so freaked out by my snake form. I understood now how he felt. Simone was radically different from John's Serpent — darker, more disturbing and slightly unnatural.

She dived again, holding me tight, and this time the journey was easier. Still, it seemed to last forever. We travelled under the water for hours, her snake form writhing above me. Each breath was a struggle against the pain in my chest, and my hands and feet became numb from the cold. My diaphragm would be aching for hours from the struggle to breathe, my ribs were bruised by her grabbing me, and my feet felt like they'd never be warm again.

Eventually her movement changed, her grip on me tightened and we surged out of the water onto a long, lonely beach. Both of us lay on the sand, sucking in air. I rolled over to see her, and she was still in snake form. I heard a shout some distance away, carried by the wind.

'Change to human,' I said through the gasps. 'We don't want anybody to find you like that.'

She grunted with effort and changed back to human. She rolled onto her back, gasping. She'd lost her clothes and was naked.

'Great, I don't have the energy to put anything on.' She raised her head slightly and dropped it. 'That was exhausting.'

I staggered to my feet and, with great effort, peeled off my soaking jeans and sweater.

She stared at me. 'What are you doing?'

I fell to sit. 'Wear my clothes.'

She raised one hand slightly without moving otherwise. 'But you'll be in your undies and a T-shirt.'

'And neither of us will be stark naked.' I pushed the clothes at her. 'Dry them off and put them on.'

She struggled to her feet and took the clothes. She pulled the sweater on, realised that it only went to her waist, and put the jeans on as well. She flopped to sit cross-legged, then fell backwards to lie in the sand.

'Give me a minute and then I'll contact Leo and tell him where we are.'

I was too tired to sit upright so I lay next to her. My whole body was racked by uncontrollable shivering, so hard it hurt my muscles.

A military helicopter roared low overhead and both of us flinched. It headed inland, losing altitude.

'We're right by the air force base,' I said.

'I hope Leo can drive through to the beach.'

'He'll find a way. Oh, he's here already.' I sat up to see a jeep driving towards us and waved one arm at it.

'That's not Leo,' Simone said.

The jeep stopped and two men with rifles got out.

'Oh shit. Run!' Simone said.

I pulled myself to my feet, but only managed to stagger a few metres before I collapsed. Simone fell to sit next to me, then lay face-down, obviously just as exhausted.

'Run, Emma, they'll shoot you,' she said.

I didn't have anything to run with. No second wind, no last-minute surge of energy, nothing. I was done, and they were going to shoot me.

'Go into the water. They want me,' I said.

'No. I'll stay with you to the end.' She put her hand out and touched me. 'I love you, Emma.'

I wanted to argue with her, but it was hard enough staying conscious. I closed my eyes and waited for them to come.

Their feet made crunching noises in the sand, and they stopped next to us.

'I wish there was some other way,' one man said.

'You know there isn't,' the other said.

The first man's voice was full of remorse. 'I don't think I can do this. Look at them.'

'Let me then,' the other one said.

A voice shouted a long way away from us, and a shot rang out.

'Oh shit,' the first man said.

Another shot and more shouting.

'Run!' the other one said, and they both took off over the sand.

I raised my head and peered around. I wasn't dead.

'What happened?' Simone said.

A pair of army boots trudged through the sand and stopped next to my face. Someone put their warm fingers against my neck. I was too exhausted to fight them. I tried to speak but nothing came out.

'We're from the base, lass,' a man said. 'I don't know why these assholes were trying to shoot you — you don't look like you have anything worth stealing. Hold on.'

A crinkly silver emergency blanket was wrapped around me. 'On three.' They lifted me onto a stretcher. 'Let's get them back to the base and warm them up.'

Someone felt my pulse in my wrist. 'Hypothermia, exhaustion, dehydration.' A drip was slipped into my arm, then I heard someone speaking unintelligibly over a radio. 'Understood. We're bringing them in now. Two females, one early twenties, one mid thirties, they've been in the water for a while. We scared two men away; looked like they were about to shoot and rob them.'

They hoisted the stretcher and I was too exhausted to do anything but let them take me.

They're soldiers from the base, they're looking after us, Simone said. *I think we're safe.*

'Just rest, my love. We'll contact your family when you're sorted,' the soldier said. 'You're in safe hands now.'

I told Leo. He's coming.

I relaxed into the movement of the stretcher. I felt a jolt when they pushed me into the back of a van, then the doors were closed and they drove us away.

* * *

I woke in a sunny room, in a bed. I was clean and deliciously warm and wearing a hospital gown. Simone was lying on her back in the bed next to me, a drip in her arm and her face peaceful. The room looked more like a dormitory than a hospital ward, although there were consoles at the tops of the beds for oxygen.

I tried to pull myself up and out of bed, and felt a thrill of accomplishment when I succeeded. I pushed the IV stand along next to me and went out into the corridor to see what was happening, making a quick stop at the bathroom on the way.

A man in fatigues sat behind a desk in what appeared to be an ordinary office. He looked delighted, then concerned, when he saw me. He quickly rose and came around the desk to me.

'You don't need to get up,' he said. 'Just call and we'll come help you.' He held my arm to support me. 'I'm a nurse, my name is Darren. I'm afraid we don't have any women medical staff here, but if you're uncomfortable with me looking after you —'

'That,' I began, and stopped. My throat was very dry. 'Not a problem.'

He gently led me back into the room. 'Is there anything I can get you to make you more comfortable? Are you up to filling out some forms so we can contact your next of kin?'

'No. Yes,' I said. I was about to ask for something to drink when I saw the water jug on the night stand. 'No. Forms are okay.'

He sat me down on the bed and wheeled the IV next to it. 'Just rest, I'll bring the forms in. The doctor's already taken a look at you, and he's concerned about your ribs. They're heavily bruised and may be cracked. The X-ray staff will be along soon to take some photos of them. Is that okay?'

'No X-rays,' I said.

'Are you pregnant?'

'Possibly.'

He nodded. 'We'll do an ultrasound instead; that won't hurt a developing foetus at all. Is that all right?'

I nodded a reply and rested on the pillow. Just that small walk had exhausted me. He poured some water into a cup and handed it to me.

'How long have I been out?' I said.

He checked his watch. 'They brought you in about six last night, and it's nine in the morning now.' He saw how exhausted I was and tucked the blanket around me. 'Just rest. I'll put the forms on the table here, and when you're up to it, fill them in.'

'Has Simone woken up?'

'Is that her name? She was frantically worried about you, but as soon as we told her you were okay, she settled down. After she talked to the police last night she passed out and hasn't woken since. She doesn't seem injured, just exhausted like you.'

That wasn't surprising; she'd probably messed with the police officers' heads to make our story believable. I tuned back in to what the nurse was saying.

'I'm surprised the sound of us talking hasn't woken her up. Are you related?'

'She's like my stepdaughter, but I haven't married her father yet.'

'I see.' He patted my arm. 'I'll be back later to check on you. If you need anything, just call for me. We don't have buttons like a hospital, but I'm just outside the door and will hear you.'

'It's possible my friend will come looking for us. You'll know him if you see him: he's six five, African-American, and his name's Leo Alexander.'

He smiled slightly. 'I'm sure we won't miss him if he does show. I'll let the gatehouse know.'

'Thank you.'

I sipped some more water, then leaned back and closed my eyes.

I was woken by Darren speaking outside the room. 'Yes, she's in there.'

Leo came in, accompanied by my stone. They rushed to us and held each of us in turn.

'Careful, I hurt my ribs,' I said.

Leo pulled back. 'Are you sure you're all right?'

'We're fine, we just needed to rest,' Simone said.

'There's a young man with a gurney outside for you, Emma,' the stone said. 'Says he's here to take an ultrasound.'

'They want to look at my ribs,' I said.

Leo nodded. 'Good idea, it's important to make sure there's no complications. So who'll go with her?'

'You go, I'll stay with Simone,' the stone said.

The young man came in with the gurney. 'Emma Donahoe?'

'That's me,' I said. 'Do you mind if my friend comes along?'

'I'll help you lift her,' Leo said.

The young man looked Leo up and down and obviously liked what he saw. 'Any day.'

Leo grinned.

They lifted me onto the gurney, sat my IV bag next to me and wheeled me out. It was only a ten-minute drive to the clinic, which was a new building next to the large shopping centre just out of town. They wheeled me in, had me sign some forms, then took me into the examination room. Leo waited outside.

An older woman came in, holding the forms I'd filled out. She sat next to me and turned on the ultrasound machine. She put a sheet over me, then lifted my hospital gown to reveal my ribs.

'Oh my, there is some bruising here. Tell me if I hurt you too much while I run the wand over you,' she said kindly. She took my IV bag from beside me and moved it so that it sat behind my head. 'Just relax and we'll have you out of here in no time.'

She squirted gel over my ribcage and began to run the wand over me. As she did, a young man came in holding a clipboard.

'This Miss Donahoe?' he said.

'That's right,' she said.

'I just need to ask you some questions, if you don't mind,' he said to me. He pulled up a chair and sat behind my head. 'You haven't filled in a middle name here.'

'I don't have one,' I said.

'I see.' There was a crinkle of plastic. 'You're a Hong Kong resident?'

'I am. I have full travel insurance if that's what this ...' I closed my eyes; it was too hard to keep them open. 'If that's what this is about.'

He continued talking, but what he was saying was difficult to understand. It dawned on me that I really was feeling very sleepy. I wanted to turn around to see what he was doing with my IV bag, but my eyes wouldn't open. I tried to call for Leo, but the sound wouldn't come out.

'She's out. Bring the other one in,' was the last thing I heard.

22

Zhenwu

John stormed out of Court Ten still furious about Judge Pao's deliberate delays.

Report, he said to Leo.

We escaped the Holyhead people, but they blocked the bridge, Leo said. *Simone swam Emma off the island and exhausted both of them. They were found at the air force base and taken for medical care, and they have recovered well. I'm driving them back to London right now, and I'll have them safely there in two hours.*

Good, John said. *I'll meet you there.*

A number of Immortals stood in the forecourt outside Court Ten, obviously waiting with questions for him. He avoided them all and teleported straight back to the Earthly.

He landed in water off the coast of China, changed to his biggest Turtle form and swam. He kept a good distance from the shore because his wake was enough to disrupt sea life and overturn small boats. He became one with the water, passing through it at speed, but it would still take him all night to reach the other side of the globe.

Are you all right, Simone?

We're fine. I'm not as good at taking people underwater as you are and Emma found it hard. But we're okay now, no major damage. We're safe with Leo, and we'll be back in Kensington soon.

Good. I'll be there tomorrow morning your time. Get some sleep.

Hurry, Daddy.

He heard her tone. *Is something wrong?*

No, everything's fine.

You don't sound sure.

Just hurry back.

He dropped his Turtle head and tried to go faster.

The choking muddy waters of the Thames weren't as polluted as they had been back in the seventies, and he was able to travel all the way up the river to the closest point to the house.

I'm five minutes away, he said.

Emma can't wait, Simone said with humour. *She was worried. We all were.*

He changed to human form, made himself invisible and rose out of the water. He didn't bother summoning a cloud, he just manipulated his own energy centres and flew to the Kensington house, drying his clothes as he went. It was surprising how little of the city landscape had changed in the past forty years. He rematerialised in the basement and charged up the stairs to find them. They were in the living room and he raced in to hold both of them, just to make sure they were safe.

Simone flew into his arms. He glanced at Emma and froze.

'What's the matter, Daddy?' Simone said. 'You look like you've seen a ghost.'

He thought quickly. 'Just a jolt of the future. Nothing to worry about.'

He carefully controlled his demon-destroying capabilities as the demon posing as Emma hugged him.

It pulled back and gazed into his eyes, its own full of genuine delight. 'It was only a day but it seems far too long.'

It put its hand around the back of his neck to pull him down for a kiss, and he nearly resisted for a moment. The demon foulness was buried deep inside it; no wonder Leo and Simone were deceived.

'Is something wrong?' it said, sensing his hesitation.

Where the hell was the real Emma?

'Everybody sit and tell me exactly what happened,' he said. *Tea*, he added in the general direction of the household staff. They needed to be checked as well. 'Is Franklin still living here?'

Leo shook his head. 'He went home. He said he'd rather be dead and free than alive in a cell, and that they weren't coming after him any more.'

'He has a point,' John said.

He sat next to the Emma copy, holding its hand, and thought about how to handle this. Simone sat on the other side of him. The Emma copy seemed to be unaware of its true nature; otherwise it would be terrified of him. It obviously thought it was the real Emma.

If he told Simone and Leo telepathically, their reactions would give it away and the copy could explode. He had to find out how much this one knew, and when — and where — the replacement had been made.

Peta brought tea; fortunately, she was real.

'Have Paul come in as well, Peta,' John said. 'I want to talk to him.'

'Yes, sir,' Peta said, and went out.

'Now tell me what happened,' John said, feeling relief as he was able to loosen the copy's grip and pour tea for himself.

Paul came in while Simone was recounting their escape, and he was genuine too. John made a poor attempt at asking him something on pretence and then let him go.

'And they did an ultrasound, brought her back to the base, and we all climbed into the van and came home,'

Simone said. 'They said they'd send the ultrasound along if they found anything.'

'Was Emma left alone in the ultrasound room?' John said. 'Leo, were you there with her?'

'There wasn't enough space for me to be in there as well, and she was only in there for about five minutes,' Leo said.

'Why do you ask? Do you think they did something to me?' the Emma copy said. It took his hand. 'There. You nearly flinched away again. What do you sense in me?'

'We have to go back immediately,' John said. 'Give me a second and I'll ask Peta to arrange accommodation for us, off Holy Island this time, slightly further away on Anglesey.'

'The Jade Emperor's not letting you give up?' Simone said. 'I thought all duties were cancelled if you died.'

'In this case, it is most important,' John said. 'But first I need everybody to come down to the basement with me to discuss which weapons would be most suitable to take. We will not be surprised like that again.'

The Emma copy shrugged. 'I don't need anything; I'll just summon the Murasame.'

'I didn't know we had weapons in the basement,' Simone said.

'Firearms,' John said, 'in a locked chest. These are humans and I won't take any more chances with them.'

'Oh,' Simone said.

'Good idea,' the Emma copy said. 'Shoot them before they shoot us.'

Simone glanced at the copy, obviously wondering if it was joking.

'Right now?' Leo said.

'Right now. Let's go,' John said. 'We'll sort out weapons, then pack and return and carry on from there. Today.'

'What's so urgent?' Simone said.

'It's a long story. I'll tell you on the way. Right now, we go down and sort out weapons, then we pack clothes and go.'

'Trust you to put weapons before clothes,' the Emma copy said with humour.

That was exactly the sort of thing that Emma would say, and John nearly let the anguish and frustration overcome him. They had her.

Down in the basement, he went to the corner and pulled out the chest. He put one hand over the lock and moved the tumblers inside. When the lid opened, he turned back and kept his expression carefully neutral.

'Emma, do you know what gun oil looks like?'

'Yes.'

'Good. You're probably the only one. Check in Franklin's cell, will you? I think it's on one of the shelves in there.'

He turned back to the chest and watched the copy with his Inner Eye. It trusted him completely and didn't hesitate; it walked right into the cell. The minute it was at the shelves on the back wall, he turned to face it and slapped one hand through the air, slamming the door shut. He locked the door with a twist of his wrist.

To its credit, it stood completely still at the back of the cell. 'You'd better have a very good reason for doing this.'

He walked up to the cell bars. 'Move to the other end of the room, Simone.'

'What are you doing, Daddy?' Simone said. He felt her Inner Eye on him and he summoned a small amount of yin. 'Okay, I get it, you're you, but what's going on?'

The Emma copy fell to sit on the bed and ran its hand over its forehead. 'It's me, isn't it? Has the Jade Emperor passed an Edict about me after he saw what happened?'

'Tell me what happened in Holyhead,' John said.

'We talked to Ruby at the quarry. Then we went back to the inn, they took us to their clubhouse, they shot at us and we ran away.'

'What colour is Ruby's hair?' John said.

'Uh ...' The Emma copy looked confused.

'Oh shit, no,' Leo said under his breath.

'What happened at the clubhouse?'

'They took us to their clubhouse, they shot at us and we ran away,' the copy said. It stopped. 'That's exactly what I said last time.'

'After you ran away, what happened?'

'We swam until we ended up on the beach near the air force base, and the soldiers found us.'

'How many soldiers?'

'The soldiers found us,' the copy said automatically, and appeared even more confused. Then its expression cleared. 'They brainwashed me? I seem to be reciting something told to me.'

John went down on one knee on the other side of the bars from the copy. 'Tell me exactly in your own words what happened in the ultrasound clinic.'

'They wheeled me into the clinic and I filled out forms. Then I went in, and the woman did the ultrasound, and then they took me out again.'

'Do you remember who wheeled you into the examination room?' John said.

'No.'

'Do you remember who wheeled you out?'

'Oh yes, that's much clearer. There was a young man looking after me, he made sure I remembered everything. He kept asking me what had happened, having me tell him the story over and over.' The copy looked stunned as it realised. 'Everything's just a story until I was taken out of the ultrasound. That's when the real Emma was replaced with me.'

John didn't reply.

'No, John. Please, no.' The copy put its head in its hands and moaned. 'Oh god, after what happened in Singapore this is my worst nightmare. Tell me it isn't true. Tell me I'm the real me.'

'Leave us,' John said. 'Leo, Simone, prepare to return there. We don't need to pack; we'll be flying, the three of us.'

'I want to stay with her,' Simone said.

The copy visibly rallied, and in an impressive display of courage worthy of Emma herself it rose to speak to Simone. 'Go and find the real me.' Its voice cracked slightly and it took a deep quivering breath, very close to tears. 'Whatever happens now, it's what I want. Let me spend some time with him, and then go find the real me. She's probably alone and afraid and you need to get her out of there. I can only imagine what they're doing to her. I'm safe and I won't hurt anybody here. Go.'

'Come on, Simone,' Leo said. 'Let's get ready to find her. The copy's right.'

At the word 'copy', the demon collapsed to sit on the bed and leaned its head on its knees.

'You know the cruellest thing about all this?' it said into its knees.

'What?' John said.

It glanced up at him and smiled through the tears, its voice thick but controlled. 'They didn't program me to explode. I don't get the kindness of a quick end. They knew we'd be here like this, and you'd have to murder your love.'

'I think they knew very well it would end like this,' John said.

The copy wiped its eyes and rose. It took a deep breath and stood straight and strong, looking him right in the eye. 'I'm ready. I love you. Do it.'

'I'm not doing anything,' John said, rising as well. 'I'll leave you here with instructions for Peta and Paul to care for you, but to be extremely careful. When I return with Emma, it will be her choice what to do with you. If

I know her, she will show the compassion your creators didn't and allow you to live out the rest of your life on the Mountain.'

'You can't trust me unless I'm tamed.'

'I can't trust you even if you are tamed. If you're programmed to explode that will override everything.'

'True. But if I'm tamed I'll follow orders, and it will bring me peace.' The demon knelt and lowered its head. 'Better to do it now before Emma has a chance to protest. Protect me, my Lord, I am yours.'

It stayed on its knees and waited for the next order.

'Rise,' John said.

The demon's expression was no longer full of misery; it appeared calm and at peace.

'Put out your hand.'

The demon put its hand out. John took it and fed the Fire Essence Pill into it. He checked it: it was tamed.

He ran his hands over his face. 'I never want to see another tamed Emma as long as I live.'

'Find the ones who created me and you won't,' the copy said.

'Good point. Now I need information.'

'I'll try to remember as much as I can.'

'I need to know where you were created. Think past the story to images you may have seen.'

The demon closed its eyes. 'This is hard.' It took a deep breath and relaxed. 'I have fragments of visual memory in between the bright hard words of the story. I see windows. Many, many really big windows, and the view from them is high above everything. Lots of glass.'

'Well done. Do you have memories of people?'

'Strange faces. Many faces.' The demon concentrated and its face twisted. 'That *bitch* Kitty Kwok. I remember ... a man with Kitty — with the Demon King. An older European man. His name wasn't Semias, it was something else.' It shook its head. 'That's all. If I think of more, I'll have Peta call you.'

John put his hand through the bars and onto the side of its face. It closed its eyes and raised its face slightly to welcome his touch.

'You have done well,' he said. 'Stay here and stay quiet and harm no one. I will return as soon as I have found Emma.'

'My Lord,' the demon said. 'I will wait.'

It sat on the bed and watched him as he headed up the stairs.

Simone, Leo, Peta and Paul were waiting in the entrance hall.

'Is she all right?' Simone said.

'It's tamed. It'll behave,' John said. He turned to Peta. 'That's not Emma in the basement cell —'

'What?' Paul said.

'I don't have time to explain,' John said. 'Emma's been kidnapped and they put a copy in her place. The copy's in the basement cell. Do not under any circumstances release it from the cell. Any circumstances, even if the house is burning, you leave it in there. Understood?'

'I can't just —' Paul said.

'You can and you will,' John said. 'It may be tamed, but it can't be completely trusted until it's proved itself — there may be previous programming. It could explode if it's let out. Don't let it out.'

'What about feeding it and such?' Peta said.

'No need. It's a demon. It won't need to eat anything for a week, and we should have returned before then.'

'We're going right now?' Simone said.

'Yes. We're flying back as fast as we can right now. Where's the stone?'

'Still asleep upstairs,' Leo said. 'He's exhausted.'

'*Stone!*'

Sorry, my Lord, on my way.

This. This. And this.

By the Grandmother. I never sensed it.

The stone appeared next to them in human form.

'We're going to find her now,' John said. 'We'll start at the ultrasound clinic.'

'Did the copy have any idea where they might be?' Simone said.

'It mentioned many large glass windows from a high vantage point; that's where it was created. It may be one of the big houses that Emma mentioned.'

'She's out there alone and I'm not with her,' the stone said. Its voice became fierce. 'I should have stayed in her back!'

'Do you need me to carry you?' John asked Simone.

'I'm okay. Maybe ask me again in an hour or so.'

John teleported to the sky above the house and waited for them. Leo appeared next to him and summoned a cloud. Simone just floated with the Jade Building Block in True Form next to her. John didn't have the energy to make the whole journey without a cloud. He summoned one, nodded to Leo and Simone, and they took off.

* * *

It took them nearly two hours to arrive back at Holyhead. After an hour, Simone had joined John on his cloud and he was feeling the strain from travelling halfway around the world and being so far from his Centre.

When they reached the outskirts of town, it became obvious why the centre was deserted and many of the shops had closed. A supermarket chain had opened a shiny new building away from the centre, a chain hardware store had opened nearby, and a couple of strip malls had sprouted up next to the huge car park. People were streaming in and out of the supermarket.

They landed behind the buildings and went around to the front of the strip mall where the ultrasound clinic stood. John didn't hesitate at the 'closed' sign; he teleported inside. The interior appeared to be a normal clinic but completely bare. There were no papers or files, the drawers in the desk were empty. A computer was the only thing remaining.

Leo opened an inner door to an examination room. 'Ultrasound was through there,' he said.

'Stone, we may need Gold to come and help us with the technology,' John said.

The stone was floating in midair in True Form. 'Don't assume I'm inferior with technology just because I'm older,' it said. 'I taught Gold everything he knows.' It rested on top of the computer box. 'Give me a second to run through these drives.'

'I see,' John said.

He went into the examination room. The whole setup had been minimal, thrown together in a hurry. The examination couch was still there, but the machine was gone. Another door led out to a back alley and he went through it.

'Stone,' he called.

'My Lord?'

'Call the ...' He rechecked the label on the machine sitting next to the back door. 'Penrhos Stanley Hospital in Holyhead. Tell them that their stolen ultrasound is here and appears reasonably unharmed.'

'One of these costs a fortune,' Leo said, putting the machine back on its wheels correctly. 'I'm sure they'll be thrilled to have it back.'

John lifted the lid of the dumpster and pulled out some papers. They were all blank. He picked up a manila folder; it was full of blank pages. He floated above the dumpster to move the papers out of the way.

'That's rank,' Leo said. He dropped his voice when he saw. 'No way.'

The body parts had been cut into pieces, presumably to lessen the chances of discovery. The heads were under the limbs.

'Some of those bits are black,' Leo said.

'Yes, it's a copy of you, and one of Simone,' John said. 'Obviously they weren't needed.'

He yinned the contents of the dumpster. Anyone finding these demons would ask the real Leo and Simone too many difficult questions.

He returned to the ground. 'Let's see if the stone found anything.'

'The computer's completely empty,' the stone said when they returned. 'It's brand new and nothing was put on it.'

John closed his eyes and reached into the energy flowing through the room. He sensed Emma's presence from the previous day; Leo had been there as well. There was no dark trace of any demon having been there. It appeared that only humans had been present in the room in the past twenty-four hours. He leaned on the desk; he was exhausting himself again but he couldn't afford to rest yet. They had to find her.

'Next stop the air force base,' he said. 'There were no demons here. Let's see what the soldiers have to say for themselves.'

They landed in the infirmary room at the base and John checked the area. He felt a moment of dizziness and leaned on the bed, then sucked in some energy from the air around him and straightened.

'Whoa, it just went real cold,' Leo said.

'That was me,' John said. 'Is the same nurse outside this room?'

'Yeah, same guy,' Simone said.

'Put your watch under the bed you were in.'

'I'm not wearing a watch,' she said. She pulled her mobile phone out of her pocket and put that under the bed instead. 'Ready.'

They teleported outside the front door and Simone knocked on it, then went in. Darren was sitting behind his desk, and rose as they entered.

'I wasn't expecting to see you back here,' he said. 'Did you leave something behind?'

'Yeah, I think I left my mobile here somewhere,' Simone said. 'Mind if we check?'

'Go right ahead, but there isn't much chance of finding it. The cleaning staff have already been through.'

Simone shrugged. 'I'll have a look anyway.'

'Sure.'

He followed them into the room and leaned against the bed as Simone rummaged underneath it. 'This your dad, then?'

John held his hand out to Darren. 'That's right. I'm Simone's father, John Chen. Thanks for looking after them.'.

'I'm glad I could help,' Darren said, shaking his hand.

John tightened his grip, pulled Darren closer and put his left hand over Darren's face. He quickly shuffled through Darren's mind before he had time to resist. When he'd seen enough, he released him. Darren took a huge breath and fell backwards slightly.

'What was that?' he said.

'What was what?' Leo said.

Darren shook his head. 'Nothing. Never mind.'

'Found it,' Simone said, rising and waving the phone in triumph. 'Thanks, Darren.'

'No problem at all,' he said.

'We'll be on our way then, many thanks,' John said.

'No problem at all,' Darren repeated, obviously still slightly stunned.

They left the office through the front door and John headed for the beach, Leo and Simone following him. He landed on the sand and they stood next to him.

'What's the verdict?' Leo said.

'As far as he knows, he called the hospital for an ultrasound and the hospital sent someone to collect Emma,' John said. 'He was unaware of the deception.'

'We're back where we started,' Simone said. She ran her hand over her forehead and turned away. 'We have to find her.'

'We will. We still have some leads we can follow,' Leo said.

'I'll contact Ruby as well,' the stone said.

'Good idea, we'll speak to her first,' John said. 'She should know what's happening. We can check the houses that Emma and the King's Number One were talking about; she's probably in one of them. We just have to find the one with the big windows.'

'Good idea,' Leo said.

'Daddy, you're cold, I can feel it coming off you,' Simone said. 'Do you need to rest?'

'Yes,' John said. 'But not yet. Let's go.'

23

Emma

I came around in a heavy dark-wood four-poster. Pale green velvet swags fell from the sides and the bed itself was carved with twining vine patterns. The room was like something from a European palace. The ceiling must have been four metres above me, with much decorative plasterwork and a heavy crystal chandelier as the centrepiece. Tall panels on the walls showed Art Nouveau style paintings of blissful country scenes, with men and women in gorgeous flowing robes riding horses and hunting with dogs.

I sat up and looked around with my Inner Eye. I was in a tower that stretched enormously high above a lush island. It appeared to be made of obsidian; its polished sides shone in the sunshine. Many curved glass windows of random sizes punctuated its walls; the window to my room was one of the smaller round ones. A tall, narrow dome of transparent crystal covered the tower, like the glass dome over a mantel clock.

I was still wearing the hospital gown I'd been kidnapped in. The fact that I was still alive was both worrying and reassuring. It meant they wanted something from me. Probably John's cooperation, and the stupid damn Turtle was so in love with me he'd do anything they asked. I had to get out. I didn't have the stone either, so I had to get access to the internet somehow, to send them the necessary information.

My Inner Eye didn't give many details of my surroundings, so I walked to the window, admiring the parquet flooring as I went. At the centre of the room, the wood had been inlaid in an Art Nouveau design of a giant rose, surrounded by vines and leaves. It was disturbingly reminiscent of the story of Sleeping Beauty.

I leaned on the carved wooden window ledge, and the view took my breath away. The dome's surface was close enough to the window to touch, but it was completely transparent and almost invisible. I was so high up it was like I was flying. Gently sloping hills spread below me, covered in brilliant green grass and copses of trees. A river ran between the hills, its water reflecting the sky and its small white clouds. The sky was the impossibly intense blue of the Celestial Plane. The view resonated within me: this was Western heaven, one of the places from my dreams. I was finally home where I belonged — but as a prisoner.

I pulled myself together, taking deep breaths. I couldn't let this place get to me. I had to remember who and what I was, and the people who loved me and had lost me.

I took another look around with my Inner Eye, this time at the interior of the tower. My room was at least six hundred metres up the tower. Horror crept over me as I saw that the only occupants of the building apart from me were all demons. Every single one. And there were *thousands* of them.

I tried the door; of course it was locked. My Inner Eye showed no physical locking mechanism. There wasn't even an old-fashioned keyhole.

I turned back to the window. It was a single sheet of glass and didn't open. I checked the room for something to break it with, and saw a wooden chair with legs and arms that were carved into vines. The Art Nouveau theme appeared everywhere, and in different circumstances I would have found the whole place enchanting.

I picked up the chair, took it to the window and threw it as hard as I could against the glass. A couple of the legs cracked as it hit the glass, then fell to the floor. Okay.

I was about to try calling the Murasame when a movement caught the corner of my eye. It had come from the mirror above the dressing table. I checked the room: empty. The movement came again and I gingerly shifted so that I could see my reflection in the mirror.

A small, plump European woman — obviously a Shen from her wise expression — was standing where I should be and looking straight at me. She wore a tan and gold gown that fell to the floor, with roses embroidered on the bodice. I looked around — okay, she was just in the mirror. She gestured to me to come closer, then put her palm against the mirror's glass. I put my hand on hers, and a distant lilting melody came to me, merry pipes and a drum. Her compassionate essence moved through me.

I cannot reach through time in person, she said, *such a thing is forbidden. But you will need assistance if our mistakes are to be made good.* Her expression changed and I felt her sadness. *I will bolster your strength until you can break their control.*

How will they control me? What do I need to do to stop them? I said.

A tall man with long blond hair entered the room behind her. He was wearing a pale blue tunic and trousers with snowbells embroidered down the sleeves and pant legs.

'Hurry, my love, the dance has already begun,' he said, then saw me. 'And what is this?' He smiled slightly. 'Find some suitable apparel, little one, and join the dance.'

'She will not be joining us today,' the woman said, turning away from me. 'But she must remember to touch the glass.'

Both of them faded and I removed my hand from the mirror. Okay.

I returned to the door and was considering breaking it down when the handle turned. I jumped back.

The door opened slightly and the Demon King poked his head around. He was in his mid-twenties male human form with blood-coloured hair in a short ponytail.

'There are clothes in the dresser,' he said. 'Put something on, there's a good girl, and I'll be back in five minutes.'

'What are you —' I began, but he closed the door on me.

I considered for a moment, then went to the dresser to find something that wouldn't leave my ass hanging out in the open air. The drawers were filled with clean new clothes, fresh with the scent of lavender. I found some underwear, a pair of soft moleskin pants and a white shirt that seemed to be made for me.

'Are you decent?' the Demon King said from the other side of the door.

'Yes,' I said.

He opened the door and gestured with his head. 'Come on then. Time to meet our host.'

I took a quick glance at the now-unremarkable mirror before following him through the door. Two large Western demons in True Form were waiting outside.

The hallway was three metres wide, with the same high ceiling and a polished stone floor inlaid with a design of twining ivy. The ivy theme continued in carved wood up the wall columns, joining at the ceiling to create an artificial bower. The hall appeared to stretch the width of the tower, with windows at either end. The window behind me was a floor-to-ceiling circle filled with a single sheet of glass painted in translucent colours, with flowers and more ivy curling around its edge. The window at the other end of the hallway was so far away it was barely visible.

'Is this Tara?' I said.

'I heard you'd been doing some research,' the Demon King said. 'No, this is Caer Wydr.'

'The Glass Fortress.'

'Or Glass Citadel, something like that.'

'Why are you here? This isn't a demon place, it belongs to their gods.'

'Ah, good question.' He smiled slightly and gestured towards the other end of the hallway. 'Wait until we meet up with our host and I'll explain everything.'

'Who's our host?'

'One of the Four Kings of this part of the world. Lord Semias.'

As we walked, I checked for stairs or an open window to run through. When we reached the middle of the hall, there were stairs down. I summoned the Murasame, cut one of the guards in half before they could react and jumped over the body. I didn't bother with the King or the other guard, I just ran to the stairs, hopped up onto the guardrail and dropped off to float down the centre of the stairs. I checked each floor as I passed, hoping to find a way out. Nothing.

When I reached the bottom, I bolted into the hallway and found more stairs down. I sliced through some confused-looking demons and ran down the stairs, hoping to find some sort of fire escape. Instead, I came out in the receiving hall of what was obviously the castle's dungeon. A couple of burly demon guards jumped to their feet and dropped their playing cards when they saw me.

There was a small round window in the wall to my right. I launched myself at it with the Murasame, and nearly broke my wrist when the sword hit the glass and didn't go through. I stepped back, confused. Nothing short of a shield of Celestial Jade had ever blocked the dark blade before.

The Demon King appeared behind me and grabbed my sword arm in a grip that I couldn't free myself from.

'Damn, you're fast,' he said.

He squeezed the pressure point between the bones of my weak and withered forearm, effectively paralysing my hand, and I dropped the sword. It floated slightly above the floor and the demons stepped back from it, intimidated.

'Help me,' an elderly man called from the cells. 'Please, if you can hear me —'

'Shut up, old man, nobody's coming to help you,' the King shouted over my shoulder. He spoke into my ear. 'Some guests are never satisfied. Try something stupid like that again and you will be punished. There's no way out of the tower unless I open it for you. Now.' He twisted my arm painfully behind my back. 'It's a very long ride back up again, and we're going to make it together.'

'What about the sword, my Lord?' one of the demons said, studying the Murasame. His expression changed to avarice. 'Is that a legendary weapon?'

'It's yours if you can hold it,' the Demon King said.

The demon glanced at him. 'Seriously?'

'Any demon that can hold this sword can take possession of it,' the King said. 'Its name is the Murasame, the Destroyer. It's a legendary weapon from the East.'

The demon edged towards the sword. He held one hand out, gingerly took the handle and immediately exploded into demon essence, some of which was siphoned into the King as he held me.

'This will be fun,' the King said. He nodded to the other demon. 'Anyone who wants can try to take the sword. Limit of twenty a day, though. I can't afford to lose too many of my soldiers. Do you want to try?'

The second guard was more cunning. 'Will it destroy me too?'

'Oh, absolutely,' the King said.

The demon shook his head and returned to his station. 'Then I'd prefer to just leave it.'

'Smart man,' the Demon King said, and led me into an elevator that mirrored the Art Nouveau theme.

Back at the top of the tower, we went into a room that was obviously on the corner; it had two walls of glass from floor to ceiling. Once again, the view over the green hills was breathtaking. This room had an oak motif: oak leaves and acorns were twined around pillars and embossed into the wooden floor. A Western demon, who'd taken the shape of an elderly European man, sat on the couch. He was wearing a hooded tan robe that fell to the floor in old-fashioned druid style, the hood thrown back from his long, elegant face.

He rose when we entered. 'Let her go, George. There's no need for this.' His voice sounded exactly like the elderly man I'd heard calling out in the dungeon.

'Try her out first,' the Demon King said. He shook my arm, which he was still holding painfully behind me. 'Say hello to Lord Semias, Emma.'

'You're not Semias, I heard him in the dungeon,' I said. 'You're a big —'

'Shut up,' the Western demon said, and I was silenced.

I attempted to speak, but couldn't get any words out.

The Semias copy changed form to a European man in his early forties wearing a tailored navy suit with a white shirt and maroon tie. 'You were right,' he said to the Demon King. 'It was just a matter of me being from the right region and much bigger than her.' He studied me. 'Barely enough demon in there to count. One more generation and I wouldn't be able to control her. Kneel,' he ordered me.

I had no choice; I fell to my knees. The Demon King released me as I dropped.

'You think she's pretending?' he said, coming around in front of me to study my face.

'I doubt it,' the Western demon said, 'she's tiny. Hardly worth bothering about. This is what you put all that effort into?'

'She's pretended to be controlled before,' the Demon King said.

'Let's be sure,' the Western demon said.

He stood in front of me and started to undo his pants. I wanted to move away but couldn't. I was frozen and helpless. He jammed his crotch in my face and I could smell him. A wave of nausea ripped through me.

'Oh no you don't,' the Demon King said. 'You made a promise. No sexual assault.'

'Haven't you ever wondered how good she is?'

'Beside the point. No women are forced to do anything sexual while we hold them. I made that clear at the start.'

'But you're quite ready to impregnate her with a demon child. How is this so different?'

Another wave of nausea went through me.

'That's a medical procedure,' the Demon King said with emphasis. 'This is rape. Now put that away.'

'Your origins betray you, Kitty, and one day they will be your downfall.'

'Whatever,' the Demon King said. 'Find another way to prove she's obedient.'

The Western demon fixed his pants and waved one hand at the window. The glass of the window and the dome disappeared.

'Bad idea,' the Demon King said.

'Stand up,' the Western demon said.

I rose and faced the window and my freedom.

'Could she manipulate her centres and survive that fall?' the Western demon said.

'Could you, Emma?' the Demon King said.

I tried to reply but couldn't.

'She needs permission to speak,' the Western demon said. 'Answer him.'

'Easily,' I said.

'Well then, there's your freedom; all you have to do is jump,' the Western demon said. 'Now sit on the couch and put out your left arm. We're taking blood.'

More than anything in the world I wanted to leap through that window to my freedom. A chill breeze swept through the room, full of the fresh cool air of the Western Heavens. Instead, I sat on the couch and put my arm out. I had no choice.

The Western demon put the glass back with a wave of his hand, then picked up a kidney dish covered with a cloth. He took out a large syringe, put a tourniquet around my upper arm, and slipped the needle into the vein. He took nearly three hundred millilitres, more than enough to fill a large drinking glass. He squirted half the blood into an oversized wine glass, leaving half of it still in the syringe. He took a sip of the blood in the glass and then held it away, his expression rigid. A golden glow exploded around him and he trembled, his eyes closed, then he dropped his head and panted. He took another sip and made soft noises of effort.

'Did you just come in your pants?' the Demon King said with amusement.

'Nearly.' The Western demon held the glass up to the light. 'Dear God, George, it's pure DDOMA serpent, the real thing. I haven't tasted anything like this in close on a thousand years.' He turned his attention to me. 'How is this possible? Look at her, she's tiny. She's mostly human; far too fragile to be good for anything. There's hardly any demon at all, and what is there is weak and useless. If I ran into her on the Earthly, I'd just eat her and count her as a snack.' He raised the glass again. 'Why is she like this?'

'Years of hard work. The Dark Lord has trained her to be a perfect blend of physical power and energy control, and it all fits together to make her greater than the sum of her parts. I knew he wouldn't be able to resist a double-heritage DDOMA. I couldn't believe my luck when I found an O'Breen-Donahoe in Hong Kong.'

'We must have her teach our armies what she's learnt.'

'That's the plan,' the Demon King said.

He smiled slightly and held his hand out, and the Western demon passed him the glass. He raised it to me. 'Cheers, Emma. I finally have you in human form and we'll make sure he won't find you this time. I have a chance to do some very nice work with you now.'

He sipped the glass and looked confused. He raised it in front of his face. 'Interesting. I've been waiting years for this, and she just tastes like an ordinary human to me.'

The Western demon took the glass back. 'That's because she's from here. You're the wrong nationality to fully appreciate it.'

'Shame.' The Demon King concentrated, and a small skinny Eastern demon wearing nothing but a lab coat came in. The King waved one hand at the syringe in the kidney dish. 'Is that enough?'

The demon checked the syringe. 'More than enough.'

'Full blood work. I want a complete DNA as well. Everything you have on it,' the King said.

The Western demon took a gulp from the glass. 'You're not having this. It's sublime.' He looked over the rim at me. 'How much could we take from her each day without killing her?'

'Not more than what you have here, and over a long enough time it would kill her anyway,' the skinny demon said.

'Damn,' the Western demon said. He shrugged. 'Hurry up and do what you want to do with her, George.'

'It depends on what this blood work shows,' the Demon King said. 'If she's capable, I'll change her into a Mother again and have her producing young. If not, I'll mess around with her human genetics and see what comes out.'

'If you impregnate her yourself, the spawn will probably obey you,' the Western demon said.

'That's what I was thinking. They should be exceptional, quite capable of acting as generals in the army.'

I wanted to throw myself at him and tear him to shreds, but I couldn't move.

'She's shaking,' the Western demon said. 'She doesn't like that idea.'

'Do you have complete control?' the Demon King said. 'She won't free herself with a giant act of will or anything?'

'Don't be ridiculous, there's no chance of that. She's too small. She'll do whatever I tell her.'

'You should take away her awareness and sentience, just to make sure.'

No!

'But she's more fun fighting it! Look at her. Completely unable to do anything.'

'Trust me, she might win.'

'Oh, all right.'

The Western demon put the glass down and came to me. I quivered with effort as I tried to move away from him. He put his hand over my face.

'When I say "now", you will stop having any independent thoughts and exist only to obey my orders until I tell you otherwise. Now.'

I fell into a bottomless black pit.

24

Zhenwu

Ruby and the stone arranged a meeting at a pub in a small village on the island of Anglesey, which sat between the mainland of Wales and Holy Island. The pub was located across the road from a ruined castle.

Simone stopped when they entered. 'Wow. Nice.' The interior had been renovated in cream and gold, with fine linen and flowers everywhere.

Ruby was waiting for them at one of the tables and waved when she saw them.

'Why isn't anyone else here?' Simone asked as the four of them sat.

'The restaurant's not open for lunch,' Ruby said. 'But they know me — you can get a sandwich or something from the bar.' She picked up her glass of red wine. 'I had no idea they were planning an ambush. Snakes are supposed to be smarter than that; looks like being human for too long went to their heads.'

Is she telling the truth? John asked the Jade Building Block.

I should be offended you even ask that of one of us, the stone said. *But under the circumstances ... Yes, she is.*

'I've already updated Ruby on what happened,' the stone said out loud.

'The copy of Emma said that it was created somewhere high with a lot of windows,' John said. 'Does that sound like one of the big houses around here?'

'Can't be the castle across the road,' Ruby said, gesturing with her head towards the window. 'That's just old stone walls.'

'We should check anyway,' Simone said.

'We will,' John said. 'What about the other two houses Emma knew of?'

'One was the residence of the Marquess of Anglesey, but it's a museum now,' Ruby said. 'It has big windows overlooking the strait between Anglesey and mainland Wales, but it's not very high up.'

'Sounds like we should still go there,' Simone said.

'The other place is a mansion, not very old, on top of a cliff overlooking the water,' Ruby said. 'It's unusual because it's so black, but it has big windows as well.'

'Which is closer?'

'The castle here, then the manor, then the black house.'

'We'll check the castle first,' John said. 'Then head for the manor.'

'One other thing,' Ruby said. 'Holy Mountain itself is the highest point anywhere around; the demon may be remembering the Heavenly analogue.'

'After the big houses, we'll check that too. Eastern Number One said that they were building a demon army in a big house.' John rose, eager to start. 'Let's go.'

The castle was three storeys tall, but had no roof, internal flooring or fixtures; it was just bare stone walls. It had been an impressive fortress in its prime: the walls were high with battlements and the corner towers had slits for archers. An artificial inlet from the sea had been dug right up to the walls to create a moat around the building. It would have been a centre for town trade a thousand years before, and John wished he had been there to see it.

He heightened his senses as they split up and walked around inside the castle's yards, now just lawn between the walls. He couldn't feel more than a few centimetres below the surface, even though it was soaked from the British rain, so he pulled his boots and socks off and held them in one hand while he felt the ground beneath him.

'Ruby,' the stone said.

'I know.'

'What?' Leo said.

'Something here isn't right,' John said.

'I can't sense anything,' Leo said.

John dropped to one knee in the wet grass and put his hand on the ground. 'Below thirty centimetres I can't feel anything. This is the same as Kowloon City Park.'

'No,' the stone said.

'Take True Form and scout the area,' John said. 'There will be an entrance here somewhere.'

'You mean they're dead? All those stones are dead?' Ruby's face was ashen.

'Some could still be imprisoned. We will find them,' John said.

Ruby changed to True Form: an uncut ruby the size of a human fist. 'And avenge them,' she said, her voice full of menace.

John stood again and felt the ground beneath his bare feet, looking for the entrance. The bare feet triggered his change to his basic form and his hair came out of its tie and quickly tangled. He ignored it as he checked the corner towers. Their partly-hidden interiors would be ideal for a secret entrance and exit.

What he was looking for was in the second tower.

I've found it.

They gathered inside the remains of the circular stone tower. Water ran down its walls, making the round black stones shine.

Simone gestured towards the shoes in his hand. 'Your feet are filthy, Dad. You are absolutely impossible.'

'I can feel things more effectively barefoot.' He pointed at the ground. 'Under here.'

The stone and Ruby changed to human form, shared a look, then both crouched and put their hands on the ground. They stayed there unmoving for a full minute, then Ruby shook her head and stood.

'We can't open it, it's not in tune with our nature,' she said. 'It's something demonic.'

'Of course it is,' John said. 'Move back.' They stepped back slightly and he waved his hand at them. 'Further.'

He put one hand over the centre of the entrance and released a tiny amount of yin. A black circle, thirty centimetres across, appeared, showing the tunnel entrance. It wasn't big enough, and he hoped they didn't see him quivering with the effort of controlling the rush of yin through him as he opened it further. This fine work required an immense amount of restraint; the yin wanted to flood through him and take out most of the stars in that part of the galaxy. It was made doubly difficult by the fact that the coating on the wall wanted to grow back and cover the opening, and he had to maintain a flow of yin just to keep it open.

The circle expanded to reveal a stairway leading down, its walls and steps made of the same wet black stone. John held his arm out to stop anyone from rushing in, and climbed down the first few stairs. He sent his awareness down, sensing what he could, and came up against a blockage at the bottom. There was a door there, covered in the stone coating.

'How many have died?' the stone said quietly.

'I can't feel past the door,' John said.

He sat on the damp stairs and put his socks and boots back on, not enjoying the enclosed feeling around his feet. He made an attempt to tidy his tangled hair, roughly braiding it to keep it out of the way.

'Simone and Leo, remain up here. Ruby and Building Block, in True Form with me.'

He moved down the stairs with the two stones in True Form floating at his shoulders. He pressed his ear against the door. His heightened senses might not be able to see anything on the other side, but there was still basic physics. There was no sound, so he pushed against it. It didn't open, and had no handle. He put his palm against it and pulled it towards him. It swung open and he stopped it at a five centimetre crack.

The Building Block floated through the gap. *Clear*, it said.

John pulled the door all the way open to reveal a corridor, its walls and ceiling lined with the same black stones as the castle above. The floor was packed earth. The tunnel smelled of damp mud and mould and the death of the stones that had been made into paint and used to coat the walls.

It was only forty centimetres wide and one and a half metres high; he had to stoop and turn slightly sideways to fit. He glanced at the stone; this couldn't be good for its claustrophobia.

Stay there, he said to Leo and Simone, still on the surface, then released the yin and let the hole seal itself.

The two stones rested on his shoulders so they could communicate.

It's getting narrower, the Building Block said.

It isn't, that's just you, John said. *Try to keep it under control.*

The tunnel appeared to follow the contours of the castle, suggesting it was part of the structure. It opened on the right into one of the circular corner towers, two metres across. The room was made even smaller by the shelves lining the walls. Ruby changed to human form and picked up one of the many shoe boxes on the shelves.

'Dad?' she hissed, picking up a stone from one of the boxes and cradling it in both hands. 'Mummy?' She fell to her knees, bent protectively over the stone. 'Please talk to me.'

'I'm sure I heard something,' a voice said down the corridor.

They're coming. We need to get out, the Building Block said. 'Go, Ruby, take your parent. Lord Xuan, take her out. I'll stay here and monitor.'

Ruby didn't respond; she seemed to be stricken with grief.

I'll just destroy them, John said.

They'll call for help and you'll have all of them down on you. They'll probably kill you. Simone needs you up there.

You won't be able to communicate! John said.

'In the stone room?' another voice said, and John made them invisible.

A pair of Western demons filled the doorway.

'Nothing here,' one of them said.

'Something's not right,' the other said. 'Listen.'

Ruby was softly sobbing, unaware of her surroundings.

'I'll be damned, listen to that,' one of the demons said. 'Haunted. How cool is that?'

Just go, the stone said. *I'll find out where they're holding Emma and make my way back to you.* The stone took the form of Ruby's parent and floated to lie in the shoe box.

John hesitated.

'I don't think that's a ghost,' one of the demons said, and both drew their weapons. 'Get backup.'

John grabbed Ruby and teleported them both out of the room and into the corridor behind the demons. As the demons entered the room to investigate, he moved as silently as he could, taking her back up the stairs. He opened the ground again to see Simone and Leo waiting. He pushed Ruby at them. 'Take her back to the pub and wait for me there.'

He dashed back down the stairs and made himself invisible, then sent his awareness down the corridor. The demons were still checking the stone room.

He pushed his awareness as far as he could, and sagged with disappointment. This was a stone laboratory occupying the old tunnels beneath the castle. There were only five rooms branching off the corridor, and all of them were full of stored stones. A circular area at the end held a nasty-looking variety of saws and crushers. The walls were covered in stone stuff, but there were no other doors. Emma wasn't there.

He eased down the corridor, wincing as he brushed against the stones. He was so low on stamina that just the invisibility was as much as he could handle; he couldn't manage the added effort of making himself soundless. The demons walked out of the room and headed down the hall away from him.

I'm back. Go out. I'll check around, he said.

The stone didn't reply.

Stone? He went to the box and touched the stone lying in it. *Stone?*

Emma's not here, the stone said.

I know. Let's go.

Let me stay here to do some reconnaissance, the stone said. *I'll learn as much as I can and meet up with you.*

John hesitated. *What if they catch you?*

Finding Emma is more important than losing an old tired stone, Turtle. Come back after you've checked the other two houses and I'll meet up with you.

You'd better, John said. *I will return for you.*

He went back up the stairs and walked across the road to the pub. He stopped at the door and raised his face into the misty rain, absorbing the energy of the natural water. So far from his own Centre, it didn't do much. He dried himself and went inside.

Leo and Simone were sitting at a table with Ruby, who was still clutching her parent in both hands.

'I have to find help,' she said when she saw him. 'We have to go in and stop them.'

'Where's the Jade Building Block?' Simone said.

'It stayed behind to scout the location,' John said.

'You should not have let it do that!' Simone said. 'It'll get itself killed, like Ruby's parent.'

'Don't say that, my parent isn't dead,' Ruby said. 'I just need to find the other stones and they can help me.'

'Have you ever seen anything like this before?' John said, sitting across from her.

'Never.' She took a drink from a glass of red wine. 'You should not have left the Jade Building Block in there. The same thing will happen to him.'

'He's old and crafty,' John said. 'I have faith in him. Can you show us where the next house is?'

'I'll show you where they both are, then I'm finding help to destroy everything down there and free those stones,' Ruby said. 'You can go to the houses yourselves.'

John looked from Leo to Simone and opened his mouth.

'Don't even think about it. We're coming with you,' Simone said.

John closed his mouth. Waste of time arguing with them. He stood up. 'Let's go then.'

* * *

The manor was only half an hour from the castle, on its own large estate between Anglesey and the Welsh mainland. It was rectangular, two hundred metres long, three storeys high, and made of brick with large double-storey windows overlooking the strait.

'This could be it,' Simone said as they landed in the grounds.

John extended his senses around and down. The earth below him wasn't blocked; there were no tunnels beneath this building.

They entered a three-metre-wide, double-storey hall with huge Renaissance paintings that filled the entire height of the room. From there they went into the ballroom, which was largely empty except for the portraits along the walls. Only about ten other people were present in the museum, and when they were alone in the ballroom John quickly dropped to one knee to concentrate on the floor. The building didn't have a basement and he could sense the sodden earth for a long way down. He stood up, went to a wall and leaned on it to send his awareness through the building.

On the other side of the manor was a dining room and parlour, each ten by five metres with a six-metre-high ceiling. A magnificent mural covered an entire wall of the dining room and John wished he had time to admire it. These rooms had double-storey windows overlooking the strait, but there was no trace of demonic presence anywhere and no trace of Emma.

'She's not here,' John said. He led them to the dining room and gestured towards the windows. 'These may be what the demon copy was talking about, but if so it must be the Heavenly analogue because there's absolutely nothing untoward here. We need to find the gateway to the Celestial Plane.'

'Is there one here?' Simone said.

'Leo, check the gardens. Simone, stay with me and we'll look around,' John said.

Leo dropped his head and disappeared.

'The top floor's occupied by the Lord of the manor,' Simone said. 'The rest of it's a museum. Where do we start looking?'

'The stables,' John said. 'The big building next door.'

He took her hand and they teleported to the stables. They were as large as the house and a similar shape, with gothic arched windows. The interior wasn't as well-kept as the house; assorted junk from the house had been stored there and the paint on the concrete walls of the loose boxes was peeling. They walked the length of the building and found nothing.

'Back to the house, but I'm sure there's nothing there,' John said. 'Go straight onto the roof.'

The villages and hillsides on the other side of the strait were clearly visible from the roof. John walked around, feeling for anything different, and found nothing. Simone crouched and put her hands on the roof tiles, then shook her head and stood up again.

'I don't think there's a gateway here. We need to find one somewhere else.'

'There's one near Holyhead: two stones that are obviously a way to the Celestial Plane. This house looks too much like what the demon was describing to be a coincidence. We'll go straight there.'

Meet us on the roof, he said to Leo. *There's nothing here.*

Already on my way back, Leo said. *We're wasting time and need to find her.*

* * *

They flew over the gateway twice before Simone spotted the field halfway up Holy Mountain that held the stones. The ocean was visible a long way below them. The stones stood behind a grey cottage with a stone wall behind it and a line of laundry flapping in the cold autumnal wind.

'Just keep an eye out for those crazy snake people,' Leo said.

'They were after Emma, not us,' Simone said.

She hesitated when she neared the ponies in the field, but when they didn't act aggressively she moved towards the stones with more confidence.

Where are you, Father? Martin said.

You should not have come, you have duties to perform in the North, John said, well aware of Martin's reasons for coming with the squad. *Lock onto my location. We are at the Penrhos Feilw standing stones, preparing to sortie into the Western Celestial Plane. You will take Simone and Leo home before I go.*

Understood, Martin said.

'Don't touch them!' John yelled at Simone when she put her hand out towards one of the stones. 'Remember that stone that One Two Two used — it was a teleporter to take you to him.'

'I remember,' she said, pulling her hand back. 'These don't look anything special. I can't even feel how old they are.'

'We should have made the Jade Building Block come along,' Leo said.

'Stand back from them,' John said.

He opened all of his senses and prowled around the stones, looking for the gateway. They were mossy slabs of rock, thirty centimetres by five centimetres, three metres high and three apart. Simone was right: they appeared to be ordinary stones.

Martin and the squad appeared down the hill from them. Martin waved as they approached. He quickly embraced Leo and Simone, then fell to one knee in front of John. 'Xuan Tian.'

'Rise,' John said. He turned to the stones. 'Before you go, take a look at these.'

Martin studied the stones without touching them. 'I see nothing interesting at all about them except for the fact that they were put up here about three thousand years ago.'

'They should be a gateway,' John said, putting his hands on his hips. 'I'm loathe to touch them; something isn't right.'

Martin nodded. 'Let me then.'

John gestured with one hand towards the stones.

'No, Ge Ge,' Simone said. 'Stop him, Daddy.'

'We can't risk our father right now,' Martin said.

He summoned shen energy and put it into his hands, then gingerly rested them on the closest stone. He stood for a moment, investigating the stone with the energy, and John could see that he achieved nothing — it behaved as if it was an ordinary stone. Martin tried the same with the other stone, then looked back at John and shook his head.

Here goes, he said, and walked between the stones.

'No!' Leo said, then, 'Huh? Nothing happened.'

Martin turned around and walked back through the stones.

John approached and gingerly put his hand on the stone. The minute he touched it he felt the life gone from it.

'This stone was once alive,' he said, looking deeply inside the granite's core. 'Both these stones were once alive, and they were a gateway. But someone has killed them.'

'And I think we have a good idea who,' Leo said. 'We'll have to find another way up.'

'I will find another way up,' John said. 'You and Simone are returning with Martin.'

'I am staying here and finding Emma!' Simone said.

John went to her and took her hands. 'I know you want to, but you will slow me down and I will be concerned about your safety. Let me do this alone, quickly and dangerously.' He put one hand on the side of her face. 'I can do this much more effectively alone.'

'Your father's right, Simone,' Leo said.

Simone screwed up her face and turned to Martin, but didn't say anything.

'Thank you, Simone. I will be reassured to know that you are safe in the East,' John said. He nodded to Martin. *Take care of her.*

Martin put his arm around her shoulders. *She is my little sister.*

Simone turned back to John. 'We need to stop in London and collect our stuff. I want to check that Franklin's okay.'

'You do that. I will return to the East as soon as I have found Emma. And I will find her, Simone.'

Simone's eyes widened. 'Didn't you already find her in Hell?'

'The Little Grandfather did,' John said.

'So this is it. You have to find her. She's lost,' Simone said. 'Why didn't you say so before?'

'I hoped that finding her in Hell was enough. Obviously it wasn't. Now go home and be safe,' John said.

Simone ran to him and hugged him fiercely, pressing her face into his shoulder. 'Find her fast, Daddy.'

He held her close. 'I will. I have promised.'

She went back to Martin, who summoned a cloud. The three of them rose and flew away.

John headed back to the ruined castle to meet up with the Building Block, trying to control his panic. He was running out of options. He needed to find a way up to the Western Celestial Plane. As he travelled on a cloud, he cursed himself for his lack of curiosity all those years ago. He'd been preoccupied with the interesting events on the Earthly in the seventies and hadn't thought much about the Celestial Plane. When no Western Shen had sought him out and he hadn't found any gateways, he'd just shrugged and concentrated on the humans and, to a lesser degree, on studying the fascinating Western demons.

Huge mistake.

He hoped the stones would have more intelligence for him. Just flying upwards wouldn't guarantee entry to the Celestial Plane; he needed to know the correct harmonics of the gateway. If he died in this region, he would just end up in Eastern Hell again. On top of everything, he was close to complete exhaustion. It was all he could do to stop the cloud around his feet from turning to ice and falling out of the sky. He had to find the gateway soon; hopefully being on the Celestial Plane would reenergise him. He couldn't stop now and let the trail go cold.

The castle was an impressive sight from above, its black walls elegantly laid out in an almost perfect square, with the towers punctuating the walls and at the corners. He made himself invisible as he came in to land on the street in front of it. He nearly used his Inner Eye to check inside the pub for Ruby, then changed his mind. He had to conserve his strength. He went to the windows and looked in; she wasn't there.

He walked across the road, quietly teleported inside the castle's walls and went to the tower. He took a deep breath and had even more difficulty controlling the yin as he opened the ground. He slipped down the stairs again. Lights blinked at the edge of his vision and he shook his head to clear them. He pulled the door open a crack and had no choice but to send his awareness down into the corridor. The ground froze under his feet as he did.

He sensed nothing, so he pulled the door open further and went in without making himself invisible. He turned right into the first stone storage room and stopped. The shelves were empty. He leaned against the wall — the demons were gone. He eased himself back into the corridor and checked all five rooms; all had empty shelves. The equipment had been removed as well.

He checked his watch, having difficulty focusing on it. The tunnels had been cleared out in the three hours it had taken him to go to the standing stones and return. His thoughts were so sluggish. He needed a stone to help him find the Jade Building Block, or to help him reach the Celestial Plane. The only stone he knew here was Ruby, and he had no way of contacting her directly. But the serpent people knew Ruby and they possibly knew a way of reaching the Western Celestial Plane.

Ice formed under his feet as he walked back out of the tunnel and up the stairs. The walls appeared to be moving around him; he didn't have much left. He stopped at the exit from the stairs. He couldn't bring out enough yin to open the ground without destroying the entire town. There was no other way out; he had to rest.

He staggered back down the stairs and into the first room, then sat cross-legged on the damp earth and leaned his back on the wall. Ice crystallised and spread from him, covering the walls, floor and ceiling as he relaxed into a trance. Only for five minutes, and then he would move again.

25

Emma

I landed and it felt like I'd fallen about five centimetres. I staggered and put my arms out to balance myself. I was holding the Murasame in my weak right hand.

I looked around. I was in a training room. The wall to the left of me was four-metre-high windows, the glass decorated with dandelions and clover. The room stretched away from me for twenty metres, with a mirror on my right. About fifty demons stood watching me, all with weapons.

'Now let's try it again,' the Western demon said. 'Show the squad the basic Wudang sword set.'

I moved into the starting position and froze. The order to do the set warred with the Jade Emperor's restriction on me teaching, and the restriction won. I couldn't move.

'Show them,' the Western demon said, becoming irritated.

'I can't.'

'You said that before. Why not?'

'The Jade Emperor himself commanded me not to teach anyone.'

'You're not under his jurisdiction here. Do it.'

'I'm under his jurisdiction wherever I am; I pledged allegiance to him.'

'This is ridiculous.' He pulled out a mobile phone and speed dialled. 'I need you. Something's gone seriously wrong here.' He smiled slightly. 'No, no, she hasn't broken free of my control; you worry too much. Come down and see this.'

He pressed the button on the phone and walked to the mirrors and back again.

I used the time to relax and study the room. We were on a lower floor of the same tower, but I had no idea how much time had passed. I was in different clothing: someone had dressed me in a Japanese martial arts gi, fortunately with a T-shirt under the wraparound top because they always gaped horribly. I didn't feel violated and I wasn't sore anywhere, which was reassuring. I studied my arms: needle tracks. They'd taken more blood, at least half a dozen times from the looks of it.

John, I called telepathically in desperate hope. *John, Leo, Simone, Jade Building Block, I'm in Caer Wydr.*

I repeated the message as loudly as I could in my head. If they heard me, it would be a simple task to look up the Glass Citadel and find out where on the Western Plane it was.

I touched minds with the sword and found that it was full of glee at the amount of mayhem it could wreak if I let it. It was absolutely no help at all and showed no sign of sentience.

The Demon King came through the door at the other end of the room and approached us. 'What's seriously wrong?' He put his hands on his hips and studied me. 'I can't see anything wrong with her.'

'Stand back,' the Western demon said, pulling the Demon King to the side. 'Watch this.' He raised his voice to order me. 'Do the first-level Wudang sword set.'

Once again I raised the sword into the start position and was unable to take it further.

'Told you she'd break your control,' the Demon King said.

'It's not broken. She says the Jade Emperor has ordered her not to teach and he takes precedence over me.'

'Well, he would,' the Demon King said, crossing his arms over his chest. 'Jade Emperor, one; King Francis, zero.'

'He knew she'd end up here?'

'Possibly. Or the Jade Emperor was just being a dick; he's done that before.'

'What am I supposed to do? She won't teach them for me.'

'Find a workaround. Have her do the sets and video her or something. You'll find a way.' He turned back to the door. 'Oh, I need you to stop taking blood for two or three days. The lab's nearly ready for her.'

I couldn't stop the sound coming from my throat as I tried to break his control.

The Demon King turned back to me. 'See? She's working her way out of it already. You should put her under again.'

'What do you want to say?' King Francis said with interest.

'Don't do anything to me! I don't want to have your children. Leave me alone!'

'Oh, okay, I won't,' the Demon King said. 'I'll just leave fifteen years of research sitting in the lab and won't put it to good use.' He walked out of the room, waving one hand behind him. 'Day after tomorrow we'll be prepping her for the procedure. I suggest you find a workaround before then.'

King Francis glared at me. 'When I say "now" you will lose all individual thought and will and exist only to serve me.'

'No!' I screamed.

'Now,' he said, and grinned.

* * *

340

I was sitting alone in my room when I saw the movement in the mirror again. Even though I hadn't been told to approach the mirror, something about it called to me. I placed my hand on the glass and everything snapped into focus.

It was the same woman, this time wearing tan breeches and a soft white tunic.

You must work harder to free your will, she said. She smiled, and the whole world filled with the joy only a Shen could share. *You do not need much help, Emma, you are already breaking his hold when he frees your thoughts. It will not take long before he has no control at all. Remember that.*

What's your name? I said.

Emmaline, the same as yours.

You're my ancestor?

No. If you were descended from me you would be much more powerful.

Wow, thanks.

You're welcome. Someone is coming. I suggest you pretend to be still controlled, and concentrate on breaking his hold.

I have an idea how I can do that, I said.

Well done. She faded away.

I sat back in the chair next to the window and mentally linked King Francis's orders with something so terrible that it would break anyone's hold over me: memories of the Demon King's experiments.

Zhenwu

John jerked awake, but was unable to move. He was completely encased in ice. He had a moment of disorientation, then melted the ice around him, causing a small flood out of the stone-walled room.

As he stood, he checked his watch: the ice had killed it. He pulled his mobile phone out of his pocket and pressed the button to wake it, but it didn't. He tried to turn it on or off and nothing happened. Either the battery was dead or the moisture had killed that as well. He opened the back of the phone and water dripped out. Dead.

He sent his now-stronger senses out and saw that the tunnels were still deserted. He went back to the stairs, opened a portal and climbed out. It appeared to be early morning; he'd slept the whole night. Ruby wasn't anywhere nearby.

He prowled the town looking for a phone box, but when he found one it had been vandalised and was useless. He walked to the sea, checked around to ensure that nobody was watching him, climbed over the low breakwater wall and fell into the water. He swam around the north side of Anglesey and into the harbour at Holyhead. He pulled himself out close to the point where the train and ferry stations intersected, and dried his clothes. He then walked up the hill to the inn run by Mabel Defaoite.

There was no reply to his rap on the front door, so he put his hand over the lock and unlocked it. The house was quiet; the clock in the entry showed that it was 6:30 am. They were sleeping in their bedroom on the ground floor at the back of the house. Unlike the rest of the inn, it was full of clutter, with clothes and possessions thrown all over the bed and the floor. The warm fug of sleeping mammal hit him as he entered the room, both of them breathing in slight snores. A cat curled up at the end of the bed saw him and ran away.

'Mabel,' he said.

Her partner heard him before she did. He turned over and sat up, blearily studying him. 'What the holy fuck are you doing here?'

He struggled out of bed and looked around, obviously searching for a weapon. Mabel sat up and peered at him, half-asleep.

The man didn't have anything to grab, so he rounded on John and jabbed his finger at him. 'I don't know what you want, mister, but it's fucking 6 am. You can just get out before I call the police.'

Mabel saw John and scrambled away from him to cower against the bedhead.

'I won't hurt you,' he said. 'I just want to talk to you.'

'I have nothing to say to you,' she said, turning away and picking up a purple floral dressing gown.

'I need to find Ruby. My stone's missing, and she's the only one who knows where it is. You serpent people have to help me to find Ruby and then the gateway to the Celestial Plane so that I can stop the demons. They're planning something big.'

'What the fuck are you talking about?' Mabel's partner said. 'Stones? Demons? You're making no sense.'

Mabel rose, the dressing gown clutched around her. 'Come with me into the breakfast room. It's all right, Ross, go back to sleep.'

'Oh, sure I'll go back to sleep while you're entertaining this big man in your nightie,' Ross said. 'I'm coming with you.'

Mabel turned on the lights in the breakfast room and put the urn on to boil, then sat at one of the tables. 'I want you to know that it wasn't my idea. I thought we were going to talk. Margaret just said to bring you to the hall, and then it all went stupid.'

'Margaret? Doctor Margaret?' Ross said.

'You killed me,' John said. 'I was sent back to my own Hell. It took me a full day to return here, and by then the demons had taken Emma.' He leaned towards her. 'You are all responsible for this and you will —'

'What are you talking about, man?' Ross said, interrupting. 'What do you mean, they killed you?'

'He's not one of you?' John said.

'Of course not, we never marry our own kind,' Mabel said. 'He's no part of it.'

'Is this some sort of joke?' Ross said.

John touched Ross's mind and slowed down the connections to mildly sedate him. Ross sat back, dazed.

'What did you do?' Mabel said.

'Calmed him. We need to talk.'

'You didn't hurt him?'

'A couple of pints of beer would have more effect on him.'

'All right then.' Mabel rose and went to the urn to make herself a cup of tea. She raised the teaspoon to John. 'Tea or coffee?'

'Tea. Strong and black.'

'How strong?'

'British Rail.'

She smiled slightly. 'You sound very British sometimes.'

'I spent a few years here in the early seventies, studying your culture.'

'That was forty years ago. You hardly look more than forty yourself,' Ross said, amused. 'Who's your plastic surgeon?'

'Lao Tzu, the Ancient Sage, and the Holy Buddhas,' John said. 'I have studied the Way and attained Immortality.'

'I found it hard to believe you are what you are,' Mabel said, fussing with teabags and cups. 'But I saw the bullet hit you, and then you disappeared, and now here you are back again.' She turned and put cups in front of John and Ross. 'Ruby was the only one who could do that.' She poured herself a cup and sat. 'We should have listened to Ruby when she said to give you the benefit of the doubt.'

'I am one of the biggest gods of the Eastern Plane,' John said. 'The demons have been taking advantage of a difficult situation, and they're preparing to make a move against not only my Heaven but I think yours as well. It's possible they may have infiltrated the other regions and are planning to take over the entire Earthly Plane. The riots you saw in 2011 would be nothing compared to the destruction an army of demons could produce.'

'Is this a movie script or something?' Ross said.

'I could explain it for you, love, but I doubt you'd believe a word of it,' Mabel said.

'I need to find Ruby,' John said. 'The demons are holding Emma, the woman who came here with me, and now they've taken her stone companion as well. I need to find out where they are and stop them, and Ruby is the only supernatural creature I know in this part of the world, apart from you.'

'We don't qualify, we're too human,' Mabel said.

'You have the same sort of heedless courage that Emma does, and that makes you more than human.'

'We don't want to be.' She stood up. 'I'll call Margaret, you should talk to her. She has access to the DDOMA archives and might have something for you.'

She went to an old-fashioned dial telephone sitting on the sideboard. 'Margaret, sorry to wake you, love, but that Chinese god is back and says he can help us find Ruby. Will you talk to him? No, he's not mad, he just wants to find Ruby. Yes, come on up, we're in the breakfast room. Okay. Bye.'

She put the phone down. 'I am so sorry about all of this, Ross. You were never supposed to be involved in any of our secrets.'

Ross was staring at John. 'Chinese god?'

'Where I come from we're not called gods, we're called Shen.'

'You both sound like you actually believe this,' Ross said.

'We're concerned about Ruby,' Mabel said to John. 'We'd appreciate your help. It's not like her to disappear for a week. She's normally very careful about keeping her pharmacy open, and she has regular customers who need her.'

'I saw Ruby yesterday,' John said.

'That's reassuring,' Mabel said. 'We've called her several times on her mobile phone and there was no answer. We really were beginning to worry.'

John felt a shock of concern. 'Wait a moment — what day is it?'

Margaret looked up at a calendar on the wall. 'Friday.'

'But yesterday was Friday.' John saw the calendar and shot to his feet. 'I passed out for a week. I need to use your phone. Can I use your phone?'

'You pay for it if you call international,' Mabel said.

'I don't even know my daughter's phone number; it was stored in my phone,' John said, picking up the receiver. 'I have to call my house in London.'

Peta answered. 'Chen residence.'

'Just tell me yes or no. Is Simone safe?'

'Yes. Where have you been? We've all been frantic! There's a team out looking for you. They went to that castle you visited, and couldn't find a way in.'

'Have you heard from Emma?'

'No, sir. Gold advised us not to call the police, but we are very worried about her.'

'I passed out from exhaustion and slept for a week,' John said. 'I didn't mean to do it. I'm back in Holyhead, talking to the serpent people. Listen carefully, Peta.'

'Just let me get a pencil,' Peta said. 'Go.'

'Call Simone's mobile, let her know I'm okay and that I'm looking for Emma. Call Gold, tell him the Jade

Building Block was last seen in a stone laboratory in Wales. Have him contact the stone network and start looking.'

'Already doing that, sir,' Peta said. 'Anything else?'

'Has anyone been … Is everybody all right?'

'Everybody's fine, but we're missing Emma and the Jade Building Block; and until now we were missing you. Apparently Simone is driving everybody on your Mountain completely nuts. She was convinced you'd rejoined.'

'I'll buy myself a new phone right away and give you the number so you can contact me.'

'I'll pass the message on to everyone.'

'Good.'

Mabel's doorbell rang.

'I have someone I'm talking to right now,' John said to Peta. 'I'll be in touch as soon as I've bought a new phone.'

'If you need anything at all, just contact me,' Peta said.

'Emma did exactly the right thing hiring you.'

'Thank you, sir.'

'Bye, Peta.'

'Bye.'

John put the phone down and immediately thought of half a dozen things he should have told Peta. Mabel came into the room with Margaret, the middle-aged woman who'd opened the hall and sent him and Emma into the ambush. Margaret stopped in the doorway, her face unreadable.

'I won't hurt you,' John said. 'I just want to talk to you. I need to find Ruby.'

Margaret visibly relaxed and sat at the table. 'I hope you understand why they did what they did. It was a town vote.'

John sat with her and took a sip of the bitter Ceylon tea. 'Explain.'

'Your friend is dangerous. We're all dangerous, but she's more dangerous than any of us. She's more demon than human, and one day she'll go berserk and kill everybody around her. It's happened before.'

'She has control,' John said. 'I've been teaching her the Way of the East.'

'What happened when she saw the mountain? Holy Mountain?' Margaret said.

John didn't reply.

'They see it, and they remember what happened up there. They want to taste blood again; they go wild.' She shook her head at her teacup. 'We're stronger than ordinary humans, and when one of us turns into a snake and goes stupid, people die.' She looked up at him, miserable. 'Many people die. Last time one of us went mad with bloodlust, he killed twenty-six men, women and children.'

'And he went for the children first,' Mabel said.

'The demons have Emma,' John said. 'They've been doing genetic experiments. They want to make her stronger and breed from her to make a new race of demons.'

Margaret was quiet for a while. 'That's even worse than us breeding pure snake people. The result will be monsters. We have to get her out of there.'

'I need you to give me a guide to the Celestial Plane. There's a building somewhere with big windows, either in your Heaven or Hell, where they're working. I need that information so I can find them.'

'Come with me down to the town hall and we'll see what we can find for you,' Margaret said.

She rose and nodded to Mabel.

'Help him find his girlfriend,' Mabel said, still sitting. She looked down at her tea and dropped her voice. 'And when you find her, do it again and this time don't miss. I can't bear the thought of all that happening again.'

'Come on,' Margaret said, gesturing for John to follow her.

'Thank you for your hospitality,' John said to Mabel.

'Just find your girl,' Mabel said, 'and do what's right.'

'You'll have to forgive Mabel,' Margaret said as they walked along the icy street in the grey dawn. 'Her son was one of the children I was talking about.'

'Killed by the berserk serpent?'

'Yes. The serpent was her other son. Her first husband came from Yorkshire and we didn't check his bloodlines. Turns out he was DDOMA as well; his mother didn't follow the Welsh tradition of keeping her family name. Their oldest went mad when he turned fifteen.'

'He was so mad with bloodlust he killed his own brother?'

'He killed his brother and his father, and tried to kill Mabel. Ripped her open. I was only just able to save her. Mabel's had health problems ever since. After he'd finished with his family, he headed up the hill to the school and killed the children.'

'I'm only just beginning to understand the depth of the blunder I've made by bringing Emma here.'

'You sure you're a god?'

John smiled slightly. 'Sometimes it's debatable.'

'So tell me what happened after you were shot.'

John brought her up to date as they walked to the hall.

When they arrived, she unlocked the padlock. 'Nobody inside with guns, I promise.'

'Even if there are and they kill me, I will be back in twenty-four hours asking the same questions — and extremely annoyed.'

The interior of the hall didn't match the run-down exterior at all. The windows along the tops of the side walls let in the early morning light, but it was still gloomy until Margaret turned on some fluorescent strip lights on the ceiling. The walls were faced with polished stone from the quarry, and at the far end of the hall was a large stone frieze showing the serpent people fighting the Romans in both human and snake form. Cupboards stood along the wall underneath it, and bookshelves lined the other three walls. A rectangular stone slab provided a conference table in the middle of the room, with modern office chairs around it. The slab had words carved into it in a language John didn't recognise.

'It says "Never kill again",' Margaret said, tapping the table top as she passed it. She went to a computer set up underneath the frieze and woke it up, then typed into the search box on the screen. 'G for gateway. Let's see what we find.'

John leaned on the bench next to her and she gave him a sly sideways look. She was slightly younger than his current human form and the attraction was obvious. The thought of being with a human woman again just made him miss Emma more fiercely.

'I thought you didn't keep written records,' he said.

'We didn't. But we were forced to keep records of our bloodlines to stop any more children, and over time notes were added to them, until eventually we had something of a history.'

'How far back does it go?'

'Not far. We only started keeping historical records in about 1500; before that it was just the serpent family birth records. We wanted to disappear completely, but we had to make sure that what we are capable of never happens again. The story must be told.'

He looked down at the bench, and the row of round stones that sat along its edge. He picked one up and turned it over in his hands. It was the size of an apple with a hole through it. He put it down and checked the others; they all had holes through them.

'Something about these stones stirs a memory and I don't know what it is,' he said.

'Those are serpent eggs,' she said, reading from the screen and taking notes. 'Our people used to wear them to identify themselves. With the right sort of energy treatment, they're a potent protective amulet.'

John opened his senses into the stone he was holding and felt nothing. 'They're not sentient stones like Ruby?'

'No, just rocks. We're deliberately letting them fade. We want nothing to do with that stuff any more.' She sat straighter and wrote something on her notepad. 'Aha.'

'Found something?'

'This hasn't been translated in a while: document 554556. Let me see.' She rose, went to a shelf and pulled out a large volume bound in green leather. 'It's the job of the town headman — or woman — to keep updated versions of every document. As time passes, we pull them out, update the language and put them away again. That way the information is never really lost. This one hasn't been redone since 1750. It's on my to-do list.'

'Don't you lose meaning across the translations?'

'We do our best not to. It's part of the job to be an expert in old languages, and we keep the originals.'

'You're an expert in languages as well as a doctor?'

'Most of us are smarter than average.' She put the book on the table and flipped it open. 'Gateway, gateway.' She glanced up at him. 'How do you do alphabetical order in Chinese? Do you even have an alphabetical order? Isn't your alphabet enormous?'

'We sort them by the number of character strokes in the basic part of the character, then the number of strokes in the whole character,' John said, leaning over to see the book. 'Every character is made up of other characters, and if you know what the base one is and the number of strokes ...' He put his finger on the book. 'That's the Penrhos Feilw stones.'

'That's your gateway,' Margaret said. She peered at the text. '*Gateway to Heaven. We cannot use this gateway any more; it required our serpent forms. We would take the form and walk through the stones, which are alive, although slow in thought, and act as a gateway to the gods.'*

'The stones are dead,' John said.

'How do you know?'

'I went there a week ago and touched them. They were alive once; now they're dead. The demons we're dealing with are experts at manipulating stones. Look at the laboratory under the castle I told you about.'

Margaret glanced up at him. 'How do you kill a stone?'

John shook his head. 'Theoretically it's impossible. The stones are terrified.'

'What about poor Ruby?'

John tapped the book. 'This is why I'm here. I need to find her. Is there mention of a gateway to Hell?'

She put her hand on the picture of the Penrhos Feilw stones. 'You can't use these?'

'No.'

'Okay.' She left the book on the table and John flipped through it, fascinated, while she went back to the computer. 'This is an older one: 29798.' She rose and went to the shelves again.

The hall doors opened and a group of men came in carrying guns, although they were pointed upwards rather than at John. Nevertheless, John immediately raised his hands to demonstrate he was harmless.

'You okay here, Doctor Margaret?' one of the men said.

'No trouble. I'm helping this gentleman here with some research,' Margaret said.

'Isn't that the one ...?' one of them said, his voice trailing off.

John didn't lower his hands. 'You killed me when you tried to shoot my girlfriend.'

'You don't look dead.'

'Right now I feel it,' John said. He leaned on the desk and wiggled his fingers. 'May I?'

'He all right, Doctor Margaret?'

'He can help us find Ruby. Put the guns away.'

The men's expressions changed from suspicion to relief. They went to the cupboards at the end of the hall, unloaded the ammunition from the rifles and stowed the guns away, locking the cupboard doors.

'Leave us to it,' Margaret said, studying the volumes on the side wall. 'I'll let you know if we find Ruby.'

One of the men came to John and clapped him on the shoulder. 'Find her for us. We're lost without her.'

'I will find her,' John said.

They appeared satisfied with that and went out.

'Here,' Margaret said, pulling down another thick volume. 'I didn't want them to see this. The information in here can be disturbing and we only share it on a need-to-know basis.'

She flipped the book open. Unlike the previous one, the lettering was spidery with many vertical strokes. Margaret put on some reading glasses and flipped through the pages, studying the text and occasionally referring to notes she'd written while looking at the computer.

She stopped, leaned back and stared at the book. 'Good Lord, I never knew. I used to mess around down there when I was a kid. No wonder we were so strongly warned not to go inside.' She spun the book around on the table so that John could see the hand-drawn picture of two vertical stones with a third stone horizontally over them. 'Trefignath burial chamber,' she said. 'There are three chambers; the oldest two have fallen down, but the most recent one is still intact.'

'How old?'

'As old as Penrhos Feilw, maybe older.'

'And that's the gateway to Hell?'

Margaret read the text: '*Come under these stones at your own peril; place your hand on the end wall, then make it in your mind as the wall unseen ...*' She winced. 'Old terminology, they mean ...' Her expression cleared. 'Seriously, this is hard to believe and I know it must be true. *Make the wall invisible in your mind*,' she read from the book, '*and you shall be transported to the netherworld. Beware, this is not the world of the fae and our fathers, the Sidhe, but the world of demons and the dead. Go you hence and you will never return; only the dead may enter the domain of the dead, and if one who is alive should enter, they are henceforth dead and will never return.*'

'Definitely sounds like Hell,' John said. 'Where's this chamber?'

'Down past the Tesco's on a bike track. It's on top of a little hill — you can't miss it.' She picked up her car keys. 'I'll show you. I want to take another look myself now.'

'It would be quicker to fly,' John said. 'I can carry you and you show me the way.'

She was silent for a moment, then, 'Fly?' she said weakly.

He saw how terrified she was at the concept. 'Never mind. You can drive.'

26

Margaret parked in a car park at the end of the bike trail and they got out of the car. The land around was low treeless rolling hills with the outskirts of the town behind them. There was a small group of houses nearby, and the occasional passing car was audible from the motorway a hundred metres away. They followed the bike track, which ran parallel to a row of metre-tall standing stones, each spaced ten metres apart over a kilometre. They passed a few people walking dogs or strolling, who looked at them curiously.

The burial chamber was on top of a low hill. A group of teenage boys and girls were sitting with their backs against the stone, smoking and sharing a six-pack of beer. They scrambled to their feet when they saw John and Margaret approaching.

'Heads up,' one of them said loudly, then they all dropped their stuff and ran into the trees.

'Oh shit,' a voice said loudly, and a girl and boy, half-dressed, rushed out of the chamber and into the trees as well.

'I hope you're using a condom, Tiffany and Stuart!' Margaret yelled after them. 'I'm not here to fix your mistakes.'

She dropped her voice to speak to John. 'Like I said, we used to come down here and mess around. The archaeologists hated us; we used to move the smaller stones to piss them off.' She gestured towards the chamber. 'This is it. I never saw it as anything unusual before, just a pile of rocks.'

The chamber wasn't big: only a metre high, the same wide and two metres deep. John had to crouch to go inside.

'Make the back wall invisible, you say?' he said.

'That's what it said.'

He crawled back out of the stone chamber and stood up, pulling his wallet out of his back pocket. 'I don't know how long I'll be. Will you do something for me while I'm gone?'

'What?' she said, eyeing his wallet suspiciously.

He pulled out a wad of fifty-pound notes. 'Buy me a phone. I don't care what it is or what plan it's on. I'll only need it as long as I'm in the UK, so put the contract in your name and you can have it when I'm done.' He handed her the money. 'Keep the change, just get me a phone.'

'How long should I wait for you?'

He glanced back at the stones. These ones were definitely alive, but not sentient.

'If I'm not back by nightfall, call my house in Kensington and tell them where I went.' He told her the number and she recorded it on her phone.

He turned back to the burial chamber, crawled to the end and put his hand on the wall. He closed his eyes and made it invisible, and the transition was easy.

He landed on an island in a Hell that looked very much like Eastern Hell, except it was devoid of buildings or plants. The only life — if it could be called life — was a long line of defeated-looking individuals waiting to pass a couple of bored-looking guard demons to access what appeared to be the gateway to rebirth.

He approached the demons and they studied him curiously.

'What the hell's going on?' he said, doing his best to sound irritated. 'I wasn't supposed to be here. I have a job to do.'

One of the guards gestured with his spear. 'Just get back in line.'

John snorted with derision. 'You have me mistaken for one of *them*, my friend.'

'Whoops,' the other demon said with amusement.

'Sorry,' the first demon said. 'Where are you supposed to be?'

'On a mission for the *fucking* King himself, something to do with that new Eastern ally,' John said, taking a gamble. 'And I ended up here. Someone's in serious trouble.'

A woman broke from the line and ran to them. 'I'm not supposed to be here!' she said. 'This isn't Heaven! I did everything I was supposed to so why aren't I in Heaven? Someone's made a terrible mistake.'

'No mistake, my love,' the first demon said. 'Heaven's a place for better people than you.'

'But I promised my faith and my soul,' she said.

'Yeah, and you probably weren't a terribly good person,' the second demon said. He saw her face. 'You know I'm right.'

'It doesn't matter whether you're good or bad because you're forgiven,' she said, her voice becoming desperate. 'As long as you have faith, it doesn't matter how nasty you are to anyone ...'

'Yeah, doesn't work like that,' the second demon said. He pointed his spear at the woman. 'Now get back in line like a good little girl, drink what they give you and be on your way.'

'It's not poison, is it?'

Both demons doubled over with laughter.

John feigned joining in the merriment. 'Do you seriously think that matters now?' he said. 'Just do as the guards say and you'll move on to the next life. And this time, try to be a better person — you know, help those less fortunate, work for equality and justice, detach yourself from worldly needs, stuff like that.'

'Communist propaganda,' she spat at him, but returned to the line anyway.

'I love those ones,' the first demon said, wiping his eyes. He turned to John. 'So where are you supposed to be?'

'Heaven.'

'A mission from the King himself,' the other demon said with awe. 'Did you actually meet him?'

'No,' John said. 'I hatched, and they told me what I had to do and sent me out and I landed here. I'm supposed to be in Heaven.'

'This isn't it,' the demon said.

'Obviously. Do you know where I'm supposed to be? The building with all the glass? I have no clue.'

'Don't ask us, we just poke these people with our pointy sticks. Why do you look like an Oriental?'

'Need to know, my friend,' John said.

'He mentioned the new Eastern ally,' the other demon said.

'I never said anything about that,' John said urgently. 'Don't talk about it, or I'm in serious shit.'

The demons nodded; this they understood.

One of them shrugged. 'Well, I can call the boss if you like, although he'll be pissed. If you can make your own way back up ...' He gestured towards the gateway with his spear. 'Just go on through, head back to where you started and make them deliver you where you're supposed to be.'

John put his hands in his pockets and surveyed the bleak landscape. 'I might hang around here a bit before I go, just to have a look around.'

The demons seemed incredulous. 'Really? There's nothing to see here but us.'

'You know in Asia, everyone's judged, and if they were real dicks when they were alive, they're punished? Keeps the demons occupied. Hell over there is full of games.'

'Sounds like fun, but pretty pointless, if you ask me,' one of the guards said. 'They forget anyway, don't they?'

'Does knowing what's coming stop them from being dicks when they're up top?' the other demon said, pointing its spear towards the ceiling.

'Nope,' John said, digging one heel into the ground. He shrugged. 'Pointless fun — doesn't get much better than that, eh? They should do the same thing here.'

He winced inside as he spoke. It was he who was responsible for the punishments in Eastern Hell; it was one of the terms of surrender he'd brokered all that time ago with the demons. They'd agreed to stay in Hell on the condition that they could play with those condemned by the Courts. At the time it had seemed completely logical to torture the wicked, but times had changed.

'Our relief will be here soon,' one of the guards said. 'You can stay and ask them if you like. We'll be parked.'

'Point me at the gateway to Heaven before you leave?' John said. 'I'll try to make it there myself.'

The demons shrugged. 'No idea.'

'Will your boss know?'

'Don't think so. We're down here from the day we hatch. Your best bet is to go back up through the gate and kick some heads until they send you to the right place.'

'Here comes the boss,' the other one said.

The boss was a bigger demon in True Form, three metres tall with a bat-like head and many protruding uneven teeth. It saw John and stopped, staring, then summoned a weapon and ran towards them.

'What's wrong with him?' one of the demons said.

John didn't hesitate; he didn't want the demons to know he'd been there. He grabbed the spear out of the closest guard's hand, filled it with shen energy and ran it through him, making him explode. The second guard raised his spear in defence, but John pushed it aside and ran the spear he was holding through the demon's head. He turned and threw the spear through the head of the oncoming demon boss. As he checked that they were all destroyed, a siren started to wail.

He ran through the line of people, knocking some over, and out the gate.

* * *

It was nearly dusk when he charged out of the burial chamber. He thought Margaret had gone, then saw her sitting with her back to the rocks, reading a book.

She stood up when she saw him. 'So did you really go to Hell?'

'Yes.'

'What's it like?'

'I can't tell you. Did you find me a phone?'

She handed him a mobile.

'Thank you.' He quickly called Peta to find Simone's number and called Simone.

'Hello?' Simone said, sounding suspicious.

'It's me. I have a new phone, this is the number.'

'Oh my *god*, where have you been? We haven't been able to contact you telepathically —'

'Stop.'

'We've had people looking everywhere for you. Emma's still gone —'

'Stop.'

'It's *chaos* up here and they expect me to make decisions for them —'

'Simone, stop.'

She was silent.

'Thank you. I am looking for Emma. Stay close to the Mountain and stay safe. Are there any major developments that I need to be updated on?'

'No, not really. We just need you to find Emma.'

'Has the stone checked in?'

'No. The stones here are going crazy. Gold came back up from setting up house on the Earthly. He's worried about his kids.'

'Everybody is. Liaise with the Lius on running the Mountain —'

'Dad,' she said, interrupting, 'Actually, you don't need to worry about the Mountain. I'm handling things here; me and the Lius are looking after it. Ge Ge and Jie Jie are managing the North. Everything's under control. I was just really worried about you.'

'I'm fine.' He let the frustration leak into his voice. 'I'm running out of leads. I need you to contact the Archivist and find me a gateway to Western Heaven. It looks like demons have taken over the Heaven here and I need to get up there.'

'Will do.'

'This is my new number if anybody needs to call me, but tell them to only call if it's an emergency. I'm blocked from direct communication; I don't have the strength. I'll only take direct calls from you.'

'Understood. I'll let everybody know. Don't worry about things here — we have it under control.'

'I'm so proud of you, Simone.'

'Just find Emma for us,' she said, her voice strained, and hung up.

He turned the phone to silent. Within the next hour he would receive at least twenty phone calls and messages that he didn't need.

He turned back to Margaret. 'Thank you for your help.'

She held her hand out, full of fifty-pound notes. 'Change.'

'Keep it.'

'I'd prefer not to.'

He took the money, and as he did she brushed her fingers over the back of his hand, then moved closer. He didn't move at all.

'In another situation, I would be both flattered and tempted, Margaret. But my wife is out there, and I will remain completely loyal to her as long as she lives.'

She stepped back. 'She's your wife? I didn't know.'

'She is to me.' He raised one hand and made a portrait of Emma appear in the air. 'This is what she looks like. If you see her, please call me.'

Margaret studied the picture. 'Can you give me a hard copy of that? I'll help you look for her. Someone might have seen her.'

'I'll have my daughter text one to you.'

'Thank you. Where are you going next?'

'The black house Ruby told us about. Could you do me a favour?'

'Anything.'

'Search your database for a building in Heaven — a tower with big windows, lots of glass. That's my only other lead.'

Her face went strange. 'Lots of glass?'

'That's what the demon said.'

'That could be Caer Wydr, the Glass Citadel. Let me look it up for you and see if I can find a way there.'

He bowed slightly to her. 'Thank you. I also have a name: Lord Semias.'

She frowned. 'That's not possible, he's one of the Great Fathers.'

'That's what Emma said. Do you know about him?'

'There are four cities in Heaven, and each has a Castellan — an administrator — who runs things. Semias is one of the Castellans ...' Her brows knitted. 'I think it's the northern city. Gorias? Finneas? I'll look it up for you.' She shook her head. 'Up until you arrived, this was all second-hand, more folklore than real. Ruby was our only genuine touch of the supernatural.'

'That gives me an idea. Can you email me the locations of any really old stone circles in this region?'

'There's one up behind the school,' she said.

'I'll go there first.'

'I can take you.'

'I'm sure you have better things to do than traipse around with me.'

She smiled slightly. 'Right now I don't think so.'

'Don't you have patients?'

She pulled a phone out of her pocket and checked it. 'Yes, I have forty-three messages from the surgery.'

'Then they come first.'

'But you don't know where the circle is,' she said.

He put his index finger on her forehead. 'Think about its location.'

The information flowed into him, together with the unfortunate fact that she had developed an extremely strong attraction to him. It was understandable: he was a powerful, good-looking mystery man who'd dropped out of the sky.

'Thank you,' he said. 'I know where to go now.'

'That's amazing,' she said, wide-eyed. 'Do you need a lift?'

'No, I can make my own way there faster.'

She nodded. 'You're a very impressive man, and I don't even know your name.'

'John Chen.'

'Is that your real name or just an English version?'

'I have many real names. My true name is Xuan Wu.'

She repeated it, tasting the strange consonants.

He saluted her, but she obviously didn't understand the gesture. 'I appreciate your help, Margaret.'

'If I find something, I'll let you know.'

He nodded to her, then shot straight up into the air and headed for the stone circle.

* * *

When he arrived at the school playground, it was obvious that the stones had been stolen. Only indentations remained in the dirt, some of them up to sixty centimetres deep. The demons must have been desperate to take a circle of stones from such a public area.

He put his hand on one of the indentations, hoping to find a trace of what had happened, and heard a tiny click. He rose and looked around; the sound had come from the other side of the circle. He walked the ten metres across and put his hand in one of the indentations on that side. This time the click sounded like a sharp intake of breath right behind him. He stood and turned, looking for the source of the noise, and saw nothing. He stretched his senses out and heard something very much like a small child's sob.

He examined the indentation again and found what he was looking for — a small stone, barely more than a pebble, half-buried in the dirt but obviously alive. He didn't touch it; he just crouched to speak to it.

'What happened here?'

The stone didn't reply.

'I can see you, I know you're there,' John said. 'You're a little stone, I won't hurt you. I have friends who are stones, I know all about you. I want to protect you.'

'They'll come back,' the stone said in a child's voice, scarcely more than a whisper.

'If they do, I will be here and I will protect you,' John said.

The child's voice filled with hope. 'You will?'

'Yes. What happened? Was your parent here?'

'Yes. When the bad people came, my parent dropped me and buried me so they wouldn't find me. Can you help me find my parent?'

'I'm here to look for all of them.' John held his hand out. 'What's your name?'

'I don't have a name yet,' the stone said, floating out of the ground to settle on his palm. 'Please help me find my parent. Those were bad people.'

'Can you take a human form?'

'I'm not big enough yet.'

'Do you have any idea where they took the rest of these stones?'

'Up?'

'More than that?'

The little stone sounded embarrassed. 'I don't know.'

'Do you know if there are any other stone circles around here?'

'There are others?'

'I see.' John stood up and looked around. 'The places I'm going will be too dangerous for you. Do you have family that can care for you while I look for your parent?'

'All my family were here in this circle,' the stone said, forlorn.

'Can you call the Grandmother? She can look after you.'

'I have been calling her. But my parent said that the Grandmother is … slow.'

John understood. The Grandmother worked on geological rather than biological time, and was a thousand times slower than any living thing. For her, an immediate reply could take a couple of weeks.

'Can I put you in my pocket until I find someone to look after you? You'll need to stay quiet if anything happens.'

'I want my parent,' the stone said.

'I know you do, little one. And I will find your parent. You can help me, all right?'

'All right.'

John put the little stone in his pocket and flew towards the black house.

The house was modern, built at most in the last century, and sat proudly on its own small promontory overlooking the water. Its two storeys had a multitude of chimneys and gables, giving the impression of a single large mansion. It was constructed entirely of dark stone, making it almost black, and John admired the colour scheme.

He made himself invisible and teleported inside. The entry hall looked completely normal: a tiled floor and a staircase with a wooden banister. There were two doors with numbers on them on this level, and two more on the landing above: the house had been divided into apartments. The letterboxes inside the lobby were stuffed with advertising pamphlets that had overflowed onto the floor — all of the letterboxes, not just one. The whole area smelled of death. Something had died in here, and more than a couple of days ago.

He went to the door in front of him — apartment one — and held his ear next to it. Nothing. He pushed his senses to the other side of the wood, hoping not to trip any alarms, but sensed nothing.

Stay very quiet, he said to the stone.

Okay.

He put his hand on the doorknob and pressed his palm against the deadlock above it. He moved the tumblers inside, then realised that the door was open. He pulled it towards him to open it a crack, then pushed his senses inside. Nothing.

He opened the door to five centimetres, crouched and put one eye to the opening. All he could see was the white wall of the apartment's entry. He summoned Dark Heavens and pulled the door open slightly further. The white hallway had no furniture.

He stood, hefted his sword and eased himself around the door and into the hallway. He stopped and listened: nothing. He sensed no life and no demons.

He moved silently to the end of the hall and opened the door a crack. This door opened away from him and again he crouched and put his eye to the opening. The smell of death was much stronger here and he saw the corpses on the ground.

Don't look. Close your eyes, he said to the stone.

I don't have eyes, the stone said, bewildered. *What do I do?*

Just don't look.

The apartment doors were a sham. The interior of the house had been drastically altered to make a nest. The ceiling rose two floors above him; they'd taken out the internal floor, but had done the job roughly and the edges of the floor still ran around the sides of the large single space. The doors on the landing above led to empty air. The floor coverings had been removed and the floor reduced to bare concrete. The walls and windows were splashed with black demon essence, with what appeared to be dried blood crusted in the corners of the floor. Splashes of blood and essence had sprayed onto the ceiling. Clumps of mud ran across the floor from the door to the office area on the left. The office held three desks, one of them overturned.

The rest of the interior of the house was taken up by three large nest hollows. Two held dead Mothers and clutches of eggs. He went to the first and saw that the Mother's top half was a copy of Simone. He resisted the urge to run his hand over her honey-coloured hair, and moved one of the eggs, watching the dead demon shift inside the shell. It was another copy of Simone.

The second nest's Mother was an Emma copy. He quickly knelt, his heart thumping, to make sure that it *was* a copy of Emma and not her Snake Mother form. He rose, relieved. It was another copy. Her eggs held copies of herself.

The third nest had just eggs in it, all containing Michael copies. From the staining around the nest, it was possible that this demon had exploded rather than dying without dissipating as the others had.

He went to the desk and rifled through the drawers, but found nothing except a few ballpoint pens and paperclips. They'd killed the Mothers and taken everything. An inter-demon coup? Possible.

He exited through one of the large windows that overlooked the ocean and searched for the rubbish bins. He found them on a rear terrace, melted down to nothing. The demons had filled them with paper and some sort of accelerant and set them alight.

He returned to the interior and went to each nest in turn, yinning the Mothers and eggs. He had to lean against the wall when he'd finished. The control needed to stop the yin from destroying everything was exhausting.

He teleported out onto the pebbled beach of the promontory, where the low waves of the cold, black sea called to him, and pulled out the phone. There were about twenty messages from people on the Mountain and in the Heavens asking him to call back urgently. He ignored them. No messages from the Lius or his children. He called Margaret.

'John,' she said, sounding relieved. 'Did you find anything yet?'

'That stone circle behind the school has been stolen. The black house had dead demon nests in it; it was an abandoned demon base.'

'There were demons there?'

'Yes. They probably wouldn't leave their eggs, so they were destroyed. The postal workers must know the house is deserted but they didn't report it. I'm not surprised considering what was in there. You need to call the police and tell them about the house. Do you have any leads on the gateway to Heaven?'

'Yes. I think I have a way for you to reach the Western Watchtower.'

'Where are you?'

'In the town hall.'

'I'll be right there. Do you have children, Margaret?'

'What? No. Why do you ask?'

'I need you to stone-sit.'

'To what?'

'I'll explain when I get there.'

27

The day was fading when John arrived at the town hall, and lights from inside shone through the high windows. He stopped and tapped on the front door.

A man opened the door and nodded brusquely. 'In you come.'

The snake people were grouped around the conference table, with Margaret sitting at the head. John recognised Jamie, the owner of the café, his blonde daughter, and Mabel Defaoite, but none of the others were familiar. Tea and coffee were laid out on the table, as well as what resembled a pot-luck dinner Western-style. The smell of the food made John aware of the fact that he hadn't eaten in days. Normally this wouldn't be an issue, but he needed to keep his energy levels up and carbohydrates would definitely help.

Margaret gestured for him to join her at the end of the table. 'Come and tell us about the demons.'

He sat and leaned forward on the stone table top. 'The interior of the black house was gutted. It had been set up as a demon nest.'

This caused consternation among the group.

'You said they were all dead?' Margaret said.

'They seem to be closing down their Earthly operations and moving everything to Heaven. I need to get up there.' He eyed the food on the table. 'Is any of this vegetarian?'

'I'm afraid not,' Margaret said. 'We really enjoy meat.'

'I can understand that, I'm half-snake myself,' John said. 'You said you've located a gateway to Heaven?'

Margaret fetched a glossy modern book written by an archaeologist about the ancient Celts. She flipped it open to a page marked with a post-it note and pointed. 'They've studied our people, and found a vast amount of valuable weapons and armour in this lake. The people threw them into the lake as a sacrifice, believing that they'd go to Heaven and be with the gods.'

'Where's the lake?' John said.

She placed a map of the island on top of the food bowls. The lake was circled with a black marker. 'There. Does this help?'

John placed his finger on the marker for Holyhead, then traced a route to the lake, running his finger over the topology and noting the hills and landmarks. 'Thank you. I'll go straight there.'

She returned the map to a side table. 'Will you need scuba gear or something?'

He smiled slightly and shook his head. 'I am one with the water. I am the water.'

'So you're, like, the Chinese version of Poseidon?' Jamie said.

'I'm the Chinese god of water, so probably, yes. I don't know too much about your gods. My wife, Emma, did the research and I was counting on her wisdom and knowledge to help me find them.' He rubbed his hand over his eyes. 'I'm lost without her.'

Margaret put her hand on his shoulder. 'We'll help you. Anything you need to know, we're here.'

'Thank you. I do need your help with something.' John pulled his pocket open. 'Out you come, little stone. You should stay here.'

The stone floated out of his pocket and hovered in front of him.

'That's not Ruby, is it?' one of the women said.

'No, this is a baby stone. Its parent and family were stolen from the stone circle behind the school. Its parent hid it, and it escaped being captured.' John nodded to Margaret. 'Can you care for it while I'm searching?'

'Can I stay with you, black turtle?' the stone said.

'No, little one, where I'm going is too dangerous,' John said. 'These people have a friend who is a stone, and they will care for you until I bring your parent back.'

'Is there anything special we have to do?' Margaret said, studying the stone.

'No. You don't need to feed or care for it in any way except to keep it close, talk to it, and don't let whoever took its parent find it.'

'I'm scared,' the little stone said.

'I'll look after you,' Margaret said, her face softening.

'Hold your hand out,' John said, and she did.

The little stone floated to sit in her palm. 'Hello,' it said, its voice soft and shy.

'Hello,' Margaret said.

John glanced around at the people sitting at the table. 'The little stone has called for help from the Grandmother of All the Rocks. If she comes, treat her with respect, give her my regards, and give the stone to her.'

'What does she look like?' Margaret said.

'You'll know her when you see her. And the stone will as well.'

'She's really big!' the little stone said.

'I'll head for the lake immediately, and I'll call you if anything happens.'

'Just find our Ruby for us,' Jamie said, gruff. 'I wish I'd never yelled at her now.'

* * *

John called into the Tesco's supermarket, bought a bag of grapes and ate them while he flew west over the island to the lake. It had muddy edges full of weeds and rushes; his favourite sort of environment when he was a land turtle. His boots squelched in the mud and he lifted himself slightly to float over the surface until he was past the reeds and over the water itself. He sent his senses down to the muddy bottom, thick with algae and weeds and full of life.

He dropped vertically into the water and sent his awareness through it. There was a deep hole near one of the banks that the archaeologists had missed; inside were a couple of weathered bronze swords and the remains of a wooden rectangular shield the height of a man.

John merged with the water, becoming one with it, and was dazzled by the entrance to the Western Heavens: a vast, blindingly white gate that occupied the entire lake floor. He pulled his human form back together, then changed his mind and turned into his Celestial Form, so tall that the top of his head nearly protruded from the surface of the lake. He drifted down through the opening and emerged into the sky of the Western Heavens. The land spread before him, green and lovely, and the dark water of the lake entrance shimmered above.

What had Emma said? 'Green and crystal and beautiful.' This was definitely it. A cluster of impossibly tall glittering towers rose from the plains, their many spires linked by soaring walkways. The low hills were covered in green grass, rolling forever.

There was absolutely no sign of life, but John wasn't concerned. He had a start, he was in the Western Heavens, and it was just a matter of time before he found the Glass Citadel. The crystalline towers were a good place to begin.

Bells went off in his head and he stopped, hovering under the gateway. He opened himself to communication and Simone linked up with him. She was shouting.

We need you here right now! There are hundreds of them!

She sent him a mental image of an army of demons attacking the Mountain. The Disciples were seriously outnumbered.

On my way. Less than an hour. Just hold them off until I get there.

He took a deep breath, lowered his head and tried to suck energy out of the Celestial air around him — but it was the wrong Centre; there was nothing there for him. He teleported to the Earthly, and landed in the river in London. He tried to pull energy out of the water, again without success, and teleported again. It would take less than an hour to return to the Mountain, but after making the journey he would be dead from the effort within two hours.

He put that aside and teleported again. His Mountain needed him.

* * *

He contacted Liu Cheng Rong as he neared the Mountain. Cheng Rong sent him a mental appraisal of the battle situation and it wasn't good.

The demon force was around two hundred, all between level thirty and fifty. In the old days before the Attack, they would have easily routed them, but in its current undermanned state, the Mountain was struggling. Only two hundred Disciples remained actively fighting against the overwhelming force.

The demons had somehow managed to carry a hydraulic crane up to the southern gate and were close to being able to use it as a battering ram. The hook on the end of the crane's arm had been removed and a pointed steel cap put in its place.

All the reinforcements are out, Liu said. *That's everybody.*

Casualties?

More than you'll be comfortable with. Most of the Celestial Masters have already fallen. His voice changed slightly. *I was on the verge of sending out the first years.*

That won't be necessary, John said. *Retreat. Pull them into the walls and shore up the gate. I'm ten minutes away.*

I've already called them in, Liu said. *We're threading energy around the gate, but we don't have much. Hurry.*

Have you asked for help?

Northern Palace is under attack from a single large demon that's trying to destroy the castle itself. Prince Ming says it is under control but it's keeping the entire Northern Imperial Guard busy. West is besieged by insects — small, seemingly natural ones, which are deadly toxic if they bite you. Thirteen wives have died and twenty-three more are close to death. I have asked for the Phoenix and Dragon to help us and they are both sending reinforcements; they weren't attacked.

John arrived at the familiar mountains of Celestial Wudang and saw the demons driving the crane into position to destroy the southern gate. He couldn't risk using yin so he took Celestial Form, summoned Seven Stars and threw a massive ball of his remaining shen energy at the crane. The Disciples loudly cheered from the battlements as the crane hissed and melted, steam rising from the structure.

The demons abandoned it and scattered. Some stood their ground, and a couple of them fired at him using modern automatic weapons. He was hard-pressed to dodge the fast-moving bullets. He landed behind the crane and hacked into the demons with his sword, mercilessly destroying them. He couldn't block all the bullets and did his best to ignore them as they lodged in his thick Celestial skin.

Some of the demons were trained and could parry a few of his blows, but they were completely outclassed. They retreated to the other side of the melting crane and gathered into a group of a hundred, then charged in an effort to topple him. He leaned into the weight of them and they didn't knock him over. He summoned his aura and those closest to him disintegrated.

A sword was plunged into his shoulder. He reached around, ripped it out and used it in his off hand to destroy the demons in front of him. He swung the swords wide, Seven Stars singing its deadly bass song, and blunted the pain of the blows that he received as the demons tried to use force of numbers to overpower him. Another weapon hit him in the left shoulder; even he couldn't battle a hundred at once without taking some damage. Blood ran down his left arm, making his grip on the sword slip. The demons saw the damage and one of them attacked with a vicious axe blow that took his left arm completely off. He didn't have time to cauterise the wound; he continued to swing one-armed at the demons around him, his vision blurring and red from exhaustion and blood loss.

A shout rang out overhead. The demons panicked and scattered as a wash of flame destroyed everything for metres in front of him.

Clear the field, someone said from above.

John staggered towards the gate and looked up to see fifty of the South's Red Warriors in crimson phoenix form. They swept over the battlefield and flame jetted from their beaks, engulfing every demon below. The demons' screams rose in pitch and the acrid smell of burning demon essence spread over the landscape.

Lord Xuan, you need to move. We don't have precise control over the flame, the lead Red Warrior said.

John fell to his knees next to the gate, deafened by exhaustion and barely able to see. *I'm finished. Forget that I'm here and do what needs to be done.*

We will work around you.

Destroy everything, including me, and that is an order.

A phoenix lifted him in its claws, carried him to the battlements and lowered him gently onto the stone.

'Move away, give me room,' Edwin said. 'Simone, freeze the stump for me.'

'What? No!' Simone said, distraught.

'We're losing him; we need to stop the bleeding. Do it.' Edwin's voice changed to regret. 'Never mind, there's no pulse. He's gone.'

'Please don't rejoin, Daddy,' Simone said, her voice full of tears.

John went deaf; he tried to concentrate on Court Ten as everything spun away.

* * *

He felt a wash of relief as he landed, standing, in Court Ten in Celestial Form, facing the dark furious face of Judge Pao.

'Kneel before your judge,' one of the court officers said.

'Go to hell,' John growled.

Pao pushed his chair back and stood. He stomped down the stairs towards John and stopped in front of him, glaring. They were of equal height and John matched Pao's stare, not shifting his gaze from Pao's black-skinned face, darker than his own.

'You have a choice,' Pao said. He paced in front of John, one hand on the belt over his yellow silk judicial robe. 'The Celestial Himself has summoned you —'

'I'm heading straight back to find Emma.'

Pao spun and glared at John. 'The Celestial is well aware of your ridiculous weakness in regards to human women. So you have a choice.'

'Humans are our reason for existence.'

'Your choice is this,' Pao said, ignoring him. He walked back to stand in front of John and they matched stares again. 'Either go immediately to audience with the Celestial, or face punishment in *every single level of Hell*. Your choice.'

John tried to leave to find Emma, but couldn't.

'Choose,' Pao said.

'I am First Heavenly General, Pao, you can't do this to me —'

'I can and I have. I answer to none but the Celestial Himself,' Pao said with quiet fury, stabbing his index finger at the floor between them. 'You do not have precedence over me.'

He walked back up the stairs to the top of the dais and sat at his desk. 'Personally, I would love to send you through all ten levels and teach you the meaning of responsibility. You are failing in your duty to protect the Celestial realm. People — your oh-so-dear-humans — are *dying*, Zhenwu, and you are running around the far corners of the world chasing a single worthless woman. These are not the acts of an Immortal Worthy.' He dipped his brush meticulously into the ink on the inkstone and held it over the judgement scroll. 'Choose, Turtle. Heaven or Hell.'

'Release me to Heaven and I will attend the Jade Emperor immediately,' John said through gritted teeth. 'He is the one who sent me to the West —'

Pao didn't let him finish as he wrote the judgement onto the scroll. 'Very well. You are released.'

John stomped through the Celestial Palace, but carefully held his yin in check — the palace didn't need to suffer for his fury again. The buildings were full of activity; fairies were fitting every window and door with insect screening.

He entered the Jade Emperor's informal meeting room and fell to one knee. 'Ten thousand years.'

'Come and sit, Ah Wu,' the Jade Emperor said from his yellow silk cushioned chair, its rosewood carved with six-toed dragons.

John sat in one of the guest chairs that faced side-on to the Emperor's throne and the Jade Emperor poured tea for them both. John tapped the table next to his cup in thanks.

'Don't worry, Ah Wu, I will release you to find her,' the Jade Emperor said. He saw John's relief. 'We still need to find out what's happening over there. You are no good to us here fretting. You have already demonstrated what happens when you're distressed: the palace itself suffers.'

'That won't happen again,' John said.

He sipped the tea and let its pure fragrance ease his worries slightly.

'Good tea always takes away some of the horrors,' the Jade Emperor said. He sipped, then put his cup down and opened a box and tipped out an enormous wasp, fifteen centimetres long. 'This is one of them. The other three Winds are on their way; together you must study these new demons and find a way to deal with them before you go. They are deadly.'

'Was it the stings that killed the wives?' John said, studying the insect without touching it.

'Yes. They contain a large amount of toxin because of their size. We have never seen a poison like it. One of the wives suggested it may be a variant of snake venom because of the speed of death. She said it was like an Australian viper of some sort. She was stung herself.'

'Australian? It wasn't Emma's friend, Louise, was it?' John said, concerned.

'We'll ask Thirty-Eight. She was there, and she's waiting outside to speak to me.'

'What escorted these demons to Heaven?' John said, lifting the wasp's stinger with the end of one of the Emperor's writing brushes.

'A cockroach the size of a bus. It wasn't poisonous itself, but its sharp legs did quite a lot of damage to the walls of the Western Heavens. Largest insect-type we've ever seen.' He answered John's question before he asked it. 'The Horsemen took it apart.'

'Did any of these wasp things invade here? You're having screens put in.'

'No. Only the West.'

'But you're taking precautions,' John said.

'Better to be safe. I have many mortals here as well.'

John contacted Yue Gui. *Number Two, have the entire Northern Heavens insect screened. Tell the Lius to do the same to the Mountain. Liaise with the Celestial Palace, they are having it done now.*

Already being arranged, Yue Gui said. *Father, there is much that we need to discuss —*

Later, he said, and cut her off. 'You said Thirty-Eight is here and she saw what happened?' he asked the Jade Emperor.

'Yes.' The Jade Emperor raised one hand and a beautiful slender Chinese woman in her mid-forties entered the room.

She fell to one knee. 'Ten thousand years.'

'Thirty-Eight,' John said, nodding to her.

'Lord Xuan.' She sat on the other side of the Jade Emperor, her long fingers clutching the arm of her rosewood chair. 'My Lords, I seek your permission to take True Form and sortie into Hell for you. I will gather intelligence on what is happening.'

John glared at her. 'That is too dangerous, Sophia. They'll see through you and destroy you.'

'The King is never there; and hardly any of the new generations know me.'

'They'll see you've turned.'

'No, they won't.'

'You can't do this, Sophia, you're close to regaining your free will. Don't throw it away like this,' John said.

'Three of my best friends were attacked by those horrible things!' she said, distraught. She sniffled and wiped the back of her hand over her eyes. 'I *love* Xiao and Louise and Yuko like sisters, and two of them are in a coma and one is dead. So many of my dear friends and sisters died.' She gulped a huge breath. 'I must go down and find out what's happening.'

'Wait ... Louise?' John said. 'Emma's friend Louise?'

'In a coma,' the Tiger said as he entered. He fell to one knee. 'Ten thousand years.' He sat next to Thirty-Eight and held her hand in both of his.

'How are they?' she said.

'We won't know for a while. They're on life support so they won't die, but the doctors need to wait and see how much damage has been done.' He lifted one of his hands from hers and rubbed his face. 'It's possible they'll be fine. It's possible they'll end up vegetables. It's possible they'll never wake up at all.'

She dropped her head and sobbed once, quietly.

'Be strong, Sophia,' he said gently.

'I'm so damn tired of being strong,' she said. She pulled herself together and glared at John. 'Don't try to stop me. I'm going down there to find out what's happening.'

'You will be dead within two hours,' John said. He switched to silent speech and spoke to the Tiger. *She's not yet gained free will. Forbid her or lose her.*

'Sophia, please,' the Tiger said. 'I don't want to order you to stay out of there. Let the experts handle it.'

'I'm a level seventy-eight Mother — I'm more expert than anyone!'

'I am a greater expert and I say you will not last five minutes in there,' John said.

'You don't know me,' she said.

'Sophia, darling,' the Tiger said.

She ripped her hands out of his. 'I am not your darling right now.'

'I really don't want to spoil what we have by ordering you. Give it up and we'll find another way.'

'Why can't I leave?' she said. She glared at the Jade Emperor. 'Are you stopping me from going?'

'Of course I am, dear one, because the men are right. Listen to them,' the Jade Emperor said.

'Oh, the men are right, are they?' she said with a sneer. 'Of course, the *woman*,' she said the word with such malice that John flinched, 'is wrong and you know best. They were like *sisters* to me, something I've never had, and I want this to stop.'

'Thirty-Eight, I order you —' the Tiger said.

'No!' she yelled. 'Take my free will and I might as well be dead. Just let me find out what's happening.'

'I order you to return to the Western Heavens immediately and stay there until I order otherwise.'

She went ice-cold. 'I cannot believe you would do such a thing to me. I may not be home when you get there, *darling*.' She angrily shook his hand free from hers and stormed out.

The Tiger shook his head. 'Set her back by a hundred years.'

'It was her will or her life,' John said. 'I would have done the same thing.'

'You know what, Ah Wu?' the Tiger said, studying John carefully. 'I think you would let your wife die rather than take her free will. But that's just me. Now.' He leaned over the dead wasp on the table. 'My kids in the lab are looking into these — they're a nasty reptile-insect hybrid the like of which the Celestial has never seen.' He looked up at the Jade Emperor. 'They are making new and more fearsome hybrids all the time, and we need to find where they're making them.'

'Ah Wu has my mandate to return to Europe,' the Jade Emperor said.

'Good. Do you want to take anyone with you?' the Tiger asked John. 'I'd come myself, but I have too many mortal wives to protect. Take some of my Horsemen.'

'No, I'm faster working alone,' John said. 'I made it into the Western Heavens just as we were attacked. I think the fact that we were attacked at all demonstrates that I was in the right place.'

The Jade Emperor rose and bowed slightly to them. 'The Phoenix and Dragon are here. I will leave it to the four of you to coordinate your plans for defence. If you require Er Lang to attend, he is nearby supervising the reinforcement of the palace walls.'

John and the Tiger stood, then fell to one knee as the Jade Emperor glided out of the audience hall. He stopped at the doorway and spoke to someone outside. 'They're in here.'

The Dragon and Phoenix came in, and the four Winds pulled their chairs closer together.

The Tiger gingerly picked up the wasp by its wings. 'There's a snake in Australia, tiny little thing, kills you in thirty minutes. This is the same venom.' He dropped the wasp and brushed his hands against each other, then glanced at John. 'So what's the word in Europe? I hear you found Emma's people.'

'Hybrid snake-demon people. Bred by their Shen to fight human conquerors, but it all went bad.' John ran his hand over his face. 'They say that all their Shen are gone, and it looks like the demons have taken Heaven.'

'That's really not good,' the Tiger said.

'Understatement of the century,' the Phoenix said.

The Dragon jumped; his mobile phone had gone off in his pocket with a Japanese pop tune accompanied by an impossibly sweet girl's voice.

'That's a vocaloid,' the Phoenix said with amusement. 'You are far too old to be listening to that.'

'I own it,' the Dragon said as he checked who was calling. 'I was developing software to see if demons could be controlled by a voice at a particular pitch, and it turned out the voice sounded magnificent when it was singing. I had some of my kids match it to a cute girl model and I'm making a fortune; it's hugely popular.' He smiled slightly. 'Never did get the demon thing working.'

He sharpened his voice and snapped into the phone, 'What? I left strict instructions that I was not to be disturbed.' As he listened, his eyes widened and he glanced at John. 'No. Don't tell anybody. Need-to-know basis only, do not share this. No, we all know she's alive anyway, so don't tell anyone. YouTube? Okay.'

He pulled the phone from his ear and glared at it as he cut the line. 'Ah Wu, there is something very important that you have to see,' he said.

He placed his phone on the table face up, waved one hand over the device and a transparent computer screen appeared hanging in the air. A keyboard made of light shone onto the surface of the table below it.

'This technology isn't released yet, so mind who you tell about it,' the Dragon said, tapping on the keyboard. 'My daughter says there's a YouTube video with a password attached so only we can see it.' He quirked a small smile. 'They know way too much about you, Ah Wu: the password is "genbu".'

John stiffened slightly. It wasn't common knowledge anywhere outside the present company how much he hated his Japanese name. The name itself — Genbu — wasn't an issue, but the Japanese had turned his spiritual nature into a creature of humour and disrespectful parody in anime and manga far too many times.

The Dragon brought the video up on the screen and tapped the table where the volume button was, then pressed play. It was Emma, sitting alone in a chair and facing the camera. She had the blank face of a …

'Demon under control?' the Phoenix said. 'How is this possible?'

'All her snake ancestors are part-demon,' John said. 'A very small part. They're so close to human —'

Emma started talking and he stopped.

'Don't come back for me,' she said. 'Don't try to …' She choked on the words. 'To. To. To. Don't. Try.' She stared at the camera, eyes wide and frightened, then screwed up her face with effort.

'Read the card,' someone ordered off screen. It wasn't the Eastern King of the Demons.

Emma panted a few times, staring into the camera with desperation, then spat the words out quickly. 'Don't try to enter this Plane again, they've closed it. We will …' She dropped her head and shook it. 'Will. Will. No.' She raised her head. 'John! I'm at Caer —'

The sound was turned off, but they could still see her mouth moving. It was obvious that she was saying 'Caer Wydr, the Glass Citadel'.

'Oh, well done, Emma,' the Tiger said softly.

John didn't remember standing but he was on his feet.

On the screen, two guard demons grabbed Emma and bundled her out of the chair. A man moved into view, slightly out of focus. The sound returned.

'I hear you've vowed to destroy us all,' the man said. 'What if she's a mix? Part-human, part-demon? What if one of us can control her? What happens to your vow then? I *can* control her, so from where I'm standing she's a demon, and you've vowed to destroy her. Funny when things are only in black and white, isn't it?' He grinned at the camera. 'George wanted you out of the way so we could seal everything up.

There's no way into the Western Heavens now. Be good, sit tight, don't attempt to attack either of our realms and the *demon woman* won't get hurt. You can see we haven't harmed her, and as long as you stay put she won't be.' He waved one hand dismissively at the camera. 'That's enough. Turn it off.'

The Dragon waved one hand over the phone to make the screen and keyboard disappear, then picked it up and speed dialled.

'That video,' he said. 'Yes. I want it pulled apart pixel by pixel. I want to know who that is and where it is. That demon has to have an Earthly identity. Anything you can find. No! I don't want excuses. I want information.'

He hung up. 'So where now?'

'Caer Wydr — I thought so,' John said. 'It's just a matter of finding the entrance again and then finding the castle. Emma probably knows a great deal about what's going on there, including the source of the demon hybrids.'

'We'll send some soldiers with you,' the Phoenix said.

'My guys are better utilised as tech backup this end,' the Dragon said. 'Tiger?'

'I won't leave my wives,' the Tiger said with regret, 'but I should be able to spare some Horsemen.'

'I will give you some of my Red Warriors,' the Phoenix said. 'That will be all that is needed. The Southern Palace won't be attacked; the demons fry just from the proximity.'

'That may not be the case with these new hybrids,' the Dragon said.

John saluted the Phoenix. 'Thank you for the assistance; your Red Warriors were invaluable in yesterday's battle. But all of your armies are better utilised here. The Red Warriors can be a shock force if anywhere is attacked — they seem to be immensely effective. The realms must be defended and I'm relying on you to see it done. I'll go alone, and if I need backup I'll let you know.'

'Just leave your damn phone on,' the Tiger said, gruff.

John winced. 'I promised my contact in the serpent people I'd give it to her. I still have it.'

'Let me give you one of mine,' the Dragon said. 'A variation on Gold's work with Celestial Harmony and artificial stone AI, and linked to us through the Tree. My kids have done some great work with advanced tech.'

'Can you load it with information and addresses for Kitty Kwok's biotech labs?' John said.

'Done. I'll load it with everything I have on Europe, and the AI will respond to verbal questions.' He smiled slightly. 'Do you speak Japanese?'

'What, the actual language without Celestial translation?'

'Yes. Do you speak it like a human does?' the Dragon said.

'As a matter of fact I do.'

'Excellent. Speak to the phone in Japanese rather than English. English is too hard to understand, too many words. It will work like an artificial stone.'

'Good. I hesitate to take a stone with me; I've already lost two.'

'Emma's stone is with her?' the Phoenix said.

'Emma's stone is lost. A Western stone is also lost. The stones in Europe have been disappearing, probably to be used in experiments.'

'Has the Grandmother heard of this?' the Phoenix said.

'Yes. I expect her to move soon.'

'Good. Angering her is a very bad idea.'

'Don't tell her about my phone technology, okay?' the Dragon said. 'You know how she feels about artificial stone AI.'

'Don't worry, Ah Qing, nobody will,' the Phoenix said.

'Is there anything else?' John said. 'The trail is going cold. I need to get back to that lake. If I'm quick I may get there before they close it up, it will take them a while to seal something that big.'

'Just a minute,' the Dragon said, and dropped his head, his turquoise eyes intense. He shook his head. 'They are so slow.' He gestured towards John. 'The phone will be here in ten minutes. Sit and drink and tell us what's happened so far.'

John hesitated, then picked up his teacup. He needed that phone.

After ten minutes of him bringing the other three Winds up to date, a young woman raced into the room. She was in her late teens, with brilliant blue hair and wearing skinny jeans and a T-shirt with a design of a cat on it. She stopped when she saw them and quickly fell to one knee, head bowed. 'My Lords. My Lady.'

'Don't worry about that, give me the damn phone,' the Dragon said, holding one hand out. 'Is this the latest version?'

'This has pina colada running on it,' she said.

'Is that four or five?' the Dragon snapped. 'Just use numbers; these code names for versions are ridiculous. Completely meaningless.'

'Five point five. Six is still in beta,' she said.

'Phone,' the Dragon said.

'Please ask me a question,' the phone said.

'Where are Penrhos Feilw standing stones?' He glanced at John. 'That's how you pronounce it, right?'

'Yes.'

The phone replied in a sweet synthetic female voice, sounding almost like a child. It was similar to the vocaloid. 'The Penrhos Feilw standing stones are fifty metres back from the road at ...' It gave the map coordinates.

The Tiger glared. 'I prefer the natural way of doing things.'

'That's why you'll always be trailing behind,' the Dragon said. He handed the phone to John. 'As you can see, it's marked the stones on the map for you, and knows where you are in relation to them.'

'Where is the Glass Citadel, Caer Wydr?' John said to the phone.

A map appeared on its screen. 'The Glass Citadel, also known as Caer Wydr or the Glass Fortress, is thought to exist in the Western part of the Western Celestial Plane. It is surrounded by low rolling hills and there is a river nearby.'

'I programmed that in after the Archivist gave us the information,' the Dragon's daughter said with pride.

John rose. 'Thank you. I've wasted enough time; I need to find Emma and find out what they're doing over there.'

He clasped hands with each of the Winds in turn and headed directly out towards the West.

28

Emma

'Now tell me what you really think,' Francis said.

I had to answer him, but I managed to hesitate before I did. 'I'm home.'

'That's more like it.'

We were standing on a forest trail, among trees that had trunks three metres across and canopies so high they were almost invisible. The ground was covered in fallen leaves and moss, and sunlight rippled through the trees above, green and comforting. Birds called from a distance and answered closer, and an impossibly huge bright blue butterfly meandered through the tree trunks. The air was fresh with the scent of the trees and the earth and I breathed it in deeply.

Francis started to walk and gestured for me to follow him. I looked around, ready to make a break for it.

'Don't try to escape,' he said.

As I followed him along the trail, I resisted his control by mentally visualising Kitty Kwok filling me with demon essence.

'Where is this?' I said. 'I can't see the Citadel anywhere.'

'We had to move. You told him where our main base was, and he was being a pain.'

I felt a little thrill of satisfaction. John was looking for me and must have been close.

Francis linked his hands behind his back as he walked, looking for all the world like an English gentleman in his slacks and hound's-tooth jacket.

'You said you feel that this is your home?'

'I've been dreaming about this place forever,' I said. 'I belong here.'

He stopped and turned to me, his pale blue eyes full of amusement. 'We own it now. If you want to live here, you have to talk to me.'

'What happened to the gods?'

He turned back to the path and raised his head slightly into the sunshine. 'Wonderful, isn't it? Why would anyone throw this away?' He dropped his head again. 'Sometimes, if you have a good heart and you make too many mistakes, you can't live with yourself any more.' He shook his head. 'Something new came along. They thought it was a better option than themselves, so they moved aside to let it take their place.' He grunted a short laugh. 'If only they could have seen where it would lead.'

'They're gone completely?'

'Yes.'

'He'll find me, you know.'

'He already did; he found you in level six of your Hell. As long as we're one step ahead of him, we can keep you as long as we like.' He studied me. 'You're so tiny. If you'd never met him, you'd be nothing.'

'No. If I'd never met him I'd still be me, and that's not nothing.'

'Compared to us you are. The world will be ours. Kitty has her hand in so many schemes that not even I can keep up with them all. She really is very impressive, but it wouldn't hurt to have another lady around when she's off doing her stuff.'

'You and George ...?' I said.

'Match made in Heaven.'

'He'll betray you.'

'I've never met anyone like him before. Friend, lover, sister, brother — he's everything I've ever wanted in a partner. And you know what else? He feels the same way. We share something very special.' He turned to walk on. 'But you and I could have something very special too. If you were to turn and join us, you could have this.' He raised his hands slightly to indicate the magnificent forest. 'Pledge allegiance to us and you'll be free to join the winning side.'

'Oh, so that's what this is about,' I said. 'You want me to renounce my oath to the Jade Emperor so I can teach your army.'

'Fuck, yeah,' he said with quiet amusement.

'No.'

He shrugged. 'Worth a try. George is ready to inseminate you; I just wanted to see if I could get you to turn on your own before we do it. He's right about crossing you with demons — that kid he made in Wales really was exceptional. With a female DDOMA, the demon spawn will be magnificent.'

'Inseminate me?' I said weakly.

'As soon as he's back, we'll make some lovely little demon babies. He couldn't infuse you with demon essence directly while your arm's so damaged, so he'll get you pregnant instead. Don't worry, it'll be a clinical procedure, and you'll be under my control and unaware. George isn't into rape. One of the things I really like about him.'

'It is rape.'

'Well, you don't have to screw him. You'd probably break my control if he tried to fuck you.'

I filed that away for future reference.

'One last chance to accept my offer,' he said. 'Join us and we won't do this to you.'

'No.'

'Suit yourself. You will lose all original thought —'

'No, wait —'

'— and obey me without question when I say "now". Now.'

* * *

I followed the two guards into the new place. It looked like the manor that had belonged to the Marquess of Anglesey; it must have been the Celestial equivalent. It was three storeys tall, with high windows and mock battlements along its faux towers. It overlooked the Heavenly analogue of the strait between the island of Anglesey and the Welsh mainland, but instead of houses and fields there were rolling grasslands and a forest of immensely tall trees.

The guards took me through an elegant entrance lobby decorated with Renaissance-style paintings, through the massive two-storey dining room, then downstairs to the servants' quarters in the basement. One of them pushed me through the door of a small room, and they both stood in the doorway and grinned at me.

'Completely controlled,' one of them said.

'I wonder,' the other one said, and moved closer and squeezed my breast.

I grabbed his hand in my left and viciously chopped down with my right on his forearm. On a human this would have been a crippling break, but the demon was wearing bracers and they protected him, but he still howled. I took advantage of his pain to lift his hand from my breast, unlock his elbow with my right hand and smash the back of his hand into his face. Then I yanked his hand back, slipped my foot between his to unbalance him and toppled him face up onto the floor. I loaded the first two fingers of my stronger left hand with energy and rammed them into the front of his exposed neck. He disintegrated without a sound.

The other demon raised his weapon, then changed his mind when he saw my expression. He slammed the door in my face and I heard his footsteps as he ran away.

I sighed and sat on the bed. The room had beige carpet and white walls, and held a simple dresser and a metal-framed double bed. There was an ensuite bathroom, with basic fittings, visible through another door. The windows were high in the walls and barred. This was much more secure and less luxurious than the Citadel; but it was possible I was in a cell rather than a guest room.

I saw movement in the mirror on the wall and went closer. It was the same small woman from the Citadel, against the same background. She put her hand against the glass and I put mine up to it.

I do not need to strengthen your will, she said. *You are breaking their control by yourself. When you are free, you must find Semias. He will help you.*

She glanced towards the door and I heard it too: they were coming.

She looked back at me, urgent. *You are in Heavenly Plas Newydd. You must go West and return to Caer Wydr; they are holding Semias there. You must free him!*

The door opened and she disappeared.

It was a couple of demons with rifles. One pointed his gun at my feet while the other went to the mirror and pulled it off the wall.

'We saw that. What was in there?'

'My reflection,' I said. 'I feel like I'm losing my identity and the person in the mirror isn't me at all.'

'Damn, Dad will be pleased when he hears that,' the demon pointing the gun said.

'Hell, yeah,' the other said. 'Won't be long before she's completely his.'

After they'd gone, I searched the room thoroughly, looking for any way out. I could jump up to the window, but it was only fifteen centimetres high and I couldn't squeeze myself through that, even if I did manage to bend the thick steel bars on the other side. I shimmied down again and checked the bathroom; the window in there was even smaller. My only chance would be to wait until the middle of the night when everything was quiet and make a break for it using the Murasame's particular gifts.

I flopped onto the bed, exhausted. Whatever they'd been doing to me was wearing me out and I had trouble staying awake. As everything faded away, it occurred to me that my food or drink had been drugged.

* * *

I was dimly aware of the movement as they wheeled me into the operating theatre. Kitty was there in her human form, grinning with menace, George was next to her, and Francis was behind them. No, hold on, that was wrong. Weren't Kitty and George the same person?

I decided I didn't care. Whatever. I was awake and aware and I was out of there.

I ripped my arms free of the bindings and jumped off the trolley into a long defensive stance.

Everything shattered around me and I was in the room in the manor house, panting with effort. I'd had a dream so vivid that I'd leapt out of bed.

Whatever they'd given me must have worn off because I was feeling *mean*. I was still wearing the clothes I passed out in; obviously nobody had ordered me to shower and change in the past twenty-four hours. I felt filthy, but I had much more important things to think about. I had to head to Caer Wydr and find Semias.

What the Demon Kings didn't know was that the Murasame was close to unstoppable by any solid object short of a shield of Celestial Jade. I checked with my Inner Eye: one alert guard on the other side of the locked door. I carefully positioned myself on the other side of the door from the guard, then slid the Murasame straight through the door and into its throat. It collapsed without a sound.

I slipped the sword around the edge of the door and unsealed it. I opened it a crack and checked around. Nobody. I checked further with my Inner Eye: the basement only held captive demons.

I crept out of the cell and went left, remembering the way the demons had brought me in. The hall turned left at the end and stairs led up from the corner. I checked around me again: nobody. I crept up the stairs in the dim light to the entrance hall, where the huge Renaissance paintings showed grim scenes of hunts and death.

Two guard demons stood on the other side of the front door. I shoved the blade of my sword through the door into the one on the left. As he crumpled, the other one crouched to check him and I pulled the Murasame back and shoved it through the door again into his head. Both of them were down.

I opened the door and, hugging the wall, examined the clearing around the house. The Western Celestial sky blazed as brightly with stars as the Eastern one did, and I felt a twinge of loss for the beauty of the Mountain and the man who was one with it. All I needed now was to find him.

I quickly checked the demons for mobile phones; no such luck. I continued along the side of the house and edged around the corner, looking for cover to make a run for the trees. The scent of the sea a hundred metres below the house wafted up the damp lawn, full of the sound of the small waves on the shore.

Something grabbed me around the throat and lifted me so that my feet cleared the floor. An enormous demon jammed his face into mine. I swung the Murasame at his head, but he grabbed both my hands in his free one and held my wrists. I was still holding the sword to one side and helpless.

'Can't have any of that now, can we?' he said, then added with delight, 'I've been trying to get a promotion. I think you just got me one.'

I kicked him in the abdomen, but it was like hitting a rock; he didn't even seem to notice. He must have been level eighty equivalent; way too big for me to handle even with a weapon. If I ever got away from these demons, I was taking that damn Elixir as soon as I could and gaining the strength to take down anything. I wanted to fight them on equal terms.

'Breathing okay?' he said, but didn't wait for me to reply. 'Yeah, you are. Let's show you off.'

I dangled like a doll as he carried me back into the house and up the stairs.

'Wake the master,' he said to the demons guarding the upstairs hallway. 'I found a little wanderer.'

The Demon King, in his Kitty Kwok form, came out of the first door on the left, wearing nothing but a pair of old-fashioned striped cotton pyjama pants. King Francis followed, wearing the matching shirt. Both of them stopped when they saw me.

'Found her wandering around outside,' the huge demon said.

'Emma, drop the sword,' Francis said.

'I can't, the demon's holding my hand around it,' I said.

'Release the sword when he lets go of your hands,' Francis said.

I realised with a jolt of joy that I was no longer under his control. I was free of them. But when the demon released my hands I dropped the sword anyway. Fighting both of them at that moment would be pointless.

'Good. You will lose all free will and exist only to obey me when I say "now". Now.'

It was like being drugged. My consciousness became slower and sluggish, and I was only dimly aware of being carried back to my room and placed onto the bed.

* * *

I woke and stared at the ceiling, unable to move. Sleep paralysis — I knew this. My body was asleep, but my mind was awake. There was something I could do to break it ... I looked towards my right arm. It was withered and weak from where Kitty had infused me with demon essence. That was not happening again. I jumped out of the bed into a long defensive stance.

Okay, now I was definitely free.

I didn't have long to plan some way of getting out of there before morning came; the sun was already shining through the window high on the wall.

Someone tapped on the door and I froze.

'Get dressed and get ready,' the demon on the other side said. 'We'll be back for you in two minutes.'

Francis opened the door while I was still pulling on a clean T-shirt. 'Hurry up, we're waiting for you.' He looked me up and down. 'We haven't been running you around enough. You're getting fat.'

I meekly followed him, hoping for a chance at freedom when we got up to ground level, but he led me further along the basement hallway to a rough brick wall with a metal door in it. He rapped on the door and it swung open.

'In,' he said to me. 'You have your will back.'

A guard demon closed the door and pushed me to stand next to a large steel crusher. I had a moment of panic when

I saw the cylinders inside the crusher, full of sharp grinding teeth, then pulled myself together. Even if they did throw me into it, I wouldn't give them the satisfaction of showing them my fear.

The Eastern Demon King, in male human form, stood next to the crusher wearing a black rubber apron and gloves. He put his hands on his hips and glared at me. 'I told you that if you tried to escape again you'd be punished.'

He gestured with his head towards the guard demon, and it took a wooden fruit box from a shelf and turned back to the King.

'I have four stone Shen in this box, Emma,' he said. 'How many do you want me to kill?'

'They can't be stone Shen. They wouldn't sit quietly like that,' I said.

The Demon King lifted one of the stones from the box and held it out towards me, then removed a rubber band from around it.

'What's your name, stone?'

The stone didn't reply.

'Say something and I won't crush you,' the King said.

The stone still didn't say anything.

'See, not a stone Shen at all,' I said.

'Suit yourself,' the King said, and dropped it into the crusher.

'You won't get us all!' the stone yelled. 'We will stop you.'

'Oh my god, it is a stone Shen,' I said. 'Don't do this! Let's talk about it.'

The King pressed the button and the machine roared into life. The noise was tremendous, vibrating through the floor, and becoming even louder as the stone was carried through its teeth and a fine ribbon of dust fell into the bin at the bottom. The King pressed the button again and the machine ground to a halt.

'No!' I said. 'Tell me what I need to do to stop this!'

He put his hand out and the guard demon picked another stone out of the box and dropped it into his glove. He took the rubber band off it and raised it towards me.

'Say hello to Ruby.'

'Ruby?' I said.

'Run away,' the stone said in Ruby's voice. 'Get out of here.' Her voice raised to a shriek. 'Oh no! No, please!'

The Demon King held her over the crusher, ignoring her screams. 'We need you to stop running away, Emma.'

He dropped her into the machine and held his gloved hand over the start button.

'Anything,' I said. 'Just tell me what I have to do. Don't do this to Ruby!'

'No!' Ruby screamed.

The King grinned at me and stabbed the button. Ruby fell into the grinding cylinders, her shrieks cut off as she passed through them. I covered my face and turned away.

The King turned the machine off and gestured towards the guard demon. The demon placed another stone in his hand and he dropped it into the machine.

'I don't have to crush them, you know,' he said. 'These ones are useful whole. But every time you run away, a whole boxful of them is going in here.'

He raised his hand over the button.

'No!' I shouted.

His grin grew more malicious and he hit the button. He watched with amusement as the stone was destroyed.

'Anything!' I said.

He held his hand out to the demon again. 'Last one.'

'Uh, there were only three in that box,' the demon said.

'That's fine, honey, some of the boxes have more, some have less; it's easy to lose track when we have so many of them,' the King said. He leaned on the crusher to speak to me. 'Every time you try to escape, a box of stones will lose their lives. In front of you. So be a good girl and do as you're told and nobody will get hurt.' He raised his voice. 'Francis, love?'

The Western Demon King entered the room. 'You done here? She killed three of my best.'

'Oh, she's paid for it,' George said. 'Let me finish up here and then we'll have some fun with her.'

Francis focused on me. 'You will lose all individual thought and exist only to obey me when I say "now". Now.'

His words filled me like a mild sedative and I pretended to go completely dull. It was definitely time to get out of there.

George turned back to the machine, pulled on a transparent eye shield and waved at the demons. 'Take her back to her room. We'll get started as soon as I'm done here.'

As I walked out, a tiny stone skidded from behind the door and jumped into my shoe. I nearly hopped with pain as it burrowed around and under my foot, and had to pretend that I'd just lost my balance slightly.

Keep quiet, it's me, the Jade Building Block said.

I nearly wept with relief as I did my best not to hobble back to the cell.

When they closed the door on me, I did what I'd done every time I was controlled: I sat in the chair next to the wall and didn't move.

I'm so glad to see you! I said.

Are you okay? the stone said.

Yes. They had control over me but I freed myself. I'm waiting for the right moment to try to make a run for it — again. I hesitated. *I am so sorry about those other stones.*

Those stones caused a diversion with their dying screams so I could get away, it said. *Every stone in existence will hear of their courage.*

Nobody should die to get me out, I said. *That was wrong!*

He's been killing stones non-stop for days, the stone said. *They knew they were going to die anyway, so they died as loudly as possible to give me the chance to join up with you. Now all you have to do is sit tight, because very soon the Grandmother will come to crush these monsters.*

I have to get out today! I said. *They're planning to inseminate me.*

The stone, horrified, was silent for a long moment. *Inseminate you with what?*

Probably the Demon King's semen.

Has he been sexually assaulting you?

No. They're planning to do it as a lab procedure.

The stone was silent for another long moment. *I don't think there's any way we can avoid this. It may be a while before the Grandmother comes. You know how slowly she works and she's only just waking up. Are you sure they don't plan to hurt you, just get you pregnant?*

They won't hurt me. They want to use me for breeding experiments.

Then I suggest you let them do what they want, and when the Grandmother comes we'll get you out and fix everything up.

I shook my head with disbelief. *All my life I've been so careful not to have an unwanted pregnancy because I didn't want to deal with the trauma. And now I'm facing the possibility that a termination will be forced on me.*

Don't think about it. Just wait for the Grandmother to come and we will fix everything once we've pulled you out.

That's easy for you to say. You won't have that disgusting black stuff forced inside you and growing. Just describing it made me feel sick.

Black is what you're used to anyway, the stone said with amusement.

My expression must have shown my shock. *How the hell do you know about that?*

Word gets around.

John will be horrified; he's very private about these things. Do you know where he is? They moved me because he was close. He can't be far away.

I was with him a couple of weeks ago, but we separated when we found the stone-processing laboratory on the Earthly. I lost track of him when they carried me up to Heaven in the box. They seem to be moving their entire operation up here. We're underground here, and I can't talk to anybody. We need to get out so I can link in and find out what's happening.

A couple of weeks? I said, horrified.

You didn't know?

They've been keeping me hypnotised or sedated or something like that. I've been unaware of the passage of time. Two weeks? Really?

Yes. But don't worry, we'll have you out of this today.

We have to go to Caer Wydr and find Lord Semias. He'll help us; he's one of the Shen that was here before. He's being held captive in the Glass Citadel.

Do you know where that is?

West, apparently. One of the lost Shen was talking to me through the mirrors, but they saw it and took the mirrors away.

Good. They're helping us. The stone's voice became brisk. *All right, you stay here and I'll have a look around. I'll check to see if there's a distraction I can create to keep them busy and stop them from doing these awful things to you; and I'll hook into the network and let them know where we are.*

Thank you.

I wanted to pace the room, but I had to appear as if I was still controlled so I sat, silent and unmoving. I tried not to think about what they were planning for me, but the idea of that black stuff inside me made me want to run as far and as fast as I could.

403

After half an hour I heard them coming and made a snap decision. I hadn't tried changing to snake before because of the possibility that I was pregnant. I hadn't had a period in a long time, and it was probably because I only had one ovary but there was always the slight chance I was pregnant so I hadn't risked it. But if they were doing this to me then I couldn't be pregnant, and I needed to change. My human form couldn't teleport, but I'd done it a couple of times as a snake, and any chance was better than none.

I stood up and attempted to change to snake. Nothing happened. I put everything I had into the effort, thinking hard about my serpent nature, John's serpent nature, the yang spinning inside me — nothing.

The door opened and I threw myself at them, summoning the Murasame as I ran. They were ready for me with a net similar to the one they'd used on John, and it was heavy enough to knock me to the ground, face down. As I tried to turn over, tangled in the thick rope of the net, someone grabbed my sword off me and yelled with pain as they tossed it away. The net was gathered around me like a cocoon and I was hefted over the big demon's shoulder.

'I'll give you your freedom, your life, a home on the Mountain, anything, if you stop now and let me go,' I said.

The demon stopped in the hallway, its voice full of amusement. 'That's the best you can do?'

'Money. A life on the Earthly. Anything.'

The demon hefted me again. 'Sorry, sweetheart, but you killed two of my brothers. I think it's about time our King showed you who's the boss.'

I pulled at the rope, trying to break it, but it was stronger than I was.

'Stone!' I shouted.

There was no reply.

I filled my hands with energy and pressed them into the demon's back, but the armour stopped the energy. I gave up with frustration and thumped his back.

'You're like a girl from a sixties show, thrown over my shoulder and hitting my back with your cute little hands,' the demon said. 'Have a kick too — I wish we had a video camera. All you need is a spanking and you'd be right where you belong. Always nice to see a woman put in her place.'

'Gah!' I shouted. 'Stone!'

'What stone?' the guard accompanying us said.

The demon holding me stopped. 'Yeah, honey, what stone?'

I thought quickly. 'Ruby!' I yelled.

'You saw Ruby die,' the demon holding me said, walking on. 'Don't you remember that?'

I went still and filled my voice with tears that weren't completely feigned. 'No, I don't remember that. Ruby's dead?'

'This just gets better and better,' the demon said. His tone changed to one of deference. 'My Lord.'

'Did she just shout "stone"?' It was the Demon King, but I couldn't see him.

'Yes, my Lord,' the big demon said.

'You, bring her into the kitchen,' the King told the demon carrying me. 'You, gather everybody who isn't busy relocating people and search this whole building from top to bottom. Use the stone-detection equipment — there's a rogue stone loose in here. It's an ancient piece of jade that's been around the Eastern Heaven forever. It's her little friend, and when we find it,' his voice filled with satisfaction, 'there are some very fun things I want to do with it. Anyone who finds it will be promoted.'

'Yes, my Lord!' the other demon said, his voice full of delight, and ran back down the hallway.

'All right, let's get started,' the Demon King said.

'This one seriously needs her attitude adjusted,' the demon holding me said. 'A good hard fuck would sort her out nicely.'

'Why do men think that raping a woman will somehow tame her?' I shouted.

'Feisty,' the demon said. 'I like a woman with spark. So much fun when you slap it out of her and show her who's the boss.'

'I will talk to you later,' the King said. 'Don't worry, Emma, you won't feel a thing. I don't have that sort of medieval attitude.'

I closed my eyes and tried to change to snake as the demon lugged me along the hallway.

29

The old-fashioned kitchen still had the original wood-fired stove, but everything else had been removed to make way for medical equipment. It looked like the treatment room at the Tiger's fertility clinic. A gynaecological examination table stood under a large light in the middle of the tiled floor.

The demon dropped me onto my feet and I stood with the net still tight around me.

'Chains on her wrists and ankles, then remove the net,' the Demon King said, and three huge demons hurried to comply. 'I told Francis you'd break his hold eventually.'

As they removed the net, I tried to break the chains. The Demon King watched with amusement. The chains were rated for my strength and I couldn't shift them, and my hands and feet were too close together to do anything else.

'Cut off everything below the waist,' the Demon King said, then turned away.

'Can't watch?' I said.

'Wrap her in a sheet when you're done and put her on the table,' he said.

The demons carefully ran their knives down the side of my pants, taking the underwear with them. The whole lot fell away and I was naked from the waist down. I didn't let them see my fear and made no attempt to cover myself. I wouldn't give them the satisfaction.

The demon who'd been holding me stood back and leered. 'Can't we take the top off too?'

'Wrap a sheet around her,' the King said, still turned away. 'That's an order.'

As the demons pulled the sheet around my waist, the big one leaned forward, grinned right into my eyes and shoved his hand between my legs. I slapped down with my chained hands but it was too late. I felt more violated than I had when I was naked. I bent over, trying to protect myself, then raised my hands and shoved the chain under his chin to push him away.

'Doesn't matter, copped a feel,' he said, triumphant.

The Demon King turned back. 'You said you wanted to be a Mother, One Five One.'

'More than anything, my Lord,' the big demon said, still grinning. 'I hope my assistance here is satisfactory.'

'Take yourself outside, stand in the middle of the front lawn, shout "I am a worthless piece of scum" and die. Slowly. Take a good half-hour about it. *And that's an order.*'

'What?' the demon said, but its feet were already moving. 'No, my Lord, I apologise. Majesty, no! I have served you well!'

'I suggest the rest of you check my history,' the Demon King said mildly. 'Put her up on the table and lock her in.' He looked around. 'Where's the little doctor?'

'Your history? Were you originally female, Kitty?' I asked as the demons lifted me onto the table.

He leaned on the cabinet behind him and crossed his arms, watching as they fastened my chains to the table. 'My feet were bound when I was four. They cut the soles open and broke all the bones to bend them double. They gave me so much opium to dull the pain that I was addicted before I was five, and I never shook the habit. They sold me to a rich old man when I was ten. He got sick of waiting until

I was old enough to do my job and raped me when I was eleven. He fucked me so hard he broke my pelvis, and it wasn't completely healed when I gave birth. The baby was a girl. He made me hobble out of the house, still covered in blood, and leave my naked crying daughter in the gutter to die. He said I could keep the girls after I'd had a boy.' He made a soft sound in his throat. 'After I'd turned in Hell, I went back and made him suffer for nearly a year. It wasn't long enough. People still think that house is haunted.'

'After all that happened to you, you'll do this to me?' I said. 'Use my ovary instead. The one you took from me. You don't need to do this.'

'I would, my love, I really would,' the Demon King said, 'but the idiot gweiloh Francis let it die. I wouldn't be risking everything by having you here if I had a choice, believe me. I survived, and you will too. We won't cause you any physical pain, and you never know, you may like what comes out the other side.' He smiled slightly. 'You're a demon, after all, and your little demon spawn — *our* little demon spawn — may just steal your heart. All the spawn of Hell are my own lovely children. I'm making sure that even if some of them die in the fight, others will see the light of the sun, live on the surface and never die in the gutter.'

I lay back and closed my eyes, feeling horribly exposed. They could put anything inside me and I couldn't stop them.

The Western Demon King came in, smiling and excited. The small doctor demon was behind him.

'You will never believe what this little idiot discovered,' Francis said.

'Sounds like someone heard some good news,' George said.

'Oh, the very best.' Francis pushed the small demon forward. 'Tell him.'

The small doctor wore a pair of reading glasses, incongruous on its demon features. It pushed them up on its nose and held up some documents on a clipboard. 'My profoundest apologies, my Lord, but I've made a terrible mistake. I was expecting her chemistry to be normal human, and I've been watching her menstrual cycle carefully to see when the best time would be to inseminate her.'

'I know that. You said you couldn't tell because it's all messed up, probably because she only has one ovary, and to just try anyway.'

'I miscalculated. She's already pregnant.'

I felt a jolt of joy and a stab of desperation at the same time.

The Eastern Demon King's mouth fell open and he stared at Francis. He looked back at the small demon. 'Are you sure?'

'Positive, my Lord. Her chemistry is so different — probably because of the snake essence — that it took a while to show, but she's definitely with child.' He glanced at me. 'We should do an ultrasound to see how far —'

He didn't finish, because George whooped and threw his arms up, then he and Francis embraced, laughing together. They stood like that for a moment, sharing the embrace, then kissed and pulled back, grinning like idiots.

'We need to work out what we'll do with it!' Francis said, excited. 'Ransom? Hostage?'

'I like the sound of hostage, we have both of them,' George said. He embraced Francis again. 'This is the best news ever!'

Francis turned to look at me. 'Now what do we do with her until she's had the child?'

'Let's start by putting some pants on her and work it out as we go along,' George said. He slapped Francis on the back. 'Did I tell you today how much I love you?'

'Leave the chains on her until you have her safely locked up in her room,' Francis told the demons. He turned back to George. 'I can't believe she broke my control so quickly, what a will of iron. This kid will be exceptional, and then we *must* make some demon babies with her. You are so right, my darling.'

George and Francis put their arms around each other's shoulders.

'Let's go celebrate,' George said. 'All of this has made me incredibly horny. Nothing like a bit of bondage to whet the appetite.' He turned to the demons who were unlocking me from the table. 'Keep a very close eye on her, kids. She's smart and fast, and if she gets loose it's your collective guts for my dinner.'

'Don't worry, my Lord, we know how to deal with ones like her,' one of the demons said.

'No sexual assault! Particularly now that she's pregnant. That woman remains untouched, you hear?' George said from the doorway.

'Unlike some idiots, my Lord, I know your history and would never treat any female with disrespect,' the demon said, bowing.

'About time someone understood,' the Demon King said, and he and Francis left the kitchen wrapped around each other.

* * *

When they returned me to my room, I checked outside the door with my Inner Eye. The guards had learned their lesson: they weren't standing right on the other side where I could get to them. The hole in the door had disappeared as if it had never been there, suggesting that this building was alive in a similar way to the Celestial Palace.

I went straight into the bathroom and jumped under the shower; I smelled like gym socks after so long without bathing. The water pressure was terrible, and the water squirted in all directions from the large steel shower head over the claw-footed bath. I quietly mourned my regular toiletries and fresh-smelling shampoo as I used the basic toiletries they'd provided for me. I'd heard of women scrubbing themselves raw after being sexually assaulted, and I understood the feeling, but I had to save the emotional backlash for later. I couldn't help quivering every time I thought about the demon's face as he'd touched me, but I was carrying our child and I had to get us safely out of there. I wondered where the stone was and how long it would take the Grandmother to arrive.

The whole building shook, hard enough to nearly knock me off my feet.

Another tremor shook the floor, and I wondered if it was an earthquake, until the explosion outside my bedroom window made me instinctively duck. The shock was so great that I was surprised the building was still standing. Another explosion went off and the building rocked again.

I charged out of the shower, dried myself quickly and pulled on some clothes. The window high on the wall was cracked. Another shockwave hit the building and the heavy central light fitting rocked. I was nearly thrown off my feet again. The window went black as something slammed into the side of the building. A writhing tentacle of stone plunged through the glass and thrashed around inside my room, nearly hitting me, then withdrew just as quickly.

The door flew open to show three terrified demons in the doorway. Two of them carried guns and the third held handcuffs. As I readied to defend myself, long green spikes shot out through their faces and they crumpled. The stone stood behind them in human form.

It pulled back the long, sharp fingers it had used to stab the demons, then bent and grabbed the handcuffs. It took my arm and dragged me into the room. 'Come on, Emma, not like you to be so slow,' it said, pulling my wrists out.

'I'm pregnant with John's baby,' I said.

It paused in fastening the cuffs over my wrists, then grinned ruefully and shook its head. 'Splendid.'

It carefully pushed the cuffs closed without snapping the locking mechanism into place, then concentrated and took the form of a Western demon.

'I was about to say walk in front of me and look blank, but you're one of two already.' It raised its demon head and unfocused for a moment. 'The Grandmother says to move your shit, she's trying to bring the whole place down. Let's go.'

As we passed the dead demons, the stone bent and grabbed one of the rifles. 'Interesting how some of the Western ones don't explode, eh? Wonder what they're made of.' It gently pushed me in front of it. 'Left and up the stairs. We're going out the back door, then we'll try to find a boat to carry us around the island.'

We climbed the stairs, largely ignored by the terrified demons. The shocks through the building worsened; the Grandmother really did seem to be trying to knock it down. I broke into a run, worried the whole thing would collapse on top of us.

The stone stopped in the ground-floor hallway that led towards the back of the house. 'Not this way.' It turned back and pulled me towards the front door. 'Grandmother's helping us.'

In the entrance lobby, the chandelier had crashed to the floor. One of the huge paintings had fallen off the wall and was leaning across the room, blocking the stairs to the higher floors. The demons were all heading towards the back of the house to escape that way.

The double front doors were made of solid hardwood. They had holes caused by the Grandmother's attacks but were still largely sound.

The stone pushed my head down with inhuman strength. 'Duck.'

It covered me while the Grandmother plunged a couple of her stone tentacles through the doors, knocking them off their hinges with a shower of wooden splinters. The tentacles receded, but there was only darkness in the doorway. The Grandmother was leaning against the side of the house, preventing any daylight from entering.

The stone pulled me upright, led me to the doorway, and dropped the gun. 'Stop hesitating, I know what I'm doing,' it said as it pulled me into the stone mass.

We entered a cave made of morphing, almost liquid mud. We were inside the Grandmother herself. As we neared the far wall, it receded and the opening behind us closed.

'Gah,' the stone said, pulling me along faster. 'She'll suffocate us.'

'I understand how you feel,' I said as he led me through a tiny air pocket that opened and closed around us. 'This is horrible.'

Thank you very much, the Grandmother said.

'I appreciate this,' I said.

You're welcome.

We emerged from the Grandmother onto the grass. The stone looked left and right, then pulled me next to the side wall of the building. I dropped the cuffs from my wrists and looked up. The Grandmother was bigger than the house, towering over it, a shapeless mass of mud that grew stone tentacles to plunge into the building's windows and walls to destroy it. Now that we were free of her, she pulled her full weight back and slammed into the manor's front wall, making the ground shake and tiles fall from the roof.

More than twenty stones, each a metre tall and twenty centimetres across, were pursuing the demons across the grass, leaving deep grooves in their wake. When they reached the demons, they leaped into the air and crushed them.

One of the stones slid across to us and spoke with a young woman's voice. 'There's a boat hidden in the trees to the left about three hundred metres away behind the stables. I'll escort you but I suggest you run.'

A regular hammering noise grew louder above us and the wind picked up.

'How the hell did they get a fucking *helicopter* onto the Celestial Plane?' the female stone shouted.

'Worry about that later. Let's use it as a distraction to get to the boat,' my stone said.

We ran together for the trees, the other stones crushing any demons that tried to follow us.

The Grandmother flailed her tentacles at the helicopter, but it dodged her and landed on the grass near the water. She broke off her attack on the house and ponderously turned to pursue the chopper, the stones gathering to assist her. The two Demon Kings raced to the chopper, jumped in and closed the doors. It rose into the air. The Grandmother tossed the metre-tall stones at it, but couldn't get sufficient distance to damage it.

'Go, Emma,' the stone said, pushing me forward.

We threaded our way through the trees along a path that at any other time would be a pleasant walk, and arrived at a stone wall, the water lapping against it. A three-metre-long wooden boat, shaped like a swan with a graceful head, bobbed next to it.

'In,' the stone escorting us said.

The Jade Building Block hesitated. 'I'm still stone inside; I don't have the strength to be fully human. If I stay like this, I might sink it.' It changed to True Form and returned to my ring. 'Okay, Emma, go.'

I hopped into the boat and looked for oars or an engine. There was nothing.

'Caer Wydr,' the stone said, but nothing happened. 'Put your hand on the neck of the swan and tell it to go there.'

I did as the stone said; nothing happened.

'It was worth a try,' my stone said. 'Any ideas, Basalt?'

'I thought that was how they ran,' the female stone said. 'How about the stables? I know there are horses in there.'

'Natural or demon?' I said.

'Big natural ones; they're all screaming and scared.'

'Waste of time then,' I said, climbing out of the boat. 'It would take me too long to get the gear on one, and riding a hysterical horse through this would be suicide.'

'Heads up, incoming,' Basalt said. 'Damn, a lot of them.'

Demons crashed through the trees towards us, shouting to each other. I moved to a clear space; about time I had something that I could take down. I felt a rush of satisfaction as I called my sword and readied myself.

Five of them — really big ones — emerged from the trees and stopped in front of me. I filled the Murasame with my chi and hurled it from the sword into the ground at their feet.

'No, Emma!' the stone shouted.

I pushed the energy under their feet behind them, pulled it out and ran it through three of them. Basalt crushed the other two. I let the energy return to the sword, and it hit me with so much force that I was knocked backwards off my feet. I sat on the ground gasping and still holding the sword and hoped there weren't any more coming for us.

'What the hell do you think you're doing?' Basalt said, full of fury. 'You're pregnant! You can't do that.'

'I'm okay, I'm not drained at all.'

'That's not the point!'

'Nobody told her,' the stone in my ring said. 'Up you get, Emma, we need to move.'

I rose, then stopped and stared down at myself. My stomach looked larger, and the baby inside me was moving even though it was far too soon for me to feel it.

'What the hell?' I said.

'Move, Emma,' the stone said. 'And don't work with any more energy. It hurts the baby.'

I held my stomach as I pushed through the branches blocking the path. 'Working with energy hurts the baby? I thought it would just drain me and that's why John said not to do it.'

'Nothing to do with you. When the energy backlashes into you, the baby eats it up and ... changes.'

'Dear Lord, what have I done to it?' I said, my voice hoarse with horror.

'No, it's nothing like that. Don't stop! You haven't hurt it. Yet,' the stone said. 'The energy forces the baby to grow. If you force it too much, it will become too dark and too strong —'

'The baby will turn into a demon?' I said, still catching my breath as I pushed through the trees.

'You already have some demon characteristics,' the stone said. 'You know the Dark Lord's nature. Feeding the baby energy will strengthen it too much until it's not really human. Just don't work with energy and both of you will be fine.'

'Okay, I understand.'

We came to a clearing with the sun shining through the leaves. I stopped to check the area.

'Nobody around. Go. Move fast,' the stone said.

I slipped across the clearing to the trees on the other side and the sounds of battle faded behind me. 'How's the Grandmother doing?'

'They have destroyed nearly all the demons and they are in the process of freeing the captive stones,' Basalt said. 'The biggest demons escaped in that helicopter, which is a shame.'

'There's a road up ahead that we can follow west to the other side of the island,' the stone said. 'They'll be looking for her. How about you take her form and lead them on a chase?'

'I can't leave you,' Basalt said. 'What if you run into someone?'

'I can make us invisible,' the stone said.

'You'll kill yourself, Jade,' Basalt said. 'You don't have enough left to do that after what you've just been through.'

'The Lady herself helped me out before we came,' the stone said. 'I'll be fine.'

'No, you won't,' Basalt said. 'Wait.'

'That's them coming now,' the stone said. 'You'd better go.'

'It'll take more than a day to walk to the other side of the island. Can you live off the land?' Basalt said.

'I've downloaded the info from the other stones here,' my stone said. 'We can do it.'

Basalt turned in the small groove she'd been making in the ground and changed to a copy of me, looking pale and haggard with red-rimmed eyes. She nodded to me. 'All the best, Dark Lady.' She reached out and touched my hand, then crashed through the trees back the way we'd come.

'Don't worry, I'll look after you,' my stone said. 'Let's go.'

'Has anyone contacted John yet?' I said as I walked along a path that seemed to be going in the right direction.

'There's no contact with anyone outside this Celestial Plane,' the stone said. 'It's strange. We can talk freely among ourselves, and we're keeping track of what's happening, but we have no link to the network down on the Earthly.'

'When one of the stones returns there, they can tell John, I suppose,' I said, disappointed.

'We need to go further left — watch for a road or something that travels in that direction,' the stone said. 'The Grandmother is having trouble staying in this Heaven. She says it was a tremendous effort to bring herself and all of the stones here; there's some sort of barrier to stop us. The only reason she managed it was because I was already here and had my free will — I could open the way for her. As soon as she's rescued all the stones and all of the demons

418

are destroyed, she'll be leaving. It's too hard to stay here, and she belongs on the Earthly.'

'What about us?'

'When she arrives on the Earthly, she'll tell the Dark Lord where you're headed and give him a stone escort to contact me. The Shen in the mirror said to go west, and Holyhead is as far west as you can go without travelling across to Ireland, so it's probably there. If you take it easy, you can be there by nightfall tomorrow. It's quite possible the Dark Lord will meet us before we get there. I doubt it will take long once he knows where we are.'

My spirits lifted at the thought of meeting John in this lovely land and sharing the joy of our new child, and I picked up my pace with new purpose. I could be in John's arms before dark and home tomorrow, and I could tell Simone and Leo we were adding to the family.

The stone guided me along the trails, some of them very overgrown, but eventually it became quiet. I trudged on in silence, trusting it to warn me if I was travelling in the wrong direction. I distracted myself by making plans for the baby. I could clear out my mock-office in the Residence and make it a nursery. Whether the baby was a boy or a girl was immaterial, as long as it lived. I decided not to make any serious plans until I'd reached my first trimester and there was less chance of me losing it. But shopping for baby furniture with John would be tremendous fun; we'd probably argue non-stop about the best choices, and Leo would have to have his opinion heard as well. I smiled slightly as I thought of the entire family sharing this wonderful experience. I couldn't wait to tell Louise and my family as well. My heart lifted with joy as I thought of the bright future this child would bring. The look on John's face when I told him would be truly wonderful.

I tried to work out how far along I was, and failed. I hadn't had a period in ages. It could be anything from two weeks to three months. I looked down at myself and wondered if that really was a bump, or Francis was right and I was just getting fat from inactivity. Probably somewhere in between.

The sun sank lower in the sky in front of us, and my stomach grumbled so loudly it must have woken the stone.

'I don't think it would be a good idea for you to stop to eat,' the stone said. 'Even if we catch something, cleaning and cooking it will be a pain.'

'I'm vegetarian.'

'There's no plant matter around here that's even remotely edible without complex preparation and cooking. Do you think you can manage without food for a day?'

'Of course, but dehydration is another issue. I need to find something drinkable otherwise I'll be seriously weakened by tomorrow.'

'Oh, good point, I forgot,' the stone said. 'This is the Celestial Plane, so any water you run into should be drinkable ... Let me see.' It was silent for a moment. 'It will take us out of the way somewhat, but it's worth it to keep you strong. The next time you see a way to head off to the right, take it. There's a small stream about two kilometres that way that you should be able to drink from. It may even have fish in it. If it's life or death, will you eat fish?'

'Yes. What time is it?'

'Oh dear, I must have dropped off — it's already four thirty. I'm sorry, Emma. You did well to continue going in the correct direction.'

'It's not difficult to follow the setting sun. It seems it'll be cold tonight, though. I hope I can find somewhere warm. Has the Grandmother left the Plane yet?'

'Not yet, she's still pulling out stones. They were in some sort of stasis, and it needed the combined effort of a number of our people to make them strong enough to travel. She says she's nearly done and will be heading down before the hour is out. There's a fork in the path; go right.'

I followed the stone's instructions, glad that my shoes weren't giving me blisters. Nevertheless, I was dreadfully out of shape and seriously beginning to tire. My stomach growled loudly again, and I thought about all the different types of fungi that I'd ask the staff to prepare for me when I returned to the Mountain. I hadn't had wood ear in a while, and some white fungus in a sweet soup with lotus seeds sounded really good. A really good rich soup of dried bak choy with lots of bean curd and fresh tasty straw mushrooms ...

'Watch where you're going, Emma, you're drifting off the path,' the stone said.

'Sorry, I was thinking about mushrooms.'

'Don't even think about eating any; some may be very toxic.'

'I wasn't.'

'The water's another kilometre dead ahead; you're doing great. I suggest you stop for a drink, then look around for a cubby hole to spend the night. There doesn't seem to be anything alive here larger than a bird, so you should be safe.'

'Has the Grandmother left yet?' I asked again. I was impatient for her to link up to the network and tell John where I was.

'She's just about to leave; some of the stones will stay behind to keep an eye on things. She says to keep safe, and the Dark Lord will be here as soon as she tells him.'

'Tell her thank you. For everything.'

The stone didn't reply. I continued along the path, listening for the sound of water.

'Am I going the right way?' I said.

Again the stone didn't reply. I moved to tap it in the ring and stopped — it was gone from its setting.

'Stone?'

Nothing.

'Jade Building Block?'

Still no reply.

I moved slightly off the path into the trees and sat on a rock to wait for it to return, wondering what had happened to it and trying not to panic as the sun slid down the sky.

After nearly half an hour, thirst drove me back to my feet. I kept the setting sun on my left as I blundered along the darkening path looking for the water. I smelled it before anything else, and the fresh moisture quickened my protesting muscles.

I turned the corner to find a lovely spot that must have been artificially created when the Shen were still there. The trees opened out to a small clearing next to a shallow three-metre-wide stream with a rocky bed. There were no steep muddy banks or brush-covered edges as I was used to in Australia; the grass went right to the edge of the water, and river sand was visible in the bottom of the stream between the rocks. To my left, the clearing narrowed along the stream's edge and a deep pool was visible, reflecting the autumnal colouring of the trees above.

I fell to my knees next to the stream, aware that I'd regret getting my pants wet when the evening became cooler, and drank my fill. Then I fell back on the grass and lay there for a long time, revelling in the feeling of softness beneath me. I refused to worry about the stone. I had an idea what had happened: the Grandmother was holding all the stones in Heaven, and when she'd left, they'd all been taken with her. I was sure the stone would return; and even if it didn't, the Grandmother would find John and I would be okay — *we* would be okay.

This spot was heavenly. I smiled wryly; technically, I was in Heaven. If I could catch fish to eat and somehow make a fire to keep warm, I would be able to manage until John found me. Or until I moved further west to find Semias.

Ruefully, I remembered how John and Leo had been fascinated by survival shows on the television, but I hadn't wanted to watch with them. I'd gone into the other room to play something on the Playstation, and couldn't even remember what it was.

'You're not interested, Emma?' John had said.

'She finds it boring 'cause she's an Aussie,' Leo had said. 'They wrestle alligators before they can walk over there.'

'Crocodiles,' I'd said on the way out the door. 'And no, I'm not interested. I'll never need to use any of that. I much prefer civilisation, thank you very much.'

John had shrugged and Leo had grinned. And the unremembered game on the Playstation was really doing me a lot of good now.

30

Zhenwu

It took John nearly a day again to travel back to the West in his Turtle form, but this time he didn't force his speed. He had to trust the Jade Emperor's judgement. The JE didn't seem terribly worried about Emma so he had to hope that she was okay. The demon menace was equally worrying; the new insect-things were fast and deadly. The realm needed to be protected, and getting intelligence was as important as finding Emma.

He went straight to the lake on Anglesey and entered the water, then took Celestial Form — only to find the gateway gone. He did his best to recall the particular tone of the Celestial Harmony that had opened the way, but it refused to resonate. This entrance to Heaven had been closed as well.

He rose out of the lake and shot straight into the air, moving fast enough to leave a contrail behind him. At a thousand metres he slowed, looking for the gateway into the Celestial Plane. He hung in the air and resonated in the right Celestial Harmony, but there was no answering vibration. He moved in a search pattern and received no reply at all. The gateway was gone.

He descended to Holy Mountain and pulled out the Dragon's phone, hoping that it was waterproof.

'Phone,' he said.

'Please ask me a question,' the phone said.

'Find the location of a Holyhead medical practitioner, first name Margaret, surname either ...' DDOMA. 'Defaoite, Donahoe, O'Breen, MacLaren or Anathain.'

'Searching,' the phone said, its high-pitched female voice incongruous with its businesslike tone. 'Doctor Margaret Anathain, Medical Practitioner.'

It gave the address in Holyhead and showed him where it was. He summoned a cloud and went straight there. The building was a square grey house with a large glass enclosure at the front. He landed in the car park behind it and went in.

Benches along the side of the waiting room held red-eyed mothers with coughing children, and old people obviously in discomfort. A couple of toddlers sat on the floor playing with faded plastic toys. Everybody eyed him suspiciously as he approached the desk and he regretted not changing his appearance into something less intimidating. He was in his usual tall human warrior form, wearing black jeans and a black shirt under a knitted black sweater, with his long hair tied in a topknot.

The middle-aged woman at the desk glared at him as he approached.

'I need to see Margaret Anathain,' he said. 'It's an emergency.'

'Is this your first time here?' she said, looking around on the desk and picking up a clipboard.

'I'm not a patient. This is personal.'

'Then see her after she finishes work. We have a long list of people here more important than you,' the woman snapped, not looking up from the clipboard, then she gasped and lowered her voice to speak angrily to him. 'Are *you* the reason she's not been in? I don't know what business you're in, but it's not good, is it?' She picked up the telephone

425

handset and waved it in his face. 'How about I call the police, eh? Would they be interested in you? How about that?'

'Go right ahead,' he said mildly. 'My name is Doctor John Chen, PhD from Cambridge. If you have the internet there, you can look me up.'

'Sure you are,' she said, dropping the phone handset. 'And I'm the Queen of Sheba. I'll tell Doctor Anathain you're here, but you need to sit quietly and wait because we don't put walk-ins before legitimate patients with real appointments.'

He lowered his voice as well. 'Please tell her it's a DDOMA issue.'

That obviously meant nothing to her. He looked around, saw that there was nowhere to sit, and leaned against the wall instead, his arms crossed over his chest, waiting to see if he needed to contact Margaret telepathically.

The receptionist called Margaret. 'There's a man called Chen here to see you, Doctor Anathain,' she said, then cupped her hand around the mouthpiece so that he couldn't hear her. 'He looks like some sort of Chinese gangster — you're not in any trouble, are you? Do you want me to call the police for you?' She glanced at John, her hand still cupping the phone. 'He lied about being from Cambridge, and he looks like he could murder us all any time.' Her expression shifted to surprise. 'Really? You're *sure*?' She sighed. 'Okay, but if there's any trouble at all you just look at me and I'll call the police for you.'

She put the phone down and glared at John. He placidly matched her gaze.

Margaret came out of one of the offices, accompanying a young man. She gave his file to the receptionist, then approached John with her hand out. 'Doctor Chen, so nice to meet you. I read your thesis, fascinating work. Come into my office.'

She shook his hand and guided him towards the office, nodding to the receptionist, who was still scowling at John.

'This won't take long,' Margaret said. 'I'll be right back.'

'Buzz me if you need anything at all,' the receptionist said.

Margaret led him into her office and he sat in the patient's chair.

'Sorry about her,' Margaret said. 'It's her job to stop people from jumping the queue. We have way more patients than we have time for, and sometimes young idiots come in trying to score drugs. She's very good at what she does.'

'I can see she is.' He leaned his elbow on her desk. 'I don't want to take too much of your time. You have people who need you.'

'From what you say, the whole world needs you more.'

'That's true.' He rubbed his eyes. 'I used the lake gateway to enter your Heaven, but I was called back home by an emergency. When I returned, it had been sealed. I tried to find another gateway but it was closed. I need you to find another one.'

'I did some research and I've found another likely spot. The information is back at the town hall.' She rose. 'Let's get it for you.'

'You can just think it at me,' he said, pointing at her forehead.

She shook her head. 'It's marked on a map. It's in the middle of the ocean — I have to give you coordinates.'

He knew why she really wanted to go with him and his heart went out to her. She really had fallen hard.

He sighed. 'Let's go then. How's the stone?'

'I'm here, black turtle,' the stone said from a paperclip box on Margaret's desk. 'Oh, sorry, Margaret.'

'That's okay, Stacey, he knows who you are,' Margaret said, her voice warm with affection. She picked up the box. 'Let's help Mr Chen find his wife.'

She led him out of the office and stopped at the reception desk. 'I'll be right back, I won't be more than five minutes.'

She turned away before the woman could say anything, nodded to John and they went out together.

'Why does Stacey call you black turtle?' Margaret said as they walked up the hill towards the town hall.

'That's what I am,' John said, sending his senses around and finding nothing unusual. 'And giving the little stone a name was a very bad idea; I suggest you stop immediately. If the Grandmother finds out you've named it, she'll be furious, and when she's angry it can be very bad.'

'I didn't know that,' Margaret said. 'I just thought it would be nice to name the stone after my ... little sister.'

'You have a sister?'

'Not any more; she was ... she was working in the school. When it happened. My brother Jamie has never really got over it; both his wife and his sister were at the school.'

'Jamie from the café?'

'Yes.'

'I see. It might be best just to call the stone "stone" and don't give it a gender,' John said. 'Stones are very touchy about the fact that they're not gender-differentiated like us animals.'

'Oh,' Margaret said softly. 'I guess I'll just call you stone, then.'

'I don't mind, Margaret,' the stone said.

'What do you mean you're a black turtle?' Margaret said, realising what he'd said. 'I looked you up and found your PhD at Cambridge, but that was forty years ago. When I looked up your real name I didn't find anything.'

'Xuan is spelled with an X,' he said. 'You probably weren't looking for that.'

'Oh, I thought it was "sh".'

She opened the town hall doors. A group of men and women were eating their lunches on the central table. They swivelled to watch as Margaret led John to a map laid out on a side table.

'Here,' she said, pointing at the location.

John pulled out the Dragon's mobile. 'Phone.'

'Please ask me a question.'

John read out the coordinates that Margaret had written next to the dot over the ocean. 'Save these. How far away is that?'

'Three hundred and twenty kilometres west of your current location.'

'Can you guide me there?'

The phone was silent for a moment, then said, 'Method of transportation?'

'Flying.'

'Celestial flying?'

'Yes.'

'What does that mean?' Margaret said.

'It's a long story,' John said. 'Phone, guide me.'

A large arrow and a number appeared in the air above the phone.

'That will do,' John said.

He turned to Margaret, pulled the other phone out of his pocket and gave it to her. 'As promised.'

'No need, really,' she said, waving her hands in front of her.

'I said I would, and I am a creature of my word,' John said. He put the phone on the table next to her.

'Good luck. I hope you find her,' Margaret said.

He nodded to her and teleported out, floating a hundred metres directly above the town hall. He followed the phone's arrow and flew west as fast as he could.

It took two hours of travel, then another ten minutes of fine-tuning, before the number went to zero, the arrow changed to a green circle and he was there. He looked down: he was over a tiny island west of Ireland, dotted with small farms and green fields. He attuned himself to Celestial Harmony again and saw a faint shimmer in the air. He tried to control his excitement, then his disappointment as it faded. It had been blocked as well.

'Phone.'

'Please ask me a question.'

'Can you just say "yes" instead of that?'

'Yes.'

'Good.' He took a quick breath. 'Locate the Earthly equivalent of the Glass Citadel.'

'There is no Earthly equivalent.'

That stopped him; it was unheard of for a Celestial structure not to have an Earthly equivalent. He gathered himself, taking more deep breaths. 'If there was an Earthly equivalent, where would it be?'

'Reduce your altitude by three hundred metres.'

He dropped the required distance and hovered just above the grass.

'You are now at the location of the Earthly equivalent of the Glass Citadel.'

He tried again with Celestial Harmony and failed. He seriously needed something to hit.

* * *

It had been very hard waiting for everybody to leave the British Museum, but they were all gone now and John had the place to himself — apart from the motion detectors in the corners of the rooms, the CCTV cameras everywhere, and the bored-looking guards. None of them detected him, however, as he drifted into the forty-metre-wide circular Reading Room. Most of its lights were dimmed, which suited him more than the daylight brightness and he moved quickly through the comfortable dark. The domed ceiling high above had been renovated when the museum had been redeveloped, and the papier-mâché interior had been repainted in stunning pale blue, cream and gold.

As he slid quietly between the silent desks, he flashed back to the early seventies, when he'd spent a great deal of time here researching Arthurian mythology and the Romantic movement. One of the young staff members, who was full of fire to change the world, had pursued him relentlessly and he wondered where she was now. He'd turned down all her advances. Back then, he'd had a strict no-human policy, afraid of what would happen should they be exposed to his life of violence and destruction.

The Reading Room was now used for exhibitions, but still had bookshelves all around its circumference: an impressive sight. John recalled his resolution to build something similar on the Mountain to hold his martial arts and philosophy collections. It had never happened. He'd met Michelle instead, and thrown away all his reservations about liaisons with humans. The minute he laid eyes on her he was defeated; she had glowed with courage and spirit, unlike any other he'd seen until he met Emma. He'd deserted his realm and his Mountain for her.

He felt a twinge of guilt, then straightened. After three thousand years of living to serve the realm, he deserved a small piece of happiness for himself. His resolve flagged again when he remembered where that had led Michelle, and where Emma was now. He would find Emma, and he would find out exactly what was going on here; but to do both these things he needed to break into their Heaven.

The main book collection had been moved to a different location, but the reference system here would tell him what he needed to know. He just wished the Archivist would come back to him with whatever the Eastern Archives had.

He selected a console in a secluded location, pulled out a chair, and stopped halfway to sitting as a pair of security guards just outside the doors had a loud conversation in

Hindi, discussing their kids' grades with obvious pride. When they'd moved away, he turned on the computer and jumped when the welcome ping sounded. He needed a login to access the system, and his old pass to the collection was well and truly out of date.

He put the phone on the table next to the screen. 'Phone.'

'Please ask me a question.'

'I thought you could say "yes" instead of that?'

'I can,' the phone said.

'Well, why don't you?'

'You didn't tell me to.'

'Say yes in future. Understood?'

'Understood.'

'Good.' John waved one hand in front of the monitor. 'Can you break into this computer and locate anything in the collection about entry to the Western Heavens or the Glass Citadel?'

'Yes. I can also cross-index with the Archivist's information in my memory.'

'Do so.'

'Accessing,' the phone said, and the screen flashed. A login screen appeared, the box filled with asterisks, and then the screen started to flick through thousands of images inhumanly fast. The resulting blur made John feel slightly nauseous and he turned away.

'Done,' the phone said, and a map and list appeared in the air above it.

John leaned forward to study the map. 'Remove any locations that I've already been to.'

All of them disappeared, and John thumped the table.

'Return the locations,' he said.

The list reappeared.

There were four: the castle with the stone lab; the Penrhos Feilw standing stones; the lake; and the Earthly analogue for the Glass Citadel.

'Widen the search to anything that could be remotely listed as a gateway,' he said.

The Trefignath burial chamber appeared at the bottom of the list, marked with a note that said: *This is probably a gateway to Hell not Heaven — Archivist.*

'Why isn't there anything else?' John said, frustrated. 'This is ridiculous. We have many more gateways than that in the East.'

'Accessing,' the phone said. The list disappeared and a snippet of text appeared above the phone.

Mostly oral history. These stupid fuckwits never wrote anything down; they kept it secret by transferring the information by word of mouth. What a bunch of useless retards. If they'd had something like the Shang/Zhou war with resulting Jade Emperor like we had, this would not be an issue; their Jade Emperor analogue would have forced them to start recording shit. As it was, one of their gods created a transcription method for them and it was never used. I salute their bloody-minded devotion to this idiocy. — Archivist.

John sighed, rubbed his eyes and turned away.

The security guards passed again, now talking about food. One was boasting about his cooking ability, and the other was keen to visit and share a meal with the family.

John went home to Kensington.

He let himself in the front door and called the staff.

Paul charged out from the back of the house, his face lined with worry. 'Did you find the real Emma?'

'No. I've been looking for days and I'm running out of leads,' John said. 'Is the copy safe? Have you been feeding it?'

'Simone showed us what to do and we've been looking after her, sir,' Peta said, coming up from the basement and closing the door behind her. 'But she hasn't given us much useful information that could help you.'

'Good. Soup noodles, ho fan, bak choy, in the study.'

Peta and Paul shared an amused look, and Peta said, 'Yes, sir.'

'What?' John said, glancing from one to the other.

'Emma warned us you'd be like that,' Peta said.

He sagged slightly; he knew what they meant. Western manners were different, and Emma would have said something about him being abrupt or rude if she was there.

'I'm sorry,' he said, waving one hand. 'It is my way, and I've been so long away from the West it will take some time to adjust. If you could bring me the noodles to the study, please.'

He turned to go up the stairs; each one felt a hundred metres high.

In the study, he fell to sit behind his desk and pulled out the phone. He checked for the Archivist's number and called.

'Go away, it's four o'clock in the morning,' the Archivist said.

'Are those the only gateways to the Western Heaven you could find? You haven't found one since, or anything related to them?'

'Did you read my note about their oral history?' the Archivist said.

'Yes. Has anything turned up since you wrote that?'

'No. They were fucking useless.'

'I checked all of those gateways and they're just as useless.' He rubbed his hand over his eyes. 'I'm out of leads.'

'Come home then. The Jade Emperor will know what to do.'

'I have one of the Dragon's AI phones here. I'll break into the national library files and see what I can find.'

'Keep a copy of anything interesting,' the Archivist said.

'I've also been in contact with some people here, and they've been keeping records for about four hundred years. Do you want to get in touch with them?'

'Absolutely,' the Archivist said with enthusiasm. 'Who do I talk to?'

'Margaret Anathain. I'll text you her phone number when we've finished talking.'

'Excellent. About time you discovered something useful,' the Archivist said, and hung up.

Twenty minutes later, Paul came in with the noodles on a tray, together with a steaming pot of tea, and John nodded his thanks.

Paul hesitated before leaving. 'Do you want to speak to the Emma copy?'

John made a show of studying the screen containing the library records. 'I don't think that's necessary just yet.'

'I understand. If it was a copy of Peta and she was gone, I wouldn't want to see it either.'

'Has it remembered anything new?'

'Only more detail about what sounds like the Glass Citadel.' Paul pulled a notebook out of his back pocket and put it next to John's notes. 'This is everything.'

John checked the notebook; only a couple of pages of notes but the information could be useful if he ever made it up there. 'Tell her thank you from me.'

'Anything else, sir?'

John realised it was late and they were human. 'No, that's all, thank you, Paul.'

'Good luck, sir.'

'Thank you,' John said, not really hearing as he continued to search the library files.

* * *

435

A vibration shocked him awake; he had fallen asleep over the keyboard. He checked the date on the computer and was relieved that it was only half an hour after he'd last checked it. The ground shook again beneath him and he searched for the source. When he saw what it was, he jumped to his feet and teleported directly above the house. The Grandmother had landed in a field next to Stonehenge.

Grandmother, he said, his tone respectful, as he flew as fast as he could towards her.

Oh, thank the heavens, Emma's stone said. *She's alive, and last I saw her she was free, Turtle.*

John dropped slightly in the air with relief. *How do I get up there!* he said, frantic.

We can't, the stone said, its voice rich with remorse. *It's all closed off. It was all the Grandmother could do to escape with our fallen brethren. The demons have sealed everything.*

There has to be a way! John said.

There is none, the Grandmother said, interrupting. *I could only enter because the Jade Building Block was already there. You will only be able to enter when they exit. I suggest you put guards on watch on each of the gateways, to slip in when the demons come out. There is no other way. Even I am unable to return there now all my stones have come out.* Her voice changed slightly. *This is powerful demon sorcery and it greatly disturbs me.*

What are they planning? John said.

Meet up with me and I will tell you everything I know, the stone said. *By your leave, Grandmother.*

Please permit the stone to share information with me, John said, keeping his tone respectful.

The Grandmother was silent for a long time. John knew the problem: on a visit to Australia, Michelle had climbed the Grandmother, an insult that usually resulted in the Grandmother never speaking to the person or their family again and banning every stone Shen from having anything to do with them. The Grandmother had made a special exception for John, but she found it hard to forgive him for loving a woman who had treated her with such contempt. John thanked his absent-mindedness in leaving the Dragon's phone on his desk; its presence would be enough to tip the balance, and not in his favour.

I'm just north of Stonehenge, the stone said.

John raised himself in the air and moved faster.

The Grandmother sat in the middle of the field, looking like a large amorphous, vibrating clod of dirt. She'd sunk into the ground and it rippled around her. Smaller stones hovered above and around her, occasionally disappearing inside her. As John approached, he saw a pattern emerge: the smaller stones that spiralled into the Grandmother did not reappear.

He landed next to her and bowed politely. 'Grandmother.'

The Jade Building Block hovered in front of his face. 'Thank the Grandmother, Turtle, Emma was alive and free when —'

'Do not thank me,' the Grandmother said, her voice a vibration through their feet. 'Just stop these demons. They have killed so many of my children!' The ground vibrated again. 'You must stop them.'

The Grandmother appeared to shrink and John leaped back as he realised she was sinking into the ground.

'Stop them,' she said again as the final few stones merged with her, and she disappeared completely, the turf closing with a small sucking sound as if nothing had been there at all.

31

'But why didn't you stay with her?' John said for the third time.

The stone was perched on the desk in the Kensington house study. 'I was pulled out when the Grandmother left; all of us were. I wanted to stay with her, believe me.'

'So she's definitely safe?'

'Yes. She had water, and she can easily survive without food until we find her.'

'Then what aren't you telling me?' John said.

The stone was silent for a long time.

'She broke their control. Yes?'

'Yes,' it said.

'You helped her get free. She's in hiding on the Western Celestial Plane, in a place where there should be nothing to hurt her, and the Grandmother's destruction up there will slow the demons' search for her. All I need to do is find a way up there and she will be waiting for me, tired and hungry but safe. Yes?'

'Yes. But ...'

'But. What?' John said, slowly and clearly.

'She's carrying your child.'

'Sweet snake-tailed Nu Wa,' John said. He leaned back and rubbed his hands over his face. 'I suppose I should be pleased. Holy shit, this is bad.'

'It's not that bad. You find her, you free her, she comes to the Mountain and you can be happy parents. The end.'

'What if the demons find her and get their hands on our child?'

'They won't hurt it —'

'Of course they won't hurt it. The mix of me and one of these Western serpents will be immensely powerful, and if they can find a way to hold and brainwash a little child …' His voice became more frantic as the full implications came crashing down on him. 'If they can brainwash and control this child, it will be a weapon that could devastate everything we hold dear. Simone is already one of the most powerful things on the Plane and she doesn't have Emma's unique ancestry behind her. This child could be unstoppable.'

'Nothing is unstoppable.'

'I am the only thing that could stop it, and I will not kill my own child. Again,' John said with force. 'I don't care if the Celestial falls. I. Will. Not. Do. That. Again.'

'So find a way up there and pull both of them out. You have ten months.'

'No, I don't. She won't last more than a couple of weeks without regular food, particularly as she's pregnant. How far along is she? Her menstrual cycle was all over the place. She said it was because of the fertility drugs, but it was obvious the missing ovary was a factor. Work it back from her last menstruation; you were there.'

'I try not to involve myself in these extremely personal matters,' the stone said with dignity.

'Cut the bullshit. You know everything that goes on with her, and you like to watch. When did we conceive this child?'

'I really haven't been watching, Turtle. I have too much respect for her to do that.'

'That's beside the point. Last menstruation. Work it back.'

The stone was quiet for a full minute. John checked his email while he waited. Nearly thirty messages, but none from his children or the Mountain. Mostly updates on the attacks and reports on the nature of the demons. It was important information and he needed to read it later. Nothing from the Archivist.

'She could be up to twelve weeks,' the stone said.

'Already?' John said with dismay.

'She hasn't had a period in ages. It could be anything from that time in the bath in this house a couple of weeks ago, to just after her last menstruation three months ago.'

'You said you didn't watch.'

'I liked the bubbles.'

John remembered the bubbles and the joy of being with her, and nearly lost it. He took a deep gasping breath, straightened and rubbed his eyes. He would find her; he had promised.

'So where to now? Has the Grandmother posted sentries at the gateways to Heaven for when someone comes down?'

'No. She has retreated to her home and taken nearly all the stone Shen with her. They are huddled together in the middle of Australia, mourning the loss of many of our kin.'

'But you stayed here?'

'I have family here. Other stones who have human families have stayed with them. Gold refused to go as well.'

'The Grandmother can't sulk like this. We need her help.'

'Four hundred of her children have died in the last twenty years. That is nearly half of our population, Turtle, and a geological minute. She is broken.'

A terrible feeling of dread filled John. A time of great anguish and loss was descending over all the Planes. The other Immortals had to feel it too. A small horrible part of him rejoiced at the amount of death and destruction about to come crashing down on all of them, but the rest of him filled with dismay.

He called Kwan Yin and received no reply.

'Phone,' he said.

'Yes?' the phone said.

'That thing is creepy and unnatural and should be destroyed,' the stone said. 'You have me now.'

'Can I use you as a phone to call Er Lang?' John said.

'Yes,' the phone said.

'Oh,' the stone said.

'What time is it in Beijing?'

'Seven am,' the stone and phone said in unison.

'Destroy it and buy a dumbphone,' the stone said. 'If the Grandmother discovers you have this, she'll be even more broken.'

'Good,' John said. 'He'll still be asleep; he's a late starter. Call Er Lang and put him on speaker.'

'By all the Buddhas, Number One, this had better be good,' Er Lang said, his voice thick with sleep.

'Touch the future.'

'What?' Er Lang said.

'Do it. I don't care about the rules, have a look.'

There was silence for a moment, then Er Lang said, 'Lady have mercy. I need to alert the Jade Emperor. I'll get back to you.'

'Wait,' John said.

'What could be worse than the future before us?' Er Lang said.

'The demons are building an army in the Western Heavens and the way into it is blocked. Not even the Grandmother can enter. They have already destroyed half the stone Shen population. Emma is up there as well and with child, although she escaped from their hold.'

'Tell me you've turned to join them and the bad news will be complete,' Er Lang said.

'Of course not.'

'So, your woman. Can you bring her down?'

John wasn't surprised the information hadn't filtered into Er Lang's sleep-fuddled brain. 'I can't get in. All the gateways are closed.'

'Talk to the Shen — ask them to open it up again. If they think you're too scary, I can come talk to them as well.'

'There aren't any Shen. They're all gone. Demons have taken over the Heavens here and closed them.'

Er Lang was silent for a long time, then said, 'Not possible.'

'Confirmed by the Grandmother herself. She just went up there to rescue a bunch of stone Shen that were being held by the demons. Half the world's stone population has died.'

'Can we enter the Western Heavens and pursue them? This isn't our corner of the world.'

'Some of them are our demons, we can pursue them. The Grandmother says that the only way up is when one of them comes down through a gateway and opens it; it will be open long enough for one of our agents to sneak in. We need to post good people — *really* good people — at the locations of all the gateways we know.'

'Imperial Elite Guards.'

'I'll send you a list of the ones I want.'

'Come back here and select them yourself.'

'I won't leave here until I'm sure someone is watching the gateways.'

'And as soon as they are being watched, you'll return here.' It wasn't a question.

John didn't reply. He wanted to be there when a gateway opened.

Er Lang's voice dropped with emphasis. 'You're needed here, Number One. We must prepare for what's coming. Don't make the Jade Emperor order you back, because you know he will.'

John rubbed his hands over his face. 'All right,' he said, his heart breaking both at the decision and the knowledge that he was doing the right thing. 'As soon as the gateways are monitored, I'll head back.'

'Deal. Head home as soon as you can, Ah Wu, you have responsibilities here.'

'I know,' John moaned.

Er Lang hung up without another word. John pulled up the list of Imperial Elite Guards to select some of the best.

'I'll stay here and monitor a gateway,' the stone said.

'No. There's a woman in Holyhead called Margaret Anathain; she's holding a stone child that was hidden when one of the circles was stolen. I need you to take that stone child home.'

'Why is she holding one of us?' the stone said, its voice sharp.

'Because the stone child didn't know any other stones apart from those in the circle, and the circle is gone.'

'Oh,' the stone said, its voice softening. 'I'll tell the Grandmother. Are you really heading back to the East?'

'I don't want to.'

'But you need to. You need to prepare for whatever it is you see.'

'What I see is war.'

* * *

John himself had trained the eight Imperial Elite Guards he'd selected when they were juniors and knew them well. He waited for them next to the Penrhos Feilw standing stones, fidgeting with impatience.

Each guard wore the simple fitted black silk pants and jacket of their stealth field kit under modern Kevlar body armour. They stood in a semicircle around him as he briefed them: two dragons — one female, Cloud, and a male, Hazel; a stone, Marble, in female human form; two turtle Shen, a male Vincent and female Black Ice; and three humans, Red, Eagle and Wind, all male due to the historical Earthly bias against women learning the Arts that he was working so hard to break. The next generation would have a much better gender ratio — if they survived the coming war.

'Cloud and Hazel to the Caer Wydr gateway,' he said. 'That's a small island, so one dragon rest and hunt in the sea while the other watches the gateway.'

He gave them the coordinates, they plugged it into a GPS with a waterproof cover, and flew away west.

'Turtle Shen to the lake, take True Form and sit on the edge. If the gateway opens you'll know about it.' He transferred the location to Vincent telepathically and they disappeared.

'Marble, our gratitude for staying with us when the Grandmother called all of you back,' John said to the stone.

'I am an Elite Guard, my Lord,' Marble said. 'My duty comes before our grief.'

'You and Red, go to the town near the castle, stock up for a long campaign, and meet me at the entrance. I'll let you into the tunnels. You'll stay in there until you run out of supplies or a gateway opens.'

'Length of campaign, sir?' Red said.

John considered the future warning he'd received. 'What is the maximum amount of time you can stay this far from your Centre?'

'Two months maximum.'

'That's it then.'

'Understood.'

The guards saluted him and headed down to the castle. The human, Red, was the only one of that pair who would need supplies, and hopefully Marble could work on a way to get in and out of the tunnel.

'Wide Eagle and Gentle Wind, you stay with these stones. A human family lives in the house over there.'

'Understood, my Lord,' Eagle said.

'Contact me the *second* anything happens.'

The two humans saluted him. He rose into the air and headed towards the castle to let Red and Marble in. Afterwards, he flew to the top of Holyhead Mountain and settled on one of the ancient Roman walls. He pulled his boots off and dug his feet into the damp spongy ground, then recoiled at what he felt. He had expected power, but this was pure death.

The ground was full of the dark energy that the serpent people had conjured when they'd performed their sacrifices. The saturation of death in the ground had been building over many years, casting a dark pall over the entire area. Any other creature would have found it horrifying, but John's nature resonated with it. He reached out with his consciousness and searched the area, looking for something approaching a gateway. He found nothing, but the amount of dark power focused on top of the mountain was so intense that a gateway had to have existed there.

He pulled his phone out of his pocket and arranged for two more Elites to guard this location as well, hoping they wouldn't be too affected by the nature of the lingering corruption.

As he waited for them, he looked out over the town of Holyhead and the mountains of Wales beyond. He hoped that Emma was managing on her own in Heaven, and allowed himself a small elation-filled burst of excitement at the prospect of sharing the joys of parenthood with her.

He would find her. He would find both of them.

32

Emma

I searched the riverside clearing in the fading light, looking for shelter and enough dry wood to make a fire. I found neither, even though the clearing was edged by large trees and smaller bushes. Everything was damp from the cool autumnal air. I curled up under a tree, wrapped around myself as much as I could, and shivered as night fell.

I tried to distract myself from the cold by planning for our child. Cloth or disposable nappies? I could use cloth because I was lucky enough to have Er Hao to help me. There weren't many births on the Celestial Plane, and the demons would be thrilled to bits, to the point that we may even have to warn them off being around the baby too much.

I sighed and shivered. The *baby*. I remembered holding Louise's baby and thinking that I may never get there myself; and here I was. It was worth the cold and the misery to be free, and to know that by the time the sun rose I may be in John's arms and we could go home.

I must have dozed despite the cold, and it was bliss to feel the morning sun touch me with its warmth. I uncurled myself, stiff from cold and exertion and nearly unable to move. I vowed never to take warmth for granted again as I wriggled my hands and feet, trying to return some circulation to them. It took me a couple of minutes in the weak sunlight before I was warm enough to stand, and even then I hobbled towards the stream with stiff joints.

Hunger drove me to the edge of the water; I summoned the Murasame and plunged the blade into the pond. Its special curse as the Destroyer meant that anything alive would be pulled into its blade. After a couple of minutes, it was obvious that nothing was alive in the water. For a moment I saw movement and readied to grab whatever it was, then relaxed as it became apparent that some weed had dislodged from the bottom of the pond by the force of the dark blade's pull.

I put the blade aside, took a long drink of the icy-cold water, trying not to get my clothes wet, then stood up. I moved to the centre of the clearing to catch as much of the sun as I could, and performed a fast-moving Tai Chi set to warm myself up. It was like moving through mud: my muscles were painful from the cold and lack of movement. If it rained, I could quite easily die of exposure in the cold night air; my clothes were definitely not made for this.

I put the rising sun to my back and headed west, hoping that the Glass Citadel's immense height would soon make it visible. Occasionally I felt what seemed to be kicks from the baby, but dismissed the idea. No way would I be feeling anything this early; it was possible that the foetus was only two weeks old and the size of a full stop. I ignored the fact that I hadn't had a period in twelve weeks and the baby could be more than five times that. I concentrated on walking, still not moving with my usual ease. It would take some time before I loosened up. I smiled grimly; by the time I was warm, the sun would be gone again.

A path led through the forest in the right direction, and it was possible that the picnic or camping ground could have been a daytrip ride out from the Glass Citadel. I hoped they hadn't been in the habit of hunting large carnivores because the lack of prey meant that the large carnivores would hunt me.

I'd just had that merry thought when three demons appeared on the path in front of me and one dropped to land behind me. I was surrounded.

I summoned the Murasame, but I was too slow. The one behind me grabbed me and held my arms to my sides, while the others prepared some cuffs.

I dropped the sword, then bent forward and down onto one knee. The demon behind me was forced to drop with me, and I grabbed him around the ankles and flipped him over onto his back. When he was down, I lifted him by the ankles and swung him into the other three, using him as a bludgeon to take them down.

I picked up the Murasame again, feeling the stiffness and difficulty of my movements, and sliced two of the demons in half. They didn't disintegrate, just oozed black goo. The other two scrambled to their feet and backed off before I had a chance to fell them, and their faces filled with cunning.

I moved into a long defensive stance, sword raised.

Each demon reached up and grabbed a weapon out of the air. They came at me together and I couldn't parry both of them; I wasn't fast enough.

Sorry, I said to the child, filled the Murasame with my chi and blasted them. Again the backlash slammed me backwards, but I was ready for it and wasn't knocked off my feet. A rush of nausea filled me and I bent, retching. Wonderful. Morning sickness on top of everything else.

That wasn't a kick I felt as I dismissed the gleeful sword and checked the demons for any sort of communication device, without success. I headed west again, listening carefully for anything following me.

After another couple of hours of walking, it became obvious that I was in trouble. What started as mild digestive cramps turned into full-on suffering, waves of agony coming at regular intervals. Each time, I had to stop and hold on to a tree, too weak to block the pain.

'I will not lose you,' I said to the baby, continuing to struggle towards the west.

I stopped after an hour of misery, aware that I was losing blood. I checked the path behind me and nearly collapsed: I was losing a lot of blood. I couldn't afford this after all the Demon Kings had taken. I fell onto the dirt and sat with my head between my knees, the rich scent of my own blood filling the air around me, then fell sideways as another wave of agony racked me.

Two demons slid noiselessly out of the trees on the path behind me. I tried to put my hands up and failed.

'She's hurt,' one of them said. 'Did the other group injure her?'

I attempted to get to my feet and they pulled weapons. I stopped on one knee and panted for a moment, trying to get my breath. They eased to stand in front of me and I kept my hands where they could see them.

'I surrender,' I said. 'Get me to the Demon King. Either of them. Hurry, I'm losing the baby!'

One of them concentrated, communicating, and the other carefully slipped its arm under mine and helped me to my feet. A wave of spasms went through me and I cried out, nearly making it drop me. I hung from its grasp, shaking as the pain tore through me, then collapsed when it stopped.

The helicopter hovered overhead; I hadn't even heard it coming. A rescue stretcher was lowered and the demons strapped me into it. The stretcher was lifted, and I had a horrible, helpless eternity of nausea, sure that the stretcher would swing too far and I'd fall out, or the rope would break. Then strong hands grabbed me and roughly pulled me into the helicopter, smashing me into the side in their haste.

The next thing I knew, I was lying on my back in a white room and the Demon King was yelling at demons who were running around me. I couldn't make out his words, but he sounded angry.

'Save the baby,' I said to him, and he looked down at me, blurring in and out of focus.

'Don't worry, love,' he said. 'This baby is worth more than all my armies put together. We'll make sure it lives.'

'Save it, then let us go,' I said.

'Not fucking likely.'

The light was bright in my eyes and I whimpered and tried to turn away. There was a drip in my arm and I thrashed weakly at it, then collapsed, exhausted.

* * *

I prised open my eyes and saw a hospital room — again in the hospital, this was becoming too much of a habit — and a demon exiting it. She closed the door behind her. I breathed deep and remembered where I was. I quickly put my hand on my stomach, and wondered if they'd managed to save the baby. Everywhere inside ached. From the amount of cotton wadding wrapped around me I was obviously still losing blood, which was a very bad sign.

The female demon returned with George, who sat next to my bed.

'Did you save it?' I said.

He took my hand and shook his head, his face grim with remorse. 'It didn't die in the gutter.'

I snatched my hand away and turned towards the wall to hide my anguish.

'Let it out, you need to have a cry,' he said.

'Fuck off.'

'Feisty. I like a woman with spark,' he said, his voice rich with sarcasm.

'So what will you do with me now?' I said to the wall. 'Impregnate me again as soon as I'm useful?'

'Nobody will be impregnating you ever again. Too much damage.'

That pushed me over the edge. Our baby had died and I'd killed it. This was completely my fault, I should never have used energy. I'd made a horrible mistake and our child had paid the price. I would never be able to hold my baby in my arms and share the joy with my family. I was completely empty inside and it *hurt*.

I tried to hold the grief in, and gasped a huge sob as it overcame me. I squeezed my eyes shut and held my breath, and when I couldn't hold it any more another wheezing sob escaped me. I tried to control it and shook with the effort, tears cascading down my face. I used the sheets to wipe my face, and a box of tissues landed next to me. I ripped a few out and blew my nose, but didn't give him the satisfaction of seeing my face. I gulped air a few times, my throat raw, still shaking with the effort of holding it back.

'You have a choice now, Emma,' he said, his voice becoming casual. 'You can agree to turn and help us train our armies, and we'll look after you exceptionally well; you'll be a queen among us. If you choose not to help us, we'll take you outside and drop you halfway to nowhere, because like this you're completely fucking useless and a waste of resources.'

'Leave me out there. He'll find me.'

'He already did, sweetheart, when you were in Hell. And you won't last the night out there. If he does find you, he'll find you dead. You've lost a hell of a lot of blood and you're still bleeding. Francis doesn't want to drain you because of the contamination, so if you won't turn we'll throw you out of the car onto the side of the road. You have an hour to make your choice.'

'I don't need an hour,' I said.

'Oh, that's very good news. I have a gorgeous suite ready for you, with five servants and a really big hot spa full of the natural mineral springs that come out of the ground here. The water's like magic; should heal you in no time. There's a vegetarian banquet waiting for you, although if you turn you may as well go all the way and eat some meat. A rare steak would do you a hell of a lot of good. Designer outfits — choose what you like, we have a personal shopper. All yours, Queen of the Damned.'

'Side of the road, please.'

'Suit yourself,' he said, rose and went out.

They put me in the back seat of a four-wheel drive. I couldn't stay upright, but they didn't go far; only ten minutes and they stopped. A big demon threw me over his shoulder and followed the King into a stand of trees that thickened and grew blacker as we went deeper in. The chill of the air made me gasp. Something was seriously wrong with this place; something had died here. Many things had died here.

The demon dropped me in a clearing in the trees and I cried out as I hit the ground. It was cold and black and something inside me writhed at the contact, but I couldn't tell whether it was pleasure or pain. Everything hurt.

'Last chance, Emma,' the King said, standing over me. 'Warm spa, mineral water, bubbles, servants, great food, a big soft bed. Your choice.'

'Bye, Kitty,' I said.

'Humph.'

He led the demon away and I lay alone in the gathering darkness, well aware that in this state it was unlikely I'd survive the night. I was beyond caring. I didn't feel cold any more. I was strangely at peace.

I rolled onto my back and looked up through the trees. Darkness was falling and the sky was a soft, delicate violet. Stars were beginning to emerge. The silhouettes of the trees were different: dark and menacing. They leaned over me as if they wanted to shove their branches into me.

He would find me. He would. And I'd be alive, because he had to Raise me. He would find me.

I began to shiver, and tried to curl up around my aching insides. He would find me, and I would have to tell him that I'd killed our child.

33

Zhenwu

People rushed out of the way as John and Er Lang, both in Celestial Form, strode together to the War Room in the Celestial Palace. The double doors opened and they went in; the Council were standing next to their chairs in a traditional show of respect. John and Er Lang halted inside the door, accepted salutes from everyone in the room, then John walked around the table to take his place at the head, with Er Lang on his right. The entire wall behind them was a specially commissioned ink painting of warriors on horseback and on foot, in both human and True Form, during the Shang/Zhou.

As John sat, the other members of the Council sat too, carefully following order of precedence.

'Time frame?' the Phoenix said. They'd all been briefed.

'Less than six months,' John said.

'Celestial says prepare now,' Er Lang said. 'We will be attacked by early softening skirmishes almost immediately. Main force late spring, just under six months from now.'

'The Mountain is so understaffed,' Ma said with frustration. 'Is it too late to recruit?'

'Yes,' John said.

'The Western Heavens are closed. We need to find out how the demons did that and duplicate it,' the Dragon said.

'And pull everybody in before we do. Full evacuation of everybody on the Earthly,' the Tiger said.

'Hell?' Michael said.

'All civilians are to be evacuated from the Celestial side of Hell and we will bolster its defences,' Er Lang said.

'Where will they start?' the Dragon's Number One said. 'Do we know their first target?'

Nobody replied.

'Do we have *any* intelligence at all?'

'As soon as the Elites are in we'll know a hell of a lot more,' said the Phoenix's Number One, a small fragile-looking female Red Warrior.

She was a new Number One for the Phoenix; John tried to remember her name and couldn't. The Red Warriors kept mostly to themselves, in the Southern Palace under the volcano, and the heat of the location made socialisation for most of the residents impossible.

'We should try to lure them out so they open a gateway,' the Phoenix said.

'Good idea,' John said. 'Team to brainstorm that?'

The Phoenix's Number One, Michael and the Dragon's Number One, Golden Dragon, raised their hands slightly.

'Done.'

'Join us, Prince Ming,' the Phoenix's Number One said.

'I'll be busy organising accommodation for the Twelve Villages, Flute,' Martin said. 'I'll give you Yue Gui. She's smarter than me anyway.'

'Three of you are sufficient. Yue Gui has another role here,' John said.

He contacted her at the Northern Palace. *Yue Gui, I am about to nominate you to coordinate preparation for the full evacuation and housing of refugees from the Earthly and Hell. If we are going to bring everybody up here where it is safe over the next six months, we need to prepare now.*

My Lord.

'Yue Gui will coordinate the evacuation; we'll use her as a central administrator,' John said.

There were general nods of agreement around the table; Yue Gui's efficiency and competence were legendary.

Move to the Celestial Palace, the job is yours, John said.

My Lord.

Zara. Zara?

No reply.

Yue Gui, I was about to give you my stone secretary but it has gone with the Grandmother. Take the Jade Girl to assist. She has admirable skills in dealing with people and they are wasted just doing public relations for the Mountain.

Thank you, Father, most appreciated. Her voice changed slightly in his head. *I hope we find Emma soon.*

We will.

'What else?' John said.

'If you coordinate the defensive lines, I'll set the forges to work,' Er Lang said.

'I suggest we return to our realms, arrange our defences, then meet back here this time tomorrow to map out the full Heavenly strategy,' the Phoenix said. 'The Number Ones can work together and see what they come up with from here.'

'Agreed. Any other business?'

'Defending the Earthly?' Ma said.

'They won't attack the Earthly,' the Tiger said. 'They don't want the humans to know any more than we do. They'll come straight here.'

'The riots in 2011 in London were them,' John said. 'They will start something similar in this Centre.'

'There has been unrest all over Europe,' the Phoenix said. 'This is them?'

John nodded.

'Tiananmen all over again,' the Tiger said. 'And innocents will be pulled in just as they were before.' His voice dropped with restrained rage. 'Demons massacring humans for fun, and the government looking on with delight.'

'Directly after this meeting I am gathering the Thirty-Six to discuss the defence of the Earthly,' John said. 'The four of you concentrate on the Celestial.'

'We need the stones back,' the Dragon said. 'Does anybody have a special bond with the Grandmother?'

'I'll talk to Gold,' John said. 'Anything else?'

'A safe journey to you and Emma, my Lord,' the Phoenix said more gently.

'I will find her. I have promised,' John said.

'Just don't spend too much time there once you do. In and out like a White Tiger; let the Elite gather the information,' the Tiger said.

'I will be here when I'm needed,' John said. 'Enough?' From their expressions, they were eager to start work. 'Dismissed.'

* * *

After the meeting with the Thirty-Five Generals, John headed back to the Mountain and spoke to the Lius about the preparations there. He went to his office in the early evening and flipped through his emails. Exhaustion was making him see double; he would have to stop soon.

Simone came in and sat across from him while he tried to read the reports on the demons.

'Any word on Emma?'

'She's free. She's safe. All I need is one gateway open and I'll be up there to pull her out.'

'The demons have really taken over the entire West?'

'They have.'

457

'The Celestials say there's going to be a war.'

'We are preparing,' he said. 'Stay in the Mountain where you're safe.'

'I want to fight too.'

He glanced away from the computer to her determined face. 'You're too young.'

'I'll be eighteen in a few months; I'm nearly an adult. Have them make me a weapon. I want to help.'

He opened his mouth and closed it again.

'That's right,' she said, smiling slightly. 'This is the reason I've trained all my life, so I can help you defend the Celestial. This is *our* Mountain and *our* home and *our* realm and I'll be damned if I let any demons come over these walls again.'

He leaned on the desk to face her and pulled out a scroll.

'Don't try to stop me, I'm helping,' she said fiercely.

'What sort of weapon?'

Her eyes widened. 'What, that's it?'

'I think something with a bit of reach on it — maybe a halberd or polearm? You're not a great expert with a sword, but two smaller knives to match your speed? A pair of wakizashi-sized daggers; you've always reverse-handed well and you move so damn fast they'll never see them coming. Or a staff. I can have something very special made and you can load it with energy, or even yin.'

'You'll give me my yin back?' she said, eyes even wider.

'What you said about the damn wall. And frankly ...' he leaned back and pulled his hair out of its tie, 'the idea of having you fight next to me to protect our Mountain is the coolest thing anybody's said to me all day. One condition, though.'

She quirked one eyebrow at him and he wondered when she'd learnt to do that.

'Study Internal Alchemy and pursue Immortality or all bets are off.'

'Deal.'

She rose and held her hand out. He stood as well, grasped hers and released the binding he'd placed on her control over yin. The yin had always been there, but she hadn't been able to touch it. Now she could, and she shivered. Her eyes went black for a moment as the yin flooded through her, then returned to normal and she gasped. She released his hand and flopped into her chair, which was instantly covered with satisfying ice.

'An hour a day on controlling that,' he said. 'Don't work with it alone until I say so. Your Arts are weak as well. We'll have to spend some serious time together to bring you to full potential.'

'Okay,' she said, obviously still slightly dazed.

'How about a staff of Seven Stars? I can have chakra vessels put into it and it will hold your energy the same way the sword does.' He sat back down at his desk. 'It will take some time to make, though, and I have a very fine pair of daggers that would be perfect for your build and reach until it's finished.'

'Um ...' She stopped, thoughtful. 'Can I have a smaller version of Seven Stars? Give me intense training on sword work and bring me up to speed.'

'You want the same thing as me?'

'That sword is completely bad-ass.'

'No,' he said, and she frowned. 'I won't give you the same as me. You are your own person, and let's face it: your style is different. A pair of short broad blades with the stars in both of them? You've seen me pull Seven Stars apart; this would be the same thing, just all the time.'

'Curved blades, sickle-shaped,' she said. 'Something with a curved tip that I can use to slip into throats and bellies to rip stuff out, and slip behind heads to take them off. If they're curved, they'll be less likely to get stuck in demon shells; I can lever them out.' She frowned. 'I don't remember what they're called, but they were used a long time ago. I think they'd suit me.'

He scribbled on the scroll. 'The blade is called a khopesh, and you're right, they're very ancient. First one I saw was in India about three thousand years ago. Perfect for you: they'll give you the impact of an axe and the finesse of a sword, and the tips for ripping. They're also an excellent weapon to wield on horseback.'

She smiled. 'Freddo will be thrilled to bits. Lisel might agree to teach us again.'

'They don't need to be completely sickle-shaped,' John said, drawing on the scroll. 'A flatter curve is more powerful than a circular one. I'll have them sharpened on both sides so you can backhand if you want. Sounds ideal.'

'Can they be black? And I need armour; I'm not skilled enough to summon my own yet.'

'Your livery's dark blue, I've seen it. Armour and weapons both in that colour.'

'Oh,' she said, eyes wide. 'Damn, Dad, that really does sound very cool. Dark blue armour, and blades with chakra vessels?' She smiled slightly, and suddenly the little girl was gone and she was all woman. 'Best eighteenth birthday present a girl could ever ask for.'

He finished the order on the scroll and rolled it up. 'Give this to Moaner in the forge. Tell him to give them priority, but not to rush. It will take them some time to create the right alloy to make the blades blue, and fixing the chakra vessels is a precision task. You'll need to be there when he creates them, so arrange a time with him.'

'I'm not taking resources away from the war effort, am I?'

A small part of him died when she said that. A war effort meant death and deprivation and suffering.

He shook his head. 'No. You'll be as important as me when the demons come.'

'Are you sure they're coming?'

'It's just a matter of time. They've been building up to this for years.'

'I suppose we all knew it was coming. It's just …' She sighed. 'You try not to think about it; and now people are heading up here to be safe, you can't not think about it.' She bent closer and touched his temple. 'Come home and rest, Dad, you're wrecked. Your hair is even going grey.'

'As soon as I've checked these reports. Have the staff keep some food warm for me.'

'I'm waiting up for you, so don't be too late,' she said.

She patted his hand and went out, leaving him feeling very old.

He returned to the emails, flipping quickly through the reports and scanning the information. The details on the new demons, the insect/snake hybrids, were seriously disturbing. He read the first two paragraphs of an email from the Tiger's Number Two about Freddo's mother and moved to the next one, then went back and undeleted it. He'd seen the word 'unusual'.

The horse is unusual in that it has not come from any of the regular racing stables that supply the Jockey Club. It appears to have been bred on a stud attached to the Anglesey Manor; records show it was born there. This is the only horse ever to go through the Jockey Club from that stud, and further research shows that it's the only horse ever to have come out of that stud ever. The stud bred one horse and Freddo's mother is that horse.

He picked up his phone and called the Tiger's Number Two, Rohan.

'My Lord,' Rohan said.

'Freddo's mother is the only horse ever to come from the Anglesey Manor?' John said. 'Really?'

'If any others were bred there, they weren't entered into any stud books,' Rohan said.

'The stables there have been deserted for a very long time. I estimate at least seventy years since they've seen a horse.'

'I wonder where the horse came from then?'

A small ferocious ray of hope lit up inside John. 'I'm heading over to have a look. Thank you for your assistance.'

'No need, my Lord. The Number Ones are about to head over there to try to lure a demon out through one of the gateways. They're just doing the handover to us Number Twos before they go. I'll tell them to take a detour on the way and check out the manor.'

John hesitated, then realised he was right. 'Very well. Tell Michael to call me the minute he finds something.'

'My Lord.'

John pushed his chair back, grabbed the phone and went out to the Imperial Residence. He missed Zara's comforting presence outside his office. Dinner with Simone and hopefully Leo would help to take the pain away, and he really was exhausted.

* * *

Emma

Something moved next to my head: a silver scaled leg with a cloven hoof, glowing in the darkness. I flopped onto my back to see it better, and wished I had the energy to appreciate it more. It morphed between an Eastern qilin and a Western unicorn: one minute it had two antlers and a scaly goat's body, and the next it was a horse with a single horn and cloven hooves.

'Hello,' I said. 'You're beautiful.'

It fell onto its front knees and curled its hind legs behind it to lie down next to me. Warmth and light radiated off it and I immediately felt more alive.

'You're not,' it said, and its voices sounded like three speaking in unison: a man, a woman and a child. It dropped its head slightly and blew warm sweet air on me. 'You're very ordinary-looking, and I like that. You're true to yourself.'

'Thank you. I try. Why are you here? I'm not nearly important enough to merit a visit from you.'

'You aren't, but if the future is to be resolved, you need to be in it.'

'I'm that important?'

'You, no. The things around you, yes. Kind of.' It shook its head. 'You're not important, but you're vital and real and full of life. And there's a thing that will need to be done. And it needs you.'

'I've done enough,' I said, snuggling into it. 'Your scales are lovely.'

It nuzzled me with its horse nose. 'Most people are awestruck into silence when they meet me.'

'Hey, I've slept with the Xuan Wu and seen its Turtle form. I've yet to see anything top that,' I said. 'Whoa. Is your presence making me high or something? I feel really … good. Euphoric.'

'Either my presence, or the blood loss and exposure. Probably a combination.' It snorted gently with amusement. 'I wonder if I'm habit-forming.'

'You should be a controlled substance,' I said. 'Is it okay if I sleep until he finds me? You're lovely and warm, and I feel like I haven't been warm in forever. You won't leave me, will you?'

'Go right ahead.'

'And of course, if I'm hallucinating, I'll just die and that'll be that.'

'Yep.'

'You're a big help,' I said, and fell asleep curled up next to its satiny scales.

34

Zhenwu

'I decided not to go with that sword shape because the horse people use them on *Game of Boobs*,' Simone said over breakfast the next morning.

'Don't let that stop you,' Leo said.

'What's *Game of Boobs*?' John said as he sat with them.

'Fantasy series on HBO,' Simone said. 'They call it that because of the gratuitous nudity. It's full of unnecessary boobs.'

'When's it on?' John said.

'Dad!'

'I want to see the depiction of the khopesh.'

'Like I believe you,' she said with derision.

'Leo's right, don't let that stop you. They probably use that shape because it is the right shape for that purpose. It will be the most suitable weapon for you.'

'And nobody has to see your boobs,' Leo said.

'Leo!'

Leo grinned into his bacon.

Simone laughed, and John heard how forced it was. They were trying to cheer him up. It was probably obvious that he was fretting now that he'd run out of things to keep him occupied.

'I'll need to give them names,' Simone said.

'Yang and Yin?' Leo said.

'Cliché,' Simone said, stretching the word out with derision.

'Penn and Teller.'

'Oh, I like that.'

'Siegfried and Roy?'

'The Tiger would adore that. How about Cloud and Squall?'

'I don't get the reference,' Leo said. 'But weather terms are always good.'

'Stop thinking of male names and honour some famous women,' John said. 'Scientists, leaders, warriors.'

Simone and Leo shared a horrified look.

'I didn't even realise I was doing that,' Simone said. 'How about Ada and Marie?'

'Who are they?' Leo said.

'Only two of the most famous women —' Simone began, but John's phone rang and she stopped.

He snatched it up. It was Golden Dragon, the Blue Dragon's Number One.

'Talk to me,' John said.

'We're three li from the manor, and there's something my wood nature felt the minute we got here. It's … strange. Damn, it's like the most evil spot I've ever been; there's these trees and they're … grotesque. Really, really creepy, and it's the middle of the night, which makes it worse. Whenever I attune to the harmony you gave us, something seems to happen with the trees, then stops.' His tone changed to chagrin. 'There's something here, my Lord, but my dragon nature isn't wood-based enough to make it resonate. You need something seriously wooden. I suggest you have a tree take a look.'

'Text the coordinates to my phone.'

'My Lord.'

After he'd hung up, John looked from Leo to Simone. 'I need a tree.'

'Aren't the trees kind of boycotting you?' Leo said.

'Yeah,' Simone said. 'They all hate him.'

Yue Gui. I need a tree. He shared the information with her. Her son was a tree; she had to know one that would help him.

Father. Hold, she said.

John ate while he waited, excitement building within him. If this was a tree-only gateway, and he could find a tree who was willing to assist, he could finally break in there. Demons were completely unable to work with tree essence; trees were too natural and pure.

Father. Sang Shen will help you in return for a pardon. He is genuine.

'What, Daddy?' Simone said when she saw his face go grim.

'Sang Shen will help, but I need to free him,' John said.

'Yue Gui can't help it,' Leo said. 'She's just being a mom.'

'Are you about to make a pact with the devil?' Simone said.

'No,' John said. 'The devil's about to make a pact with me.'

Will he cease this ridiculous vendetta against Emma? Yes.

One condition. He has to act as a representative for Emma with the trees, and work to rebuild their goodwill towards both of us.

Yue Gui was silent for a long time as she relayed the message to her son. John wondered if he'd asked too much. He needed a tree and right now Sang Shen was probably the only one who would help.

He agrees. He is on the Earthly, hiding in Hong Kong's forest park. Do you need to go to him to free him?

466

No. He's free now. Confirm.

Confirmed. Her voice changed to relief. *My thanks, my father.*

Sang Shen spoke to him. *My Lord.*

How soon can you be in the UK? John said.

I've never travelled that far.

Do you know where it is?

Sang Shen was silent. He wouldn't admit that he didn't know where to go. John cursed the tree's pride.

Can you meet me in Hong Kong, Sang Shen?

My Lord.

Top of One Black Road. Do you know where that is?

Sang Shen's voice sounded impatient. *Of course I do.*

John put down his spoon and rose. 'He's meeting me halfway, then I'll take him to the UK.'

'Wait, Daddy,' Simone said.

She rose and came to him and put her arms out. He pulled her into a hug, and she used the contact to feed him Shen energy, brisk and pulsing with her youth and fervour. She stopped the feed just as quickly, impressing him with her control.

'Enough?' she said, studying his face.

'More than enough.' He put his hand on her cheek. 'You impress me more and more every day. I'll keep you posted.'

She glowed with pride as the room dissolved around him and he headed down to the Earthly.

* * *

Sang Shen was already waiting for him on the black-stained roof of the Peak apartment, the low clouds flowing around him. John landed across the roof from him and waited.

Sang Shen jumped as he remembered, then fell to one knee and bowed his head. 'Dai Yeh Yeh,' he said, calling John 'Grandfather'.

'Sang Shen,' John said, 'call me by my full title. You are no longer any child of mine.'

'Xuan Tian,' Sang Shen said.

John waited.

'Shang Di,' Sang Shen finished, his face dark with humiliation.

John paced around Sang Shen, not yet giving him permission to rise. 'Four hundred stone Shen are dead. These demons have control over fire and metal elementals. How much do you value your life and that of the other trees?'

Sang Shen's face went expressionless. He obviously hadn't known this.

'Repeat these words,' John said. '*I do not know.*'

'What words?'

'Say the words *I do not know.*'

'I do not know,' Sang Shen said, obviously confused.

'What is the way to Britain?' John said.

Sang Shen didn't reply, his expression still full of humiliation.

John stopped in front of him. 'Your life and the lives of every other resident of the Celestial are at stake. The demons are readying for war; they will try to take our Heavens. Will you risk all of that to save your stupid pride and refuse to admit your ignorance when you don't know something? Save us all the time and effort, and if you don't know, say so. Your pride is not worth your life.'

'I do not know the way to Britain,' Sang Shen said, now understanding.

'Good!' John said. 'Up you get, lad. You trees can't handle immersion in salt water, can you?'

'Not for long periods,' Sang Shen said.

'Very well, we'll have to fly. Can you summon a cloud? How do you travel long distances?'

'You don't know?' Sang Shen said.

John pointed at his own face. 'Listen to me when I say this. No, I don't know. Trees have always graced the Heavens, but they have been silent beauties that kept to themselves. I admit I took you for granted. Now the Heavens are in danger and we need your skills. So let's share information.'

'I can burrow under the earth to travel long distances, but the furthest I've been is Delhi.'

'Right,' John said. He waved Sang Shen closer and put his finger on his forehead. 'This is where we're going. Can you meet me there?'

'Yes,' Sang Shen said, eyes unfocused as he processed the information.

'How long will it take you to get there?'

'Eight hours, but when I reach that body of water before the large island, I will need a lift. I can't travel through the ocean without a tunnel or something.'

'There's a tunnel, you'll be able to cross the Channel. This is where the entrance is; meet me there,' John said.

He was well aware that Sang Shen could break his oath and take off. He had to trust him.

Sang Shen bowed once sharply. 'I will meet you there.'

He jumped off the roof and changed into a ball of roots as he fell. John leaned over the edge and watched as Sang Shen quickly burrowed into the earth and disappeared.

John flew to the ocean, changed to Turtle form, and swam. He met Sang Shen at the Channel and showed him the way across, briefing him in more detail on the situation on the way.

When John arrived at the location Golden Dragon had given him, he found all three Number Ones standing at the edge of the copse looking uncomfortable, and Michael's white Horseman uniform was splashed with blood. Sang Shen erupted out of the ground nearby as a ball of jutting roots, changed to wood shaped vaguely like a human, then reverted to full human and joined them.

'What happened to you?' John asked Michael.

Michael glanced down at himself. 'Nothing. This is part of the ruse. We splashed me with blood and I pretend to lie injured under one of the gateways, hoping a demon will come out and grab me.' He grimaced. 'Hasn't worked yet.'

'Where are these trees?' Sang Shen said.

'In there,' Golden Dragon said, indicating the thicket. 'Michael thinks it might be a druid grove, but druid groves weren't supposed to be this ...' He searched for the right word.

'Wrong,' the Phoenix's Number One, Flute, said. She nodded to Sang Shen. 'I hope you can help us.'

'Let's have a look,' Sang Shen said, and gestured for Golden Dragon to lead the way.

Michael fell into step next to John. 'How long has Emma been by herself?'

'Nearly three days now.'

'That's not good. I hope we find her. I heard you two are going to be parents?'

'The stone said she's pregnant, so it's very urgent we find a way up there,' John said, distracted by the nature of the trees they were passing. 'What the hell?'

Sang Shen spun around, rushed back up the trail, and stopped to vomit. He retched for a long time, gasping.

The Number Ones all shared a look and hesitated at the edge of the clearing. The trees were stained with what appeared to be dried blood for a good three metres up their trunks from the ground. Their branches were bare and they were obviously dead. The small clearing had originally held a stone circle, but all that was left of it was dents in the ground, also stained with what appeared to be blood. The area was completely lifeless.

John went to one of the dents, picked up a clod of the earth and smelled it.

'Is this what we think it is?' Michael said.

'Both. Blood and demon essence,' John said. 'Humans and demons were sacrificed here.' He opened his vision. 'Nobody's died here for a very long time, but the stain remains. The area is even more contaminated by the fact that the serpent people really enjoyed what they were doing. The power they gained from the deaths here was a massive high.'

He closed his vision. 'Sang Shen.'

'They bound humans to these trees and tortured and killed them,' Sang Shen said. 'They thought they were worshipping the trees and giving them power; instead, they drove them mad and killed them.' He came to the edge of the clearing, leaned on one of the tree trunks, then jerked away as if it had bitten him. 'So. Much. Death. No tree could take this many years of torture and survive with its mind intact.'

'Is there a gateway?' John said.

'Let me see.' Sang Shen glanced down at the ground, then up at John. 'I need to take tree form. I will feel everything that has happened here.' His face screwed up with distaste. 'Everything.'

'Can you endure that?' John said.

'If we're to find a way to stop these demons, I need to,' Sang Shen said. He moved closer to the rest of the group. 'It may prove too much. Destroy me if I make any move to attack you.'

'It won't come to that, man,' Michael said.

Sang Shen coughed and moved away to retch again, bending forward. John went to him and held his shoulder while Sang Shen worked it through. Eventually, Sang Shen straightened and moved to the centre of what had once been the circle of stones.

'If my leaves start to change, kill me,' he said.

'You can't be killed,' John said.

'I can here,' Sang Shen said. He nodded to Michael. 'If my trunk or leaves change into something ... different, you can't let me contaminate the rest of the forest. You must destroy me. Yang me to ash and make sure nothing's left.'

'Stop him, my Lord,' Golden Dragon said. 'This is suicide.'

John didn't reply.

Sang Shen glared at John. 'I hope I survive this, because if I do you will owe me more than you owe any other Celestial.'

John didn't have a chance to answer. Sang Shen changed into a mulberry tree, his canopy completely covering the sky above the clearing. His branches thrashed above them although there was no wind.

'Touch the sky, do not let this affect you,' John said. 'You can do it, Ah Sang.'

A gateway opened next to Sang Shen's trunk and John leaped through. All sound ceased; he was deaf. Then he arrived on the Celestial Plane and sound returned.

'Do it!' someone shouted, then a scream. 'Do it!'

There was a brilliant flash of yang, making the air sizzle around him, and the portal closed.

* * *

The grove on this side was green and full of life, not contaminated at all. The trees were a warm welcoming presence around him, clearly unaware that one of their own had died to get him there. He sent out his awareness, touching the land around, feeling it resonate with a beauty that was possible only on the Celestial Plane.

The demons were five kilometres away to the east. He would have to be stealthy to avoid patrols.

There was a dirt road just outside the grove, showing the recent tracks of a car. He opened his awareness: Emma had been in it. He followed the tracks for two kilometres, and saw that the car had stopped, turned around and headed back again. He sent his awareness out and felt another of the tortured tree groups a hundred metres away to his right, together with something glowing that definitely wasn't Emma.

He moved as silently as he could along the path until he reached the dark stand of trees. The glowing energy seemed benign, it wasn't demon energy. He crept cautiously through the trees and came to a small dark clearing, where he stopped and stared in wonder. Emma was there, curled up next to, of all things, a goddamn qilin lying in the middle of the trees as if it was the most normal thing in the world.

The qilin looked up and saw him, and he quickly fell to one knee and bowed his head.

'Hi,' the qilin said. 'Emma's great fun — did you know that? When she gets high, she's hilarious.'

John pulled himself to his feet and eased around the qilin to Emma.

'It's okay,' the qilin said. 'Don't be afraid.'

John knelt next to Emma. She was in pyjamas that were soaked with dried blood. He touched her face. 'Emma? Emma?'

'She's out,' the qilin said. 'You'll need to find her medical attention before you can take her back down.' It nuzzled her hair. 'Take her to Caer Wydr, the Glass Citadel. The demons evacuated the place; only Semias is there, still locked up. Free him and he can help you.'

'What happened to her?' John said, feeling her pulse. Her skin was ice-cold.

'Demons dumped her here to die.'

'Why?' John said, but when he looked up the qilin was gone.

He picked Emma up like a child, summoned a cloud and headed west. The phone guided him for a while, but Caer Wydr soon appeared on the horizon and he didn't need to use it any more. The tower floated above the land, encased in a crystal dome. Its many windows were round and all different sizes, cascading around the tower in an organic pattern like seeds on a sunflower. Water flowed down the outside of the dome, creating a waterfall at its base, which was filled with rainbows from the light of the morning sun. The land around the tower was green and healthy, with fields of short grass and copses of trees. The tower floated above it all without touching it.

John landed, passed through the curtain of water and peered up at the base of the tower fifty metres above him. Water from a stream rushed into the air and entered the tower through an opening in its base. Close enough.

He laid Emma on the grass on her back and felt a flash of concern at her paleness. She'd obviously lost a lot of blood and needed help quickly.

He became one with the water flowing into the tower, and arrived in an entry hall that encompassed the entire bottom floor. The water streamed into a marble pool, and overflowed into white stone grooves that ran to the edges of the room and then up inside the walls. The walls and floor were white stone carved with fish and birds; and the ceiling was a stained-glass dome showing an illusory sky. Large containers around the area held healthy-looking plants, but there was no animal life.

John opened his Inner Eye and located Semias immediately: he was two floors above in a jail cell. Not a single other living thing was present, human, Shen or demon, so that had to be him, as the qilin had said.

John checked around for an exit from the tower, and found a set of double doors on the far wall next to a staircase leading up. He approached the doors and they opened. He summoned Seven Stars, changed it to spear form and jammed it between the doors to prevent them closing. He walked through and was on the grass next to Emma again. He gathered her up and turned to find the doors hanging in midair behind him. He carried her through, dismissed the spear and hurried to the stairs.

* * *

The dungeon was bright from the round window, and there were only four cells. Semias was curled up in a corner of his cell, looking haggard, but he jumped up with delight when he saw them. John carefully rested Emma against the wall, then went to the cell and tried to freeze the bars, without success.

'Just use brute force, you look strong enough,' Semias said.

John grasped a bar with his left hand to steady himself, then pulled at the bar next to it with his right. It took all of his strength, but he managed to bend it. He did the same to the bar next to it and Semias could slip through. He ran straight to Emma and checked her pulse, then lifted her eyelids.

'We need to move her to the infirmary straight away,' he said.

'Give me a cup and a knife,' John said. 'My blood is a potent healing agent.'

'Come with me,' Semias said.

He led John out of the cells and up twenty-four flights of stairs, moving inhumanly fast, then raced out of the stairwell into a long wide corridor. He turned left, ran to the end, then left again and into what was obviously the tower's infirmary. Four desiccated corpses lay in hospital beds with tubes hanging out of them.

Semias stopped dead. He dropped his head and shook it. 'I couldn't do anything for them.'

'Deal with them later,' John said. Emma was barely breathing. 'Knife. Cup. Quickly.'

'Yes,' Semias said. He went to one of the hospital trolleys and stared at the contents. 'I don't recognise any of this.'

John laid Emma on the floor and went to a cabinet. He pulled out a sterilised scalpel in its bag and a kidney dish. Close enough. He tore the scalpel open, stabbed himself in the vein in his left elbow and let the blood run into the kidney dish. Semias went behind Emma's head to lift it, watching John with close attention. When the dish had enough in it, John went to Emma and poured some into her mouth. It dribbled out the sides, but Semias helped her to swallow it by massaging her throat.

Some must have gone down, but she wasn't reacting. John squeezed more blood into the dish and poured it into her. She remained unmoving.

'Whatever this is supposed to do, it's not working,' Semias said.

'I'm too far from my Centre,' John said.

Emma's breathing had slowed to nearly nothing; she was lost. John gathered her into his arms and crushed her face into his shoulder, feeling her last breaths against him and treasuring her scent and touch before he lost her forever.

'I will travel to your Hell and I will find you,' he whispered into her shoulder, hoping she would hear his reassurance without the lie in his voice. Once she was in Hell finding her would be close on impossible.

Her breathing was almost undetectable, and John strained to impress on his memory the sweet feeling of holding her before he would never feel it again. The noise whirled around him and he ignored it, concentrating on his last moments with her.

Semias smacked him sharply on the side of the head and he glared up.

'Bring her into the next room,' Semias said. 'We're not done yet.'

John lifted her, ignoring the trickle of blood coming from his elbow, and followed Semias through the double doors at the end of the room.

The circular room on the other side was five metres across, its floor, walls and ceiling faced with white stone tiles. A black rectangular stone altar stood in the middle, with a pentagram inscribed into its surface and another on the floor around it.

'Put her on the table,' Semias said, gesturing towards the altar. He went to the far end of the room and tapped the wall, which slid open. 'This will take a minute, so go back and find something to wrap that arm while I set it up.'

John went back into the infirmary and quickly found some gauze and a bandage. When he returned to the altar room, Semias was placing coloured candles at the points of the pentagram on the floor, and smooth coloured stones where the lines intersected.

'Flower of Life would be more effective, but that's another hundred floors up and takes too long to etch,' he said, almost to himself as he placed the stones. He glanced up at John. 'Does she have any particular elemental alignment? Is she water, like you?'

'She's one of the Welsh serpent people,' John said, watching Emma's chest rise and fall and expecting each breath to be her last. 'Apart from that, no elemental alignment.'

'None of *your* elements,' Semias said, lighting the candles with his fingertip. When they were all lit, he pushed the end of a stick of incense into one of the flames and waved the incense above Emma. 'The spirits forgive our haste, our need is dire.'

He put the incense into a holder between Emma's feet and pulled a black-handled dagger out of his robes. He stood at the head of the altar and raised the dagger, reciting silently. Then he moved to the northernmost point of the pentagram, pointed the dagger outwards at waist-height, and walked clockwise around the edge of the pentagram, creating a visible circle of blood-red energy around himself, the table and Emma.

'Choose now: in or out,' he said without slowing his stride.

'I'm in,' John said. 'I lived here myself for a few years and I've done this. Anything you need, let me know.'

'Great Rite?' Semias said, and winked at him, grinning.

'I don't think that's really appropriate for this situation, but I appreciate the offer,' John said. 'If we could hurry this ...'

'We can save her,' Semias said, and closed the circle with an audible snap. A dome of red-tinged energy surrounded them. He quickly ran the tip of the dagger along the lines of the pentagram on the floor and they lit up with a similar red fire.

'This isn't in any of the rituals I've studied,' John said.

'That's because this is the real thing,' Semias said.

When the pentagram was complete, the lines from the floor ran up the sides of the altar and made the pentagram beneath Emma glow, bringing her into relief above it. Semias stood next to Emma's head and gestured for John to join him. John hesitated about walking over the pentagram, and Semias gestured again impatiently. John moved next to Emma's head on the other side of the altar from Semias, feeling nothing as he crossed the glowing red lines.

'Wait, Welsh serpent?' Semias said.

'Yes.'

'Wrong flavour then. Just a minute.'

Semias concentrated and the glowing red energy turned a deep shade of purple-black. John admired its purity; it was an energy that resonated with his own, dark, soft and yielding.

Semias's face went serene, and a low bass thrum sounded through the floor, a rhythmic pulse slower than a heartbeat. With each beat, the circle lit up from the edge to the centre, dark purple light flowing in circles through the pentagram. The light flowed up the sides of the altar and into Semias, so that he too was glowing with pulsing black-purple energy. His face became beatific and he put his hands on Emma's chest, thumbs touching, fingers wide. The energy flowed into Emma from his hands and back down through the pentagram on the altar. The purple-black light spread slowly through her, lighting her up from inside with a glowing dark aura.

Semias lowered his head, grimaced, and went stiff for a moment. He grunted with effort and the energy went red. The whole room was bathed in a shifting red aura that continued to move from the edges of the circle to the middle, with Emma at its centre. The energy entered Emma through Semias's hands and flowed through her, reverberating up and down the sides of the table. Semias's long thin hair lifted in the energy current and John could feel the heat. The light snapped off, the circle around them disappeared and Semias collapsed.

John raced around the altar and lifted him. He weighed hardly anything and John could feel how emaciated he was underneath his robes. Semias didn't respond as John pulled him up; he was unconscious. He put Semias's arm around his shoulder to hold him, then checked Emma. She was still out, but she had much more colour. He touched her hand and it was warm.

'Thank you,' he said to Semias as he lifted him like a child and carried him out to the infirmary. He put Semias gently on the floor, and hunted in a cabinet for bed linen so he could remove the corpses from the beds and make them up freshly for Emma and Semias.

35

Emma

The light was too strong and I opened my eyes. Another hospital room, but this one was bright and cheery and smelled wonderful. I hadn't realised how bad the places infested by demons had smelled, but it was obvious now I was clear of them. I looked right and my heart exploded with joy: John was dozing in a chair next to me, his arms folded, his chin on his chest. Semias was in the bed behind John, his face peaceful in sleep. I snuggled down. I didn't need to wake them; let them sleep. I revelled in John's presence until I couldn't keep my eyes open any more.

The next time I woke, they were sitting together on the other side of the room, speaking softly.

'John,' I said.

He turned and his face lit with a huge grin, making his eyes crinkle up. I was filled with both joy and pain.

He came to me and held my hand. 'How do you feel?'

'I lost our baby,' I said.

He squeezed my hand. 'I know. But you're alive.'

'There'll be others, Emma,' Semias said.

'No,' John said. 'There won't. Saying there will be others is like saying there are plenty more women in the world when your wife's just died. This baby was unique and there will never be another one like it.'

'And there won't be any others anyway,' I said. 'The Demon King said I was too damaged inside to have any more babies. That's why he threw me away. I wouldn't teach his armies, and I'm no good as an incubator.'

Semias grimaced and turned away.

I dropped my voice. 'John, I am so sorry. I killed it. I used energy when I was pregnant.'

'You did?' John said sharply. 'I thought I told you not to do that?'

'You never told me the reason why not. It was life or death, and I thought it would hurt me, not the baby.'

'My fault, I should have told you.' He bent over me, concerned. 'How many times did you use energy? How much?'

'Only twice. The first time I killed ...' I struggled to remember, it was all a blur of fear and running, 'three big demons. Second time, I killed another four, and I lost the baby straight ...' I held my voice together. 'I lost the baby right after.'

'That wouldn't have hurt the child, particularly early on,' John said. 'If anything, it would have made it stronger and more likely to survive.'

Relief flooded over me. I hadn't killed the baby; it had been the stress of running and hiding. The baby was still gone, but at least I wasn't responsible.

John saw my face. 'Don't blame yourself, Emma. It wasn't your fault.'

'Why doesn't that make me feel any better?'

'Because that child was unique. Remember, once you're Raised things will change,' he said.

I smiled and my heart lifted. He was right. 'I hadn't thought of that,' I said. I turned to Semias. 'Anything to eat around here?'

He shrugged. 'They took everything with them when they left. There's nothing here. If we were in Murias, it would be different, but it's still overrun with demons and I can barely hold myself together.'

'What's Murias?' John said.

'One of the Four Cities up here,' I said. 'Something analogous to our Four Realms. He's the North Wind.'

'No,' Semias said, shaking his head. 'I'm not the spirit of the North like Xuan here. I'm the spirit of the city.'

'You're the city of Murias?'

'Yes.' He straightened. 'If I wasn't infested with demons, I'd appear much younger and better-looking, and you'd drop your man in a second for me.'

'What are you doing in the Glass Citadel instead of looking after your city?' John said.

'They locked me in here,' Semias said. 'I'm severely weakened being so far away.'

'What about the other Castellans?' I said. 'Are they looking after their cities?'

'I'm the only one left. Everybody else returned to the Earth.' Semias gave us a wry grin. 'I drew the short straw and was left guarding the Heavens.'

'Alone?' I said.

Semias's smile disappeared. 'It's been very tough. Even tougher now that the Heavens are full of demons making plans to take over the whole world. I cannot stop them, and our gods are gone.'

'How are the demons blocking access to the Heavens?' John said. 'If we can find a way to bring our army up here, we can take the fight to them.'

'When the gods left, they sealed the gateways,' Semias said. 'They could only be opened from this side. Or so we thought. One of the Eastern demons is highly skilled in the art of energy manipulation; it took him thirty-five years to break the ward, but he managed it. He let the others in, the demons from this part of the world joined them, and from what I can see they're building a formidable army.'

'This is very bad,' John said, rubbing his eyes.

'We need to go home and warn everybody,' I said.

'I already did. The East is preparing for war. We have less than six months before all the demons flood out of here and attack.' He turned to Semias. 'I have to take Emma home, but I'll need to be able to re-enter here.'

'I can let you in,' Semias said. 'I'll keep a low profile here, and open the Citadel gateway for you.'

'What about food?' I said. 'You'll have nothing to eat if they took everything.'

He quirked a smile. 'I'm a city; I don't eat. I'll be fine.'

'We need you stronger before we can take you down to the Earthly,' John said to me. 'I know you lost the baby, but you have many, many needle tracks — what were they doing to you?'

'Bleeding me out,' I said. 'Apparently I taste very good.'

'Is that what they were doing to the other humans here?' Semias said. 'Draining the blood from them because they tasted good? That doesn't make sense; all of them were sick.'

'Wouldn't being up here heal them?' John said.

'They were very far gone, close to death. They didn't deteriorate further up here, but they couldn't get better,' Semias said.

'Would they want the blood of serpent people if they were sick?' I said.

John shrugged; Semias looked blank.

A jolt of dismay hit me. 'They were AIDS patients.'

'Why would they want AIDS patients?' John said.

'What's AIDS?' Semias said.

'Remember what happened to my arm when the demon essence hit the AIDS in my bloodstream?' I said to John. I quoted what the Demon King's Number One had said: '*Cut them, break them, nothing can harm them.*'

'Sweet Mercy aid us,' John said. 'They'll be unstoppable.' He turned to Semias. 'Have you seen any demons coated all over with shiny black armour?'

'No,' Semias said.

'Let's just hope they haven't worked out how to do it the other way — AIDS blood into demons,' I said. 'It seems these were the only AIDS patients they had.'

'Tell me about this AIDS, it sounds important,' Semias said.

'That's quite recent. Where was I up to?' John said.

'About fourteen hundred? Things were happening in Italy — you said a new beginning.'

'Okay.' John turned to me. 'I'm giving him a potted history of the world since the Shen left him alone here. Go back to sleep; you need to rest and get better so we can go home.'

'Are we safe here?' I said.

'They left you for dead, yes? They think Semias is still imprisoned, and they don't know I'm here. I doubt they'll come back.'

'There's nothing worth coming back for,' Semias said. 'Since the gods left, everything has been slowly dying. The animals first, then the plants.'

'When did the gods leave the Heavens?' I said.

'About two hundred AD,' John said.

'You've been here nearly two thousand years alone? How did you stay sane?' I asked Semias.

'Cities can't go mad. No, I take it back; we can, but it takes more than a couple of thousand years of neglect to do that. I slept mostly, and dreamed of a past when I was full of joy and song.'

'I hope we can find a way to bring that back to you,' I said.

'The gods cannot return,' Semias said, his voice flat. 'They are gone. It is all gone. The important thing now is to drive these demons back into Hell, then you can leave me here alone to listen to the lost songs.'

'Tell me what happened to them?' I said. 'I'm awake now, and it will help to take my mind off things.'

John squeezed my hand; he understood. Semias looked to Jóhn, who nodded.

Semias pulled a chair up next to my bed. 'About four or five thousand years ago, our gods were beginning to take form and arrive at self-awareness. Humanity was new and wild and fierce, and the gods loved humans dearly.'

'That's about the same age you are,' I said to John, and he nodded again.

Semias continued. 'One of our most powerful spirits, the spirit of the sea, was entranced by a human and shared a family with her. They had eight sons, who chose to live on the Earthly. Their father gave them and their wives an island paradise full of magic and beauty.'

'Atlantis really existed?' I said. 'The Archivist said it was a myth.'

'Hush, I'm telling a story,' Semias said. 'The sons of the sons were greater than ordinary humans and wanted to see the world outside their island. They heard tales from traders of mighty deeds and battles fought, and how a man can only be a hero if he conquers wide lands and returns with the spoils to make his clan rich.'

'That's the way it was back then,' John said. 'You gained wealth by conquest.'

'They invaded the surrounding seas, destroying whole civilisations in their zeal. They became known as the sea people, and terrorised half the world.'

'And their father sank the island?' I said.

'Yes. He couldn't bring himself to kill his children, so he took their land away and made them homeless. He vowed to have nothing more to do with them. They were accomplished seafarers so they took their boats and found a new home.'

'Where did they go?' John said.

'They found an island far to the north where they would be safe, and settled there. They had to fight the existing people for it, but they were still stronger than humans and had little difficulty. The local people revered them as gods.'

'Ireland?' I said.

'I believe that is its name now,' Semias said.

'What happened next?' John said, obviously fascinated.

'They started invading the island next door, and moved to the lands further east. They spread their culture by conquest ... again.'

'Are these the serpent people?' I said.

'No,' Semias said. 'The gods were unhappy that their descendants, who had the gifts of superior strength and speed, were set again on conquest, but again they could not bring themselves to destroy their own children. Instead, they helped a small growing civilisation to become strong enough to stop them. They went down and lived among the people, shared their stories, had families, and built a fair and just system of government with them that all people could participate in. They hoped that this positive, peaceful society would influence their children by example.'

'Greece,' I said.

'Then Rome. Rome developed as Greece weakened, so the gods moved into Rome and helped the people. They armed them with the knowledge and strategy to defeat the brutal children of the gods that were sweeping over the continent, and compassionate philosophies to enlighten them. More children were born: mighty warriors and talented strategists. Of course, the Romans did what everybody else had done: they started to conquer the lands around them and descended into tyranny. They swept through Europe, destroying everything in their path. They murdered and raped and mutilated, committing atrocities that still cause me nightmares. They had to be stopped.'

'So the gods did it again? They created us serpent people after failing twice to control their children? Didn't they learn anything?' I said, exasperated.

'They went to Ireland and took their remaining descendants, now much weakened by time and interbreeding with humans,' Semias said, 'and mixed them with captive demons, to create an even more powerful race that could change to serpent. The gods hoped that by making the people snakes, they would have the wisdom and healing inherent in that noble spirit and would resist repeating the same bad patterns. It didn't work. The serpent people had a demonic thirst for blood and violence. They helped push the Romans back, but at the cost of many lives. The gods saw what they had done and retreated to the Heavens. At the same time, a new religion was spreading across the land, based on compassion and selflessness, purity of heart and freedom from the pursuit of worldly attractions. The gods decided that it was better than anything they had ever done and so they elected to destroy themselves by releasing their spirits into the Earth and sealing the Heavens. They hoped that the new beliefs would make the world a better place without them.'

'That sounds like the teachings of a Buddha,' I said. 'I never thought of it like that.'

'It probably was the teachings of a Buddha, but it didn't work,' John said. 'One: the demons are here in the Western Heavens; and two: that new belief system has probably led to more deaths than the gods' folly.'

'Religion doesn't lead to deaths,' Semias said. 'It's the people who twist the teachings into something cruel and poisonous.'

'Which seems to happen all the time,' John said with regret. 'Humans twist meaning to suit their own agendas.

Teach them to respect all life and look after each other, and watch them turn it into bigotry and oppression.' He sat straighter. 'I like to think that they have matured enough now not to need our guidance and are capable of making their own moral decisions. We can control the demon menace and leave the humans to build a society based on reason and their marvellous sciences.'

'Are they capable of building a caring society without your supervision?' Semias said.

'Some of them, yes; they live their lives protecting the world and helping others. Other humans are still full of pride, and their need for dominance over their brothers and sisters saddens us. But I think that very soon they will become a compassionate civilisation without our stupidity affecting their lives so badly.'

'You're not that stupid,' I said.

'I've made some terrible mistakes that have resulted in many lives destroyed,' John said mildly.

'So did our gods,' Semias said. 'Each decision worse than the last, and the Welsh serpents the most frightening of all.'

'And that's me,' I said.

'Xuan says you have been greatly changed by being with him, but you're still a demon-god-human mix, yes,' Semias said.

'I have been a demon all along,' I said to John. 'The Blue Dragon was right: you were crazy to keep me around.'

'Nobody could sense the Western demon in you. The Dragon was being his usual hysterical self,' John said.

'You must have sensed something,' I said.

'I did, but it was so small and so tenuous that I was sure it was my imagination and there was nothing there. The Demon King burned all the demon essence out of you and that should have fixed it. I made a terrible mistake bringing you here — it activated your Western demon nature.'

'So am I a demon?'

'Even if you were, you aren't now. You broke their hold on you, and they will never be able to control you again. You are not a demon; you have Ascended to fully human.' He quirked a smile. 'More than human.'

'Kwan Yin knew this would happen? She let this happen?'

'It's not that she let it happen; she would have had no choice,' John said. 'The Buddhas exist outside of time. For them, everything is happening now, has already happened, and has yet to happen. That is one of the facets of enlightenment: time no longer holds you. It means that you can never live a full human life inside reality ever again.'

'Sounds horrible,' I said.

'For someone immersed in the pleasures of the Earthly, it sounds like a sacrifice. It is not. It is a profound elevation.'

'Your people have developed a wisdom that our gods were never able to achieve,' Semias said. 'Probably because they were too busy trying to control their wayward children.'

'Some people here must have attained enlightenment,' John said. 'Have you ever been contacted by an Enlightened One?'

'Never,' Semias said. 'And looking at the mess we made of things here, I can't really blame them.'

'Can you go to the Second Platform and talk to them?' I asked John.

'What's that?' Semias said.

'Where the Enlightened Ones live,' John said. 'I can't, Emma. I tried, but this is as far as I can go. I think it's because it's the wrong region, but I'm not sure. Maybe the Lady would be able to tell us, but she's not answering my calls, and I'm not surprised.'

'Why not?' I said.

'Because she knew all of this would happen to us and she made no attempt to stop it. Even if she had no choice in the matter, it will be killing her.'

'It's not her fault, it was the demons that killed ...' I choked on the words; our baby was gone. Then I filled with rage. Those demons would *pay* for what they'd done to us, and nobody would be used in breeding experiments ever again. This would stop.

'You look exhausted, love, sleep,' John said, and put his hand on my forehead.

I pushed it away. 'No need to magic me asleep, I'm tired enough already.' I took his hand. 'And I love you.'

He kissed my fingertips.

'You two are very cute,' Semias said.

John glowered at him. 'I am not cute.'

'Sorry, John, yes, you are,' I said, and his face softened.

36

'Emma.' John's voice was insistent.

I woke to the dim light of evening. 'Huh?'

'Emma, quickly, we have to get out of here. The demons know we're here and they're on their way.'

'They're at the base of the castle,' Semias said. 'Carry her.'

John lifted me, pulling a blanket around me, took me through to the next room and laid me on a table. The sounds of many feet echoed outside the room, and Semias closed the door.

'That will hold them back for a couple of minutes.'

John lifted my hand and put a phone into it. The demons started to hammer on the door.

'This is one of the Dragon's AI phones,' John said. 'Talk to it when you land; tell it to contact anyone it can. Phone.'

'Yes,' the phone said.

'As soon as you can contact someone, tell them —'

The door opened with a crash and John turned away from me, pulling Seven Stars out of the air and taking Celestial Form.

Semias's face appeared above me. 'Ready yourself; you're about to drop about three feet.'

He put his hands out over my prone body and muttered under his breath. As the altar fell away from me, I saw John's head cut from his body and it followed me down.

I landed with a thump on my back on soft grass with a wild, cold wind blowing over me. The sky above was clear and full of brilliant stars with clouds scudding across them. The gateway was visible as a glowing white opening at an angle to me.

I sat up and looked around. John's head had landed on the grass nearby, and he wasn't strong enough to keep it going the same way the Tiger had. He was gone.

Two figures in all-black military outfits raced across the grass towards me, faster than humans, and I staggered to my feet to defend myself. They stopped in front of me; it was a man and a woman and they were from the East.

'I didn't kill him,' I said.

'It's Lord Xuan's lady,' the woman said, and I relaxed. They knew who I was. She looked up. 'Quickly, before it closes.'

The man transformed into a dragon and flew up into the open portal.

'I'm in,' he said. 'Incoming!'

He fell back to earth in two pieces, and a couple of demons followed, landing lightly on the grass near us. The female soldier pulled a pair of swords from scabbards on her back and moved in front of me. I summoned the Murasame, and unbalanced under its weight. I really wasn't strong enough for this.

'Stay behind me,' the female soldier said.

One of the demons grinned at me. 'You survived, Emma,' it said in George's voice. 'Well done. Next time, eh?'

'George?'

The demon's face went slack, then it glowered at us. 'You will survive this time,' it said in a different voice, then both demons jumped up to the gateway. It closed after them, from the centre out to the edge, with a sound like metal sliding over ice.

The soldier put her swords away then dropped to one knee next to the dragon's corpse and touched his head. 'Hazel,' she said, and lowered her own head. 'Travel in peace, brave comrade.'

She rose and turned to me, then bowed slightly. 'Miss Donahoe. Is there somewhere safe here in the West you can go until the Dark Lord returns?'

I fell to sit on the grass, the world spinning around me.

'Are you well?' she said, crouching next to me and putting her hand on my forehead. 'You are very pale.'

'I've been through hell and back,' I said. 'The Dark Lord's house in Kensington — do you know where that is?'

'No. Tell me.'

I gave her the address, and bent my head over my knees. 'Can we wait here for a while? I'm wrecked.'

'No. We need to get you safe.' She transformed into a purple dragon with pink fins and tail, lifted me in her front arms and writhed into the air. 'Rest. I will carry you.'

'Thank you. I'm sorry your companion died.'

'So am I, but he was an Elite and our lives are dedicated to the Celestial. He died fulfilling his duty.'

'You're an Elite?'

'That I am.'

'I'm honoured.'

'Thank you.'

She lifted me higher and we travelled over the ocean. I relaxed into her arms; the bobbing sensation of her flight was soothing.

'Close your eyes,' she said. 'You are safe with me.'

* * *

I woke to a moment of disorientation, then realised I was in bed — mine and John's — in the Kensington house. I relaxed with a sigh of relief. It wasn't the Mountain, but it was home enough for me.

The light outside was grey and rain was hitting the window with a comforting rattle. The same dragon, in female human form dressed all in black, was watching me from a chair at the side of the bed. She smiled slightly when she saw I was awake.

'Thanks for bringing me here,' I said.

She nodded. 'You are welcome.'

'What's your name?'

'High Cloud.'

She lifted her head slightly to listen. I heard it as well: Peta was walking up and down the hallway, talking softly and urgently on the phone.

'No, sir, she's not awake, but she's not injured, just tired. No, she's fine. No, she's still losing blood but it's easing, and we're looking after her. No, she hasn't had anything to eat because she's been asleep. No, I don't think we should wake her.' She was silent for a moment. 'No, I can't say anything except "no". Leave her be and let her rest.'

'I'm awake,' I called to her. 'Let me talk to him.'

She poked her head into the room. 'You should rest.'

I put my hand out for the phone. 'If I don't talk to him, he'll start contacting both of you telepathically and I know what a pain in the ass that is.'

'Oh hell, she's right,' Cloud said. 'Let her talk to him.'

I could hear John's insistent voice as Peta handed the phone to me. 'And whatever you do, don't let her see the demon in the basement.'

'What demon in the basement?' I said sharply.

He was silent for a long time, and Peta's face filled with guilt.

'Emma,' he said. 'Thank the Heavens. How are you feeling? If you're in pain we can arrange something —'

'It's a dull ache, but that might just be because my bladder is very full and I really want to go home,' I said. 'What demon in the basement?'

'We will deal with it when I get there. I'm leaving now; I'll be there in eight to ten hours. Rest, Emma, get better. We have a flight booked for you later tonight.'

'What's down there?'

'You don't want to know, Emma,' Peta said.

John was silent. Then he said, 'Trust me, Emma. It is for your own safety. It's not Franklin. He is on his way to live on the Mountain with us where it's safe. It's a different sort of demon. Please, I ask you, my Lady, do not go down there without me.'

'Oh, okay,' I said lightly, and could almost hear his relief over the line.

'You mean it?'

'You asked me to trust you. I do. I won't go down there,' I said.

'Promise me.'

'I promise.'

He sounded even more relieved. 'I will be there later today your time. Your flight is for ten tonight. Simone and Leo can't wait to see you. Rest, love, and heal. We will be together soon, and nothing will ever part us again.'

'You found me.'

His voice was full of quiet delight. 'I found you, and I will never lose you again.' His tone changed to urgent. 'Don't hang up, I want to talk to Peta.'

'Okay,' I said, and moved to pass the phone to her, then changed my mind and spoke to John again. 'I love you.'

Cloud made a soft sound of amusement.

'I love you too,' he said. 'I'll leave here as soon as I'm off the phone.'

'Hurry.'

I handed the phone to Peta and she took it out of the room, talking to John about what medicinal dishes he wanted her to feed me until he arrived. From the list he was giving her, I would be presented with enough food for a week.

I swivelled on the bed, pushed my feet into my bunny slippers and grabbed a robe from the chair next to the bed. I leaned on the chair, then straightened. Cloud moved next to me to hold my arm and I didn't wave her away; I'd been in this state too many times to pretend. I let her help me to the bathroom.

By the end of the day, I'd recovered enough to get dressed and have a comfortable dinner with Peta, Paul and Cloud at the little four-seater table in the kitchen.

'It's him,' Cloud said, and I heard the front door close. I pulled myself up, but couldn't run to him.

He came into the kitchen and gathered me into a huge hug, then kissed me. He leaned back to study me and ran one hand over my hair, then dropped it to check my pulse. He listened for a moment, then released my wrist, satisfied.

Cloud rose and fell to one knee. 'My Lord.'

'Rise, Lieutenant,' John said. 'I commend you for the care you've taken of my lady.'

Cloud rose and stood to attention, both hands on her left hip. 'Should I return to the gateway?'

'Yes,' John said. 'A second Elite is on her way to join you.'

She saluted him. 'We failed to infiltrate their Heavens.'

'You saved Emma,' he said, squeezing me around my waist. 'You will have another chance at the gateway, I am sure.'

'By your leave, my Lord,' she said, bowing slightly.

He nodded to her and she disappeared.

John pulled me to sit at the table and sat next to me, studying me as if he'd never seen me before. Peta and Paul rose and went out, obviously giving us some privacy.

'Eat,' he said, waving one hand over the table. 'And then we'll take you to the airport and take you home.'

'After I see what's in the basement,' I said.

His expression went blank.

'I mean it.'

'I know. You will need to see. Emma.' He looked down. 'It is a demon copy of you. It fooled Simone and Leo completely.'

I nearly choked on my food and had to drink some water. I stared at him, uncomprehending, for a long moment, and he waited for me.

'Why is it in the basement?' I said. 'Did you tame it? How much like me is it? Did it fool you?'

'It's in the basement because it is tamed but I'm not sure about an explosion imperative. It is enough like you to fool Simone. What was the last question? Oh,' he said before I could prompt him, 'no. I knew what it was the second I saw it.'

I relaxed and sagged in my chair. 'Okay. What do we do with it?'

'Up to you,' he said. 'You can keep it if you like, or I can find a place for it.'

'It infiltrated our family and deliberately misled us,' I said. 'I don't think I'd trust it even if it is tamed.'

He rubbed one hand over his eyes and sighed. 'Eat, Emma, the snow fungus will purify your blood. It didn't know it was a copy.'

I stopped with my spoon halfway to my mouth. 'It thought it was the real me?'

'Yes.'

'Oh dear Lord, the poor thing.'

'I know.'

'Are you sure …?'

'You are the real you? I cannot be fooled. Ever,' he said. That was a relief. 'Okay.'

'You can leave it here, or take it with you, or just destroy it.'

'If it's fully tamed and it won't explode, then it could be incredibly useful as a body double for me,' I said.

'I know.'

'But that's only if it isn't too traumatised by the fact that it thinks it's me and it isn't. How does it feel about you?'

'The same way you do.'

I studied the snow fungus for a while. It loved him as much as I did, and would never be able to have anything with him.

I glanced up. 'But it's tamed now?'

'Yes. It is content.'

I was in no hurry to go down there and see it; I needed some time to prepare myself.

'Let me finish here and then we can go down and talk to it,' I said. 'I was starving.'

'I'm glad.'

* * *

We went down to the cellar together later. I felt a rush of pain when I saw the copy sitting in her cell and looking blankly at the wall. It was the same way I had been when I was a tame demon. She went from inanimate to vibrantly alive when she saw John, jumped to her feet and approached the bars.

'My Lord Xuan Wu,' she said, her hands on the bars, obviously wanting to reach through to him. 'I have waited for you.'

I leaned on John. I knew exactly what was going through her head because I'd been there myself.

'Emma,' she said when she saw me, and put her hand through the bars to reach me. 'Emma.'

I backed away. She'd broken his order to stay in the cell by sticking her arm through the bars. John moved in front of me.

She jerked her hand at me, reaching for me. 'Emma. I need to touch you. Emma? Come closer. I must touch you. Please.' She pulled her hand in and moved sideways from one side of the cell to the other. 'Let me out — I need to touch Emma.' She reached through the bars again, her fingers outstretched. 'I must touch you.'

'Stand down, demon,' John said, but she ignored him, still trying to come through the bars at me.

'John,' I said urgently when I saw what was happening — she was losing her shape and oozing through the bars. Her face became grotesque and twisted as it pressed into the bars and liquefied around them.

John put his hand on top of my head and pushed me down behind him. I backed up to the far wall and watched as he concentrated on the copy. He moved faster than was visible, his hand glowed with chi and he plunged it into her head. It went straight through as if there was nothing there. He summoned Dark Heavens, shoved it through the bars and ran it vertically through her head, cutting her into two black, oozing pieces.

'I suppose that answers that,' he said. He held his hand out over the body and hesitated. 'What the hell?'

He bent to study something between the bars, then opened the cell and went in. He put his hand out over the floor. 'Damn.'

'What is it?' I said, approaching cautiously.

'One of their stone things,' he said, squatting and concentrating with his hand over it. 'I don't know what it was supposed to do.' He stood for a moment, thinking, then obviously came to a conclusion. 'Back up again.'

I moved to the far side of the basement and he blasted the stone with chi.

'That didn't do anything. Wait.'

He yinned it, creating a circular hole in the bars and an indent in the concrete floor.

He came out of the cell and closed the door, shaking his head. 'I didn't want to touch it, it felt so damn wrong, and there aren't enough stones left to bother giving it to them.' He turned to me, his eyes dark with emotion. 'Let's take you home to the Mountain where you're safe.'

'Your energy isn't nearly as effective in this part of the world,' I said.

'It's almost completely ineffective. I have to rely on physical.'

I went to him and leaned into him, and he put his arm around me.

'How about the half-Western hybrid demons?' I said.

'Nearly as bad. I think we will all have this problem. The Demon King appears to be many steps ahead of us in building an army that we will be unable to defend against.'

'We need to get you back to the East so you can coordinate the defence effort.'

'And we need to get you somewhere safe until the Elixir is ready, so I will never have to worry about you again.'

* * *

Leo and Simone were waiting for us in the arrivals hall at Hong Kong Airport. Simone grabbed me and pulled me into her.

'I'm so sorry about the baby,' she said into my shoulder.

'I am too,' I said, patting her on the back. She was trembling. 'Don't worry, Simone, everything will be okay.'

'It won't be okay,' she said, pulling back and wiping her eyes, 'because my little brother or sister is dead.'

'It was too early to be anything but an idea,' I said. 'I didn't want to think of it as a baby until I was further along. When you're in the early stages there's always a chance that this will happen.'

'It still hurts, Emma.'

'I know.'

Leo hugged me as well, crushing me into his enormous chest. 'It's good to have you home and safe, girl.'

He took the luggage trolley from John and led us out. John linked my arm in his, probably aware of how weak I was feeling after a sleepless flight.

'We'll drive to the gateway in Central and go up from there,' Leo said. 'Less stress on you.'

'Thanks,' I said. 'I cannot wait to be home. Is everyone okay?'

They all shared a look. My stomach fell out.

'Who was hurt? What happened? Nobody died, did they?'

None of them replied.

'What happened?'

John pulled me closer as we walked. 'They turned off Leonard's life support.'

I leaned into him as we walked out to the car.

* * *

I passed out as they transported me to the Celestial Plane; not surprising considering the condition I was in. When I came round, John was holding my hand and speaking over me, his voice soft and vehement. I couldn't move or open my eyes; the trip had really knocked me out.

'I want her out of all decision-making and not involved in anything,' he said. 'All training is to cease. Nobody is to tell her what's happening. I want her shut out of whatever's going on —'

Meredith interrupted him. 'She won't let you do this.'

'Look at her,' John said, raising my hand slightly. 'She's covered in scars. She's been through more than any

501

mortal soldier on the Earthly ever has, and her mental state has to be fragile to the point of collapse. She's done too much, and it's time for her to stop before all of this breaks her.'

'And when she's Raised?' Meredith said.

'Screw that,' I said, and used John's hand to pull myself to a seated position. I opened my eyes, resulting in a moment of dizziness that I pushed down with force. 'You don't make these decisions for me.'

I looked around; I was in the bed in the Imperial Residence back on the Mountain. I was home.

John raised my right hand so I could see the withered muscles of my forearm. 'You've done enough. If you go into any more battles, your mental state may start to crack.'

'He's right, Emma,' Meredith said.

'What if I enjoy it?' I said. 'What if there's nothing I like more than destroying demons? What if I live for the thrill of wielding my sword in battle?'

'Then you're an adrenaline addict and you need to stop anyway,' John said.

'Like Meredith said, what about when I'm Raised? You've been fighting wars for four thousand years. What about *your* mental state?'

'Bad idea bringing him into it; I wouldn't call him sane,' Meredith said.

'I'm a warrior by nature,' John said. 'It is what I am.'

'And it's what I was bred for,' I said. 'My heritage was manipulated to make me a greater warrior. It's what I am as well.'

'Touché,' Meredith said with humour.

'And look at Meredith,' I said. 'She's been fighting demons for four hundred years since she was Raised, and she's the sanest person I know.'

'I resent that,' she said.

John sighed, exasperated. 'I've seen too many soldiers

break under the pressure of much less than what you've been through. Don't you think it's time to stop?'

'No,' I said. 'I think it's time I drank that damn Elixir, because then I can really *start*.'

'Told you,' Meredith said, and rose. 'Agree to regular physical and mental checkups, Emma, and do what the counsellor tells you if they say to slow down. And slow down for a few months anyway. You can't take the Elixir until you're in top condition, and it will take you a while to regain that.'

'Aye aye, Captain,' I said, saluting her Western-style.

'You are impossible,' John said, eyeing me.

'That makes us a matched pair then,' I said, and stopped as the summons hit me. 'You have to be freaking kidding me. No way. No way!'

'This is completely ridiculous,' John said.

'What?' Meredith said.

'The Jade Emperor just summoned us into his presence first thing tomorrow morning,' John said. 'I do not believe this.'

'It'll just be to report on what's happening in the West,' Meredith said.

'Why does he want me then?' I said. 'I'm not allowed to have anything to do with Celestial affairs.'

'He wants both of you?' Meredith said, now concerned.

'Go check the Celestial records. See if there's a reason posted for our interview,' John said.

Meredith nodded to him and went out.

'When's Leonard's funeral?' I asked John.

'Memorial service. Day after tomorrow.'

'The summons won't interfere then. I want to be there. Whatever it takes. Even if it's on the Earthly.'

'You will be. It's being held here on the Mountain.'

I relaxed back onto the pillows. 'Good.' I raised my head. 'My family are coming up to the Mountain?'

'Yes.'

'I can't wait to see them. Do you think we could talk them into staying?'

'We will talk about it when they're here.'

'Oh, that's excellent news. It's just terribly sad that Leonard had to die before they would come up here.'

I raised my left hand; there was a button-type band-aid on it and my stone was still gone.

'Where's my stone?'

'A great many stones have died. The Grandmother —'

'I saw her. She was *pissed*.'

'She's gone home to mourn the loss of so many of her children, and taken all but a few of the stones with her.'

'My stone went as well?'

'No, it took an orphaned baby stone to the Grandmother and will probably return soon.'

'Did Gold go with the Grandmother?'

'No, but Zara did.'

'Zara will come back. She'll get bored,' I said.

'I hope she will.'

I looked at my hand again. 'Someone took blood?'

'Edwin checked you over while you were out, but didn't do a thorough examination. He's taken a sample to check exactly how anaemic you are and whether there's any infection. He's satisfied that the blood loss will settle as if it was a normal ...' he took a deep breath, ' ... miscarriage. Apart from exhaustion and exposure, you're otherwise unhurt.'

'I suppose he couldn't check if what the Demon King said was correct?'

'He can now you're awake, but he said it would be best to go to the Tiger's facility in the West after things have settled down. If you still hurt inside, he's given you some painkilling options; being in pain will only slow down your recovery.'

'It doesn't hurt any more, I just feel tired. Worn out.'

'That's understandable.' He squeezed my hand. 'Rest.'

'Yeah, I need to be strong to face His Celestial Ugliness tomorrow.'

'That's me,' he said.

'I meant the Jade Emperor, but you qualify.'

He rubbed his free hand over his face, his voice thick. 'You have no idea how glad I am to have you home, my love.'

I pulled him into me and we silently embraced for a very long time, both of us relishing the feeling of being together with nothing to part us.

37

The Jade Emperor saw us the next morning in his small meeting room. Three carved rosewood sofas sat in a U-shape, with tea tables at the corners. A four-metre-long screen sat behind his chair, inlaid with gold and semi-precious stones showing a stylised depiction of longevity cranes flying through China's distinctive mist-covered mountains.

The Jade Emperor nodded to the fairy who brought us tea, then turned to us as he poured. 'Your period of penitence is complete. You may return to duties.' He placed a pair of teacups for me and John on the corner table, pulling his long sleeve out of the way. 'I will not hold a public ceremony or make an announcement. You may choose to tell others whenever you please. Your precedence as the Dark Lord's promised is restored, Lady Emma, but you are no longer a Heavenly General. Ah Wu and Er Lang have those positions covered.'

'Good, I don't want it,' I said. 'Can I choose not to tell anyone until I'm stronger?'

'I'd advise that course.'

'I assume this means there is no longer any danger of her teaching the demon army in the West,' John said, glowering.

'That is the case,' the Jade Emperor said, his face bright and serene.

'You knew she'd be taken.'

The Jade Emperor didn't reply, his expression unchanging.

'Did you know I'd lose the baby?' I said.

His expression faltered slightly but he still didn't reply.

'Sometimes I wonder why I serve you,' John growled.

'Did our baby really have to die?' I said. 'There had to be another way.'

'The future is not fixed, Emma,' the Emperor said. 'There are many possibilities laid out before us. We can guide the realm in the right direction, but sometimes sacrifices must be made to serve the greater good. There was no other way.'

'I find that difficult to believe,' John said.

'The qilin said something similar,' I said. 'That things need to happen.'

The Jade Emperor put one hand out towards me. 'She understands. You are wiser than your Lord sometimes, Emma. I look forward to the two of you working together to defend the realm. Begin teaching her strategy, Ah Wu, because her intelligence will be a great asset.'

'That's what *I* told *you*,' John said, exasperated.

'And you were right. We will need our greatest minds and spirits to defend our realm, because there is a very good chance that it will fall.'

'It could still fall?' John said, his anger dissolving into concern.

'How much of the future can you see?' I said.

The Jade Emperor didn't reply; it was obvious I was wasting my time asking.

'Are we done here?' I said.

John turned and stared at me.

'Absolutely refreshing,' the Jade Emperor said.

John smiled and shook his head.

'Dark Lord. Dark Lady,' the Jade Emperor said.

He rose and we did as well. He bowed slightly to us and we returned the courtesy. I was obviously able to act as close to an equal now that I'd been re-promoted. Nevertheless, I was glad the Jade Emperor hadn't told anyone my rank was restored and I could retain my lowly status in public for a while longer.

'Go back to your Mountain and plan the defence of the Heavens in the coming war,' he said. 'Both of you will be pivotal in the times to come.'

'How long do we have?' John said.

The Jade Emperor's serene expression slipped. 'The first casualties have already occurred.'

* * *

The Tiger was waiting for us at the outdoor table setting in the courtyard of the Imperial Residence. He fell to one knee and saluted John as we arrived, and we all sat.

'Welcome back, Emma,' he said. 'It's good you're home. He'll stop traipsing halfway around the world every second day, and your knowledge of what they're up to is sorely needed.'

'You need to give me half a day to spend with Emma, and we have a funeral tomorrow,' John said. 'After that I can start work.'

'It can wait,' the Tiger said. 'You might like to know that Thirty-Eight broke my compulsion and went to Hell anyway. She lasted thirty-five minutes.'

'That's Thirty-Eight the Mother?' I said.

The Tiger nodded.

'I remember her; she and Louise were good friends. Why'd she go to Hell? She knew they'd tear her to pieces.'

The Tiger leaned one elbow on the table and put his chin on his hand; he was silent for a long moment.

'What?' John said.

The Tiger concentrated on him and John's face went grim.

'Out loud, I do not believe this!' I said.

John nodded, and the Tiger looked down and turned his teacup on the glossy ceramic of the table. 'While you were away we were attacked.'

'What happened?'

'Demons infiltrated the Western Palace. Small flying poisonous ones. Deadly.'

'Did you lose anyone?' I said.

'Thirty-six wives, thirty-five Horsemen. Sixteen of my children also died.'

'Oh dear Lord, no.' My eyes filled, and I took a deep breath. 'Not Louise?'

'Louise passed away three days ago.'

I moaned quietly. 'What about the kids?'

'Both the children are fine; their auntie has taken them in.'

'Louise's sister?' I said.

'It's a tradition in the Western Palace,' John said. 'One of the wives who can't have children acts as a second mother for another wife's children — something like your concept of a godmother in the West.' He was silent for a moment. 'Kimberley and Lucas have known their auntie all their lives and will be well looked after by her and their father.'

'I suppose that's something of a relief,' I said, wiping my eyes. 'When's the funeral?' I sipped some tea through my choked-up throat. 'Another funeral. Have you told her family?'

'She died to her family years ago,' the Tiger said, still studying his tea. 'She even went so far as to fake her death.'

'Seeing what my family have been through, I can actually understand why she'd do that,' I said.

'The funeral is tomorrow afternoon.' He looked up at me. 'Spare yourself the exertion and don't come. She would

509

not have wanted you to put your health at risk. You can come visit her grave when you're stronger.'

'I'm well enough.'

'With all due respect, Emma,' the Tiger said, 'I can smell the blood you're still losing, and you're barely able to hold yourself upright. Ah Wu says you have a funeral tomorrow morning already, and your family will be here.' He raised his teacup without drinking from it. 'Louise would not want you to make such huge sacrifices for her.'

'I will anyway,' I said. 'She was my friend. I'll see you tomorrow, Tiger.'

He rose and put his cup on the table. 'I knew you would, but I had to make the effort. It's what she would have wanted.' He rubbed his hand over his face. 'You may find this difficult to believe, but I miss her horribly. She was my wife and I loved her.'

John and I rose as well.

'She was happy, Tiger,' I said. 'Isn't that all that really matters?'

He nodded, his face grim, then saluted John and left without another word.

'He's not usually like that when wives die,' I said softly after he'd gone.

'Actually, Emma,' John said. 'He is. You've just never seen it.'

I flopped back down on one of the ceramic chairs.

'Are you okay?' he said, sitting across from me and studying me with concern. 'We need to have you checked out in his clinic as soon as you're stronger.'

I rubbed my hand over my forehead. 'I'm okay. Just tired, and sad, and worn out.' I sighed deeply. 'And empty.'

'Go rest.'

'I won't sleep; I'll just lie awake staring at the ceiling and feeling miserable. I need something to do.' I stood back up with renewed energy. 'I'll write a full report on everything

I saw and did while I was in the West. The quicker I get the information down, the more I'll remember for the defence effort.' I made for the stairs, and stopped. 'I wonder if I can take my office back? It would be good to work near you.'

'It's ready for you; just move your things back in,' John said, rising to stand with me. 'But don't carry anything. You are confined to light duties as much as possible. We need you stronger so you can take the Elixir.'

I moved into him and he wrapped his arms around me.

'Did the JE give you permission to make an Elixir for Simone when mine is done?'

'Yes. I've also talked her into pursuing the Way.'

'That's very good news.' I pulled away and took one of his hands. 'Come on, let's check out the status of my office. I bet I'll be in there a week before anyone realises I'm back in the good books.'

'The good books?'

'As opposed to the bad books.'

'Where are these books?'

'I'll explain on the way.'

* * *

I wore the plain black pants and jacket of the Mountain uniform the next morning for Leonard's funeral. I joined John and a few of the closest Retainers outside Dragon Tiger to wait for my family to arrive.

My parents got there first, with Jade, and I was shocked by how much older they looked. It had been less than two years and they appeared to have aged ten. I hugged both of them, teary-eyed with joy tempered by sadness for the reason they were here.

'Mandy stayed home,' my mother said. 'She and Allan are happy where they are. Mark's settled and they don't want to disturb him, and she's minding Jen's baby for them.'

John put his hand out. 'Brendan, Barbara, so good to see you.'

'Look at you, John, you actually seem younger each time we meet,' my father said as he shook John's hand.

'I don't feel it,' John said, and somehow that broke the ice.

Michael and Clarissa arrived in a flash near the entrance to Purple Mist, Clarissa in a long-term therapeutic wheelchair with a low back. Simone went to them first, quickly followed by Martin and Leo in his own chair. Leo went up to Clarissa and held one hand up, palm out. She stared at it for a moment blankly, then grinned and high-fived him. They spun their chairs side-on to each other and had a small sideways hug.

I stood back to let them have their moment: Michael and Simone ribbing each other like brother and sister; Clarissa's and Leo's heads nearly touching as they compared chairs. Simone bent to hug Clarissa, both their faces full of delight. Michael wiped one eye and shook Leo's hand, turning it into an embrace. Martin watched them with contentment, and I turned to see John had a similar expression.

A group of happy children all grown up, he said to me. *It's been a long road but completely worth it. Sometimes I feel very old.*

I squeezed his hand. 'I feel old too.'

'Don't we all,' my mother said from behind me, and I moved back to put my arm around her. She scolded John. 'Talk out loud.'

'Sorry,' he said. 'I just said I'm so glad to see them grown up and happy.'

'We all are.'

Greg and Jen arrived with Jen and Leonard's boys, Andrew and Colin. I went to Jen and hugged her.

'I'm so sorry, Jen.'

'I heard what happened to you,' she said, smiling sadly.

'We were hoping you'd give Mum and Dad a granddaughter. Maybe next time.'

'Maybe,' I said, making light of it. 'How's the baby?'

Her face lit up. 'He's a bundle of trouble. Terrible twos soon.' She glanced at Greg, who was standing next to her with his expression full of pride. 'We've yet to see if he can do anything special.'

'We're hoping he won't,' Greg said. 'Both of us are glad to be well out of the whole Celestial thing.'

'If he turns out special we're always here to help,' I said.

Her face froze for a moment and I silently cursed myself. Her son had been kidnapped and raped by the demons after he'd come to me asking for training. Greg took her hand in his and she brightened. 'Thanks, but Greg can handle it.'

I turned to the grief-stricken boys and hesitated. Colin was hovering protectively over Andrew, his younger brother who'd been taken by demons. Andrew had put on a great deal of weight and his face was pock-marked with acne.

'Hi, guys,' I said. 'It's really good to see you again.'

Colin gingerly hugged me, obviously uncomfortable, and Andrew didn't move at all. He was frozen like a rabbit in headlights. His expression became even more panicked when John approached.

Greg fell to one knee to salute John.

John raised one hand. 'Up, Greg.' He studied Colin and Andrew, who had also raised their hands to salute him. 'No need for formalities. I'm just Uncle John; you're family. Treat me like your uncle. Okay?'

Colin nodded, obviously relieved. Andrew didn't even blink.

John went to Jennifer and took her hand. 'I know you and Leonard had parted ways, but you had a family together and I'm sorry that's gone now.'

'Thank you,' Jen said, and Greg put his arm around her shoulder.

Clarissa went to Andrew and took his hands — she'd been in the cell next to them when the demons had held them. I couldn't hear what she said to him, but he nodded a few times, wiping his eyes. Colin hovered behind him protectively. Andrew leaned down to Clarissa and hugged her, and she patted his back.

John gestured towards Dragon Tiger. 'If you'll come this way, the hall is ready. Everybody would like to pay their respects.'

He led the family, followed by the staff of the Mountain, up the stairs into the hall. Clarissa hesitated at the bottom of the stairs, and Michael levitated her.

'You need a ramp here,' Michael said.

'We're in the process of installing them everywhere,' John said, waiting at the top of the stairs. 'Next time you come there'll be one here.'

'Took your time accommodating Leo,' Clarissa said, but her smile was wide.

'Leo can carry himself,' John said. 'The ramps will be for an injured student. He's chosen to stay even though he's lost the use of his legs. He'll be studying hand-to-hand and would like to learn financial management from you, if you have the time.'

'I'd be glad to help,' Clarissa said.

The hall had been filled with chairs and decorated with flowers and a large portrait of Leonard with candles burning on either side of it. The service was non-denominational according to Leonard's wishes, and Martin would officiate as a high-ranking Celestial.

Ben's and Tom's portraits stood on a side table in the hall, receiving offerings of incense and food for six weeks after their funeral as was the custom. I had a horrible feeling that I would be seeing a great many more of these in the near future. After this afternoon's service, I would add a portrait for Louise myself.

* * *

We had lunch together in the officer's mess after the service, and I quizzed everybody about what they'd been doing.

'Greg's my apprentice,' my father said with obvious pride. 'Natural affinity to electricity, and boy, can he lift heavy stuff.'

'They have their own company,' Jen said with similar pride. 'We'll be putting more people on soon.'

'You're not doing too much, are you, Dad?' I said. 'I thought you'd retired.'

'I run most of it,' Greg said. 'Brendan is the brains, I'm the brawn.'

'Oh, I wouldn't say that,' my father said, pleased at the compliment.

'We're vegetarian now, dear,' my mother said to Simone as she turned the lazy susan in the middle of the table for them.

Andrew wasn't eating. I tried to draw him out. 'Colin and Andrew, how are you two going at school?'

Andrew's face screwed up and he began to sob silently. Jen jumped up and ran around the table to soothe him, holding his shoulders.

'Can I go home?' he said, his voice close to panic. 'I want to go home. Can we go home now?' He gulped a huge mouthful of air. 'I just want to go home. I just want to go home.' He rocked in his chair, silently repeating the words over and over.

Colin turned away; he was breaking down into tears as well.

'I'm so sorry. Go if you want to,' I said.

Jen crouched to speak to Andrew. 'You can be brave; you're safe here. Can't you stay just a little bit longer?'

Andrew threw one arm over her shoulder and let go into her. 'Please take me home. This is all too much.'

'Take him home, it's fine,' my mother said. 'You can stay with us if you want, Colin.'

Colin had his hand protectively on Andrew's back, tears running down his face. 'I'll go with him and look after him.'

'Greg?' Jen said, turning to him.

Greg nodded to us, went to Jen and the boys, and they all disappeared.

I ran my hand over my forehead. 'I ruined it.'

'No, that was coming,' my father said. 'It wasn't anything you did.'

'He's been more than a month without a breakdown; it was inevitable,' my mother said.

'Even a boy who hadn't been through what he has would react like that to the loss of his father,' John said. 'Don't blame yourself, Emma. The boys know they have a family that loves them.'

'He did very well to make it as far as he did,' my mother said. 'A year ago we wouldn't even have been able to get him up here.'

'Just tell me when you want to go home as well. We'll arrange transport,' John said.

'We'd prefer to stay a while and talk to Emma,' my mother said, reaching out and holding my hand. 'I heard what happened. I'm sorry about the baby.'

I tried to say something, but the words wouldn't come out. 'Thanks.'

'You look like hell, Emma, what did they do to you?' my father said.

'Demon stuff,' I said, my voice thick. The boys' reactions had hit me hard.

'Would you like us to stay up here on the Mountain with you?' my mother said.

'I would absolutely love that, but ...' I shook my head. 'I think Andrew and Mark need you more than I do, Mum.'

'We want to pursue Immortality,' my father said. 'We've talked about it, and since we have the opportunity, we thought we might as well see what's involved.'

'You are always welcome,' John said.

'Maybe we can split our time between there and here? Would we be safe doing that, John?'

'Perfectly safe. We're quite capable of arranging something for you; and Greg is a fine warrior who can protect you on the Earthly.'

'That would be wonderful,' I said, choking back the emotion. They'd always been too traumatised to even consider visiting us.

'There you go, that's much better, isn't it?' my mother said, seeing me cheer up at the idea of having them around.

'I need to find you a nice residence here,' I said.

'Good, that will keep your mind occupied,' she said, patting my hand. 'Make it big enough for Jen and Mandy to come visit as well. Now let's eat, and then we can go to poor Louise's funeral.'

'You know about that?' I said.

'Greg was listening the whole time. He nearly went back up to help out, but he wanted to be sure we were safe. It was awful.'

'Yes, it was.'

* * *

After Louise's service, John and I dropped into the Tiger's medical centre and they took some X-rays and an ultrasound. The same doctor saw me in the same office. He held the X-ray up and snapped it onto the light box.

'Do you know what they did to you?' he said.

'All I know is that I lost the baby. They said I wouldn't be having any more.'

'Once you're Raised it won't be a concern,' John said, squeezing my hand.

'I'd love some more samples from you if you ever have the chance, my Lord,' the doctor said. 'You're fascinating.'

John leaned back and glared at him. 'I don't think that will be happening.'

'You have no idea what I went through to get that one,' I said. 'And now everybody appears to know about it.'

'What?' John said, horrified.

'It wasn't me, I swear,' the doctor said. 'I think it was someone in the pathology lab, but nobody will admit to talking about it. I suspect it may have been our father.' He turned back to the X-ray. 'They did a hysterectomy on you, Miss Donahoe. Everything except a very small part of your remaining ovary is gone.'

'What?' I said, as horrified as John had been. 'But there's no scarring, no stitches. How did they do it without opening me up?'

'They performed it vaginally so there'd be no scarring. It's a very common method.'

'They spayed me like a cat to make me more docile?'

'No, if they wanted that they would have taken your ovary completely and removed all your hormones, turning you into a female eunuch.' The doctor took the X-ray off the light box and put it back into its folder. 'If the damage was as extensive as it appears from the scans, then it was a valid medical option. It could have saved your life.' He shook his head. 'The surgeon was highly skilled; I couldn't have done a better job myself.'

John took my hand. 'Once you're Raised it won't matter, Emma.'

'As the Dark Lord said, once you're Raised the matter is academic. You will choose your form and physiology,' the doctor said.

I dropped my head and ran my hands through my hair. I'd heard of women not feeling like a woman at all after having this done to them, but all I felt was numb.

John took my hand in both of his. 'Come on, Emma, let's go home. You have a family there who love you and who have gone far too long without you around to annoy. Simone hasn't had a chance to sit you down and talk your ears off about the boys at school, and I'm sure Leo wants to take you shopping because your clothes are more than a week old.' He patted my back. 'And I have a big pile of budgeting spreadsheets waiting for your magic touch. We've missed you sorely.'

I looked up at him and smiled through the tears. 'Sometimes you know exactly the right thing to say.'

'Good.' He nodded to the doctor. 'Doctor.'

'Dark Lord, Miss Donahoe.'

* * *

'This doesn't change anything,' John said from behind me as we rode his cloud back to the Mountain.

'I never for a moment thought that it did,' I said. 'I know you better than that.'

'Good,' he said, and pulled me closer. 'But if you ever want to talk about how it feels, I'm here.'

'I may take you up on that, but right now I don't know how I feel.'

'I understand.'

I leaned into him. I knew he did.

38

The next day Yi Hao and I were working together on a filing system for the information I'd compiled on the Western situation when John interrupted me.

Your stone's back and in here with me.

'I'll be right back,' I said to Yi Hao, and walked as quickly as I could to John's office, which wasn't terribly fast. The stone and Zara were in human form, sitting in the visitors' chairs.

'There you are, Emma,' my stone said, rising to give me a huge hug. It released me, then folded up and returned to my ring. 'I am never leaving here again, understood? I am so sorry I left you alone up there. I blame myself for what happened.'

'Is there any way you could have avoided it?' I said. 'The Grandmother pulled you with her when she left.'

'That's beside the point; it will never happen again. I promise I will always be there to look after you.'

'That's a powerful vow to take, stone,' John said.

'I stand by it,' the stone said.

'Very well,' John said. 'Thank you for returning, Zara. I appreciate it.'

Zara rose and bowed to John. 'If I may return to duties, my Lord?'

'You are more than welcome. I've missed your skills,' John said.

Zara flushed red to her hairline, then turned into her diamond form and floated out of the office.

'I have a message from the small stone I escorted to the Grandmother,' my stone said.

'You arrived safely?' John said.

'Yes. The stone would like you to go back and visit Margaret. It says that Margaret was "very sad" when you left.'

John dropped his head and sighed.

'Margaret who?' I said.

'Margaret Anathain,' John said. 'She was the head of the serpent people in Wales. Community doctor as well as expert on ancient languages and leader of the town.' He rubbed his hand over his forehead. 'Intelligent, courageous, spirited, much like you.' He looked into my eyes. 'She helped me search for you. I never encouraged her in any way, but just my presence was enough. She'd never seen anything like me before.'

'Oh dear,' I said. 'I understand exactly what's going through her head. Poor woman.'

'She'll get over it,' John said.

A squeal drifted back to us from Zara's desk outside. 'Who has been doing your filing, my Lord?'

'Me,' John called to her.

'Oh no,' she said loudly. 'No, this is wrong, this doesn't belong here ... By the Grandmother, why is this here?' The diamond floated back into his office and hovered in front of his eyes. 'Do not even attempt to do your own filing in future. It will take me *weeks* to sort this mess out.' She rose slightly in the air and floated out, obviously in a huff.

John and I shared a smile.

'Maybe you should call her to tell her you found me, and say goodbye?' I said.

'It will break her heart,' the stone said. 'From what the small stone told me, that's a small and isolated community and Margaret has never met a man to match her in wit and temperament. She'll never meet anyone like you ever again.' Its voice became accusing. 'According to the small stone, you never even said goodbye. You just flew off, and she was waiting for you to return for a week.'

'She will get over it,' John said. 'She doesn't have a choice.'

'You've ruined her life,' the stone said. 'She'll compare every future man she meets against a god.'

'The Archivist will be in contact with her soon to discuss her records,' John said. 'After she's met him, she'll never want to speak to another Immortal ever again.'

'Oh, well done,' the stone said with awe.

Zara zoomed in. 'The Lord Venus is here to see you.'

John waved one hand. 'Show him in.'

Venus came in, and stopped when he saw me. His face went expressionless. I was becoming accustomed to this reaction to my appearance.

He saluted John and me. 'Lord Xuan. Lady Emma.' He placed the box he was carrying on the desk, then grinned lopsidedly at me. 'Come here, Emma.'

I let him wrap his arms around me and lost myself in his soft purple silk robe and the heady scents of jasmine and gardenia.

'I am so glad you made it out of there,' he said into my ear, then sighed with feeling. 'And I'm sorry for your loss.'

'Thanks, Venus,' I said, pulling back. I put one hand out towards the other visitor's chair. 'Please, my Lord, sit.'

He flicked his robe and sat, and I sat as well.

'Emma gives the best hugs ever,' Venus said. 'And I've missed her unique sense of humour.'

'Your wives will be jealous if they hear that,' John said.

Venus waved one hand at him. 'Both my wives give excellent hugs, but Emma's are terribly exotic.'

'If you're trying to make him jealous, it's not working,' I said, gesturing towards John's placid expression.

'Always worth a try,' Venus said. He sat straighter. 'Open the box.'

The box was slightly smaller than the usual Edict, and John studied Venus as he thumbed the clasp to make it spring open. His eyes widened slightly as he saw what was inside, then he glanced from me back to Venus. Venus leaned back in his chair, smug and relaxed.

John lifted a slender jug from the gold silk that lined the box. Its base was carved black glass, and the handle and top were made of filigreed silver.

'All yours,' Venus said, full of delight. He turned to me. 'You'll have to wait a few months before you're strong enough to drink it, Emma.'

'Is that it?' I said, dumbfounded.

'This is it,' John said, standing the jug on the desk with reverence. 'We'll have to put it somewhere completely secure until you're ready for it.'

'Let me smell it,' I said. 'I want to be sure.'

John raised the lid and held the jug out to me. I inhaled and the air around me burst into a brilliant symphony of colour and glowing light. The scent was dazzling to the point of making me dizzy.

'Okay,' I said, my voice weak. 'That doesn't smell bad at all.'

Venus pulled out a modern Japanese notebook with a cute puppy on the front and read from it. 'Expect the Jade Emperor to be in touch soon; he'll want regular meetings to coordinate the war effort. The demons haven't moved yet, but it's only a matter of time. The Number Ones came back; nothing they tried would lure any demons out. The trees will not sacrifice one of their own unless the need is completely dire. The Elites are still posted at the gateways, though, so hopefully we will find a way up there. We are looking for volunteers to sortie into their Hell again and do more intelligence gathering.'

'Semias will be back in that damn cell,' I said. 'We have to get him out.'

'You're not going anywhere until you've drunk that booze,' Venus said.

'Damn, you've been around Emma too much,' John said.

'We all have. Refreshing, isn't it?'

'Absolutely.'

Venus glanced down at the notebook. 'That's all. The Jade Emperor wants the first meeting next week; your stone can arrange a time. He wants to see both of you: Lord Xuan for tactics, and Lady Emma for intelligence on what they're up to.' He rose and bowed to us. 'Welcome home, Dark Lady. Dark Lord.'

'Thanks, Venus,' I said.

He bowed to us again and went out.

John rose and came around the desk, holding the jug with both hands. 'Come on, let's put this somewhere safe.'

'In the Grotto?'

'No, at least five people have access to that. In the armoury.'

We walked through the gardens together, and I revelled in the freshness of the cool air. Winter had arrived and the blue sky was full of the cotton-wool clouds of promised snow.

'Are you warm enough?' John said.

'Yes. Don't worry about me.'

He raised the jug slightly. 'One thing less to worry about.'

The double doors of the armoury were kept open during the day. We went in and passed Miss Chen, who was doing a stocktake of weapons.

She looked over her reading glasses at us. 'Is that it?'

'Yes,' John said.

'Good. About time,' she said, and turned back to her counting.

We went to the end of the armoury and walked through the wall, then John stopped before the gold-encased bars of the Celestial storeroom.

'Don't attempt to come in here. I'll do this myself.'

I didn't argue; it wasn't worth killing myself to go in.

He closed his eyes and walked through the bars, then went to Seven Stars in the centre of the room. The sword hummed gently, resonating with his presence.

'I'm having something similar to Seven Stars made for Simone,' he said. 'A dual pair of daggers with the chakra holders in them. She'll be the first person besides me able to do it.'

'She asked you for them?'

'Yes. She wants to defend the Mountain.'

'I'm proud of her too,' I said.

John concentrated and a metre-tall stone pillar with a gold top emerged from the ground. He placed the Elixir onto the pillar and stepped back. A black box appeared around the jug, polished and featureless.

'Only you or I can open that.' He glanced at me. 'If something happens to me, open it and use it anyway.'

'I won't want to. I wouldn't want Immortality if it doesn't include you.'

He turned back to the pillar and his shoulders drooped slightly. 'I don't want it without you either, but I don't have a choice.'

'See? Besides, nothing can happen to you, you're indestructible,' I said, trying to lighten the mood. 'We're nearly there.'

He walked back through the bars and held me, resting his face on the top of my head. 'I found you.'

'You did. All you have to do now is Raise me.'

'And then we can have a huge, tedious, over-inflated wedding where everybody enjoys themselves immensely except for us.'

'Sounds perfect.'

'One of three,' he said softly. 'I found you, and I will never lose you again.'

'Can I be with you for the rest of my life?' I said.

'Only if I can be with you for the rest of mine.'

'Deal. Let's go and prepare to defend the Heavens. Those demons will never come into our Mountain again.'

He took my hand and smiled into my eyes. 'Let's stop them together.'

The Serpent's eyes are glazed and cloudy;
it cannot die from heat or thirst.
Nobody has come in weeks, it is alone.
Death's release is out of reach.

The Turtle's head is full of war;
it studies the time streams, planning defence.
The streams all merge and gather
At a place that spells defeat.

Characters

(*Ordered by first name*)

Amy Leong: black dragon who can take human form. Gold's wife, mother of Richard and Jade Leong.

Andrew Black: Emma's teenaged nephew, brother to Colin, son to Emma's sister Jennifer and her first husband, Leonard. Kidnapped by demons, raped and tortured; now in hiding with the rest of the family in Perth.

Archivist, The: Immortal responsible for the management of the Heavenly Archives, a collection of all the world's literature and the Celestial Records. Usually takes the form of a twelve-year-old boy.

Bai Hu: the White Tiger, God of the West. His element is Metal.

Barbara Donahoe: Emma's mother; in hiding with the rest of the family in Perth.

Ben O'Breen: father of Tom O'Breen. Human Welshman on the run from his demon wife, who used him to produce Tom, a snake-hybrid demon.

Black Jade (BJ): stone Shen, child of Gold, created when he was damaged in battle.

Blue Dragon: Qing Long, God of the East. His element is Wood. Father to Jade's three dragon children.

Brendan Donahoe: Emma's father; in hiding with the rest of the family in Perth.

Bridget Hawkes: wife of David Hawkes; executive in a large Hong Kong company.

Chang: human, ex-Shaolin monk. Worked as an assassin/bodyguard for a demon prince until he refound the Way and returned to the monastic life.

Chen, Miss: human Immortal. Wudang Academy Weapons Master.

Clarissa Huang: human. Was engaged to Michael MacLaren until she was captured and tortured by demons, giving her lingering physical and psychological after-effects.

Da Shih Yeh: the Little Grandfather; ancient mystical demon that wanders the Halls of Hell comforting those who are in most need. Rumoured to be a demonic incarnation of Kwan Yin.

David Hawkes: human executive director of one of Hong Kong's large family-owned companies; husband to Bridget.

Death Mother: one of the four demons in the Demon King's research group, which he used and destroyed. Made undetectable copies of humans from demon essence.

Demon King (East): calls himself George. Has several male and female human forms, one of which is Kitty Kwok. His True Form is similar to a Snake Mother (human front end, snake back end) but red instead of black.

Demon King (West): calls himself Francis. Has teamed up with the Eastern Demon King and they are building an army together.

Edwin: Wudang Mountain's staff doctor.

Emma Donahoe: human Australian woman who can change into a snake; engaged to Xuan Wu.

Er Hao: tame demon, major domo of the Imperial Residence on Celestial Wudang.

Er Lang: Second Heavenly General, the Jade Emperor's left hand and John's assistant in defence of the Heavenly realm. Has a third eye in the centre of his forehead and is most often seen in the company of his Celestial Dog.

Firebrand: dragon Immortal; one of the administrative staff of the Northern Heavens.

Franklin: last vampire in existence. A hybrid of Eastern and Western demons, which makes him very fragile even though he is powerful.

Freddo: Freddo Frog, Simone's half-demon horse.

Gold: stone Shen, child of the Jade Building Block. Works as the Academy's legal adviser. Husband to Amy, stone parent to BJ, and human father to Richard and Jade Leong.

Grandmother of All the Rocks: Uluru, the massive stone in the centre of Australia. Spiritual mother of all the stone Shen in the world.

Greg White: human Immortal husband to Emma's sister Jennifer. Used to be the White Tiger's Number One son; resigned to marry Jennifer and now lives in Perth with the rest of Emma's family.

Jade Emperor: supreme ruler of Taoist Heaven, God of the Centre and the element of Earth.

James: former butler at Xuan Wu's UK residence in Kensington, now retired.

Jamie Anathain: owner of a café in Holyhead; one of the Welsh serpent people.

Jennifer: Emma's sister, mother to Colin and Andrew with her first husband, Leonard. Divorced, and remarried the White Tiger's previous Number One son, Greg. Living in hiding with the rest of Emma's family in Perth.

John Chen: Xuan Wu, the Dark Emperor of the Northern Heavens; God of the North and Martial Arts. His True Form is a snake and turtle combined together. His element is Water.

Kitty Kwok: Emma's previous employer, who ran kindergartens in Hong Kong; revealed to be the Eastern Demon King in female human form.

Kwan Yin: a Buddha, one who has attained enlightenment and has returned to Earth to help others. Goddess of Mercy and Compassion.

Leo Alexander: African-American bodyguard to Simone when she was a child; now a Taoist Immortal. Engaged to Prince Martin Ming Gui, son of Xuan Wu.

Leonard Black: Emma's sister Jennifer's first husband; father of Colin and Andrew. Human lawyer working in London.

Lily: human Immortal; one of the administrators of the Northern Heavens.

Ling: owner of the demon stallion that fathered Simone's horse, Freddo.

Little Jade: Amy and Gold's young daughter, twin sister to Richie; called 'Little Jade' to differentiate her from John's PR director, the Jade Girl.

Liu, Shao Rong: the Academy's Immortal Shaolin Master; married to Master Meredith Liu.

Louise: Emma's good friend for many years; married the White Tiger and became wife number ninety-seven. Lives in the Tiger's Western Palace.

Ma Hua Guang: Vanguard of the Thirty-Six; one of the Thirty-Six (now Thirty-Five) Heavenly Generals and John's right hand.

Mabel Defaoite: owner of a guesthouse in Holyhead.

Mandy: Emma's human sister Amanda; married to Allan with two sons, Mark and David.

Margaret Anathain: physician, and headwoman of the serpent people in the Welsh town of Holyhead.

Mark: Emma's teenaged nephew, brother to David, son to Emma's sister Amanda and her husband, Allan. Kidnapped by demons, raped and tortured; now living in hiding with the rest of the family in Perth.

Martin Ming Gui: turtle Shen, son of Xuan Wu, elder brother to Simone, younger brother to Yue Gui; Prince of the Northern Heavens and John's Number One son. Engaged to Leo Alexander.

Meredith Liu: the Academy's Energy Master; a European Immortal; married to Liu Shao Rong, the Academy's Shaolin Master.

Michael MacLaren: Number One son of the White Tiger; son of Rhonda MacLaren.

Michelle LeBlanc: Xuan Wu's first human wife, Simone's mother. Killed by demons when Simone was two years old.

Number One: an honorary title given to the most senior son (or daughter). Most rulers have a Number One to assist them in running their realms, and a Number One has precedence second only to their father/mother.

Pao Qing Tian: Celestial Judge of the Tenth Level of Hell. Responsible for releasing Immortals back to the world when they're killed; also makes the decision on who is Worthy to be Raised to Immortal.

Paul Davies: human housekeeper of John's UK house in Kensington; husband to the butler, Peta Davies.

Peta Davies: human butler for Xuan Wu at his UK residence in Kensington; wife to Paul Davies, the current housekeeper.

Qing Long: the Blue Dragon, God of the East. His element is Wood.

Red Phoenix: Zhu Que, Goddess of the South. Her element is Fire.

Rhonda MacLaren: the only one of the White Tiger's wives with the strength of will to leave him. Was destroyed by drinking the Elixir of Immortality.

Richie (Richard Leong): Amy and Gold's young son, twin brother to Little Jade.

Ronnie Wong: half-demon son of the Demon King; in hiding from his father's assassination attempts on him. Works as a Fung Shui Master; expert on demon seals. Married to stone Shen, Silica.

Ruby: stone Shen assisting John and Emma in their investigations in the West.

Sang Ye: tree spirit; half-sister to Sang Shen.

Sang Shen: tree spirit resident in the Northern Heavens. Yue Gui is his mother; his father, a tree spirit, died from lack of sunlight while John was absent, for which Sang Shen blamed Emma and tried to kill her. Currently serving a sentence of house arrest in Yue Gui's custody.

Semias: druid master of a Celestial city.

Silica: stone Shen living on the Earthly to avoid repercussions from a previous romantic entanglement; Ronnie Wong's wife.

Simone: Simone Chen, Princess of the Dark Northern Heavens; daughter of Xuan Wu and his human wife, Michelle LeBlanc.

Sophia: the Tiger's wife number Thirty-Eight, a tamed high-level Snake Mother.

Stone: the Jade Building Block of the World; the stone that sits in Emma's engagement ring. One of the stones created by Nu Wa to hold up the Heavens when the Pillars were damaged by an angry god, but was never used for this purpose. The ring Emma wears was created for the Yellow Empress.

Toi: owner of the mare that was mother to Simone's half-demon horse, Freddo.

Tom O'Breen: half-demon son of Ben O'Breen and a Chinese demon Mother. Transforms into a male Snake Mother.

Venus: God of the planet Venus; emissary for the Jade Emperor.

White Tiger: Bai Hu, God of the Western Heavens. His element is Metal. Michael MacLaren's father, and husband to more than a hundred wives.

Xuan Wu: Dark Emperor of the Northern Heavens, God of the North and Martial Arts. His True Form is a snake combined with a turtle. His element is Water. English name: John Chen Wu.

Yanluo Wang: God of the Underworld and the Dead. Administrative manager of the Celestial side of Hell.

Yellow Empress: wife of the Yellow Emperor, a fabled ruler from ancient times who taught humanity the basics of civilisation.

Yi Hao: tame demon, Emma's secretary on Celestial Wudang.

Yue Gui: turtle Shen; Xuan Wu's older daughter, older sister to Simone and Martin Ming Gui, mother to Sang Shen. Manages the Northern Heavens' administrative side.

Zara: a diamond stone Shen that works as John's secretary. Used to be the stone that was in both Rhonda's and Clarissa's engagement rings.

Zhou Gong Ming: the Tiger General, one of the Thirty-Six Heavenly Generals.

Zhu Bei Niang: one of the Thirty-Six Heavenly Generals; sister to Zhu Bo Niang. Resigned her commission when John's Serpent was captured.

Zhu Bo Niang: one of the Thirty-Six Heavenly Generals; sister to Zhu Bei Niang, also a Heavenly General. Resigned her commission when John's Serpent was captured.

Zhu Que: the Red Phoenix, Goddess of the South. Her element is Fire.

Research Notes

The research notes and bibliography for the Chinese mythology are included in the other two trilogies, so I won't re-list them here.

My work on researching druids is the basis for my lecture on research at the University of Queensland, and I'll run through some of my processes and resources here for anyone who is interested.

Many of the texts I used were out of copyright and have been digitised, with the resulting e-book available free from a number of sources. Rare books that cost a fortune in original, hundred-year-old hardcover format are now being digitised by the institutions that hold them and are freely available. This has made my task both difficult and easy at the same time. Difficult, because it's sometimes hard to pin down exactly when something was written and what references were used; and easy, in that I no longer have to seek out hard-to-find print copies of old texts.

I'm not a historian; I researched purely to find interesting facts for my planned story. My research is not academic, and when a data source becomes repetitive I drop it and seek elsewhere. I'm more interested in 'fun' than 'informative', and I had a great deal of fun researching the ancient Celts and druids.

I'd like to state upfront that modern druids are a charming, gentle group of nature-worshipping neo-pagans and I have a great deal of respect and admiration for them. I was genuinely surprised to discover the bloodthirsty nature of the ancient Celts; many depictions of them in modern literature gloss over their more brutal aspects. With further research, the reasons for this brutality became apparent: they were a product of their time, and most civilisations during the Iron Age fought constant, sometimes horrific, wars with each other.

When researching these ancient peoples, I went first to descriptions of them by their contemporaries. The most interesting and detailed account was written by Julius Caesar (yes, *that* Julius Caesar), who described his ongoing campaign against the Celtic/Gallic people (Iron Age Celts were also referred to as Gauls) in *De Bello Gallico* (available in a number of different formats and translations, many of them free in electronic form). Caesar was a prolific and talented historian who kept records of everything he did and published them for the edification of his fellow Romans as an obvious form of self-promotion. It is said that history is written by the winners, and Caesar was the winner, so some colouring of the Celts as the 'bad guys' was to be expected. He paints them as a bunch of savages who collected the heads of their enemies as trophies and whose druids presided over ghastly human sacrifices of their captives. Caesar glosses over a couple of 'unfortunate' episodes in which Gallic towns were burnt to the ground and the entire population, including women and children, were put to the sword by his 'over-enthusiastic' soldiers, but these give an idea of what war was like in those times.

An interesting aspect of ancient Celtic society, as described by their contemporaries, is their quite modern-sounding attitudes towards homosexuality and women. Men sharing sexual encounters was normal and love between men was highly esteemed. Women were treated as equals, were able to own property and were quite capable of going to war if they chose to. It was not unknown for women to be warlords and to rule clans; and archaeologists are re-examining discoveries of graves that were immediately tagged as those of men to see if they were actually women's graves. A woman chose her own husband, and if she was unhappy in her marriage she could divorce her husband and keep her property.

The druids kept an oral history and left no written records (as the Archivist is so peeved about). No records of them at all exist after about 200AD. This has made it very difficult to create a definitive profile of these people.

During the Middle Ages, some monks collected the folk tales of Ireland and Wales and 'updated' them, making Saint Patrick a superhero who converted the evil Celtic heathens. They produced wonderful manuscripts of these stories, which in turn form the basis of the Romantic classic *Le Morte D'Arthur* by Sir Thomas Malory. The original folk tales were translated into English by Lady Charlotte Guest and published as *The Mabinogion*; and were compiled into a series of three volumes by Owen M Edwards in 1902, all of which are available electronically via Project Gutenberg. They include many tales of Arthur and his court and the romanticised exploits of his knights, but there are also references to the true Iron Age society of warlords and chieftains, who led their clans in battle against each other, conquered neighbouring towns, then demanded regular tributes and took nobles' children to hold as hostages.

When I plugged 'Celtic mythology' into Google, a large number of nineteenth-century resources came up, all of which painted the druids as a gentle, nature-worshipping group of wise magicians who venerated Christ long before he was born. These are generally romanticised versions of the historical tales, based on the idea of the noble savage, an ancient magical sage who was at one with nature. I looked further into the author of many of these sources, James Bonwick, and discovered that he was a Tasmanian schoolteacher who had absolutely no access to first-hand archaeological information. Most of this material seems to be completely made up, based on the tales translated by Lady Caroline Guest. This was a type of counter-propaganda, an attempt to redefine pre-Christian people as civilised to refute the commonly held view that any peoples living before Christ were barbarians. The Irish were also regarded as sub-human savages at the time, and Bonwick's sympathetic portrayal of the druids was a noble attempt to stop persecution of the people of Ireland.

Even though most of this work is not based on factual archaeology, it does not detract from the fascinating recreation and retelling of the Celtic myths, colouring them with a sense of culture and civilisation that resonates even today. They're certainly much more readable than Caesar's brutal depictions, and seem to be the foundation of much of the modern life-affirming neo-pagan movement. Bonwick, for example, seems to be one of the first scholars to link the druids with standing stone circles such as Stonehenge, when historically they probably had very little to do with them.

After reading the wonderful reinventions of the druids, I wanted to find out the truth. Were they brutal headhunters who engaged in human sacrifice, as the Romans said, or were they an advanced civilisation of wise pacifists, as the Romantics depicted them? Modern archaeology would provide the answer: peer-reviewed scientific inquiry without philosophical ulterior motives. The archaeological evidence points to the latter. The solid silver Gundestrup Cauldron (200BC–300AD), discovered in a bog in Denmark, shows someone being drowned in a barrel. Ancient Celtic pits have been unearthed containing remains of sacrifices. The most definitive piece of evidence for me, though, was the Roquepertuse portal, a set of stone pillars from about 300BC in France. The pillars have head-sized alcoves carved into them, and *the heads were still in them* when they were discovered. There's a similar set of pillars nearby, again with head alcoves. Nobody lived near these pillars; they formed part of an ancient temple.

One name kept coming up in my research: Barry Cunliffe; or, to give him his full title, Emeritus Professor Sir Barrington Windsor Cunliffe CBE, Emeritus Professor of European Archaeology at the University of Oxford (retired, 2007). He's written some absolutely breathtakingly brilliant books on the history of Europe, and particularly on that of the Celts. *The Ancient Celts* (1999) is definitive; it's easy to read, comprehensive and has gorgeous full-colour illustrations throughout. I read many references on the ancient Celts and most of them either covered some of the same material as this book, or referred to it. Anything by Professor Cunliffe is worth reading.

Armed with all of this fascinating information about the nature of the ancient Celts and their druids, I promptly threw all of it away and wrote a story set in the present day with very little reference to what really happened, and an outrageous explanation for the origins of the sea people, Celts, Greek philosophers and the Roman war machine. My aim is purely to entertain and I hope I have succeeded.

All of the places on Anglesey and Holyhead mentioned in the book really exist: the castle is Beaumaris Castle; the manor is Plas Newydd; the Trefignath Burial Chamber really is on a bike track near Tesco's; and the Penrhos Feilw standing stones are in the middle of a field, along with a couple of extremely cute ponies who wouldn't come home with me. Images of all these places are easily found on the internet for those interested.

References

(Note: there are probably many more references that I dipped into but didn't note on my bibliography list. When I'm being a knowledge sponge, I think about how the references will aid *my* story and completely forget that I'll have to list them later.)

Anwyl, Edward, *Celtic Religion in Pre-Christian Times*, Archibald Constable & Co Ltd, London (1906).

Bonwick, James, *The Pagan Gods of Ireland*, Samhain Song Press (2011 digitisation of an 1894 original).

Bonwick, James, *The Druids of Ireland*, Samhain Song Press (2011 digitisation of a pre-1900 original).

Bonwick, James, *The Serpent Faith in Ancient Ireland*, Samhain Song Press (2011 digitisation of a pre-1900 original). The link between druids and serpents has existed for a very long time.

Curran, B, *Celtic Lore & Legend*, The Career Press (2004).

Davies, John, *The Celts*, Cassel, London (2002).

Edwards, Owen M (1902), editor, *The Mabinogion*, in three volumes, translated from the Red Book of Hergest and the White Book of Rhydderch by Lady Caroline Guest.

Edwards, Owen M, *A Short History of Wales*, Fisher Unwin Ltd (digitised from 1922 original).

James, Simon, *Exploring the World of the Celts*, Thames & Hudson, London (2005).

Laing, Lloyd Robert, *The Archaeology of Celtic Britain and Ireland*, Cambridge University Press (2006).

Leahy, A H, *Heroic Romances of Ireland* (2008 digitisation of a pre-1923 text).

O'Grady, Standish, *The Coming of Cuculain* (digitisation of a pre-1923 original).

O'Grady, Standish, *Early Bardic Literature of Ireland* (digitisation of a pre-1928 original).

Rolleston, T W, *Myths and Legends of the Celtic Race* (digitisation of a 1911 original).

Acknowledgements

I would like to thank the people of Holyhead, who are a generous and friendly bunch. I'd particularly like to thank Nerys Beaman and Suzanne Roberts at the Holyhead Information Centre, who plied us with maps, tourist information and advice for our time spent there; June Davies and Neil Abernathy at the Dublin Ferry Guest House, who looked after us exceptionally well; and Ann and Steve Roberts, who run *www.Holyhead.com* and gave me tea and told me fascinating stories of the town's history and one of the worst jokes I have heard in my entire life.

Kylie Chan
Brisbane 2012